DIRTY TALKING RIVAL

PIPPA GRANT

COPYRIGHT

Previously published as *Master Baker*
Copyright © 2019

All rights reserved. This book or any portion thereof may not be reproduced or used in any manner whatsoever without the express written permission of the publisher except for the use of brief quotations in a book review.

This is a work of fiction. Names, characters, businesses, places, events and incidents are either the products of the author's imagination or used in a fictitious manner. Any resemblance to actual persons, living or dead, or actual events is purely coincidental.

Editing by Jessica Snyder
Cover Design by Qamber Designs

1

Grady Rock, aka a master baker who's man enough to handle any jokes about his nickname, but still unprepared for today's gossip hour

"That's right, baby," I whisper as I ease deeper inside into her creamy depths. She's tight. So full already. "Oh, yeah, just like that. You feel that? Is that good for you too?"

The donut doesn't answer, but she does grunt under the strain of all the pudding I'm stuffing inside her.

Or possibly that was my pastry bag burping.

"You can take a little more," I murmur while my kitchen door opens. "I know you can. And then I'm going to eat you so good—"

"Ugh, you are so disgusting," my sister announces as she breezes in.

I smile at the donut. "Don't listen to her. You're beautiful."

"You realize if you ever bothered to talk to a woman like that, Pop wouldn't be trying so hard to set you up with every single woman in Virginia."

"Don't forget about the northern half of North Carolina too." I brush a thumb over the top of the donut—smooth and firm, just like she should be—and move on to filling the next donut. "You ever seen a batch of donuts so beautiful?"

"You say that every morning."

"The trick to life is getting better every day. You should try it sometime."

Tillie Jean angles into my lair and makes herself comfortable on the spare stool across the metal worktable in my bakery kitchen.

My rolling racks are half full of all of the deliciousness I'll sell out of before the day's over. My ovens are baking muffins and scones. My mixing bowl is waiting for tomorrow's donut dough. And my sink is overflowing with dirty dishes.

Just the way I like it.

If my bottom line would just start reflecting what my kitchen does—prosperity and productivity—life would be perfect.

I'm selling out almost every day. Hired an extra baker. Has to happen soon.

Or maybe never, because no matter how good I feel about what I'm selling every week, as soon as I sit down to trudge through my books on the weekends, I realize I'm still just barely breaking even.

Not like I can increase my clientele in a small town like this.

"You see Pop yet today?" Tillie Jean asks.

"It's five AM."

"Yep."

"On a Tuesday."

"Uh-huh."

"That's sex in the shower day. We won't see Pop *or* Nana for at least another four hours."

She doesn't answer. Not to tell me I'm disgusting again, or to sigh and hope out loud that when she's eighty, she'll be married to someone who still wants to do her in the shower.

Suspicious.

Especially since she's never out of bed before five AM either.

I finish the last of the donut filling and glance up at her.

She has this pensive look tightening her eyes and pursing her lips that I don't see often, but that always manages to inch my pulse up and make me want to stick my head in the sand.

Or maybe whip up a batch of macarons, because those take time and concentration and are an excellent distraction.

Not to mention delicious, and they particularly like it when I compliment their smooth, perfect mounds.

None of which Tillie Jean seems to be thinking about.

"What?" I ask while I reach back to grab the donut glaze.

She blinks and shakes her head. "What flavor today?"

"Mascarpone and Nutella. Why do you look like you're about to tell me my goat died?"

"Like you'd be sad if Sue died."

"Avoiding the question, Tillie Jean. What's got you in here before the sun on a Tuesday talking about Pop?"

Her lids close over her blue eyes, and I can see her fighting to keep from just blurting out whatever's eating at her when the back door opens again, this time with a slam.

Georgia Mayberry, my second-in-command, marches in with a flier in hand and outrage in her brown eyes. She's so mad that the braids at the ends of her cornrows are standing up and hissing too.

"Did you see *this*?" she demands indignantly, flapping the paper around.

Tillie Jean leaps up and grabs it from her. "No, he has *not*," she says on a high-pitched whisper, "and we're going to ease him into it, okay?"

"Ease me into *what*?"

"Freaking Duh-Nuts advertising *all over Shipwreck*!" Georgia announces. She snorts and marches to the fridge, where she starts yanking out butter and eggs. "Couldn't keep it in Sarcasm like they should've. Oh, no. They have to come over here to Shipwreck and try to steal our customers. The *nerve* of those—those—those *donut holes*."

"The nerve," I agree, because agreeing with Georgia keeps her happy, and keeping Georgia happy keeps her employed here without asking for a raise, and her blueberry muffins are better than mine, which is saying something.

Am I worried?

Of course not. Duh-Nuts has already gone out of business once since I bought Crow's Nest. They'll go out of business again.

But my blood pressure still spikes.

Logically, I know the vast majority of my limited customer base would never voluntarily set foot in Sarcasm —and yes, that's really what they call their town down the road. But it's still competition, and my profits aren't where I want them to be.

Not even close.

Plus, she said *Sarcasm*.

I used to know someone from Sarcasm. A long time ago.

Tillie Jean's bedhead swivels back in my direction, and—huh.

She's still in her pajamas. Are those—they *are*. They're dancing lips with little stick arms and feet. Cute.

And also possibly why she's still single.

I make a mental note to remember this the next time Pop tries to talk me into going on a date with a woman he's hand-picked.

Just because it's been a couple—several—fine, *many* months since my last casual girlfriend doesn't mean my goat and I need someone right now, and if I can persuade him to concentrate on Tillie Jean's love life instead of mine, bonus.

"Grady," she says quietly.

I start dipping the donuts in the Nutella glaze and lift a *yes?* brow at her.

She holds out the flier for me to scan it.

Duh-Nuts Grand Re-opening and Homecoming! it says proudly.

But that's not what makes *my* nuts suddenly retract.

Nope.

That's the next line.

Now I get why Tillie Jean's lurking around at this hour of the day.

My smile leaps off a cliff, I drop the donut in the glaze, and I feel like someone's been shoving pudding up *my* ass.

"Thinking they can be all *oh, come to our second-rate town for a grand re-opening of a donut shop that made bad donuts, it's so exciting!*" Georgia mutters with a snort while she slams flour and sugar onto the smaller worktable. "Sarcasm assholes. Who gives a chocolate chip that some chick came home?"

"So Duh-Nuts over in Sarcasm is re-opening. So what?" I try to keep my voice level and unafflicted while I fish the donut out of the glaze bowl, but I don't quite make it, because I read that second line too, and I know who's home.

"Grady—" Tillie Jean starts, but Georgia plows her over.

Verbally, I mean.

"They're trying to steal our customers. Right here. In our own town. Like they didn't steal half our tourists last month with their freaking *unicorn festival*. We've had the pirate festival every second week of June since the dawn of time, and they think they can just suddenly put a competing festival the same week?"

I let her rant while I watch Tillie Jean watching everything in the kitchen except me.

"So she's back for good?" I ask.

My sister not looking at me is answer enough.

Annika Williams is back. *Back* back.

Annika Williams, who couldn't bake her way out of a paper bag.

Annika Williams, who spent high school counting the days until she could leave our little slice of the Blue Ridge Mountains behind, but still promised me once she'd come back one day and be my business manager when I opened the best bakery on this side of the Blue Ridge Mountains.

Annika Williams, who took my heart with her when she left.

She's back.

Opening *her own damn bakery*.

Trying to steal my customers.

I thought I'd already felt everything I was ever going to feel about Annika Williams.

Turns out, I was wrong.

2

ANNIKA WILLIAMS, AKA A DAUGHTER AND SISTER WHO'S changed a lot, but is still best known for her chocolate chip cookie bricks, which means this bakery idea isn't going to end well

USUALLY WHEN PEOPLE say their lives are in the shitter, they don't mean it quite this literally.

Also, my family's life was already in the shitter *before* this, so I'm not amused at today's turn of events.

To say the least.

"Can you fix it?" I ask Roger Rogers, owner of *No Shit Plumbing*, who's standing over the toilet in Duh-Nuts Bakery's lone bathroom, staring down at the swirling gray water.

He scratches his balding head, then claps his Copper Valley Fireballs baseball cap back on. His dark beard is streaked with gray, and he keeps shooting a glance at the kitchen like he's hoping to be paid in double chocolate fudge cookies.

Which *I* won't be baking, because I've turned committing sins against sugar into an art.

"Normally a plugged crapper ain't a big deal," Roger says, "but normally the plunger ain't broke and stuck real good inside the crapper either."

I tamp down on the urge to throw the plunger handle at his head and shout *I know, that's why I called you* when his lips turn up in an ornery grin.

"Aw, c'mon, Annika. Had to give you shit about it. Heh. Shit. With a broken crapper. That's funny. 'Course I can fix it. Just gotta go grab a new plunger to plunge out the old plunger pieces, since you ripped yours in two when you pulled the handle out and left the plunger stuck in the john."

He grins at joking about plunging out a plunger head that's currently stuck in the toilet and blocking the water from flowing the way it's supposed to after *someone* attempted to flush raw cinnamon roll dough down the toilet an hour ago.

I don't grin back, because if I can't get this bakery back up and running, I don't know how I'm going to take care of my mom and sister.

I swallow a lump of tears the size of the iceberg that took down the Titanic.

Who am I kidding?

I can put Mama's building back together, but I don't know how I'm going to lure in enough customers to keep her brand-new bakery in business.

Not with my skills.

We'd be better off with me buying all the snack cakes the grocery store has in stock and sticking unicorn horns in all of them to make them "unique" than with letting me take over the baking.

But I can't tell Mama that going ahead with her plans for Duh-Nuts right now is a bad idea.

Not when it's everything she's ever dreamed of.

Not when she's *finally* managed to get her hands on it.

And not when it's the only thing getting her out of bed and coping right now.

"Hey. Chin up, baby girl. You know we got this." Roger claps me on the shoulder with his meaty hand. "Take me less than five minutes. Go on. Time me."

With a wink, he ambles out of the restroom, and a minute later, I hear the bells jingle on the front door as he exits to get his tools from his truck.

I sag against the bathroom wall, still clutching the plunger handle, and try to convince myself that I can do this. That *we* can do this.

Funny.

Ten years in the Army didn't seem as daunting as getting through today.

But then, in my ten years in the Army, I knew my mom and sister were okay on their own, I had a job where I could spreadsheet and plan the hell out of everything, which is where my real gifts lie, and I didn't need to train myself to be a master baker overnight in the midst of running Mama to doctor appointments and managing social worker and contractor visits to her house.

"Shitter cleared up yet?" Bailey, my baby sister, asks as she peers around the corner. Her big dark eyes are daring me to call her out on being crude—or on being the culprit who tried to flush my awful, thick, crusty, over-floured cinnamon roll dough down the toilet—but I have bigger problems than a thirteen-year-old pressing her luck with her mouth, especially when I know she was just trying to remove evidence of my crimes against dough so she could whip up her own batch.

Which I should've let her do in the first place.

"No. Did you finish frosting the cupcakes?" The ones that *she* made, because my cupcakes tend to look more like coal turds that even Santa would reject for the naughty kids, and those are my *vanilla* cupcakes. Don't ask how my chocolate cupcakes turn out.

"Yep. But...I made fresh frosting, and probably you should leave the cookies to me too."

That's right.

Mama's new shop is called *Duh-Nuts* and do we have any donuts this morning?

No, we don't.

Because I couldn't make a donut to save my life, and with Mama suddenly blind and unable to fry things, because *safety*, we're concentrating on the *bakery* part of her business instead of the *donut* part these first few days.

"Good thing all our customers today will be pity customers," I mutter with a sigh.

"That seems unlikely," a deep voice answers, startling both of us.

I lean out of the bathroom while Bailey's eyes go round, and I'm instantly eighteen again.

Unprepared, not entirely happy, uncertain what I'm supposed to do with the plunger handle, and very much on edge.

"Holy shit," Bailey whispers.

"Language," I say quietly, because it's either that, or I might start dropping a few creative words I learned in the Army that she doesn't need to know yet.

"Holy shirt on a shirtcake," she corrects. "He's hot for an old guy."

Grady Rock's blue eyes crinkle at the edges when he smiles at Bailey, which is an expression he wasn't aiming at me, for the record.

Also for the record, he's not *old*.

He's my age, not yet thirty, and he's aged as well as double-oaked whiskey.

"Adults ruin all the fun," he says to her.

"I can say whatever I want at home. Just not here, or Annika will swap out my mascara for her special homemade chocolate frosting. Who are you?"

"He's—" I start, and I realize I have no idea how to finish that sentence.

My former best friend?

The boy I crushed on all through high school, even though I knew better?

The guy who asked me to sacrifice my future and my independence and all my life plans to wait around for him to get back from culinary school since he finally realized, on graduation night, mere hours before I had to catch a bus to Army basic training, that he couldn't live without me?

The man I left behind because while I love my mama and would do anything for her, I didn't want to *be* her?

"I'm Grady," he says, shifting an unreadable glance away from me and holding a capable, strong, long-fingered hand out to Bailey. He's in a black *Shipwreck—We Do It Pirate-Style* T-shirt, because of course he is, and those biceps are *definitely* a new development. "I run the Crow's Nest Bakery over in Shipwreck."

Soda bubbles fill my veins.

I didn't keep up with the Grady Rock gossip after I left home. I didn't join Facebook or Twitter, I didn't sign up to get the Sarcasm News delivered to my inbox, and I didn't come home on leave and stalk him to find out what Shipwreck local he married and how many kids he had.

I needed space and distance to get over him and to start my life fresh and *be* someone, someone who could take care of herself, away from where I was *the daughter of that wild child who got herself pregnant at sixteen*.

I needed to get to know who I was when I wasn't in love with Grady Rock, because despite four years of solid friendship, after that night, he didn't call. Or text. Or email.

He completely dropped out of my life just when I needed a friend most.

But I still knew he was running Crow's Nest.

That we're basically competitors in this little slice of the Blue Ridge Mountains, though I'm competing on Mama's behalf right now, and if we can't find a real baker in the next month, he'll put us out of business with one hand tied behind his back.

And Mama's dreams will go up in smoke faster than she suddenly lost her eyesight three weeks ago.

I'm trying to be the bigger person here, to be happy for him and to be professional, one baker to the next—or one stumbling, klutzy mess of a kitchen disaster to one baking god—but my nerves have been raw since Bailey called in a panic in the middle of the night because Mama was in the ER unable to see anything, and nothing about this morning and the broken toilet and the ruined cinnamon rolls and the general panic over figuring out how much of Mama's and Bailey's lives I can fix before I run out of emergency leave and have to report back to Fort Bliss in Texas if my discharge paperwork doesn't go through, is making seeing him again easier.

"You're from Shipwreck?" Bailey asks, her entire posture going suspicious. "Then what are you doing here? Don't you have another village to plunder?"

He slides another unreadable blue-green glance at me.

There's a smear of chocolate frosting in front of his left earlobe, but otherwise, he's calm and cool and put together with his jeans melding to his thighs, two days' worth of scruff on his chin and neck, and his dark hair just long enough to curl at the edges.

"Heard an old friend was back in town," he tells Bailey.

It's clear she gets the implication when she frowns at me. "You have friends in *Shipwreck*?"

"You will too, once you start high school," I point out.

"Nope. I will *only* hang out with people from Sarcasm. It's better here. Sarcastic people score twenty points higher on IQ tests than normal people, and we all know pirates are dumber than normal people."

"What if one of them is good at volleyball?"

Her eyes narrow, because she knows I have her there. "This conversation is over." She turns to Grady with a flip of her hair. "And you need to leave."

"I liked you better when you were two," he tells her, which almost throws her off—I can tell by the slight flare in her eyes—but she's a Williams, through and through.

"Well, bless your heart," she says sweetly. "Annika, I think our crowd's starting. We should go finish those tres leches donuts and get to work on our bubble waffles."

We barely managed to put together the coffee pot this

morning, but she gets points for her addiction to Food Network and the bravado that goes with the bluff.

"Be right there," I tell her.

She tilts her head at me in the *you are not seriously going to stand here and talk nice to THE COMPETITION FROM SHIPWRECK, are you?* glare, and I barely refrain from smiling.

Family, food, volleyball, and loyalty to Sarcasm are Bailey's life.

She's pretty damn awesome.

"I have to wait for Roger to finish the toilet," I remind her.

"Roger knows where the toilet is."

"Bailey."

"If you think I'm going to leave you alone to let some random baker guy from Shipwreck besmirch your honor or throw you off your game, you're crazy."

Seriously.

I love her to pieces, and not in the least because she's willing to pretend I have any game when it comes to running a bakery.

Grady, though, I'm not so sure about.

Everything between us is more or less ancient history. We're practically strangers. I'm not the same woman I was when I left home ten years ago, and I'm sure he's changed too.

He still has his dimples, but his body is honed and his eyes are full of a depth that they didn't have ten years ago.

We've both grown.

But I can't stop the feelings about who we used to be.

And the feelings are too overwhelming on top of all the

other chaos that I can't fully color-code in my life planner right now.

"Thanks for stopping by, but the grand opening isn't until this weekend. We'll be sure to send an invitation."

I am *not* sending an invitation.

Which I think he knows, because I get the full intensity of his searching blue-green gaze, the gaze that used to smile at me over cupcakes in the cafeteria at school, that he'd dial up to coax me to *come over to Shipwreck and go roller skating tonight after you get off work, and I'll bring these toasted macadamia-pistachio cookies I've been working on*, that would calm me the fuck down when I was freaking over a test or a late assignment or getting my shoe stuck in mud at the lake and not knowing how I was going to tell Mama we had to buy me a new pair, when I knew Bailey was growing faster and needed more things than I did.

It's the same gaze that would silently ask if I was okay after some asshole in the hallway between classes would make a crack about my mama. I was *that* freshman, the daughter of a teen mom who was now single and pregnant in her early thirties with number two, because *doesn't she know yet where those come from* and *can't she keep her legs shut?*

Like it didn't take two. Like it wasn't more offensive that a man who claimed to love her and me had shoved us out of his life as soon as he found out she was pregnant.

Like she hadn't done a kick-ass job of raising me all on her own.

You ask me, she deserved a fucking medal.

But every time someone said something snide, Grady was there, asking if I was okay.

He knew I didn't need to be protected, but he offered it anyway.

Because we were friends.

"You bake now," he says.

"Never underestimate a motivated woman." I try to add a smile, because I don't want to be cranky and affected, but *god*.

I *am* affected by having him standing two feet in front of me. Who wouldn't be?

I'm also trying really hard to keep up the bluff that I can bake now, and even though it's been ten years since we've been friends, I still feel like he can see right through me.

"You bake for *Sarcasm*," he adds.

The disdain in his voice makes my attempt at a smile die a quick death. "I grew up here," I remind him.

"You opened *your own bakery* in *Sarcasm*."

"And it's so nice of you to be happy for me."

Those bubbles streaming through my blood are popping and sparking something far uglier. I don't bother correcting him, to tell him that it's *Mama's* bakery.

We stare at each other, because he's clearly *not* happy for me, and I'm not happy that he's not happy for me.

Aren't friends supposed to be happy for each other when good things happen?

And how about friends asking, *hey, how've you been? What brings you home? How long are you here? Oh my god, your mom went blind? What can I do to help?*

"You're putting fliers all over my town for *your* bakery."

"That was me," Bailey says. "Because you can't grow a business without advertising, and it's been a one-bakery county for way too long. I hit all the towns, by the way. Just in case you think I made a special trip to Shipwreck. I actually put them there under protest, because having a pirate town in the mountains is stupid, but now I'm really glad I did it."

"*You're not old enough to drive,*" he barks.

"So?"

Her total disregard—and lack of any desire to explain herself—should be funny.

But I'm not amused.

I'm pissed as hell that he's treating me like an intruder instead of a friend who came home.

"Excuse me," I say shortly. "As you can see, I have a bakery to run."

I grip Bailey's hand too hard when I grab her and pull her back toward the kitchen, but she still squeezes back.

I got your back, Annika, that squeeze says.

She's thirteen.

She shouldn't *have* to have my back. I'm supposed to be the adult. I'm supposed to be the one putting everyone's lives back in order. Figuring out how Mama's bakery can get off the ground when it's starting in the midst of a crisis.

Except we're both Maria Williams's daughters.

And I couldn't be more grateful for that than I am right now.

We're going to be okay.

We're all going to be okay.

And Grady Rock can bite me.

3

GRADY

I SHOULDN'T HAVE GONE to Sarcasm to see Annika.

I should never go to Sarcasm, period—that town has been a thorn in my town's side since before I was born—but going back to see the woman who told me to take a flying leap when I kissed her and asked her to give me a chance, a *real* chance, ten years ago before she left for the Army was an even worse idea.

Annika Williams does not now, and never has wanted me.

Re-opening Sarcasm's bakery is just more proof of how she always *really* felt about me.

Seeing her again, though—*god*, I wanted to touch her.

Hold her hand.

Wipe away that worry line between her brows.

For three seconds, I was back in high school. Admiring

her grit. Wanting to see her smile. Wishing I'd brought a fucking *cookie*.

And then every moment of graduation night came crashing down, her eyes landed on me with panic and disbelief and dread, and I knew.

I knew.

I still wasn't who she wanted to see standing there, and the knowledge opened every last scar I'd forgotten I had.

Turns out, my heart's still bruised too.

"Quit moping," Tillie Jean says to me. I'm sidled up to the bar in Crusty Nut, Shipwreck's most popular restaurant, rolling silverware into napkins after delivering cookies here for their ice cream sandwich dessert tonight, and helping install a new fridge. She's working behind the counter, restocking the liquor before the night crowd hits since she runs the place. "So you have a little competition now. So what?"

"We were friends," I tell my sister. "Friends don't open competing bakeries."

And having Annika here running a bakery—let's just say she's never failed at anything she set out to do.

Which means my bakery might be in actual danger from the competition.

"Did you ask her *why* she opened a bakery?" my mom asks as she slides onto the seat next to me and plops a nine-by-thirteen dish of dirt cake in front of me.

"Ma. You can't bring that in here," Tillie Jean objects.

"Can and did. Your brother's had a rough day. He needs a dirt cake."

"It's not even two in the afternoon."

"But he's been up since three, haven't you, sweetie?" Ma kisses my cheek, and I let her ruffle my hair and fuss while I finish the last of Tillie Jean's silverware, because it makes Ma happy, and I'm feeling shitty and it's nice to know my mom still loves me.

I'm officially that pathetic idiot.

Shouldn't have come here to Crusty Nut either, but I knew TJ would take the help until I'm calm enough to go back to my own bakery.

If I walk in there now, Georgia will chase me out, because pastries and baked goods need love, not heartbreak, if they're going to taste good.

"What he needs is a girlfriend," my grandfather declares.

He, too, strides into the dark-paneled bar attached to the restaurant, but unlike my mother, he has a parrot sitting on his shoulder.

Tillie Jean points to the door. "Pop, Long Beak Silver can't be in here either."

"Fuck you and the unicorn you rode in on," the parrot says.

"Long Beak Silver, go swab the deck."

"All work and no play makes a parrot frisky."

My sister glares at Pop.

His weathered face wrinkles more as he smiles broadly.

"Can't argue with that," he declares. "Besides, it's too hot outside. His beak'll melt right off."

Tillie Jean throws her hands up. "If the health department shuts us down, I'm moving in with both of you," she informs our elders. She doesn't own the place, but Dad does, and she's his manager.

She'll inherit it one day, if she wants to.

"Pipe down, wench!" Long Beak Silver says.

I unroll the last silverware I fixed up, take the spoon,

and dig straight into the dirt cake. It's a testament to how much my mother loves me that she doesn't chide me for my manners.

Or possibly I just look that shitty.

Annika Williams.

Fuck.

She's back.

With those expressive brown eyes. Those cheeks that could cut glass, but covered in deep olive skin so soft it rivals the silk of a good meringue. And her hair.

Her thick dark hair.

She didn't cut it in the Army. She left it long. It was pulled up in a ponytail under a hair net, and it was fucking adorable.

"Here, boy," Pop says, straddling the seat on my other side and putting the parrot between us. "I picked out a few more women for you to try out."

"Pop. He's not looking *for a fucking car*," Tillie Jean snaps. "Leave the man alone. He just came face-to-face with the one who got away. He deserves five minutes to mope. Okay?"

Huh.

I owe my sister a nice birthday present this year.

"She warned me," I tell them all. Despite the fact that my mom always shows up with dirt cakes whenever my life hits a bump in the road, I've never told her the whole story of why I needed a dirt cake after high school graduation.

And I mean the good kind of dirt cake with cream cheese and vanilla pudding and whipped cream, and gummy treasures mixed in, and topped with crumbled

Oreos, not the kind my brother Cooper used to bring in from the yard after digging for treasure.

"She told me a million times if she told me once that she wasn't interested in dating boys because she was going to college to get a degree so she could afford to buy a big-screen TV and a Toyota," I tell my family. "New. A *new* Toyota. Because that was making it to her."

"A Toyota?" Pop's frowning big-time now. "What's she want with a Toyota when Chevy's the good stuff? Here. Look at this one. Penelope Summer. Her grandpa cheats at pool, but I don't hold that against her. And if she hyphenates, she'd be Penelope Summer-Rock, and that's charming, isn't it?"

"Pop, Grady's not getting married just because a woman's hyphenated name would be charming," Ma says. "But show him Meredith. The one with the degree in plasma physics. I didn't even know that was a thing, but imagine how smart their kids will be."

Tillie Jean and I share a look.

My dad bustles out of the kitchen with a basket full of gold nuggets, which the rest of the world calls fried pickle chips, and one of potato swords, which are—you guessed it—french fries.

Shipwreck might be nestled into the Blue Ridge Mountains, but we have a long and storied history of being founded by a pirate on the run from the law, and so we pirate-ify everything.

The tourists love it.

Most days, so do I.

My whole family is in the business of running Shipwreck, so loving it is a good thing.

Dad bought Crusty Nut before I was born because he

loves to cook, and he and Ma decided to have Tillie Jean so that they'd have at least one kid who could run his restaurant one day.

I fell down on my role of running Ma's coffee shop, but she's holding out hope Cooper will come home and take it over when he retires from baseball in another ten or fifteen years.

"Heart attack in a basket," Dad says proudly, sliding the food onto the bar beside Ma's dirt cake. "Rather have you dead than moping over a Sarcasm girl."

"*Dad*," Tillie Jean says.

He grins. "What? Perspective." He taps Pop's notebook. "Did you show him Neveah yet? Fascinating name. And she took dance classes all through high school, so you know she's good and nimble. What? That's important for childbirth."

I pick up the dirt cake and the heart attack baskets and head for the door.

"Where are you going?" Pop calls. "We're just getting started."

I *should* head back to my own bakery and make sure everything's running fine, but Georgia chased me off the minute I got back from Sarcasm and said—rightfully so—that if I tried to bake a thing in the mood I was in, the cakes would fall and the cookies would come out tasting like chalk and don't get her started on what would happen to the donuts.

Makes more sense to pay her to not screw up than for me to ruin two days' worth of baking. I'll deal with what that means for the bottom line later.

Which means I'm going home.

To my goat.

Who loves me even though I never asked him to, and even though I tried my damnedest to get rid of him when he invaded my yard a year ago.

"Gonna go dig for pirate treasure," I reply. "Stress relief from being related to all of you."

I'm not three feet outside the door before Tillie Jean catches up with me in the blazing summer heat that's gonna melt my dirt cake before I make it the three blocks home.

"What?" I ask her.

"We need to find them all hobbies. You okay? For real?"

I hand her the fried food baskets so I can eat dirt cake and walk while we stroll past pirate-themed shop after pirate-themed shop.

"She looked at me like we were never anything at all," I tell my sister, which is a hard confession to make, since it involves admitting to feelings.

I've been pretty damn good at denying that I have feelings where Annika's concerned.

Time helped.

And her being gone helped.

Her coming back and opening a bakery not ten miles away *does not help*.

Especially not when it's affecting me more than it should.

It's been ten years.

Yet here I am, completely off-kilter.

"And she couldn't even bake no-bake cookies when I knew her," I add.

Tillie Jean sighs and shoves a french fry in her mouth. We pass Davy Jones's Locker, the water park in town where all the kids out for summer are shrieking and playing and having a grand ol' carefree time. This town—you wouldn't think a town based on a tale about a pirate coming inland to hide his treasure from the authorities would still be going strong in the digital age, but here we are.

Hosting pirate weddings and a pirate festival and treasure digs. Growing a little every year, tucked into a little valley in the mountains with the blue haze hanging over the spruce and firs and oaks covering the mountainsides.

It's a small town where people *stay*.

Not like Sarcasm.

Where they all leave.

Like Annika did.

"Maybe it's good that she came back," Tillie Jean says as the sound of all the kids playing in the park fades. We turn a corner and head into the residential area behind Blackbeard Avenue. "Maybe now you can get over her."

"I got over her ten years ago."

"Grady. You were secretly in love with her for four years, finally found your balls to tell her so, and she didn't just crush you, she ground your whole soul into dust, packed it into a cannonball, and shot it off over the mountains and wished you luck in finding all the pieces again. And that's the last thing she did before she left. For ten years. So, yeah, *you still need to get over her*. Face her. And get over her."

I snort, which isn't the best thing to do when trying to shove dirt cake into your mouth, but she might have a point.

I didn't go to Sarcasm with any plan other than *see her with my own two eyes*.

And possibly *have her be so happy to see me that she falls into my arms and I get my best friend back, except better.*

"When—" Tillie Jean starts, but I growl at her, because I know what she's going to ask, and I'm not going to answer.

When's the last time you dated a woman that you could've imagined yourself spending forever with?

"I gotta go do some research," I tell my sister. "Got a request for a tres leches donut this morning." And I need to look into bubble waffles.

Her blue eyes squint, and I know she doesn't believe me, but she doesn't call me on it either.

Probably because she knows that when Pop realizes I'm a hopeless cause, he's moving on to her next.

Maybe I should take one of his dates.

It'd solve one problem. The rest?

That's what Ma's dirt cake and Dad's fried food is for.

4

Annika

Mama was just barely seventeen when I was born. I know who my biological father is. He knows who I am. That's the extent of his involvement with us.

She raised me on her own. Finished high school with my grandmother's help, then cleaned houses and waited tables and baked morning shift at Duh-Nuts under the old management until she got a desk job answering phones for the county trash collector.

She loved to bake.

Loved to bake.

But it didn't pay enough, and so she changed jobs to take care of me.

She lost her job with the county after having a fling with her supervisor that resulted in Bailey joining our little family, but she got a better job answering phones for a local lawyer who was also a single mom, and she started saving.

And she kept baking.

And teaching Bailey how to bake.

Two years ago, I came home for Thanksgiving and had a foodgasm over her caramel cheesecake, and while I was warm and toasty and a little tipsy on wine and dessert, she asked if I wanted to go into business together.

Mama worked her ass off so I could play softball and go to art camp in the summer, and I was always painfully aware that the trade-off for her affording butter and flour and sugar, and for me being able to participate in sports and camps, was that we ate mac'n'cheese and whatever frozen vegetables were on sale—usually lima beans, because *gross*, who picks those up voluntarily?—so that she could afford gas and upkeep on the old hatchback that made a rattling noise anytime it went above 35 miles an hour, but still got me where I needed to be so I could have my own dreams.

Of course I said I'd go into business with her.

Help her have her dream, provided I didn't have to bake anything.

It was funny two years ago.

Two years ago, we'd both scrimped and saved enough since I left home that we could afford a down payment together, with money left over for equipment.

Today, life and all the unpredictability is giving me an ulcer, but dammit, I will *not* let Mama's dream fail.

And when I make up my mind, I succeed.

So while it might seem stupid to open a bakery in the midst of managing the doctor appointments and social worker visits and the contractors we've needed to come into her house and make it blind-accessible, not opening the bakery now isn't an option.

Mama needs this.

She needs *hope*. She needs to believe in the future. She needs a reason to get out of bed in the morning.

And seeing—*fuck*—*living* her dream coming true, *feeling* it, *hearing* it, *tasting* it, *smelling* it, are what's keeping her spirits up when her world is suddenly dark and scary because of a previously undiagnosed condition in her arteries that flared up ten years sooner than doctors usually see it.

She thought the dots in her vision that started two days after we signed the paperwork to officially buy Duh-Nuts were from too much stress with finally doing everything she had to do to make her dream work.

Or that she'd scratched her corneas, and they would heal.

Instead, she waited too long to get to the doctor, and her condition is rare enough that the extra time for diagnosis made her blindness permanent before we knew what it was to treat it.

She had her dream for three days before she couldn't see it anymore.

And I'll be damned before I fail her.

But one day after Grady crashed back into my world, the bakery is causing more stress than it's giving hope. So on a whim, after our afternoon naps—yes, naps that I've scheduled onto the calendar, because life right now is exhausting—I ask Mama if she wants to go to the Sarcasm GOATs league softball game.

I'm half-hoping she'll say no, because I know who the GOATs are playing tonight, but it's tradition to go, and she's looked so *worn* today, like she's aged seven years in the last four weeks, and I have this idea that soaking up the evening sunshine and talking to neighbors and friends and smelling the hot dogs grilling at the snack bar might cheer her up.

Though her chin wobbles, she sets her lips in a firm line and nods. "But only if we take our own popcorn," she declares.

Popcorn, I can make.

And I'm so relieved that she's not shrinking back from the idea of going out in public and braving walking around in a world that she can't see anymore, that I make triple the popcorn I should and let Bailey toss a portion in white chocolate and a second batch in caramel.

We don't have to stay long, which is good, because I doubt I make it past the top of the first inning.

And not just because we have an early bedtime to accommodate being up early for tomorrow's baking.

I thought my schedule was rough in the Army, but there wasn't the emotional toll of dealing with Mama's sudden blindness. And while I can rock a planner like I was born with it clutched in my hands, it turns out I'm not quite as adept at managing all the conflicting feelings that have been swirling inside me.

Worry. Guilt. Anxiety.

You know. The good feelings.

And knowing I'm probably going to see Grady again tonight doesn't help.

I'm driving us out to the fields while Bailey tells Mama all about how we sold out of cupcakes and donuts today. Our cake donut pans arrived yesterday afternoon, and

Bailey made blueberry cake donuts with them this morning after I tried to make chocolate lava rock donuts.

She chatters about everyone thinking she was sixteen, and that we have three orders for special occasion cakes for this weekend—which she and Mama will have to make, since the oven and I get along as well as peanut butter and sand that's so allergic to peanuts that it turns into slime shaped like a duck when they get within seven feet of each other, and yes, I know that's very specific, but I had a weird dream during naptime today, and I'm also getting a stomach ache over going to the Sarcasm-Shipwreck softball game.

Which is why I'm blowing out a slow breath and concentrating on Bailey.

One day, she says, she's going to open a restaurant next door to Mama's bakery so we can all work together forever.

She's *thirteen*.

She could be full of attitude and sass and hormones, and she could be mad at me for not getting home more in the last ten years, and she could be melting down completely at how quickly both our lives have changed since Mama's illness flared up—and we're still not talking about the fact that I'm only on emergency leave, and not actually discharged from the Army, which means I have maybe six to eight more weeks before I legally have to report back to duty if my chain of command can't get my paperwork processed—but she's not.

She just loves us and wants to be with us and completely rolls with things.

Mostly.

"Oh my god, he did *not*," she suddenly shrieks.

"What? Who? Where?" I scan the winding state road through the mountains, making sure she's not yelling about a nudist about to jump into our path, because with Bailey, you truly never know.

"That Shipwreck shithead is selling *tres leches donuts* at his bakery tomorrow!"

I glance in the rearview mirror and realize she's scanning her phone. "Are you on social media?"

Eye roll. "Yes, Sergeant Paranoid. I'm on Facebook and I'm posting nude selfies and telling all the child molesters where to come find me and that they can score a hot lady soldier and a blind chick who still has it while they're here."

So, yes, she's still a normal teenager.

Also, Grady Rock is even more dead to me now than he was when he left my shop, because *who steals someone else's donut idea?*

Bailey's right.

Shipwreck shithead. They think they're so special because they made up a story about their ancestor driving a pirate treasure in a covered wagon from the coast to the mountains to hide it from the authorities three hundred years ago so that they can call a *mountain town* a *pirate town*.

It's so ridiculous it makes my brain hurt.

"Please get off the internet while I'm driving. All your shrieking is distracting me. And distracted driving is unsafe driving. Remember that. You'll be behind the wheel soon enough."

One more eye roll.

I almost smile, because I know she's still going to curl up next to me on the couch tonight, lay her head on my shoulder, and tell me all her plans for how to best arrange whatever our special of the day will be tomorrow so that we can also post it on social media and lure more customers in, and by the way, did I see the pins she sent me from Pinterest with the geode cookies and can we *please* get a bubble waffle maker and soft serve machine?

"What Shipwreck shithead?" Mama asks, because that's clearly the more important question.

"Some guy Annika used to know who came over yesterday acting all *you can't open a bakery in my county, because I licked it first*. Ugh. I am *not* making friends with any of those kids from Shipwreck when I start at Blue Lagoon County High. Wait! I know! Annika, you should homeschool me. Then I can help with the bakery as part of my classes. It's home ec and economics and math and chemistry and social sciences all rolled into one."

"How is working at the bakery *social sciences*?"

"Because you have to *be social*. And it's a science to be social with some of those people who don't know how to be social."

God, I missed her while I was gone.

Mama too.

"I think she has you there," Mama says dryly.

"I'm not homeschooling her, and you shouldn't support the idea. I'm a terrible teacher. Remember the slime incident last Christmas?"

"I remember you both learned a lot more doing it the hard way than you would've if you'd mastered it on the first try. Tell me again how you learned to bake those delicious blueberry thyme muffins I had for breakfast this morning?"

"Bailey baked those."

"But I made a lot of mistakes and had to work hard to figure them out first," Bailey points out. "Struggling and keeping at it is soooo much more important than getting it right the first time. Which is exactly why you should stay and homeschool me. It'll make you a better person."

"Oh, look. We're here. Darn." I steer the car into the gravel parking lot at the edge of the softball fields, the two-story tan school building framed in the distance by the soft blue mountains behind it. "We'll have to stop talking about mistakes and homeschooling nonsense."

"But not about those shitheads from Shipwreck," Bailey says.

"Bailey. Not in public," Mama orders.

She raised us both on the belief that words are just words, and the only thing you do in banning them is give them more power. But she's also enforced the *don't cause trouble in public since not everyone believes the same* rule.

Which is going to prove mighty difficult for me to follow tonight too, because *dammit* and seven other much more inventive words I've learned during my decade in the Army want to spill out of my mouth.

That motherfluffing pirate ship bus just pulled into the parking lot from the other side.

I thought I was prepared.

I'm not.

I'm *so* not.

Coming home sucks. Everyone has changed. People stop in the bakery to feel out if I've become somehow weird or different or brainwashed because of being in the Army—spoiler alert, I've always been this high-strung—and I don't know who's married and who has kids and who left and who stayed, and it feels like one big bucket of gossip without anyone to decompress about it with later.

Which means I don't know who I can unload to about the fact that I'm going to once again have to look at Grady Rock, who *used to be that person that I'd decompress with*.

And instead is now the person I need to vent about.

"What?" Mama says. She swivels her head toward me, and I realize I've let out a long, resigned sigh.

"We're playing the Shipwreck Shitheads," Bailey tells her.

Mama's chin trembles.

Probably because this is *the* game of the summer.

And she can't see it.

And it will get rowdy. Because this rivalry always does.

I should've told her. I should've told her before we left who we were playing, and then she would've said she didn't want to go, and I wouldn't be here wondering if Grady will notice I'm in the stands and if he'll still be all glowery and upset about me opening a bakery and why I still care, when Mama and Bailey and the bakery are my top priorities.

Not an old high school friendship.

"It's okay," I tell her. "We can go home and try this another night."

"No." She visibly swallows, and though her eyes are hidden behind her dark wrap-around sunglasses, I'm almost positive she's tearing up.

The damage was in her optic nerves, not her actual eyeballs.

Which means her tear ducts still work fine.

"No, we're going to this game." Her voice is wobbly, but getting stronger. That's my Mama. "I never miss it."

"We don't have to stay long."

"Just help me to the stands."

We all climb out, and she struggles to snap her white cane open. Bailey looks away, and I don't know if it's pain at seeing Mama struggle or embarrassment at Mama being *different*.

Could be both at her age.

The gravel isn't the easiest for Mama to navigate, so we end up flanking her and helping her over to the stands, each of us carrying a tote bag with tins of popcorn on our other arms. A few people from Sarcasm join us, including Roger.

"Maria! How you doing there? Help you up into the stands? I got a seat right here on the end, but you can have it."

"What's that?" Bailey asks, pointing over to a folding table set up between the rows of bleachers and the small snack stand behind home plate.

Roger goes pink in the ears. "We, ah, got a bake sale going."

Three people I vaguely recognize are blocking the sign, and I feel my cheeks starting to twitch, because *I* could've baked goodies for a bake sale. I mean, Bailey could've. We could've participated and got the word out a little more about Duh-Nuts's re-opening.

"Wasn't going to tell you," Roger mumbled, "but we've been trying to figure out how to help raise funds for all those projects you got going on to fix up your house with you being—you know, now, and thought we'd guilt those Shipwreck shithead—ah, neighbor people into pitching in some."

The crowd gathered at the table shifts, and my eyes blur as soon as I read the sign.

Bake sale to support Maria Williams –we take cash and check, but no worthless pirate coins.

"The table's overflowing with cookies, Mama," Bailey tells her. "They have brownies too."

"All free for you ladies. Or I'll buy it for you," Roger offers.

"You didn't have to do that," Mama chides softly.

"Don't you go being all proud and humble," he replies, which would be funny if I wasn't so simultaneously touched at the sweetness of it all and also dealing with the sudden fury that Mama's accident happened at all.

Accident?

Illness?

Curse?

Every time I think I've grieved for her sight, the pain and anger and denial comes roaring back unexpectedly.

All the things she'll never see.

Having to live in total blackness and knowing there's a vibrant world all around her that she can only imagine now.

Fury makes me want to hit something, but I tamp it down, because now's not the place. I'll go for a run later. Or something.

"We're neighbors," Roger continues. "Neighbors who give a shit, and who don't know how to go back to giving you regular shit now that you're—you know—so we're helping the best way we know how. And we're fixing to get that railing on your front porch fixed tomorrow too, and I don't want to hear a word about it."

"I'm *blind*, Roger," Mama says softly. Her spine's so

straight and rigid it could double as a ruler. "You can say the word. And thank you. Girls, say *thank you* too."

We dutifully thank Roger—we *are* grateful, though I can see Bailey fighting tears too, and it's a huge relief when someone suddenly shouts my name from the dugout.

"Annika! Thank god. Get your ass over here. We need a third baseman. You still got your arm?"

I look at Mama, who can't see me looking at her, but she snorts softly anyway. "Don't go using me as an excuse," she says before I can say a word. "Get your little tush out there and have some fun."

"I don't have a glove," I tell her, which is only half the reason my heart's in my throat. The other half is that all of Shipwreck's softball team is staring at me.

And that team includes the dark-haired, green-blue eyed, dimpled-cheeked Grady Rock, who's filing toward the field with a goat on a leash.

A *goat*.

If that's not a taunt, then I don't know what is. We're the Sarcasm GOATs, and here he is, bringing a goat with him, though our team name is actually *Greatest Of All Time*, and has been for as long as I've lived in Sarcasm, but it doesn't fit on the team T-shirts when it's all spelled out.

Some things, at least, don't change.

But if Grady sacrifices the goat as some sort of ritual meant to terrify us like that New Zealand rugby team's haka dance, then the Grady Rock I know is well and truly dead.

"Shoot, you know Julio always carries three extra gloves in his coaching bag," Roger says. "You don't want to lose to Shipwreck on account of not having a whole team, do you? You go on. I'll watch over Bailey and your mama."

"I can play," Bailey says.

"No! I'll play," I say quickly, because the last thing I need is her getting hurt on the softball field while playing with a bunch of rowdy adults.

I glance over at the opposing team's dugout again.

Grady's still staring.

So is his goat, though the goat's also trying to pick its own nose with its tongue and it seems to be pulling on its leash like it wants to charge me.

I toss my hair back.

There might be a baseball diamond between us, but I swear he scowls harder.

"Do you have a spare hair tie?" I ask Bailey.

She pulls a black rubber band off her slender wrist and hands it over, and maybe I'm being ridiculous, but I push my chest out and lift my head to show off my neck while I tie my thick hair back in a sloppy ponytail.

"Oh em gee, are you *flirting* with him?" Bailey squeals.

"Who? Who's Annika flirting with? Who's here?" Mama demands. "Is it that Rock boy? He was always so kind for a Shipwreck shithead."

"Was," I agree. "Mama, I don't have to play if you don't want to stay."

"*Play*," she says. "I can sit at home or I can sit here. I'll sit here with the python."

Roger's eyebrows shoot up and he dances around.

A few people jerk their feet off the stands and look at the ground.

Even I jump, despite knowing what's going on.

"Hallucinations," I tell them all. "It's actually normal. She sees tigers and elephants too."

Mama's lips curve up.

The hallucinations are real—the doctors say it's a known side effect of sudden blindness, and now that Mama's getting used to randomly "seeing" animals that aren't there, she's started making jokes of it.

I lean in to hug her and kiss her cheek. "I'll take care of the python. And the Shipwreck shitheads."

"You always take care of everything," she replies.

I try.

I just hope I don't ever let her down.

5

GRADY

WATCHING Annika warm up is almost more distracting than the bake sale.

The *bake sale*.

What the hell is up with Sarcasm taunting me with baked goods this week?

"Oh, shit, that's hardcore," Georgia says beside me, pointing to the sign.

I ignore the jab at the pirate coins and take in the rest of the message on the poster board taped to the table, and my heart stops.

Full stop to the point of pain.

Maria Williams went blind?

I swing my attention back to Annika, who's stretching on the field, bending over to touch the ground, her ass high in the air, her ponytail dangling in the dirt, lean legs outlined in black stretchy fabric. She straightens and takes a spare Sarcasm GOATs T-shirt from somebody on the team, and when she starts shimmying her way into it, I have to wrench my gaze to her mom on the sidelines before I start having a pirate ship mast problem.

Ms. Williams's sunglasses aren't normal sunglasses. They're bigger. Darker. Wrapped around the sides of her eyes. And she's trying to sweep a long white cane in front of her as she makes her way to the stands, escorted by her younger daughter and the plumber I saw at Duh-Nuts yesterday.

Fuck.

No wonder Annika's home.

And I don't want to talk about the swirl of emotions choking my lungs and making me want to strangle something and go hug the entire Williams family at the same time.

Not that they'd take it from me after yesterday.

When I was a complete and total idiot.

Tillie Jean jogs over from home plate. "We won the coin toss," she tells us. "Take the field, and let's kick some GOAT ass."

That, I can control, so I swallow back the questions and worry and, yes, the guilt, and turn into the team huddle.

I shout louder than anyone for the team cheer—*Scallywags to Victory!*—and then head out to play some softball.

"Fire in the hole! Fire in the fucking hole!" Long Beak Silver calls from his perch on Pop's shoulder in the stands.

"That parrot isn't fit for family gatherings," Georgia says while she accompanies me to the pitcher's mound. She's catching, and don't even think of stealing second on her watch.

"Until you can convince it that *Go, team, go* is a cuss word, we're doomed."

"So long as you pitch good and don't let these GOATs score, I don't really care."

She jogs back behind home plate, and we start the game.

I might not play pro ball like Cooper, but I can toss a mean curveball, and I like to set the mood for the game in the first inning. I'm also fucking pissed at Annika for more reasons than I can articulate—for leaving, for coming home, for *not telling me her mom went blind*—and I channel it all into the game.

Which is why I strike out Sarcasm's first three batters.

Yep.

Totally did it on purpose.

On my way back to the dugout, I catch sight of Pop sharing a cookie with Long Beak Silver.

I can't glare at him for buying cookies off the Sarcasm booster club's fundraiser, because I'd have to be heartless to fault anyone for supporting a fundraiser, and doubly so because it's for Annika and her mom.

But I want to.

And then I feel like a total shithead for wanting to be mad.

And pissed that I feel like a shithead.

Fuck the feelings. I'm playing softball. And I'm going to strike out the next three batters too.

That'll help.

We don't score in the bottom of the first, but I keep my promise to myself to pick off Sarcasm's line-up one by one in the top of the second.

Unfortunately, I also strike out when it's my turn to bat.

That pisses me off all over again.

"We'll get 'em next time," Tillie Jean says to me as we grab our gloves and head back to the field.

Most of the team's drinking buried treasure ale from Shipwreck's brewery, but not me.

Because I have three more batters to strike out.

Unfortunately for me, the first batter at the top of the third is Annika.

She strolls to the plate like she owns not just the baseball field, but also the stands, the parking lot, the high school, and the mountains surrounding us. Her hair lifts in the breeze, her hips swing, her chest lifts under that Sarcasm GOATs shirt, and I hate pitching with a woody, but it looks like I don't get a choice.

I'm still grateful for the cup that's trying to hold my dick in check.

Fuck, this is uncomfortable.

I wonder how it feels, knowing her mama can't see her play, being home, dealing with what has to be a crisis in the middle of opening a fucking bakery, and if I let myself go there, I'm not going to be able to pitch this ball.

So instead, I remind myself that she didn't call.

She doesn't *want* my help.

We're two strangers. I can feel bad for the situation, but it's not personal.

Right.

She digs in at the plate, shifting her hips and swinging the bat while she gets into her stance, and *fuck*, was she this hot in high school, or is it the pursed lips and the dark gaze boring straight into mine while I toss the ball into my glove and pretend I'm not breaking out in a sweat for the first time all night?

"Go, Annika!" a young voice calls from the Sarcasm cheering section, and Maria Williams joins in the cheering, as does the rest of the crowd, who are all drinking wine, probably from Sarcasm Cellars.

But not the teenagers. That's good.

"You gonna pitch, or you just gonna stare?" Annika asks.

"Gonna stare," I call back. "Got something stuck in your teeth. It's distracting."

She doesn't take the bait.

Instead, she smirks. "Afraid to pitch to a girl?"

"Pitched to the rest of your team, didn't I?"

A murmur goes up in their dugout, and I know I'm asking for it, but *fuck*.

For four years, all I wanted was one chance to kiss her. To tell her she was more to me than a friend, more than some girl I randomly got paired with in biology the first week of high school, that I knew she didn't want to date, didn't want to end up a single mother at sixteen like her mom. But didn't she know I wouldn't abandon her no matter what? That we'd be careful, because she was worth it, and if the unthinkable happened, we'd handle it *together*.

And now here I am, ten years after I got my chance to kiss her and utterly blew it, letting my pride and ego do all my talking.

"Just pitch the ball," she says.

Not frustrated.

Nope.

She's *smiling*. Like the only thing she did in the Army the last ten years was hit softballs out of the park every single fucking day, and I'm the moron who thinks he can get one past her.

I'm so fucking doomed.

6

Annika

I AM GOING to strike out so hard.

It's been four years since I held a bat, and that time, I wasn't staring down the one man I mistakenly once thought I'd be able to count on forever, my heart wasn't beating an erratic angry rhythm reminiscent of some solid Alanis Morissette, "You Oughta Know," which might not be fully appropriate since technically, *I* left, but he tried to take my dream and my independence from me, and I was a complete ten out of ten mess when I left for Basic.

Not to mention all through it when I didn't get the mail from him that he'd promised he'd send before graduation night happened.

His eyes narrow as he pulls the ball back and then swings his arm forward to let the pitch fly. I make myself not swing, even though I want to smack the shit out of the ball, and am rewarded with the umpire's call of *ball one!*

Grady's lips thin.

"Good eye, Annika!" Bailey yells.

I step back and swing the bat casually while the catcher tosses the ball to the pitcher's mound.

"You're going down," she murmurs to me.

"He wishes," I murmur back.

She snorts. "Keep dreaming, honey."

I square up with the plate and pull the metal bat behind me, ready for the pitch, and ignore her.

Grady tosses me ball two, which I'm not even tempted to swing at.

And now I'm smirking at *him*.

His lips are so thin that the dark line between them is as ominous as a thundercloud, and I'm not surprised when the next ball is right in the strike zone.

I swing.

And I totally whiff.

Dammit.

"And he's back," the catcher says smugly.

Grady's not smirking though.

He's still thrown more balls than strikes. And I might not have known him for a decade, and it might've been his brother who went on to play professional baseball, but I *know* those two balls bother him.

He wants to strike me out.

I want to hit a fucking home run.

We stare each other down. The breeze rustles up a patch of dirt behind him. Everyone in the Sarcasm dugout is cheering. All of the Shipwreck shitheads are scowling at me from the field or heckling me from the stands.

And I refuse to blink, even when my eyes start watering, because Grady's not blinking either.

I should've worn sunglasses.

This whole being stared down by Grady Rock thing is making me uncomfortable in places I don't like to be uncomfortable.

My chest.

My knees.

My ovaries.

"Forget how to throw a ball?" I call.

"He's gonna strike your ass out so hard your mama will still be feeling it in *her* ass a month from now," the catcher says.

I can't decide if I'm pissed that he got the better trash talkers on his team, or impressed that she's willing to talk about my mama.

But I'm glad Grady finally decides to pitch the ball.

I don't swing, because it's low, but the ump still calls it a strike.

The Sarcasm dugout erupts in boos. I cut the ump a *seriously?* look. I don't recognize him, but then, I don't recognize a lot of people around here anymore.

But I bet he gets his donuts from Grady's shop every morning.

I'm gonna have to do something about that.

As soon as I figure out how to bake muffins and not fuck-up-cakes.

I step back from the plate and take another practice swing while the catcher trots out to talk to Grady on the mound. I played all through high school, and I miss it.

"Remember to keep your swing level," Mama calls, and I smile back at her. She played some too when she was younger, and she knows all the right things to say even if she can't see.

Bailey's undoubtedly describing everything to her though. We're learning how to help her see.

"Kick his hash browns, Annika," Bailey yells.

"You can do this, baby girl," Mama adds.

The catcher trots back, and I step up to the plate.

I'm gonna do this.

I'm gonna smack that ball right out of the park. Show Grady what he can do with his *you came back just to open a bakery to compete with mine?* ego.

And make my mama proud in the process.

Grady pulls the ball back, then swings it forward, sending it lobbing toward me in a perfect arc.

I step forward and swing that bat with all my might, waiting for that satisfying *crack* of softball on metal, and instead—

Swoosh-thump.

"Strike three!" the ump calls.

The Shipwreck stands erupt in cheers.

Sarcasm's fans groan.

I blink at Grady.

He smirks right back.

That's it.

He is going *down*.

7

Grady

It's the bottom of the fifth, and we're still tied at goose eggs. Sloane, a relative newcomer to Shipwreck who works as Doc Adamson's nurse during the day and plays center field for us now, is up first.

"Knock it out of the park," I tell her, offering a fist bump.

She smiles wryly, because she hasn't had a single hit all season, but she keeps trying. "Yeah. You got it."

Tillie Jean and Georgia cheer loudly while she makes her way out to the plate, and I step out of the dugout to warm up.

Annika's just a few feet away, playing third base, legs spread wide, knees bent, glove dangling, ready to charge or dive or move any way necessary to get the ball.

If she had to go away to the Army for a decade and

then come home to open a bakery just up the road from me, she could've at least come home ugly.

But not Annika.

She came home with more fire in her dark eyes than she left with, her body a honed temple of subtle curves, so much determination etched in the stubborn set of her slender jaw that I can't stop thinking about what she'd do with all of that focus and drive if we were naked in the bedroom.

Or on the kitchen table.

Under the stars up in the mountains.

Down by the creek that runs behind my brother's place.

Up on the roof of Crow's Nest.

In a fishing boat out on the lake.

Covered in cookie dough.

It's the cookie dough fantasy that gets me, but thank fuck, Sloane actually hits the ball just as I'm getting to the good parts of the fantasy with me licking dough out of Annika's belly button, snapping me out of the daydream.

Sloane's momentarily stunned, then she drops the bat and takes off running for first base.

"Go, Sloane!"

"Run! *Run!*"

Annika's charging the infield, because it's a slow-roller. She snags the softball bare-handed and fires it to first with the most beautiful throw I've ever seen on this softball diamond.

It's neck and neck.

Sloane versus Annika's throw.

And that throw—*fuck*, that throw is perfect.

Utterly perfect.

It lands in the first baseman's glove—and then rips it right off the dude's hand.

He yelps and doubles over.

The Shipwreck stands go nuts.

Sloane hits first base.

The ump calls her safe while the first baseman is shaking his hand, their second baseman running after the ball, Dad playing coach and hollering at Sloane to *run run run!*

She does, turning sharply to dash toward second, and the infield turns into pandemonium. The pitcher's yelling and charging first to help find the ball. The right fielder's running in. Both Annika and the shortstop are racing Sloane to get to second base first. The second baseman reaches the ball behind first base, digs it out of the glove, turns, and throws it to second.

The shortstop misses, Sloane trips and falls right into the base and hugs it, and Annika snags the ball before it can roll out to center field.

"Safe," the umpire calls again.

Our dugout's going wild, cheering and yelling and whooping for Sloane, who's trying to stand up without letting go of the base.

Our cheering section is so loud that Long Beak Silver squawks and flies off Pop's shoulder to go hide behind the concession stand.

"Throw it a little harder next time, Annika," the first baseman yells. "You didn't take my whole hand off. Fu—udge. Why aren't you pitching?"

"Pitcher wasn't sick," she replies. "Third baseman was."

"Elijah. Get sick so Annika can pitch."

The pitcher flips him off, and I stroll to the plate.

There's a runner on second. That's scoring position.

"Get ready to run your ass home," I call to Sloane while I step into the batter's box.

She gives me a thumbs-up, grinning from ear to ear and covered in dust.

"Going down, Rock," the pitcher calls.

I don't answer.

I just smile.

I let his first ball go past me, because I'm not making the same mistake I did last time.

Annika's watching. I can feel her eyes on me.

I shake my head while I get back into my stance. Of course she's watching me.

I'm *batting*.

It's her job to watch me.

The second pitch is inside, so I let it go by and I steal a glance at Annika while the catcher tosses the ball back.

She's ready to pounce.

And it pisses me off that I want her to pounce on *me*.

The third pitch is *it*.

A gorgeous straight-shooter just on the outside of the plate, which is right where I love it.

My bat connects with a *crack!*, and I haul ass. I'm rounding first base before the center fielder reaches the ball.

Everyone in the dugout is screaming.

"*Run run RUN!*" fills my ears from all angles. Sloane is dashing around third, heading for home, and I see the ball flying back my way as I'm approaching second.

I don't stop.

Because we need to score more than I need to stay on

base. Can't win if you don't score. They won't try to throw me out before they try to throw Sloane out, but I can at least be a distraction to the ball getting home, and also set myself up for Tillie Jean to bat me home.

My lungs burn. My knee pops. But I keep flying around second base.

This is why I run every day.

So I can score.

And keep the pounds off that come from working in a bakery.

But mostly so I can score.

I'm halfway to third when Sloane crosses home plate a split second before the catcher scoops the ball up three feet from the plate. Without hesitation, he turns and fires the ball at third base.

I crank up the afterburners and put everything I have into making it those last ten feet. Annika has one foot on the base and her left hand extended. The ball's coming in high, so I go for the dive, because she has to tag me to get me out, and I am *not* getting tagged out.

Not by Annika.

Not after she tagged out my love life ten years ago.

And came home and didn't call.

She shouldn't have opened a bakery.

And she should've called.

I hit the ground harder than I mean to, and my fingertips brush the edge of the base just as her glove connects with my ass.

I get tangled in her feet, and the next thing I know, I'm straining to keep a finger connected to third base and she's sprawled across me with a knee in my back yelling, "What the hell do you mean, *safe*? He's not even on the bag!"

"Am too," I grunt out. "I'm touching it."

"If that's your version of *touching*, then high school makes so much sense," she snaps back.

I crawl closer to the base so I'm *fully* touching the whole damn thing and grunt while I try to roll her off of me. "*Your* rules. *I'm Annika Williams, and I don't date, so don't even try it.*"

She grinds a knee deeper into my back. "*I'm Grady Rock, and I don't have a pair.*"

"I have a pair. I have the equivalent of *six* pairs. *You're* the one who couldn't bother to tell me you came home *because your mama went blind.*"

"And it never occurred to you to ask what I'd been up to and what *brought* me home before jumping to all the ugliest conclusions you could, did it? I thought we were *friends*. Friends give each other the benefit of the doubt."

"Get his pitching arm while you're at it, Annika!" someone yells from the dugout.

"*Maaaaa!*" my goat suddenly cries right above me. "*Maa baaa MAAAAAAAAA!*"

"Better get off before Sue eats you," I tell her.

She snorts a disgusted snort that should be followed by hawking a loogie, but instead of going for the manly—or womanly—show of pounding her chest and spitting the farthest, she shoves off of me, leaps out of reach of my goat, who is most definitely gearing up for a good head-butting, or possibly a leg-humping, and marches the ball back to the pitcher while I stand and dust my pants off with the help of the only pet I know who's more unhelpful than Pop's cussing parrot.

Because I swear to god, the goat is trying to push me toward Annika.

And, yeah, I'm also trying to convince my boner to go home.

Why can't I be attracted to a woman who doesn't want to rip my balls off? Or who at least wants me back?

I reach out and pat Sue on the flank. "Good goat. Stop shoving me. Who let you loose?"

My mom comes trotting out onto the field with Sue's leash. "Gosh, I don't know how that happened. Good slide, honey. Your brother would be proud."

"I got it on video!" Pop calls. "Right down to you belly-flopping in the dirt."

"Eat that pussy!" Long Beak Silver calls. "Eat it good!"

Annika jogs back to third and the game resumes. Tillie Jean's up to bat, and she can kill it. We both spent hours playing with Cooper—who's between us in age—until I left for culinary school.

I clap my hands. "C'mon, TJ. Bring me home."

"Always leaving a woman to finish up a man's work," she calls back with a cheeky grin and a wink.

Our dugout hoots and hollers in amusement, but as soon as Sarcasm's stands start chuckling, the boos turn to hisses.

Annika doesn't say anything despite standing two feet from me.

There are a million things I've wanted to say to her the last ten years, and I can't put voice to a single one right now, while I'm mere inches from her.

I don't want to.

I don't want to let her back into my head.

Or anywhere else.

She's already playing games with my body, even if she

doesn't know it. And I don't want her to know, so I lead off the base, mouth firmly shut.

She plants a foot on the bag, glove at the ready for the pick-off toss from the pitcher.

And Tillie Jean connects with the first ball.

I take off, but have to head back to third when it goes foul up the first base line.

My boner isn't cooling down.

And this dropping sensation in the pit of my stomach is making me realize it's not just my dick that's upset.

It's my heart.

I'm a sappy asshole right now, but fuck it.

She was my best friend for four years, when we shouldn't have been friends at all. Not with the age-old rivalry between our towns.

"You bust everyone's balls in the Army?" I grunt as I start to lead off again.

"Only when they stole my donut recipes."

"Who'd want brick donuts?"

"The same guys who wanted a piece of my tits and ass."

I swing around to face her as I dimly register a cracking noise somewhere behind me, and in the midst of trying to suppress my rage at the idea of *anyone* touching Annika, I realize Tillie Jean's hit the ball.

I'm supposed to run home.

So I do.

I turn without a second thought and run my ass to home plate…

Where the catcher's waiting with the ball in his glove, because Tillie Jean barely got the tip of it.

I'm out.

I'm *fucking out* when I didn't have to run.

All because Annika had to mention her tits and her ass and other guys getting a piece of them.

Fuck.

Fuck.

I glower at her while I make my way back to the dugout.

She studiously ignores me while she smooths the dirt out around third base with her sneaker, but I swear, she's watching me.

Yeah.

Watching me while she's ignoring me.

I have a problem.

"What the hell, Rock?" Georgia asks when I step into the dugout.

"Too much beer," I grumble, which is a total lie, and she knows it.

But I vow to get Annika back.

She's going *down* next time she's up to bat.

And dammit all over again, now I'm thinking about her sucking my cock.

While she's out there ready to play ball.

Like I don't exist at all.

"You have a problem," Georgia informs me.

"*Maaa!*" Sue agrees from the stands.

I stifle a good *ya think?* and concentrate on the game.

"Everything okay, son?" Dad calls.

I give him a thumbs-up. Pop makes a note in his Jolly Roger notebook—the one he keeps his matchmaking notes in—and Ma blows me a kiss.

Her way of saying *I still love you even though you screwed the pooch on that play.*

I make myself remember the last time Long Beak Silver gave me a play-by-play of Pop and Nana in the bedroom, and I have my cock back under control by the time the inning's over.

With us up by a single run that should've been at least two.

My head's solidly in the rest of the game, and I don't give up a single hit through two more innings.

We don't score again either, but a win is a win, and dammit, we're gonna win this game.

The crowd's getting rowdy, because it's a tight game and everyone's boozed up like we're at a frat party instead of a softball game.

Pretty sure Sue's been sneaking some beer when Ma's distracted, because he's *maa*ing a little loopy too, with his head tilted to one side, and can goats get hiccups? Because I swear that goat has the hiccups.

I take the mound at the top of the sixth, knowing what's coming.

Annika.

She's leading off.

She strolls to the plate swinging her bat like she doesn't have a single care in the world. My pulse starts playing some Apocalyptica—that's Metallica, as done on strings, and it's hardcore—and my palm gets itchy.

Just another batter, I remind myself.

One more strikeout.

She squares up to the plate, flexing her wrists to put the bat in constant motion, small back-and-forth movements as she shifts her hips in anticipation.

Her thighs are solid under those black leggings, her

booty curved and toned, and now I'm sporting a pirate mast behind my cup again.

Her dark eyes stare me down.

Daring me to try to strike her out.

I know it's bravado. I struck her out last time, I'll strike her out again.

I toss the ball casually in my hand a few times. Show her I'm not affected by her either. That I'm bored. And this will be easy.

And then I wind up for a killer curve ball that she won't see coming.

I release it, and it flies as fast as a softball ever flies, with a perfect arc, heading into a curve that would make my brother proud, and then it happens.

There's a punctuated *tink!*, and before I can move, I catch the ball.

Right in the crotch.

Pain explodes in my hard-on, radiating out to the pit of my stomach and shooting down my thighs and rendering my lungs impotent balloons.

Darkness clouds my vision.

And somewhere, in the deepest recess of my mind, behind the internal howling, I imagine Annika standing over me.

Smirking and muttering something about donuts.

8

Annika

It turns out that racking the enemy's pitcher in the balls is a good way to ensure you're welcomed back into the fold at home.

Who knew?

The next morning, Duh-Nuts is swamped with locals wanting to order cinnamon rolls and asking how they can help my mama and, most importantly, talking about the softball game.

We won two to one in the end, thanks to my lead-off single in the sixth inning that I feel incredibly guilty about.

"Not that I'd ever advocate for violence, of course, but I'm so glad you put that smug pitcher in his place. He needed to be taken down a notch or two," my former kindergarten teacher tells me.

"Try seventeen," her daughter, who's home from college, adds before moaning over her pecan roll. "And you should throw one of these at him too, because it's like sex rolled in cinnamon and sugar and nuts. Wait. Maybe you shouldn't throw it at him. We don't throw sex at shitheads, right? I can't think straight. This is *sooo* good."

"I'll be sure to tell Mama you like it," I say while I dish up another cinnamon roll for Roger, who's back for thirds.

"Your mama working in the kitchen today?" he asks.

I nod. "Bailey helped her measure and mix, but she tested the water temperature and did all the kneading herself."

I don't add that Bailey also made the caramel sauce after my attempt literally went up in flames, or that my roll was so sloppy we almost didn't have pecan rolls this morning, because people don't really need to know that.

Roger beams and scratches his scruffy salt and pepper beard. "That makes it even more delicious. You're gonna keep playing for the GOATs, right? We need your arm."

I don't make any promises, because I have someone coming in to interview for the position of morning baker later today—which will cost more than we initially budgeted for outside help, but it's necessary—and I heard from my captain this morning that my discharge paperwork hit a snag, as if military paperwork doesn't already move slower than a slug on a glacier, and I suddenly might need contingency plans for my contingency plans.

There's no time to worry about committing to playing softball permanently for the GOATs, no matter how much I want to.

When we're *not* playing Shipwreck again.

The breakfast crowd dies down mid-morning. I'm wiping off the chipped, wobbly two-person tables that need to be replaced when the doorbell dings and a familiar face breezes in from the sunny summer heat.

"Annika!" Liliana DeSilva cries. She smothers me in a tight hug, though it's awkward because she's barely five feet tall, and I have at least seven inches on her. Eight, on a good day. "Girl, I didn't know you were home until I heard about the game last night. You should've called. How's your mama? And Bailey? And oh my god, did you *really* rack Grady Rock in the nuts? I swear, if you hadn't, I wouldn't have known you were here at all. Thank god for small favors and good gossip, right? Are those cinnamon rolls I smell? Tell me your mama made them, because we all know you can't bake worth—oh my god. I'm sorry. I'm so sorry. I didn't think, I just—"

I cut her off with a laugh, because it's laugh or cry, and I'm trying to make smart choices. "It's okay. Yes, Mama made them. And how did you miss the gossip train? I've been home for three weeks."

"This heiress just bought the winery," she whispers, "and I've been working my ass off to make sure I don't get canned. Nobody knows much about her yet, but supposedly she's actually getting here to look the place over for the first time today, so I need to make sure I'm back by noon."

"You won't get canned," I tell her, though I really don't know anything about Sarcasm Cellars at all. "How long have you been there?"

"Since I graduated college."

Bailey pops her head into the dining area. "Annika, Mama and I are going for a drive with Roger. Don't wait for us for lunch."

"You're what?"

"Mama wants to get out more. So we're going for a drive. Roger offered after I assured him the wooly mammoth wouldn't be getting in the car with us."

She smiles.

It's full of mischief.

"Bailey—" I start.

Mama appears behind her, dark sunglasses on, white cane gripped in her hand. "Don't be such an old lady," she tells me. "It's just a drive. Oh. And now there are catfish swimming in the bakery. Are the walls in here still yellow?"

"Yes, Mama."

"I like the wooly mammoth in the kitchen better, but it's going to crush the sink if it's not careful. Also, we're going for a drive. With Roger. He promised he wouldn't take advantage of us."

"He doesn't have to work today?"

"Plumbing's all good in Sarcasm today," she assures me. "And do you remember his son, Birch? He's on call."

"You don't want to go rest? You've been up since four this morning. And you don't normally have two hallucinations in a row if you're not tired."

"Annika Rose, I may be blind, but I'm still your mother, and I'm also still quite the spring chicken."

"She really is," Bailey agrees, which is even more suspicious. "We left two more pans of cinnamon rolls on the counter in back. I frosted them and everything, so all you have to do is put them out."

"It's almost lunchtime. People aren't coming in for cinnamon rolls."

She smiles. "They should. The cinnamon rolls are so delicious, people should have breakfast dessert for lunch.

Or you can pack them up for customers to reheat in the morning. Awesome either way! Later, Anni-gator."

"After while, Bailey-dile," I reply automatically, though I'm still highly suspicious, but honestly, Mama getting out is a *good* thing, even if I know she'll be exhausted, because she tries to deny it, but the stress is getting to her, as evidenced by the hallucinations. "And remember Mama needs to be home for her appointment with the mobility specialist by two."

"Got it," Bailey calls.

I turn back to Liliana. "So. You want a cinnamon roll?"

"Wooly mammoths?"

"Just go with it."

She asks for a coffee and a banana, so I grab both for her and then we sit to catch up.

"What's it like seeing Grady again?" she asks, her hazel eyes sparking with curiosity as she goes straight for the kill.

"It's just like seeing everyone again," I lie.

"*Annika*. You two were attached at the hip in high school. I never understood why he didn't just ask you out. He was clearly crazy about you. And now you're back, and he's still over there in Shipwreck…"

"Being a Shipwreck shithead," I remind her.

"Please. Cooper was a shithead. Grady was *not*. He worshipped the ground you walked on."

"He did not."

"Um, *yes*, he did. Did he bring anyone else cookies and cupcakes and muffins every day? Did he beat up Garrett MacGruder for saying crude things in the locker room about any other girl in school? Or her mama? Did he come all the way here, to Sarcasm, in enemy territory, to see any other *person* besides you? No, he did not. Because he was sweet on *you*."

I open my mouth to tell her she's wrong, that we were just really good friends who clicked because he knew what to say to calm me down when I'd go too far down the path of seeking perfection, and I didn't care what his brother or sister did, unlike half of the rest of high school.

But I can't tell Liliana she's wrong, because everything he told me the night we graduated high school suggests she's right.

C'mon, Annika. You know you're it for me. You always have been. Let's make it official. Fuck the Army. Stay here. Move to Shipwreck. Come work for my family while I go to culinary school. You can take classes at the community college. I'll be home every weekend. We'll get a place together, and it'll be awesome. You feel it, don't you? This thing? We're more than friends. Let's BE more than friends. For real.

And in the moments when I'm being completely honest with myself...I knew it.

I knew he liked me.

But I was terrified of him liking me. I was terrified I was reading him wrong. I was terrified that I was reading him right.

I was terrified of having to work two jobs to support an unplanned baby while ruining both of our life plans.

"He...might've said something to that effect before I left, but he just didn't want things to change. He didn't really mean it. He just didn't want me to leave."

She gives me that *seriously? That's your story?* look. "I get it. God, Annika, if anybody gets it, you know I do. We didn't want to be our mothers, and we needed to establish ourselves before letting crazy teenage hormones change our lives forever. But…we're all adults now. You're home now. He was your best friend. Are more friends ever really a bad thing?"

I sip my own coffee and squint at her, because Liliana grew up next door to us, in a rented house with barely enough room for two people, much less three, and she always hated that I was friends with *anyone* from Shipwreck, even Grady. "What's in Shipwreck that you want? Because you and Shipwreck aren't exactly BFFs. At least, you weren't."

"I'd say this even if my new boss hadn't already sent a memo about wanting to expand local distribution to all the liquor stores in the tri-county area. Just for the record. Because you two *were* best friends, even if I was a total Sarcasm asshole about it back then. And honestly, I miss you both. I didn't realize it until you were gone, but you were my hope that my grandparents would quit calling people from Shipwreck shitheads. Like Romeo and Juliet, without the stabbings and death stuff. And I was never really sure if you two should have sex or not. Risk of teen pregnancy aside and all that. But like…if you could overcome how different your families were and the fact that our towns are rude to each other, then maybe love's possible for everyone."

"You are a total nut."

She grins and fluffs her curly auburn hair. "Some things never change."

And thank goodness for that.

Because she's right. I need a friend. Probably several.

I'm just not sure if I agree with her assessment of who I should start with first.

And after last night, I doubt he'd be interested in any kind of truce.

So today, I choose to be grateful for Liliana.

My new Sarcasm best friend.

"You know anyone in town who can bake like a goddess and *doesn't* have to go back to school in a few weeks?" I ask her.

"Oh my god, you still can't bake?" she whispers.

"Sshh! I'm trying, but so far, all I've managed to do is create something that NASA scientists came and confiscated to see if I somehow recreated moon rock here on earth, and also set fire to the stovetop."

She chuckles over her coffee. "God, I'm so glad you're home."

I am too.

Except I'm *not*.

I'm not fully home. But not fully gone.

I'm just filling space while we figure out my family's new normal.

And in the meantime, I'm trying to make all my mama's dreams come true.

9

Grady

I'm putting the final touches on a carrot cake, ice pack to my ball sack, Apocalyptica blaring in my kitchen while I whisper to the frosting.

"Beautiful, baby. So smooth. So silky. I could stroke you all day long."

Neither the cake nor the cream cheese frosting answer, but they both clearly love the way I'm smoothing the finish with gentle spins of the cake's turntable coupled with the precise caresses of my icing spatula.

The strings on my speakers rock out to "Enter Sandman," and I can almost pretend everything is completely normal.

"So perfect," I whisper. "I could lick you from top to bottom and over again."

Georgia stalks into the kitchen in her Crow's Nest

apron, hits a switch, and my music goes silent. "People are complaining about the vibe. You need to talk it out?"

"I'm talking to the cakes. And what's wrong with Metallica? This is fucking *awesome*."

"It's *orchestral* Metallica."

"It's leveled-up badass."

She levels me with a *we're done talking about this* glare, like she owns the place or something. Which she doesn't—I do, backed by a loan from my brother, the rich baseball player, which is the only reason I haven't had to shut down yet, and yes, that irritates the shit out of me too, plus adds a big dollop of guilt at the idea that I could be letting him down too—but she's the best employee I've ever hired, and I don't want to lose her.

I'd marry Georgia if that's what it took to save the bakery, even though we'd fight like cats and dogs and she's told me numerous times that I'm not tall enough or black enough for her, and she also prefers a man with what she calls *a bigger package*, though I think she's fooling herself if she thinks *that* exists.

Can't fix any of those—and honestly, we're too similar for a relationship of convenience to work—so instead, I'll let her pretend she runs my bakery.

Sales *are* up since she started here.

Just not enough to dig Crow's Nest out of that nebulous place where it's regularly making two dollars in profit after paying Georgia what she deserves and me just barely enough to not default on my mortgage.

She's right.

I can't afford to chase my customers away.

And wouldn't that be the frosting on the shitcake to

have Crow's Nest go under right when Annika opened her own bakery?

Because her mama went blind.

Fuck.

"Cake can't love you back like a woman can." She eyeballs my crotch. "But you're not getting any from that front either, are you?"

"Are you here to rob me of my joy and ruin my day, or did you actually need something?"

"Both."

"Fantastic." I straighten. My lower back gives a twinge, and if I could glare at it and threaten to fire it too today, I would.

Especially since I know better than to threaten to fire Georgia.

"You want bad or worse first?" she asks.

"Bad."

"We still have four dozen tres leches donuts left."

"*What*? Those were delicious." And expensive, and if they don't sell, today's a red day.

A red day I can't afford.

"Yeah, but they're not banana pudding donuts. Also, there's a teenager and a blind lady sitting down at the end of the row giving away cinnamon roll samples and telling people to go to Sarcasm to support the Maria Williams Foundation for the Blind by buying from Duh-Nuts."

Fuckers.

They really are stealing my customers now, and my daily profit sheet isn't the only thing going red.

"I called the sheriff. She said they got a permit. So I called your Pop instead. Got a feeling he's gonna take Sue and Long Beak Silver for a walk."

I rip off my apron and stalk around my worktable, grabbing my phone while I go. "Fucking sheriff."

"Yeah, but until we can get somebody from Shipwreck to run against her, we're stuck. Plus, there's that whole thing where crime's down forty percent since she took over. And she charmed the pants off all those rich people with houses up on Thorny Rock Mountain."

"*Cooper* owns a house up on Thorny Rock Mountain."

"And he's never here, and half of the rest of 'em up there aren't really locals either. They just put money toward the election campaign because they like their houses not being broken into during the week while they're doing their regular jobs making oodles of money in the big city."

I toss my bag of ice in the sink, and I head for the back door.

"By the parking field or by the gazebo?" I ask.

She points me toward the mountains, and I march out the back door.

I can't be a total dick, because yeah, it sucks that Annika's mama went blind.

But they're poaching my customers, and Crow's Nest can't afford to lose customers.

Fucking numbers.

If I could just bake and leave the books to someone else, I would, but I can't afford to pay for it. Every little bit of savings I stash away manages to get eaten up by an oven needing repair or a mixer breaking or a leaky roof.

Something.

And here come the Sarcasm assholes, sitting in *my* town when they could be giving away samples in any one of the little towns dotting our county.

They're baiting me.

And they're stealing my customers.

I've worked up a good, steaming pile of *mad* by the time I spot the two of them lounging on a bench beside the *Argh, Ye Be in Shipwreck Now* sign, not a full block away from my bakery.

Pop's crossing the street from the other side the same time I approach from the back. Sue's tugging on his leash, and I can already hear Long Beak Silver.

"Get the fuck out of my town! Rawk!"

"Your bird is really rude," Bailey calls to Pop.

"So's sitting a block from my bakery and stealing my customers," I tell her.

She doesn't jump at my approach from behind the bench, and I notice the same guy who was at Duh-Nuts the other day coming from the small parking lot at the edge of the park with a box of what I assume are fresh cinnamon roll samples.

"Should've known not to expect manners in a pirate town," she says.

"Bailey. Who is it?" Ms. Williams asks.

"That old man who wears eyeliner all the time with the rude parrot, and that Rock guy who thinks he owns the world or something," the teenager replies.

"He owns the best damn bakery this side of the mountains," Pop says.

"Grady." Ms. Williams turns her head in my direction with a smile. "How are your testicles today? Annika felt terrible for hurting you."

"Not terrible enough to pause before she got on base," Pop points out.

"She forgets bakers don't have the brass cojones of all

those Army men she's known the last ten years. And she *did* stop at first instead of going on to second like she could've."

Bailey snickers.

I really did like her better before she could form full sentences.

"What are you gentlemen doing in Sarcasm today?" Ms. Williams asks.

"We're not in Sarcasm. You're sitting in Shipwreck," Pop tells her.

"What? No. Surely not." She smiles, and in my more forgiving moments, I'd say she was teasing me, but I'm not feeling very forgiving at the moment. "I'd smell the pirates if we were. And if we were in Shipwreck, those mountain lions sitting over there would definitely be gnawing on someone's peg leg."

Pop and I both jump and look around, but there are no mountain lions.

And Maria's *blind*.

Even if there were, she couldn't see them.

More snickering from Bailey.

"Here you go, Maria. Last box of samples. Told you that you still had it in you to bake the good stuff." The plumber—Roger? Is that his name?—plops the box on the edge of the bench.

Sue lunges for it. He's probably just as interested in the white cardboard as he is the cinnamon rolls inside.

I don't try to stop my goat, but Roger makes a go of saving the cinnamon rolls.

"Yes, Ms. Williams," I tell her. "You're in Shipwreck. Stealing my customers."

"It's karma." Bailey makes one of those irritating teenager faces that Tillie Jean still tosses out when Cooper's in town and we're ganging up on her, though Bailey's is all brown eyes and the same bone structure as Annika's, which means she's probably going to be hit on by everything with a single red blood cell in its body in the next four years, which means *shit*, somebody's gonna have to watch out for her.

"First of all," she continues, completely unaware that I'm about to have a heart attack at the idea of teenage boys at the high school trying something with her, which is none of my damn business, but apparently I can't stop the feelings, "we wouldn't be stealing your customers if you were giving them anything worthwhile to eat. And second of all, you stole my donut idea. We're just making things even."

Yeah. Maybe I stole her donut idea.

And maybe I've been debating spending my last four hundred dollars on a soft serve machine, because bubble waffles are trending hot, and there's only one restaurant in Copper Valley serving them, which means Crow's Nest could be a trendsetter.

"You're twelve," I say instead of letting more guilt sink in. "You don't make business decisions."

"I'm thirteen, which I know you know, and I could pass economics with a higher grade than you could."

"Are you sure we're in Shipwreck?" Maria asks.

"Fewer pirates," Roger tells her. He's standing on the bench now, which is creaking under his weight while he holds the donut box over his head and Sue tries to eat his pants. "The festival's over, so the fake pirates went home and everyone finally took their annual baths. But this Pop guy has a parrot and a pirate hat."

"I could take those for you," I tell Roger. "Give them away over at my shop."

All three of the Sarcasm intruders snort-snicker.

"You used to be so much smarter," Ms. Williams says with a soft smile.

"You callin' my grandson dumb?" Pop asks.

"Dumb as a box of pins missing their hand grenades," Long Beak Silver offers. "Walk the plank! Rawk!"

"Just thought we could be neighborly," I tell Maria. "You help me, I help you."

Bailey tosses her long hair, which has some curl to it, just like Maria's, though the older woman's hair is streaked with a few strands of silver. "There's no help for you."

"I'm gonna have to ask you to leave my town," Pop growls.

"Do you know what I've never understood?" Maria says. "I've never understood why Shipwreck hates Sarcasm so much."

"It's because we got the better name, Mama."

"*Down*, you mangy goat!" the plumber barks.

"It's unfortunate that we *did* get the better name," Ms. Williams agrees, "but we've all been named for over a hundred years. Maybe it's time we bury the hatchet."

"Maybe if you all didn't cheat in softball, we could," Pop says.

"Cheater, cheater, pussy-eater," Long Beak Silver squawks.

"Your bird is truly filthy."

Leave it to the teenager to put it so eloquently.

"Pop. Nobody cheated in softball."

"She tried to take your manhood off!"

"It was an accident," Bailey insists. "If she'd been trying, we'd still be out there scavenging for his little swimmers."

"Bailey Sophia Williams."

"Just saying, Annika always does what she says she's going to do. Also, I checked her calendar, and she didn't have it penciled in to take anybody's nuts off. If she didn't schedule it, she didn't do it on purpose."

That makes so much fucking sense, and it soothes a few of my feathers to know she's still as organized as she once was.

"And you think my bird's rude," Pop grumbles.

"Speaking of rude," Maria says, "Bailey's right. It *was* rude of Grady to steal her idea for tres leches donuts. So maybe we shouldn't be sitting here handing out samples. But maybe we can all call a truce since we're even. Unless there's something else bothering you, Grady?"

That's definitely guilt gnawing at my gut, because I shouldn't have stolen their idea.

And I don't know why I'm being such a shithead.

But I'm pretty sure I wouldn't be a shithead to anyone else.

And she's asking if I want to talk about my feelings for Annika.

Which I definitely do *not*.

I grunt, because I don't like where my thoughts are going. "I'm going back to work. And Pop, you should too."

"I don't like riffraff in my town."

"You live here," Bailey points out.

"*Bailey*," Ms. Williams says again. "Hush your mouth, or I'll feed you to that dog."

"It's a goat, Mama."

"Oh. That's not a Rottweiler-poodle mix trying to eat that dinosaur bone?"

"Unfortunately not, but these hallucinations are awesome. It's a mostly-white goat, with one horn missing and a big brown patch over his eye, and he's trying to eat Roger's tennis shoes."

"Likes garbage," Pop says.

"*Pop*. Don't you have a mini golf course to run?"

"Left your grandmother in charge so I could come walk your goat."

"Fucking goat," Long Beak Silver squawks.

The sun's beating down on all of us. Roger's sweating while he bats Sue away and dribbles cinnamon roll samples onto Ms. Williams's hair. She's swatting the crumbs away like they're bugs.

And a sudden memory of Annika running from a swarm of honeybees down by the lake hits me so hard and fast that I nearly grunt in pain.

I was carrying two paddleboards from the parking lot to the lake in the middle of the Blue Lagoon nature preserve when she came shrieking up the short path, yelling for me to run, *run*, her black hair streaming behind her, eyes wide, legs pumping furiously, arms just as hard.

We were heading into junior year, and I'd been dating someone, but I'd seen the sheer terror in her eyes and I'd known in that minute I'd do anything to protect her, and that I needed to quit dating anyone else so long as Annika Williams had a pulse and still walked this earth.

Couldn't protect her from the bees, though, and we both got stung several times over.

She cried.

Said she didn't want to kill the bees. It was her fault for going where she wasn't supposed to.

That was the Annika I knew.

Soft-hearted. Strong, yeah, and fucking determined to prove she and her mama were both worthy and *someone* despite the ways society looked down on them—I've never met anyone more determined once she set her mind to a task—but compassionate to her core.

Which is part of why I never understood why she wanted to go into the Army.

She wasn't built for battle.

Built for standing up for herself, yeah. For defending her mom and her sister, of course.

But built for war?

No.

Not my Annika.

She couldn't even kill a bee without crying.

And now she's trying to kill my bakery.

Which means I have a choice.

Fight back against the one woman who's still under my skin ten years later, or let her win and watch my bakery go down the drain.

"Sue. Get down," I order. "Pop, go back to work. And you three—good luck. You're gonna need it."

I take my goat's leash and yank him down the street, back to my bakery. He's not happy with me, and he stops to try to eat flowers, a flagpole, and a stack of cannonballs piled outside the Shipwreck Gift Shop next to my bakery.

I give half a thought to taking Sue home, but he'd probably eat through the fence to go sniff out more cinnamon rolls.

Which means he's just going to have to come with me today.

While I fight fire with fire.

10

Annika

By one o'clock, I know *something* is going on, because I've had a steady stream of people in from out of town asking for cinnamon rolls. Bailey isn't answering her phone. Nor is Mama, but then, she hasn't yet mastered swiping the screen to answer when she can't see it.

Her sessions with her mobility specialist, who helps her re-learn how to do all the things she used to need her sight for, haven't yet progressed to mastering the smartphone again.

She's trying, but she all but threw the damn thing across the small house when the voice assistant thought she wanted to dance the Macarena this morning.

Mama and the voice assistant don't see eye-to-eye right now.

And that was a terrible thing to think about my blind mother.

It's amazing how often I don't even realize I'm thinking about seeing, but having Mama blind now has opened my eyes—dammit, did it again—to just how much I take my sight for granted.

I've just sold the last cinnamon roll to a blond woman about my age, maybe a few years older, in a pink pantsuit and large sunglasses who's carrying a Prada handbag that almost certainly isn't a knock-off—very unusual in these parts—when someone stops outside the bakery window with something that looks baked and sugary, but most definitely did *not* come from Duh-Nuts.

I'm about to dismiss the sight, since Rise and Grind is right down the street, and while their baked goods aren't homemade—yet—they do sell muffins and pastries, except two other people stop beside him, all of them with identical sample-sized pastries in hand.

This is either a birthday party that I wasn't invited to, or something sinister is going down in Sarcasm.

The sunny dining room is mostly empty for the moment—just a mom and her toddler enjoying an early afternoon chocolate chip monster cookie now that the lady in pink has gone—so I wash up quickly and peek out the front door.

There's a truck in my parking lot.

With a tall, dark-haired, dimple-cheeked man wearing a tight black pirate T-shirt, faded jeans, and boots, leaning against the tailgate, handing out—I squint closer—*donuts*?

He *is*.

Grady Rock is in *my* parking lot, handing out samples of *his* donuts.

"What are you doing?" I march over there so hard, I

leave dents in the concrete sidewalk. "What the *hell*, Rock?"

His eyes are hidden behind aviator sunglasses, but I know he's looking straight into my eyes by the way my skin shivers from under my fingernails all the way to my belly button.

"You hand out samples in my town, I hand out samples in yours," he says.

"What are you talking about?" I snap.

"What am I talking about?" he repeats like the fact that I'd ask is an insult to his intellect. "I'm talking about giving you a taste of your own medicine. Don't like it? Then keep your damn spies out of my town, and the same goes for your damn cinnamon rolls."

"*Mama*," I mutter.

That's where Mama and Bailey went. And Roger, to drive them.

They're in Shipwreck.

Taunting Grady and stealing his customers.

I'd feel bad, except instead of handling this like an adult, he's brought his truck, his dimples, his goat, and his donuts to *my* territory.

And I'd be willing to bet they're tres leches donuts that *he's never served before*. Bailey made me sit with her while she scrolled through the entire Crow's Nest social media feed last night to prove that not once in the last three years has he ever sold tres leches donuts, which is all the proof she needed that he made them just because she suggested it.

And now she's worried he's going to steal her bubble waffle idea too.

I like to give people the benefit of the doubt—especially people *who used to be my best friend*—but I'm becoming more convinced by the minute that she's right.

Especially since he brought his goat, which is leashed to his rearview mirror, like he's making some kind of statement about goats also being *his*, despite Sarcasm's team being named the GOATs.

And he's still missing that our GOAT actually stands for Greatest Of All Time.

Still, his goat strains the leash and bleats indignantly at me like it's hungry and I'm denying it fresh cupcakes.

Or possibly like it, too, is accusing me of sending spies and thieves to Shipwreck.

"That's right," Grady drawls softly. "Your family thinks they can steal my customers."

"So you're fighting a teenager and a disabled woman."

"That teenager is more devious than my grandfather and his parrot put together."

"You're a grown man. And you're fighting *with a teenager*."

There are no signs of his dimples as he glowers at me in the late July heat. The half-dozen people crowding around his truck slowly back up.

"Didn't realize he was a Shipwreck shithead, Annika," one of them mutters. He eyes the donut sample, takes half a bite, moans in pleasure, then winces and throws the rest on the ground and crushes it with his boot, the pain in his face telling me just how highly he regards me if he's willing to sacrifice an orgasmic tres leches donut.

"That's what I think of your baked goods," he barks half-heartedly to Grady, still eyeing the donut like it's the second coming of fresh chocolate chip cookies, which we *all* know are the best pastry in the universe, except when I bake them.

The goat bleats again and pulls so hard on its leash that its front hooves leave the pavement.

A few more of the gathered crowd apologizes to me and either stuffs the last of the donut samples in their mouths, or cringe when they, too, throw the rest of their sample to the ground and back away toward their cars or their shops or wherever they came from.

Grady's brows are so low, they've disappeared beneath the top rim of his sunglasses, and his mouth is flatter than my first drill sergeant's high-and-tight haircut.

I always thought his dimples were sexy, but I can't deny what broody, seething, wound-up Grady is doing to my nether regions. I haven't been this hot and bothered since my favorite planner line announced Wonder Woman-themed stickers and pages.

He jerks his head toward the back of my bakery.

Like he wants to talk privately. Away from my Sarcasm supporters and his goat.

I'm all in for a private conversation right now, because I'm about done with this stupid fight, but I also know Grady, and I know how hard he worked to carve out something that *he* could be the best in.

He grew up in the shadow of his little brother, who had the bigger personality, the bigger brain, and the bigger talent. And while I know he'd do anything for Cooper, that doesn't mean he's immune to having feelings about being the less successful Rock brother.

Not that *anyone* likes to swallow their pride. Grady's just always had to fight for his place, and I get it.

I'm moving in to where *he* excels.

I'm pulling a Cooper on him.

Plus, heat always makes him cranky.

It's why his mom always kept popsicles in her freezer during the summer.

"Can you keep an eye on the shop for me?" I ask the guy nearest me before I realize it's Birch, Roger's son.

Should've known by his height and bulk, but I wasn't paying attention.

He swivels his gaze between me and Grady. "Don't know that I want to leave you alone with this guy, Annika."

A muscle in Grady's jaw flexes beneath the dark shadow of early stubble, and I swear I get a hot flash. But just in my breasts. Whatever that is between my legs, it's definitely not a hot flash.

"Ten years in the Army, Birch," I say. "I've got him."

I almost miss the flick of his gaze over my body and the slow grin that starts, but I don't miss the growl Grady aims his way, despite being completely out-matched since Birch has at least four inches and fifty pounds on him, or the way the goat suddenly goes nuts.

"Oh, for god's sake," I mutter, and I turn on my heel and march to the alley behind Duh-Nuts.

"Stay, Sue," Grady orders, and I feel him following me.

Ten years ago, we would've been piling into his beat-up, rusting truck to head down to the lake for a dip in the heat.

Today, we're headed for some air-clearing next to the trash cans.

I turn slowly when we're both tucked behind the building, and I blow out a slow breath to calm my racing heart.

Arguing and I don't really get along, and Grady might not be the only one of us who struggles with pride.

Although, if I'm being honest, I tend to embrace mine rather than struggle with it. I've earned it, dammit. I went from growing up in a rented single-wide to being a successful staff sergeant in the Army, a college graduate, a homeowner, and now co-owner of a small business.

You don't make leaps by apologizing.

So meeting him halfway will be hard, but I need to do this.

Liliana was right.

I want my best friend back. Life's hard enough right now.

I open my mouth, but before I can get a word out, he's in my face, boxing me against the wall and giving me emotional whiplash.

"Seriously, Annika? Using a disabled woman and a kid to steal customers? That's the kind of shit I would've expected from some other Sarcasm asshole, but not *you*."

I shove him, because he's too close, and too pissed, and his apparent need to *not* make up sacks me in the gut and makes all my good intentions disintegrate. "That's what you think of me? That I'm the kind of person who'd do that?"

"Racking me in the nuts wasn't enough. What's next? Beating my sister at the banana pudding game? What happened to you?"

"What happened to *me*? How about what happened to *you*? Quit with the Neanderthal show and think for a minute. What the hell do I have to gain by racking you in the nuts and *spying* on your bakery?"

"Closure? More customers? How the fuck should I know what's going on in your head?"

I shove him again, but he's a solid block of angry granite that doesn't move. "Maybe because you were my best friend? Maybe because people don't change *that* much? Maybe because *I* know you're standing here having a temper tantrum because you don't like change and you don't like competition and you don't like that I left, but you don't know how to deal with it other than yelling at me. You can't be bothered to think about the fact that my entire life is upside down and even if I am being an asshole, I deserve a little leeway from the *one person* in this entire world who's ever understood me as well as I understand myself?"

Fuck, I'm shouting.

And his nostrils are flaring.

I know what the Grady Rock nostril flare means.

It means he's about to shove off this wall and walk away and put my face on a dartboard so that when he's out of ideas, he can throw darts at my nose and plot decadent creations that'll *show me* that he's the best, because he's physically incapable of admitting that he's hurting and he'd rather lash out than admit that he's upset.

And it's making me hot and achy in my clit at the same time that my heart's cracking in two, because he was my best friend.

He got me through high school. He shared so much of himself with me, and I confessed so many things to him that I've never told another soul.

That I hated myself for wanting to be *better* than my mama, when she was the best mama in the world.

That I was afraid of the Army, but I knew I needed to spread my wings, and it was all I could afford.

That I was terrified of snakes and I wanted a pet bulldog more than I wanted a baby sister.

That I didn't know if I'd ever be the kind of girl that men were interested in, and that I *cared* that someone find me attractive, but I needed to be able to stand on my own two feet more than I *wanted* to be wanted, and I had plenty of time to grow up before I fell in love.

He got parts of me that I've never shared with another person.

And now he's nothing more than another Shipwreck shithead.

"We could've done this better," he says, his voice thick and choked with something I can't read, but I don't miss the subtle accusation that it's *my* fault.

"No, *you* could've done this better. Because *nothing* about me being back is about *you*. Except in your head. Call me when you've gotten over yourself, and maybe we can be friends again."

"Fuck *friends*, Annika. You know what I want. You know what I always wanted, but you wouldn't give it to me because you never trusted me enough."

"What the hell are you talking about?"

I'm not prepared for the sudden assault of his lips on mine, but after the initial shock, my body reacts before my brain can catch up.

And I don't want to talk about my heart.

Because *this*—this kiss, this possessive, demanding, invasive kiss—yes.

Yes.

I did.

I wanted it too.

I wanted to kiss him in high school and be so much more than friends, which is the only thing I ever kept from him.

But I didn't want him at the expense of risking my future the way Mama gave up her own to have me.

I glide my fingers into his thick, soft hair and let his tongue tangle with mine, our teeth clashing, his hard thigh nestled between my legs *right* where I want it, pressing into my clit and making my nerve endings stand up and do the wave, his fingers biting into my hips, everything hot and wet and messy but *ohmygod* so right and so wrong.

So wrong.

It's high school graduation night all over again.

Change who you are, Annika. Change who you are to be with me.

I wanted him.

I did.

All through high school, I wanted him, but I couldn't bear the idea of struggling the way my mama did when I was little. Of giving in to the attraction I felt to him. Of letting him have any of me, because I knew if he had any of me—physically—I'd give him all of me, and what if we forgot a condom, because I knew once wouldn't be enough.

And Mama had Bailey by then too. She finally had a good job with benefits, but we still didn't need me with an unplanned, unexpected baby who'd grow up like I did, in worn hand-me-downs and gifts from clothing drives, my school lunches paid for by the state until fourth grade, my walls plastered with pictures of Spain and Italy and Busch Gardens, all from magazines that my friends would give to me when they were done, beside the free calendar that Mama got from the life insurance salesman in the next building over, where I plotted my path to the adulthood I wanted.

I wanted to see the world. I wanted to be financially stable. I never doubted that Mama loved me, but *god*, I knew she struggled.

I didn't want to take any risk of putting a child of mine in that position.

Especially a child that would've been half-Grady, because *god*, I loved him, and I would've done anything for his baby too.

Which is exactly why I couldn't have him.

Grady's hand slides up to squeeze my breast, and I realize this isn't what I want either.

I don't want to hate-fuck my former best friend.

So I wrench out of the kiss. "Stop."

He freezes.

He freezes so hard, the summer afternoon goes past chilly to glacial, complete with a cloud drifting in to block out the sun.

"Fucking *fuck*," he mutters.

I'm still catching my breath when he shoves back, turns, and all but sprints back to his truck.

The door slams, and I realize my cheeks are wet. I'm bent double by the time the engine roars to life.

I don't know what life did to Grady Rock, but I know one thing.

He's not the same boy who was my best friend for all those years.

And he never will be again.

11

Grady

I'M JUST drunk enough that I can't taste the alcohol anymore.

Not that I could taste it in the first beer either, because this is the light shit that Cooper keeps stocked at his place on Thorny Rock Mountain, since he tries to eat right during baseball season.

He's on a rare day off between two home series, so I'm crashing a small party he's having. Copper Valley is just an hour southeast of Shipwreck, which is awesome because we get to see him more often than when he was playing for Colorado when he first got called up to the Majors, but sucks because the Fireballs lose a lot, which isn't Cooper's fault.

He's a beast of a player on a team whose management doesn't seem to give a shit.

And I'm a jackass of a fuck-up whose temper doesn't give a shit about my heart either.

It's been three days since I kissed Annika.

Again.

And it ended exactly like it did ten years ago too.

Now, hanging here with my little brother, two of his teammates who brought women along, plus Ellie and Beck Ryder—yeah, the underwear modeling billionaire from Copper Valley who also has a house right around the corner, and his sister—and *their* lovey-dovey significant others isn't putting me in any better of a mood.

They're all eating chocolate chip walnut bars that I threw together when I got here, and I can't turn the vibration setting up loud enough on this damn massage chair that I'm sitting in to drown out the secret smiles and intimate touches going on across the high-ceilinged room while everyone else talks strategy for how to turn the Fireballs around.

And there's not enough light beer in the house to get me drunk enough to forget they're all here, being lovey-dovey and disgusting.

"You know what they really need?" Beck says, jerking his head at me. "Banana pudding donuts at the stadium."

"But maybe the kind made with love," his girlfriend, Sarah, says. She has dark hair and brown eyes, just like Annika, except nothing like Annika at the same time, and I don't appreciate the worried look she shoots my way nor the implication that I don't bake with love.

"He bakes with love," Cooper assures her. "His neck's out of whack. Just needs a trip to the ol' chiropractor and he'll be fine."

"Don't think it's his neck that's the problem," Tillie Jean mutters as she breezes through the door.

Cooper grins. "Yeah, but if he wants a dick massage, he's not getting it at my house, so I'm blaming his neck."

"You are so gross."

"Just saying what we were all thinking."

"What *you* were thinking." She lifts two white bakery bags stamped with the Crusty Nut's logo. "Somebody order banana pudding?"

Ellie Ryder and her military fiancé both dive across the room for her.

Military.

Of *course* he's military. Like Annika. Likes to growl at me and remind me that Ellie's off-limits.

Which is kinda *duh*, because while she's not a Shipwreck native, she spends enough time chilling at Beck's weekend house down the road that she's an honorary Shipwrecker, and she's like another sister, always fussing over my love life.

The *only* time I ever looked at Ellie like she was a woman was the time she asked me to pretend to be her boyfriend at a wedding, and that lasted all of three seconds—during which I was a picture-perfect, gentlemanly, *happy* fake boyfriend, I might add—before the knucklehead she's engaged to now intervened.

With her bags delivered, Tillie Jean plops down in the second of Cooper's four expensive-ass massage chairs in the airy living room. SportsCenter is muted on the massive TV that takes up half the side wall, and I make a show of watching it so she doesn't start talking to me.

Doesn't work.

"You apologize to Annika yet?"

"For me being right?" I was so wrong it made my balls hurt for two days longer than just getting racked in the 'nads should've hurt. "And then for her advertising the shit out of offering *my* s'mores cupcakes as a daily special for the grand re-opening of Duh-Nuts this weekend?"

"Who's Annika?" Ellie asks around a mouthful of banana pudding that her fiancé feeds her.

"A Sarcasm asshole trying to steal my business." I'm the asshole.

I'm *such* an asshole.

She was right. I should've been more understanding of why she's back instead of just pissed that she came back and didn't stop by to say hi. Or stalk me on Facebook and say hi. Or came all the way to Shipwreck to drop off fliers for her bakery without saying hi.

I think that last one might finally be a legitimate beef, except I also think Bailey probably got a ride to Shipwreck and Annika had nothing to do with it, because Bailey—she's like Tillie Jean.

The baby.

The plotter.

The sneak.

"Annika's Grady's best friend from high school that he had a huge crush on for four years," Tillie Jean supplies as the rest of the room turns to pay attention. "But Grady's an idiot."

"Hey, you can't blame a guy for being a guy," Beck says. "We're all pretty much idiots."

"You are *not*," Sarah says with a smile as she leans in to kiss his cheek.

Blech.

Also, *fuck*, I want to kiss Annika again.

For real.

Slow.

Gentle.

But only at first. Until she's panting so bad that she's trying to suck my soul out through my mouth and so hot for my cock that there's a waterfall coming from her pussy.

Christ.

Maybe I just need to get laid.

I glance around the room at the women, who are all happily dating—or just screwing, since I'm not sure how serious Cooper's teammates are about their dates today—then scowl at Cooper, because I *know* he knows a metric fuck-ton of single women, but the *only* single woman in the room at the moment is our sister.

Some *party*.

"You could apologize," he says, but his smirk says he knows I won't.

"You know what their Facebook page says today? It says tomorrow's donuts will be a special, exclusive flavor developed in honor of Maria Williams's lifelong dream of opening a bakery. They're playing the sympathy card so hard, I can't believe nobody's calling them on it."

Tillie Jean slugs me in the arm, and I haven't had enough alcohol for it to not hurt.

Especially since she grew up always trailing behind me and Cooper and had to get really good at defending herself, since we never listened when Ma would yell to *remember your sister is smaller than you*. I think she lifts goats in her spare time just to keep her guns in top-notch condition.

Also, I deserved that punch in the arm, and I wish she'd hit me harder.

"Now who's being the asshole?" Tillie Jean snaps. "You know you're not going to feel better until you apologize, so just go do it already."

Here's my problem with apologizing: I don't actually have an excuse for why I've been such an asshole.

If my freezer had gone out and I'd tripped and threw an entire batch of donuts all over the floor and my roof got a leak and Sue ate all my butter and got the butter shits on my living room carpet and someone crashed a car through the front of Crow's Nest and I had to shut down for three weeks for repairs and I caught Pop and Nana doing it doggy-style on my prep table, at least I'd have seventy-five percent of an excuse for being in a bad mood.

But instead, all I have is this deep-seated anger and frustration that Annika's back. She's the woman I've loved since I was fourteen, when she walked into biology in army boots and I asked her if she was trying to make a fashion statement, and instead of giving me a smart-ass *army boot* answer, she just smiled and said, *they make me happy*.

That Annika is back.

Except she isn't, because she has more stress in her life every single day than I've ever had to face in an entire year.

I was her best friend.

I'm supposed to know how to make her happy, and instead, I keep fucking up and making it worse.

Everything should be fresh and happy and I should be grabbing my second chance by the balls, yet nothing is the way it's supposed to be, because I don't know how to be her friend again.

PIPPA GRANT

I don't know how to let go of her rejecting me ten years ago.

That's my excuse for being an asshole.

And now I'm pissed that my excuse for being an asshole is really shitty.

"I don't know what you're thinking, but you might want to eat some prunes or talk to a priest about an exorcism," Tillie Jean offers. "Or possibly both. Do possessed people get blocked up? They have to, right? What demon worth his salt would possess a man and not *also* make him constipated?"

"TJ. Go easy on the man," Cooper orders. "He's doing ten years of mourning in three days. It's rough on a guy."

"I'm not *mourning*, asshole." And it's been almost a week.

"Shithead," Cooper retorts.

"Fuckwaffle."

"No, dude, I was telling you I'm a shithead. We're the Shipwreck shitheads. You want to be an asshole, you have to go to Sarcasm. Which you should do anyway, because you're not gonna get over her until you bone her."

I grab the massage chair remote and hit the *Ultimate Pain* button that sends the rollers in the back of the chair pounding up and down my spine at pressure-washer intensity, but nope, it doesn't drown out Cooper's voice.

Or make me feel better.

Although—*fuck*—that's a tight spot right there.

And there too.

I probably need six hours in this chair.

"Sarah's got a taser if you really want a wake-up jolt," Beck offers.

I flip them all off with shaking middle fingers. I think this chair is getting ready for lift-off.

"Bro, enough." Cooper rises and yanks a plug out of the wall, and my chair bounces to a stop like a rocking horse with a crooked rocker on an out-of-control train going uphill. "Step one: eat pie. Step two: admit you're wrong. Step three: grovel with...huh. Ryder. What do you use to grovel with when food won't cut it?"

Beck's features twist like he's in pain. "Food *always* cuts it, man. *Always*."

"Maybe a different kind of food?" Sarah suggests. "Like—"

"Moroccan!" Beck finishes for her.

They smile at each other and lean in to play tonsil hockey. I gag again, and Ellie snorts banana pudding out her nose.

"Sorry, Grady," she says while she chokes and tries to clean herself off and also rubs at her cheeks, probably because she has a few chunks of banana stuck in her sinuses. Her fiancé is thumping her on the back. "And *ow*. But seriously, if it's bothering you this badly, just go talk to her. You're sort of adorable in a lost puppy way when you're this miserable. That'll give you points."

"He already tried to talk to her, and he fucked it up Grady-style," Tillie Jean says.

Leave it to my sister to put all my faults out there in public.

There are exactly two things in life I can do better than anyone else.

Bake, and be Annika's friend.

Except I can't be Annika's friend, because I'm a dumbass.

And I'm in danger of losing my bakery because I'm being out-marketed by a thirteen-year-old.

So instead, I glare at my sister.

"Growth hurts," she says.

"Don't you have a restaurant to run?"

"Dad was making googly eyes at Mom. I'm not going back down to town until I get confirmation that they've been spotted at their own respective establishments again."

I shove up out of the seat, because is *everyone* getting nooky but me? "I gotta go bake something."

"Again? Awesome," Cooper says. He jerks his thumb over his shoulder at the massive kitchen taking up the back quarter of this level. "Knew there was a reason I got extra butter."

"*Away* from all of you."

"Bro, you can't be alone. Not when you're like this. First of all, you can't drive after that much beer. Second of all, remember when you made charcoal brûlée when Annika left for the Army?"

"And the time you bricked zucchini bread when Pop had to have that stent put in his heart?" Tillie Jean agrees.

"Even Sue wouldn't eat it," Cooper says solemnly, and I wish he was the type of manscaping asshead who kept throw pillows so I could throw one at him, because the only other thing he has in his house to throw is one of his eighty-seven billion Little League trophies that are littering every horizontal surface, and I don't want to have to apologize to him—and Ma—if I impale one of them in his thigh and put him on the disabled list for the rest of the season, because the Fireballs need him, and I might hate him half the time, as brothers often do when we don't love each other and defend each other, but he still plays for the home team, and I will *always* be a Fireballs fan.

"Macaron donuts," I blurt instead of confessing that I accidentally set fire to an oven full of banana bread loaves yesterday when I turned on the broiler after glazing the dough with butter instead of waiting until the loaves were cooked.

Yeah.

I have a problem.

And I don't know if cooking will fix it.

But Cooper and Tillie Jean breathe an excited "*Ooooooh,*" and yep.

That's what I'm fucking doing today, because that was the *ooooooh* of *no way he can pull it off, but if he does, he's a culinary genius.*

I'm gonna go master the *shit* out of macaron donuts.

Without setting anything on fire or burning out any of my appliances.

I don't know how, but when I do, they're gonna put Crow's Nest Bakery back on top in the greatest bakery war of this century.

And maybe actually give me a profitable day or two and ease the pressure I'm feeling to not go out of business.

I might not be able to win the girl, but I can win the fucking war.

12

Annika

It's been a good day.

Good being a relative term.

We sold out of every last s'mores cupcake during the grand re-opening, and we have orders for six dozen more for a baby shower next weekend. The cakes Bailey and Mama put together yesterday for our special orders turned out brilliant, and helped put us in the black for the week. The toilet hasn't clogged in four days. Bailey figured out the secret ingredient to make killer banana pudding.

Yes, as a matter of fact, I *am* petty enough to fight Grady's family for the title of best banana pudding in the entire state.

And in other good news, he hasn't stopped by and tried to hate-kiss me again.

I sigh over the last of the dishes at that thought.

I don't want him to kiss me.

Wait, that's not true.

I *do* want him to kiss me. But I also want him to be the Grady I knew when we were kids, and I want him to apologize for taking out his frustrations on me. I want him to kiss me because he missed me the way I missed him, and because he wants to be friends again like we used to be.

Or however that works when friends start kissing.

But, like my drill sergeant used to say, if wishes were leprechauns, we'd all be stepping in gold shit.

I never quite understood the expression, and if he meant literal shit made of gold or if shit was a generalization for *stuff*, but it seems relevant here.

Bailey and Mama got a ride home a few hours ago, and it's just been me and the college kid we hired for the grand re-opening weekend to help us clean up. I tell her she can head home while I finish everything here, and fifteen minutes later, the bells jingle on the front door.

"Hello?" a woman calls.

I rub at my sore neck and sigh, irritated with myself for forgetting to lock the front door. Who forgets that?

Not a staff sergeant with two combat patches known for her mastery of a color-coded planner and highly trained in operational security and paranoia.

I must be more tired than I thought.

"Sorry," I call, breezing out of the kitchen that really needs a paint job that I don't have time for. "We're—*oh*."

Tillie Jean Rock gives me a tentative smile. "Hey, Annika. How's your mom?"

She's carrying a to-go cup of coffee despite the late hour, which doesn't surprise me, because she was addicted to the stuff before the end of her freshman year. Her light brown hair is piled on her head, and though I'm sure she spent all day working at one of the many businesses that the Rock family owns in Shipwreck, she looks fresh as a spring rainbow.

We could've been sisters, if I hadn't been from Sarcasm and her brother hadn't proven himself to be a shithead.

"Mama's adjusting," I say neutrally. "How's your family?"

Her lips twitch, which she tries to cover behind her paper coffee cup, but her blue eyes are twinkling too big for it to fully work. "They're good."

I sigh, because *Grady* is her family, and the last time she saw us together, I was driving a softball into his man parts. "Right. Awkward question. How can I help you?"

"I just…so, please don't think this is weird, but I wanted to say welcome home. And I'm sorry about your mama. And I'm sorry you had to come home. And I'm sorry my brother is an idiot. He misses you, but he—"

"Doesn't know how to handle it," I finish.

"We all have our quirks."

"His was more endearing in high school."

"Yeah, but he bakes better now." She winces. "Sorry. I know he's being—"

"A Shipwreck shithead?"

"Spoken like a true Sarcasm asshole."

We share a smile, and my shoulders relax for the first time all day, because it's so freaking *normal* to joke about all this with Tillie Jean.

She was Grady's annoying little sister back in high school, but she was also *my* sister in a lot of ways.

"He'll come around," she says. "I'm sure you have a lot of support here, but I just wanted to let you know that if

DIRTY TALKING RIVAL

you need anything, Mom and Dad and I are—whoa. That's a lot of bananas."

I cringe as I turn to follow her gaze to the mounds of bananas sitting on the worktable in the kitchen behind me, ready for us to tackle in the morning. "Ah, yeah."

When I turn back, the warmth in her eyes has cooled considerably. "Adding fruit to the menu?"

"You could say that."

She squeezes the coffee cup until the plastic lid pops off. "Tell me you're not stooping to his level."

"That's not a very nice thing to say about your brother."

"You *are*."

My face is getting so hot that my hair's almost on fire. "I'm trying to run my mama's dream for her here."

"Oh my god, now you're *using it as an excuse*?"

"Why don't you try getting a call in the middle of the night that your mother's gone suddenly blind and no one knows what's going on and your sister's falling apart because *she's thirteen*, so of course she is, and rearranging your whole entire life on the fly from halfway across the country, only to get home to a hostile welcome from someone who used to be your best friend and then tell me what you'd do in my shoes."

"You racked him in the nuts on purpose in that softball game!"

"*Who does that?* I hadn't hit a ball in four years."

"Well, you got three in one with that swing, didn't you? And now you're going after *my banana pudding*?"

I suck in a deep breath that I have to reach all the way to my toes to find, pinch my eyes shut, remind myself that everything is going to be fine, and I hold up my hands in surrender.

"Tillie Jean. I'm not." I am. I'm an awful person, and I totally am. "Isn't what we had as kids worth more than banana pudding?"

"*No!*" she shrieks. Something green sloshes over the edges of her coffee cup and spills on her hand, and she curses under her breath while she grabs a handful of napkins from a dispenser on the nearest table.

"That's not coffee? But you love coffee. You practically needed an IV of it in high school."

"Things change," she snaps. "*You* changed. Grady changed. Cooper changed. *Everybody fucking changed*. And if you think you're going to out-bake my banana pudding, you just wait. You. Just. Wait."

She turns and stalks out of Duh-Nuts, and I sag against the bakery counter, head in my hands, rubbing my temples while my neck protests and my shoulders and lower back whine about being on my feet all day.

I need to get home and make sure Bailey was able to handle dinner.

And then I need to drown my guilt and everything about the last three weeks with a big bottle of Jack.

Except I can't.

Because I'm the only one in the house who can handle any emergencies that might pop up in the middle of the night.

The bells jingle again, and this time, I let out an audible *dammit*.

"Was that Tillie Jean Rock?" Liliana asks. "Holy turtles. You look like you need a drink."

I lift my head and meet her wide gaze.

"Where do you live?" I ask her.

"Over on Irony, by the library."

I pull a face, because Mama's place is all the way across town on Mediocre Street.

Which is all of sixteen blocks, but still.

"Want to have a sleepover and play sober adult?" I ask.

"Oh, hell, yeah."

I snort, because this is Sarcasm, and who wants to play sober adult? No one. That's who. "Never mind."

"I'm serious," she says. "I've never seen you drunk. I'll bet it's hilarious. Name your poison. It's on me."

And that's how, an hour later, we're lounging in Mama's cozy lavender living room, a bottle of Jack opened before me, a platter of the most adorable unicorn faces I've ever seen within easy reach for devouring—relax, they're treats, not real unicorns—and everything we need for a girls' spa night laid out on the coffee table.

Bailey made fajita quesadillas for dinner, along with the unicorn logs. I snort softly to myself, because they really do look like logs, though I know they're marshmallows wrapped in fondant with faces drawn on them in edible marker, which is also funny to me.

"Annika, when did you learn to drink?" Mama asks. Her nose wrinkles under her dark glasses, and she shifts her feet in the warm tub of sea salt water on the floor beside me. "And what *is* that? It's not the good tequila."

"The Army drove me to it," I declare. "And it's delicious. Tastes like denial and impending hiccups."

Bailey giggles. "Annika's gonna get trashed," she whispers while she selects an apricot face scrub. Her hair's already coated with argan oil and wrapped up in a towel, and I did Mama's hair before I got into the whiskey too.

"And then she's going to puke her guts out," Liliana whispers conspiratorially.

"All of my guts," I agree.

I'm barely a finger into the drink, but it's already warming me in all the places I need to be warm.

My belly.

My toes, which are weirdly cold despite the heat in both the bakery and the sunshine today, because late July weather is freaking brutal.

My heart.

My brain.

My brain definitely needs to be heated up.

Baked brains can't focus on all of life's troubles.

"Is this because she's secretly pining for that Rock guy?" Bailey whispers while she hands Liliana a tube of avocado oatmeal face mask stuff.

"Pining?" Liliana busts out laughing over her fingernails. "What have you been reading?"

"*Anne of Green Gables*. I love those books. And also cookbooks. Because once Annika realizes Mama and I will adjust to everything *just fine*, she'll go back to the Army and let me run the bakery and homeschool myself until she realizes on her own how much she misses us and comes home to be our accountant for our Sarcasm food empire."

Given the mounds of paperwork I'm still working on for emergency termination from the Army, I don't even want to think about the administrative nightmare that would be trying to get back *in*. And I like paperwork.

Paperwork is my happy place.

Doing homework for my accounting degree with a minor in business was *fun*.

I *like* catching up on the bakery's books every night before I go to sleep.

I am such a lame, boring nobody.

"You're schtuck with me," I tell her.

"Are we doing facials?" Mama asks. "We better not be doing those charcoal facials. You know I hate how they make me look."

"But it's so good for your skin," Bailey says. "Doesn't it feel good afterwards?"

"No."

I snort-laugh my whiskey, because Mama's being intentionally obstinate.

"Annika, don't let her lie to me and tell me she's using that nice avocado mask when she's actually putting charcoal on me, or I'll tell that mountain lion on the TV to eat her toes off."

"I—*hic!*—won't, Mama."

"I want the charcoal mask," Liliana declares. "Honey *swears* by them, so as long as it doesn't make me break out in a rash, I need to as well."

"Honey? The heiress at the winery?"

"Yeah."

"What's she like?" Mama asks while she lets Bailey rub green goop all over her face. "And is this really the avocado stuff?"

"Yes to avocado, and Honey has sparkly pink stilettos," Liliana says on a wistful sigh. "They're so...so..."

"Gross?" Bailey guesses.

I snort again, because my baby sister might love baking, but she also loves the color blue, rock band T-shirts, and Chucks, but not pink Chucks.

"They're like *unicorn shoes*," Liliana declares.

"Unishoes?" I ask.

Bailey rolls her eyes while she smears more goo over Mama's cheeks. "*Shoenicorns*, Annika. *Shoenicorns*."

"Dammit. Quit being smarter than me. *Hic!*"

"Quit making it easy."

"*Girls.*"

Bailey's eyes are bright and sparkly and dancing with unicorns. "Mama, you know we only bicker because we love each other. And because I'm totally stealing her tan suede army boots when she goes to sleep tonight, because they're seriously badass."

"I'm a badass," I declare.

"When's the last time you got drunk?" Liliana asks.

Mama frowns.

Bailey leans in eagerly.

I take another swallow of the fiery liquid and shudder. "Never."

"*What?*"

I don't know who said that. Probably all three of them.

"Never," I repeat. "Getting drunk makes you horny, and the next thing you know, you wake up naked in bed with a guy with more hair than Grady's goat and fewer brains than a chipmunk, and you realize the orgasm you thought you had was actually just a really good—*hic!*—pee."

"I...didn't need to hear any of that," Bailey says.

"Learn from my first roommate, kid. Don't drink and screw."

"Don't drink *or* screw," Mama corrects. "Not without protection. Double protection. We're very fertile. Not that I'd trade either of you for anything. Are you sure this is the avocado mask? What are you putting on my lips?"

"Yes, Mama, it's the avocado mask, and this is just moisturizer," Bailey assures her. "Remember the itty tiny baby jar that I keep on my dresser?"

"Oh, the white one? With the funny angles on the base?"

"Uh-huh."

"You never share that."

"Annika let me have some of her whiskey and now I'm going crazy."

"Lies!" I exclaim. "Quit besmirching my honor!"

All three of them giggle.

"Have you *ever* done anything crazy?" Liliana asks me.

"I fell in love with Grady Rock." I slap my hand over my mouth, because even heading into tipsy-land, I know I should've kept that to myself.

Mama purses her lips, but the edges are still dancing up like mischievous leprechauns singing *I knew it, I knew it, I bet a pot of gold that she loved Grady, and now I'm rich!*

"I was *three* and I knew you were in love with him," Bailey says, her eyes rolling so hard that they shift the gravitational pull of the earth and make me stagger in my seat. "But I didn't actually know that was him when he walked into Duh-Nuts last week, because when I was three, he was basically just this big blobby human with dark hair and a monster truck."

"He had a monster truck?" Liliana asks.

"He had a loud truck," I explain. "And now he has a loud goat. And a loud ass."

"A loud *ass*? Oh my god, did he fart at you?"

"No, he's just so *loud* with his assishness. Rubbing it all in my face. But not his actual ass. I haven't gotten a good look at his ass. His shorts were too loose at the game and when—never mind. Do you think he has a good ass now? I'll bet his ass can't beat my ass's banana pudding. Wait. Does that sound wrong to anyone—*hic!*—else?"

"How much dinner did she eat?" Liliana whispers to Bailey.

"Annika," Mama says gently, "you're not going to get closure by making banana pudding."

"Maybe not, but we'll make a fuck-ton of money," I reply. "Bailey is a cunilary—culninberry—coobinalary—shit. She's a *genius*. With bananas."

I hiccup three times in rapid-fire succession, and they squeeze my heart and assure it that another two shots of Jack is all it'll take for the hiccups to strangle that backstabbing little organ in my chest with the poor taste.

"Are we playing over-make, or are we gossiping like old men?" I demand.

"Gossiping," Bailey says.

"I think she means playing makeover," Mama murmurs.

"Here, honey, have a unimallow." Liliana shoves the treat in my face. "The sugar will soak up some of the alcohol."

"Or she'll break out," Bailey says. "Sugar makes me break out all the time. It's a curse. But I'd rather be rich than pretty, so I'm going to keep perusing Pinterest for ideas to take Duh-Nuts to the next level."

"Are you thirteen or thirty?" Liliana asks her.

"Chronologically thirteen, but I feel a strong sisterly bond with women in their forties. They're kick-ass, they know how to do everything, and they have zero fucks left to give. By the way, Annika, I asked Roger's son to take you to the roller rink next Saturday night. Do you remember Birch? I think he was a year ahead of you in school."

"*Bailey*," Mama chides while I hiccup again and the charcoal face mask goop that I just swiped onto my fingers starts to blur at the edges. "Annika can decide for herself who and when she dates."

"Actually, I don't think she can," Bailey replies. "The goats in her head keep baaing in her way."

Wait.

That's not what she said. Is it?

I squint at her.

Her nose turns sideways and acts like a diving board so her eyeballs can leap off onto the pool in the middle of the Mama's foot soak.

And that's the last thing I remember before I lay my head on the coffee table, with a bottle of nail polish digging into my cheek, and drift off to sleep.

13

Annika

Earplugs are my friend.

Earplugs, and aspirin, and frozen baked cheese bread —that *I* baked, thank you very much, because apparently I *can* operate frozen food—and coffee.

We're all up early and in the Duh-Nuts kitchen Monday morning for what we hope will be another sell-out day. Bailey's at the Viking range top, stirring a massive pot of *secret ingredient* vanilla pudding while I line up peeled bananas for slicing beside the two dozen boxes of Nilla Wafers and twelve empty pans waiting to be filled with her epic creation. Mama's kneading tomorrow's donut dough at the other worktable, and the two of them are singing Johnny Cash songs at the top of their lungs.

My headache has almost subsided by the time we flip on the dining room lights and unlock the door, but when *another* Rock sibling walks in two minutes later, not only does my headache come raging back, but my stomach threatens to revolt too.

"Dude, you grew up hot." Cooper looks me up and down, his sunglasses pulled down to the edge of his nose, and he gives a soft whistle. *"Really* hot."

Like he can talk.

He's six feet, two inches of solid muscle encased in slim jeans and a skin-tight Fireballs T-shirt, with a tattoo decorating the bicep bulging out from under his sleeve, his dimples on full display, his cheeks and chin sporting three days' worth of dark stubble.

But what he owns in the looks department, he makes up for in personality.

"Can I get two of you to go?" he adds with a brow wiggle.

"Keep it in your pants, and no," I reply.

His grin gets wider, his dimples deeper, just like Grady's.

His eyes are the same blue-green too.

They could be twins, except Cooper has about twenty more pounds of muscle and a longer face with a deeper tan.

But only just barely.

Those Rock boys give good jawline.

Dammit.

"Shitty night?" he asks.

"Galaxy donut?" I reply, gesturing to the display case full of fresh donuts. In addition to the classic glazed donut, which Bailey spent the weekend mastering when she wasn't helping run the grand re-opening, today we have a special donut topped with a smooth swirled blue, green, and black icing dotted with edible glitter, which resembles a colorful version of images of outer space.

Bailey basically absorbed all the knowledge of Pinterest and Food Network and now she's a donut prodigy from the holes to the glazes.

Bonus, they're very edibly delicious.

Having yeast donuts back in Duh-Nuts means letting Bailey stand at the fryer, but she assures me she's done far worse, which isn't actually reassuring at all.

Possibly I've already forgotten my own teen years and gotten a little uptight since high school.

"I'm not *supposed* to buy anything," Cooper says apologetically. "But I *am* supposed to talk you into a free sample of your banana pudding. And I might could be talked into buying a lot of it. Like, a *lot*. I mean, if it's good enough. And if you promise not to tell my siblings. Or my Pop. He's terrifying when he gets mad. Puts on his Blackbeard costume and shows up in the middle of the night in your bedroom pretending to be the Pirate of Sins Past and he just *knows* shit."

Cooper affects a whole-body shiver.

"Dream on," Bailey tells him from the kitchen doorway. "We know who you are."

"You want an autograph?" he asks.

"Again, dream on. Annika, do I need to make him go away?"

"Go wash dishes," I tell her.

"Not if it means you have to be alone with this guy."

"Bailey." Mama angles into the doorway too, hand on the frame, guiding herself. "Who's there?"

"Cooper Rock, ma'am," Cooper says. "Power slugger

for the Fireballs. Acrobatic second baseman. Or you could just call me a god. I'm good with that."

Mama smiles. "Ah, Cooper Rock. I should've known by the ego. How are the Fireballs this summer?"

"Full of heart, ma'am. Just like your daughter."

"Did you just subtly call my sister a loser?" Bailey demands. "Because the Fireballs are bigger losers than they are...hearters."

"Bailey." I jerk my head toward the kitchen. "Can you please go find a masterpiece for us to make tomorrow?"

"One that will bring people from *miles and miles* around?" she asks.

"Yes."

"Victory *is* the best revenge," she says tartly, and she disappears back into the kitchen.

"Now. Cooper. What can we do for you?" I ask.

"Alright. You've convinced me. Sell me all your banana pudding?"

"No."

"I'd pay you good for it."

"*No.* I'm sorry your family is upset with us, but the people of Sarcasm deserve banana pudding too. *Without* going someplace where people call them assholes just for being from Sarcasm. Duh-Nuts isn't hurting Crow's Nest. So *back off.*"

He holds his hands up. "Dude. Mellow your yellow. First of three games against Boston tonight, and the team's gonna need some comfort food when it's over, you know?"

He says it so casually, like it's no big deal that the Fireballs will get creamed, and that their injured pride will be assuaged by banana pudding, but I don't buy it.

PIPPA GRANT

Cooper Rock has *always* been a winner.

He once challenged me to a game of rock, paper, scissors that went on for *an hour* because that's how long it took for him to finally come out on top in a best of two hundred and seventeen contest. He hired a professional editor for his eighth-grade submission to the county DARE essay contest. He swapped Grady's cannoli filling for garlic butter during the annual Pirate Festival's baking contest one year, because he knew his pirate hat cookies couldn't beat Grady's cannoli cannons.

Cooper Rock does not like to lose.

At anything.

And the only thing he hates worse than losing is for his family to lose.

I fold my arms and indulge in the staring contest that he's pretending we're not having.

He doesn't crack, which is unlike him, because he hated staring contests in high school, and would always say *nah, that wasn't a staring contest, you just forgot to blink* rather than admit that he couldn't win a staring contest.

This might take longer than I thought.

"Annika?" Mama says.

"Just a minute, Mama. We're having a little contest right now."

"I'll be sure to say a nice eulogy and bury you both right here after you each die before blinking," she says. "Since I assume you mean a staring contest and you're not making out with Grady's brother while I can't see you."

"All I want is for her to go apologize to my brother." Cooper's gaze doesn't waver, and his eyes aren't even getting shiny with the need to blink.

He probably practices this in the mirror, since I doubt he'd practice with anyone else who might beat him.

"I'm not apologizing when I didn't do anything wrong," I tell him.

"You hurt him."

"He hurt *me*."

"But you're the bigger person of the two of you, so if you're ever going to be friends again, *you* have to go to *him*."

I want to growl, because I know he's right, and I suddenly feel like my entire high school experience was a lie built on coddling Grady's ego, even though I know that's not true. He had a few insecurities, but who doesn't? More often, he was fun and reliable and smart. And smiling. Always smiling.

Always bringing me baked goods, even though he knew Mama was the best baker in the world, because *I just want to see the day that you finally think I've made something as good as her*.

Always telling someone from Shipwreck to shove it whenever one of them called me an asshole.

Always grabbing me by the cheeks, saying, *Annika, look at me, it's okay if your papier-mâché Coliseum isn't to scale, because you've already earned your A, and you're missing out on the last good sledding of the season. What would you rather have, the A+, or the memories?*

"I have responsibilities that are bigger than soothing someone's ridiculous idea that he's the more injured party here," I say quietly.

"C'mon, Annika. I know you miss him too."

"I don't have time to miss him."

Mama clucks her tongue.

Cooper smirks.

And the bells jingle on the door as a dude with a huge camera pushes inside. "Coffee. I need—whoa." His sleepy eyes flare wide. "You're Cooper Rock," he says, and he lifts the camera and starts snapping pictures.

"What in the—hey! *Hey!* Get out." I step out from behind the counter as the camera flashes and the guy starts firing questions.

"What are you doing here, Cooper? Is this where you always get donuts and coffee? Can you turn to the left so I can get those awesome donuts behind you? Why are you so far from Copper Valley? Is Darren Greene with you?"

"*Out!*" I order.

Cooper's smile has vanished, and he's doing his best to avoid the guy getting a picture of his face.

"Mama, call the sheriff," I call over my shoulder.

"Solid gold," the photographer is gushing. "Solid fucking gold."

"That a baseball player would be in a bakery? *Get out* before I have to show you my combatives training. Shoo. *Shoo.*"

He backs off as Cooper finally dives behind the bakery counter.

"Jeez. Know where I'm *not* getting my coffee," he grumbles. "You seen her? Honey Wellington? The heiress who bought the winery? Can't miss that blond hair. She dating any—ow, *ow, OW!*"

"Oh, excuse me, I'm sorry, I guess my foot wasn't watching where it was going."

"Let go of my ear!"

"Quit trespassing in my bakery!"

"I could sue you for harassment."

I toss him out the door and lock it behind him, standing there glaring until he moves on, but not until after he's snapped so many pictures I have dots in my vision.

"What the *hell* was that?" I bark at Cooper.

He doesn't answer.

But Bailey does.

"Oh em gee, Annika! We have *paparazzi* in town," she squeals. "Sarcasm is going to be *famous*! And you're going to be the cranky bakery lady with resting bitch face in the background, but we'll be *famous*!"

"Who's Honey Wellington?" I ask.

My head hurts. My heart hurts. My past hurts.

Swear it does. All of my memories. They hurt.

"She's that heiress who bought Sarcasm Cellars," Bailey answers. "You know? The one Liliana talked about all night—oh. Right. You passed out drunk in the charcoal face mask and missed that part. Anyway. Honey, the heiress, is in town now and apparently the paparazzi are here to chase her."

I sigh and pull out my phone to send Liliana a warning text as all of the details about the winery and its owner come filtering back into my brain.

I also politely inquire if we'll be seeing paparazzi every morning.

"Where did Cooper go?" I ask as I put my phone away.

"Out the kitchen door," Bailey replies. "I squirted the back of his shirt with some of the whipped cream from the banana pudding though. He didn't notice. It'll get smashed all over his seat and stink up his car for weeks."

"*Bailey*," Mama and I sigh together.

She grins. "I only get to be a teenager once. Don't ruin

it for me. Also, I can't wait to hear what happens when pictures of him in *our* bakery make their way to Shipwreck. Good thing I have our next brilliant idea. You ready for this? Pirate Unicorn Fingers. Like ladyfingers, but decorated like unicorn pirates with candy corn horns. And better tasting. Boom. And you're welcome."

I rub my temples again, and realize I'm smearing donut icing all over my face in the process.

Something has to change. I have enough on my plate with Mama and Bailey and the bakery, and even though I have everything color-coded in both my planner and on the calendars hanging on the walls in both the Duh-Nuts kitchen and also in the kitchen at Mama's house, I'm running out of colors to keep my life straight.

I can't keep up a passive-aggressive war of baked goods with Grady amidst paparazzi crawling through Sarcasm too.

At least, not for long.

Three more days, I tell myself.

In three more days, if I still feel horrible and can't stop thinking about Grady, and if his family keeps stopping by, and if Mama and Bailey keep bringing him up, then I'll find some way to meet him on his turf to talk.

Even if it's just to agree that we're both moving on politely with no more of this ridiculous bakery war stuff going on.

But maybe he'll come to me again first.

Three more days.

Yeah. That sounds like an excellent plan.

And with that issue pushed back on my to-do list and highlighted on my calendar for *not today*, I go unlock the door again for Roger, who's peering in now after the paparazzi guy headed down the street for the diner.

Another day, another new normal.

I've got this.

I think.

14

Grady

I'm in the middle of making sugar cookies Tuesday morning when my phone blows up.

Sixty million people all at once need me to know that Cooper's in the gossip section.

Visiting Duh-Nuts.

I don't care that it's six AM. I pick up the phone and I call him.

"Don't go being an asshole," he says by way of greeting.

I squeeze my eyes shut and sigh. I have a mound of bad donut dough sitting on one corner of my worktable, because either I don't have enough love in my life to perfect crème brûlée macaron donuts, or it was a bad idea.

Just like practically everything else I've done in the last week has been a bad idea.

"How's Annika?" I ask Cooper.

"The better question is, who invited the paparazzi out to the boonies? There goes my privacy. Oh. Wait. You just pulled your head out of your ass. Huh. And there goes my speech. Want to hear it anyway?"

"No."

"Bro. You know I don't take bad pictures, but if I did, that one of me pointing to those galaxy donuts would be a bad picture. I made having one eyelid half-closed and my lips crooked look *good*, but you know if I'd done it on purpose to help the donuts, I would've been canoodling the pastries with my eyes."

"I said I didn't want to hear your speech," I tell him.

"I know, I know. What was I doing in Duh-Nuts anyway? Am I right? So here's the thing. I was gonna buy 'em out of banana pudding so Tillie Jean could analyze it and make sure hers was still better, no matter what that asshole from Sarcasm wrote in the *Blue Lagoon County Gazette* about the Duh-Nuts banana pudding taking Tillie Jean's ribbon at the fair this fall."

"Cooper. Shut up. How the fuck is Annika?"

"Your former best friend Annika who's dealing with a shit-ton of shit in her life right now?"

Fuck.

Fuck.

The back door bangs open, and I've never been so aggravated to see Georgia walking in phone-first. "Gotta go. Time to work. Text me, you pain in the ass."

I hang up, toss my phone back in my apron pocket, and spread my hands on the metal worktable, nodding to Georgia's phone screen. "Let me guess. They made pirate ship cupcakes."

It's what she's most likely to tell me, right?

Those Sarcasm assholes are at it again. Taunting us on social media.

Hell, I started it.

"You ever heard of *Virginia Blue Magazine*?" Georgia asks.

"Yeah. My Nana gets that."

She smiles so big that my pirate hat sugar cookies get suspicious and shrink in fear. I silently promise the cookies I'll treat them right and smother them in vanilla icing in mere minutes, and they seem to breathe a sigh of relief.

"They're interested in lifestyle pieces about friendly rivalries," Georgia announces. "Like, oh, say, a rivalry between two bakeries in towns that have hated each other forever?"

Before I can point out that *friendly* is the opposite of *hated each other forever*, the back door bangs open again and Tillie Jean marches in. "Grady. *Grady*. Look what I found in Nana's *Virginia Blue Magazine*. Look."

So this is what I've become.

The guy who would exploit an old friendship to get a little extra publicity for my bakery.

Which has been doing better and better every day since I upped my social media game to compete with Bailey.

It's the extra attention. The extra pressure.

Because of having a bakery war.

Of *course* people are coming in more.

They want to help me win.

That's what you do in Shipwreck.

Plus, I'm trying harder.

Because I can't handle the fact that the woman I've put on a pedestal for the last fourteen years is back, and she doesn't want me any more today than she did a decade ago.

Fuck.

Why would she?

I've been an ass and a half.

And my reward is my bottom line creeping further and further into the black while guilt keeps me from hitting the *buy* button on a four-pack of bubble waffle makers and a soft serve ice cream machine that would undoubtedly push me even further into the black, because it wasn't my idea.

"Do you two have anything better to do at this hour of the day than barge in here with more plans for bakery wars?"

They look at each other.

Then back to me.

"No," they say in unison.

I scrub a hand over my face and realize I haven't shaved in over a week. Then I wonder if I've showered.

"Aw, you're making my favorite pirate hat cookies. I love it." Tillie Jean hooks an arm around my neck and goes up on tiptoe to kiss my cheek, then wrinkles her nose. "Ugh, that smell. You been sleeping with Sue again? You know what they say about sleeping with goats."

I blink at her.

She grins. "It makes your package shrink."

I shake her off. "You got these?" I ask Georgia with a nod to the cookies.

She heads to the sink. "Hmm, decorate cookies by myself, or stand next to a stinky master baker who's been rolling in goat poop. What a hard decision. Where you going?"

I shake my head, because I don't know. I just know that somewhere in the last two weeks, I've quit smooth-talking my pastries, and I've quit baking for the love of it.

And I need to get that back.

I need to make a profit because I'm *good*, not because I'm being an ass.

"You're in charge today," I tell her. "Don't burn the place down."

Or do.

Fuck.

This morning, I don't care.

15

Annika

I don't have *bike ride around the lagoon* on my planner, but I haven't exercised since I got home. Mama's with the mobility specialist at home for the next two hours. Bailey's with her, and Roger's stopping by to check on them later this afternoon.

If I don't get away from the bakery, I'm going to start throwing things.

And I don't know *why*.

Okay, fine, I know why.

But when it's *there are too many emotions that I'm not dealing with well*, I don't like to admit it, because which emotion do you start with?

The sadness?

The anger?

The disappointment?

The fear?

The crushing weight of expectations pressing harder and harder every day, because while Mama *is* re-learning her way around home, around the kitchen, and around the bakery, she'll never be able to decorate intricate cookies or fry donuts, and *I can't fix that*.

So I decide that the first emotion I'm going to deal with is the *run away from it all* emotion.

I close the shop early—which is fine, since we're mostly sold out of everything today anyway—and head home. There's a small storage shed at the corner of Mama's small lot, which is where I find my old bicycle.

An hour and a trip to the hardware store later, she's back in tip-top shape, though her purple sparkle paint job has dulled over the years. But her gears work and are greased up, the tires are replaced, and I have a shiny new helmet, so I hop on, tuck my phone into my pocket, and hit the state road that leads out of town and into the preserve between Sarcasm and Shipwreck.

There *are* other little towns dotting the mountains too, but none of them get involved in this stupid fight that's been going on supposedly since the day "Thorny Rock, The Pirate" founded Shipwreck and his second cousin twice removed, Walter Bombeck, walked into whatever state department is responsible for naming towns and reported that his town was called, "Your mom," to which the state guy supposedly replied, "Seriously?" and good ol' Walter responded with, "No, that's Sarcasm."

Turns out that even in the seventeen hundreds, government employees had more of a devious sense of humor than we give them credit for, and so Sarcasm it became, though Walter never did get credit for inventing the "Your mom" joke.

Which means the story is probably as true as *Thorny Rock the Pirate*'s story.

I'm easily coasting downhill on my bike as I enter the preserve and head along the bike path beneath the deep green canopy of oak and birch trees toward the lagoon, which is actually a lake nestled in a valley, but like everything else here, it gets a cute name so that more people come visit it.

I like that about my hometown area.

It's quaint.

Most of my time in the Army has been in Texas or North Carolina, plus two deployments to the sandbox and a year in Korea, and the posts were what they needed to be, with their own culture and standards and vibes, but they weren't quirky and warm and *home*.

And even now, with August bearing down on us, there are wispy streaks of fog dotting the afternoon down here in the valley. Cool little patches of relief from the summer heat that leave my arms and legs and face feeling as though I've been kissed by an angel.

A sloppy, unexpected angel, but it's either imagine the fog as an angel or a ghost, and I'm feeling like going for the positive today.

Which is why I'm not thinking about the bike ride back up and out of the valley to get home.

I really should've considered how much uphill pedaling there would be on the way back before I got five miles from town.

But it's still preferable to thinking about the fact that I still don't have someone to fill Bailey's shoes when school starts in a few weeks, because none of the people I've interviewed have worked out.

Someone has to work out soon, because none of us can keep working six or seven days a week like this.

I catch glimpses of the lake shimmering in the sun through the trees a few minutes before the whole thing comes into view, taking my breath away with the simple natural beauty of the little hideaway nestled in the soft mountains, and socking me in the gut with hot, heavy memories at the same time.

"*Maa!*" a goat cries indignantly as it darts into the path.

I shriek and swerve, hitting the brakes and heading into a thicket of trees and brush and brambles as a man dashes out from the side path.

"Sue!" he hollers.

Grady.

My bike crashes.

I crash.

My heart crashes, my temper crashes, and my composure crashes too.

"*Maa*," Sue bleats as it follows me into the brush and tries to lick my leg.

"*Maa* yourself," I snap back at it.

It stomps a foot and snorts a goat booger at me. The fact that it's missing one horn and has a brown circle around its right eye confirms what the man yanking on its collar and trying to pull it off the path has already told me.

This is Grady's goat.

His blue-green eyes lift and connect with mine, and I see the moment realization dawns on him.

It comes with brows shooting to the treetops and lips parting and a strangled noise coming from his throat, complete with his cheeks going ruddy.

"Annika," he sputters. "Shit. Sorry. I—*Sue*. Down."

The goat *is* down, and he head-butts Grady in the leg to make the point while I attempt to pull my bike out of the bushes, which are probably full of poison ivy.

Awesome.

"Aren't you supposed to be in Shipwreck selling unicorn cookies or tres leches donuts?" I ask.

So apparently I'm grumpy.

Double awesome.

I just *love* being grumpy.

Makes life *so* much better.

His cheeks go ruddier, and his chest lifts wide and solid when he sucks in a breath and looks away.

I need to go home. Mama will be done well before I get there, and I don't need all my good memories of *this* place ruined by another fight with Grady.

"I—I'm sorry," he says.

"Are you?" I need to shut up. My problems aren't his fault.

Most of them, anyway.

But I can't help myself. Because he was my best friend, and now he's my best punching bag, because he offered himself up on a silver platter with everything he's done since the moment he found out I was back in town.

"Are you sorry, Grady? And for what? For your goat being a trail hazard? For baiting my sister on Instagram with unicorn cookie pictures, because a *thirteen-year-old whose mother went blind doesn't have enough to deal with*? For being a really shitty friend? Are you sorry for any of *that*? Or are you just sorry you didn't have your camera ready to get a picture of *this*?"

I pluck a weed out of my hair and dust pollen or dirt or powdered deer poop off my shirt to make a point about him standing there looking like a fallen backwoods angel in black athletic shorts and a gray Fireballs T-shirt and a backwards ball cap covering his dark hair.

He squeezes a tennis ball so hard his knuckles go white, and his Adam's apple bobs. "Yes," he says quietly.

"Yes *what*?" Crap.

Crap crap crap.

I learned how to suppress the tears in basic training a decade ago, but here I am, that lump in my throat so thick that I'll need the Heimlich to get rid of it, my eyes so hot I'm suddenly terrified that these tears will burn my retinas off and Bailey will be left to care for *two* incapacitated adults who are supposed to be making *her* world safe.

"I'm sorry for being a dickhead." Those blue-green eyes scan my body, and I hate that I don't know if he's making sure I'm going to live, or if he's trying to determine if this is a spy mission, and if I'm wired so that I can seduce all of his bakery's secrets out of him and immediately relay the information back to headquarters so my teenage sister and blind mother can rule this little slice of mountain heaven.

My heart bounces around my chest like a ball on one of those old wooden paddle games, because I don't want to believe we're enemies.

I don't need enemies.

I can take acquaintances, but what I really need are friends.

"I've been an immature brat, and I don't deserve you," he adds.

Now my heart's doing some acrobatics on a backyard trampoline that my safety officer back at Fort Bliss would have a few choice words about, and I really am going to choke on that lead bubble of emotion clogging my throat.

The goat stomps impatiently, bleats, and head-butts him again, propelling him three feet closer to me before he gets his bearing again. He grunts and turns, tossing the ball into the lake, and the goat goes crashing into the water after it.

My jaw hangs.

Grady chuckles wryly, and the sound wraps around my overworked heart and pets it like it's a lost puppy.

"You okay?" he asks softly.

He watches his goat wade back to shore as a cloud passes between the sun and the lake, not looking at me, but my skin is tingling everywhere as though one of those naked nightmares has come true.

I shouldn't feel naked.

But I remember feeling the same when Grady came down with a short-term case of stage fright during our freshman year production of *Beauty and the Beast* and stood there gaping at the audience on opening night instead of saying his three lines as a townsperson.

Whoever had the next line just glossed right over it, and no one knew, but *I* knew.

I *felt* his fear as if it was my own.

And I swear I'm feeling his discomfort too now.

When I don't answer right away, he glances at me.

I finally manage to swallow, and I blink four times before I'm sure I'm back in control of my tear ducts. I open my mouth to tell him I'm fine and I need to get going, and instead, I hear myself whisper, "You said you'd write."

He flinches. "Didn't think you'd want to hear from me. With…you know."

"And I never thought you were a wimp." *Shut up, Annika. Shut. Up.*

His goat crashes back to shore and charges us, soaking wet with lake water dripping off his fur, and Grady bends to wrestle the ball back from the animal while I sigh softly and finish untangling my bike from the bushes, getting sprayed by the goat's wet shakes and not caring at all. I test the tire pressure, making sure I didn't hit a rock or puncture a tire with a sticker burr, and yep.

I'll make it back just fine.

"Sue. Don't eat the ball. Give it. Annika. Wait."

"Full calendar," I say quietly.

"Can we walk you back to your car?"

I snort. "Long walk back to Sarcasm. And you probably shouldn't be seen there. They have posters up all over town with your mug on them. *If you see this man, throw his donuts back at him.*"

"I knew I'd miss you, but I didn't know how much."

His honesty surprises me—both his words and the wariness in his eyes that matches his tone and the way his shoulders hunch in, like he's preparing for me to kick him while he's raw and exposed.

He's not the only one feeling raw and exposed. Especially when his goat once again trots behind him and head-butts him closer to me.

He doesn't try to stop it. "You didn't care that I was one of the Rock boys, and you didn't use me to get closer to Cooper or to ask me to get you a job with someone in my family. You just...you were the only friend I had with no strings. No expectations. You let me be me and you didn't try to fit me in a box and most of the time you made me feel like I was pretty fucking spectacular without having to try. And I couldn't imagine my life without you in it every day."

"You were leaving too."

One dimple pops out with his crooked grin. "I'm an asshole with double standards."

The goat bleats out an agreement, then tries to lick inside its own nose.

My phone alarm rings, reminding me I have thirty minutes to get back to Sarcasm before the end of Mama's appointment.

Thirty minutes.

Five miles.

Uphill the whole way.

This was a much better plan when all I wanted was to work out for the first time in a month.

"Pre-alarm, or actual alarm?" Grady asks, and all that wobbling and hardening in my chest goes soft at the edges that he still knows I'd set an alarm to warn me that the real alarm is coming.

"I have to go."

"Need a ride?"

"No."

"Annika."

"No, *thank you*."

"It's uphill the whole way."

Yeah, my thighs will be well aware of that by the time I get home, but there's a cooler breeze blowing now, the sun's disappearing behind a cloud, and I have plenty of water.

And there are no emotional land mines involved with biking back alone.

"I need—" I start, but before I can finish, a fat ol' raindrop torpedoes through the trees and lands on my nose.

I glance up to confirm raindrop and not bird poop, and *dammit*.

"*Maaaaa!*" Sue says.

Grady looks up too as the wind rustles the woods behind us.

"I could drop you just outside town so my goat and I stay safe from the pitchforks and tar," he says while more raindrops splatter around us. "You'll still be a drowned rat by the time you get home. No one will ever know we were in cahoots to save your thighs."

It's the *Grady*-est thing he's said to me since I got back, which makes me grateful for the barrage of water droplets picking up and pitter-pattering on the leaves and in the lake, kicking up that rain smell and dotting my cheeks with moisture.

Normal with Grady threatens to make me cry again, but I can blame it on the rain if he looks too closely.

"I'll know," I say quietly. "And how do you know my thighs couldn't handle it?"

"Mine couldn't. I'm projecting."

He's lying, but he does it with a real, full-dimpled smile, rain attacking his hair and soaking his shirt, with warm green-blue eyes that haunted my memories for more years than I care to admit.

I'm struck with the desperate need to hug him.

Just *hug* him.

No kissing, I tell myself.

Just a hug between old friends who maybe, possibly, if neither of us says the words *donuts* or *cupcakes* or *cookies* or any kind of baked good, really, might be able to be friends again.

The friendly kind of friends who wave and say hi but don't confess to silly little things like crying the night she lost her virginity because even though she went into it willingly, she wished it had been him.

The kind who don't admit that when wildfires swept through the mountains south of here three years ago, she might've logged in to check the Shipwreck news as often as she talked to her family and checked the Sarcasm news.

The kind that you have inside jokes with, like the frog joke, which doesn't make sense to anyone else in the entire world, because no one else was hyped up on Mountain Dew and candy corn and that really awful orange taffy with us on Bailey's second Halloween when Mama dressed her like a turtle and we kept asking her to ribbit all night because I kept confusing frogs and turtles since they were both green.

And we're standing here, with rain picking up around us, already soaking through my shirt and making his dark hair drip into his eyes, getting heavier and heavier with each passing second and blowing in sheets over the lake while we each wait for the other to do something so we can get out of the rain before we're both prunes.

"Okay," I whisper.

I don't know if I'm saying yes to the ride or a hug, but Grady leaps into action immediately.

He swoops my bike up in one hand, grabs my hand with the other, and says, "C'mon, then," and I'm seventeen again, dashing along the path at the lake's edge with Grady and his goat while we head for the boat launch parking lot because he's going to be late for dinner, or I need to get back for a shift at the grocery store, or any of the other reasons the two of us needed to dash out away from the lake after canoeing or paddle boarding or swimming for a summer afternoon.

I miss being seventeen.

I thought all I wanted was to get out in the world, to make something of myself, to help Mama get all her dreams, but right now, I want to be seventeen again.

So maybe, for the next ten minutes, I will be.

16

Grady

When I blew off work to go look for some perspective in a place that held so many happy memories, I didn't expect my little trip to the lake would end with Annika's bike in the bed of my truck, Sue objecting to being squished behind me in my extended cab, and Annika herself strapped in beside me, and dripping wet like the rest of us while rain pounds on the truck roof, but it's all so *right* that no matter what happens ten minutes from now, I'll forever have this memory of *not* fucking something up with her.

Finally.

"How long have you had Sue?" she asks, and I'm grateful for the neutral topic while I flip on the windshield wipers and steer the truck up and out of the valley.

"Since somebody let a whole herd of goats loose to ruin the biggest destination wedding in Shipwreck in four years last summer."

"Who lets a herd of goats loose?"

"Sarcasm assholes." Okay, so maybe not a totally neutral topic.

But she snort-laughs while she points the air conditioning vents away from her wet skin, which is pebbling in the cool interior. "That's what we've come to? Turning livestock loose in each other's towns?"

I relax more at the teasing note in her voice. "Not like they could send unicorns."

"We're not Scotland," she agrees.

"What's Scotland have to do with it?"

"You don't know?"

"Yeah, hold on a minute while I pull Scotland facts out of my back pocket." I shoot her a raised brow *you're not making any sense* look, my face defaulting back to old habits, because she was almost always three steps ahead of me.

Almost.

Not that time she couldn't keep frogs and turtles straight, but most every other time.

Her dark eyes study me closely and dip momentarily to my lips before she shifts in her seat to stare out at the rain. "Scotland's national animal is the unicorn."

"Oh. So that's only stuff people from Sarcasm care about," I tease.

Tease.

I'm dripping wet, teasing Annika Williams, who's riding shotgun in my truck while rain pelts the world around us.

And I swear she just checked me out.

This is a teenage fantasy come true.

"Far better to aspire to be majestic and unique than a criminal," she quips.

Sarcasm's Unicorn Festival used to be just the plain Corn Festival, and I used to humor her attempts to tell me corn was better than pirates.

You can't eat pirate coins, and pirates always had scurvy, she'd insist.

But there's nothing cool about cornbread and grits, I'd argue back.

She pointed out once that pirates wouldn't have had whiskey without corn.

I pointed out that pirates preferred rum to whiskey, and she came back with the argument that won every time.

And there aren't any real pirates in Shipwreck anyway.

The old memories make me smile.

And miss who *I* used to be. Not just before she came back to town, but back when I used to dream about running my own bakery and going home every night to a woman who wasn't perfect, but was perfect for me, and our three or four little hellions.

It's been a long time since I thought about settling down.

Or even wanted to think about it.

"How's the Army?" I ask her.

"Army-ish."

"You get deployed?"

"Couple times."

"Going back?"

"Depends on the paperwork."

My heart lurches, and it's not because she's on the verge of walking through the door back into my life.

What happens to her mom and sister if she goes back?

"Are they being dicks?" I ask.

She shakes her head. "No. I have a good commander. But it's still paperwork."

"Harder than baking a cupcake," I wager.

That earns me a side eye and a noncommittal *hm*.

So I don't remind her she once burned boiled water in high school. "Remember the time we were out on the lake when a storm blew in?"

"I remember Mama reading me the riot act for trying to get myself electrocuted by lightning before I finished my American History essay."

"Your mama never read anyone the riot act."

"She'd read *you* the riot act."

"Yeah, but I deserve it."

Guilt and I don't get along well, and while admitting I'm wrong and I also don't get along well, I'm feeling lighter than I have in two weeks.

Right now, I'm not at war. I'm not worried about my bakery's bottom line. And I'm not alone.

She's studying me again, making my own goosebumps bumpier and goosier. I want to reach across the center console and take her hand again, feel that smooth skin, the warmth of her palm, the strength in her fingers, and I'm about to brave it when Sue bleats in my ear and nips at my neck.

"Get back, mangy goat," I grumble.

"*Maaa!*" he replies indignantly.

Annika shifts to pet his wet face, which puts her knee within easy reach. I don't grab it, because I don't know what my goat would do if I tried anything with him watching over, which is a big change from the asshole who was shoving me toward her not ten minutes ago.

Maybe he's trying to say, *Go for it, idiot, but don't take liberties.*

Who the fuck knows what's going through his head?

"What's that, Sue?" Annika says. "You don't like being called names?"

"*Maaa*," Sue tells her.

"Oh. You don't like being called *Sue*."

"You get him to answer to anything else, you can have him," I tell her, even though I'd fight anybody who tried to take my goat away from me. "I tried every name in the book, and the only one he'd answer to was Sue."

"You look like Gerald," she says.

Sue snorts all over both of us.

She shrieks and tries to wipe the goat drool off with her wet tank top, and I decide Sue's getting gourmet grilled brussels sprouts for dinner, because *hello*, flat Annika belly and adorable belly button.

"Sue *hates* Gerald," I tell her. "Don't call him *B-O-B* or *A-S-S-H-O-L-E* either."

"Maximus?" she says with a grin.

Sue nips at my ear.

"*Back*, or I'm leaving you on the side of the road."

The goat harrumphs and plops back on his haunches in the back seat.

"Maybe you should've gotten a dog or a cat," Annika whispers. "Or a hamster."

It's all so *normal*.

Except for the part where I realize her nipples are hard pebbles under her tank top, and I suddenly want to know how they taste.

Fuck, I missed her.

But I've always missed her, as much as you can miss someone you never fully had.

"I'm sorry," I say again. The words don't come easy, but they're necessary.

She's worth it.

At least, the Annika she *was* is worth it. I don't know the Annika she *is*.

But I want to.

Bakery be damned.

"Start over?" she asks softly.

I come to a stop at the preserve exit and glance at her.

The first time I got lost in those expressive brown eyes, I was fourteen years old, and I didn't know what was happening, but I knew that I wasn't supposed to be sitting in biology gaping at my lab partner, who'd just informed me that I wasn't rubbing hard enough on the faucet to really get a good sample for making mold grow.

It shouldn't have been a profound statement—mold spores aren't profound—but she was straddling this line between confidently telling me what I was doing wrong without wading into know-it-all territory, and for the first time in my life, it occurred to me that there were people who would correct me because they cared, and not because they needed to be right.

And that possibly Annika was the only person who would ever fall in that category, and I had a desperate need to know if she liked chocolate chip cookies or blueberry muffins better.

Can I sit with you at lunch? I'd asked.

And then she'd looked at me exactly like she's looking at me now.

Guarded but eager. Like she's holding her toe an inch

above a lake that might have nothing more dangerous than trout lurking in its depths, or that might be full of cottonmouths, but she really, really wants to dive in, even if it means facing her biggest fear.

We can be friends, she'd told me, *but so you know, I don't date. I'm going into the Army to pay for college in four years, and I'm not dating anyone at all until I'm financially solvent and know who I am.*

What fourteen-year-old says that?

Apparently the kind that grow into the kind of women who sit in a truck with a guy they have every right to hate and ask if we can start over.

I throw the truck into park and turn to her, hand extended. "Hi. I'm Grady Rock, and I make the best damn donuts in the world and bake muffins that can give your mouth an honest to god orgasm."

One of her eyebrows arches delicately. "That's your version of starting over?"

I smile my best smile and angle my head to use my dimples to my full advantage, because my grandmother's been telling me my entire life that dimples are lady-killers. "I believe in honesty in relationships. And I promise I won't hold it against you if you try to top me. That'll just make me work harder."

"And now that I know what your ego gets out of this relationship, what do I get?" she asks.

My hand is still extended. "Whatever you want."

Her breath catches and hangs between us, and her gaze dips down my face again, then lower, to where my wet shirt is clinging to my chilled skin, just as hers is molding to her breasts and her belly. A droplet falls off her hair and meanders down from her collar bone, taking a lazy path to the dip between her breasts, and I'm so glad I'm not fourteen anymore.

Her heavy gaze lifts back to mine, and her lips tremble. "Can I start with having my friend back?"

"Whatever you want, Annika."

She holds my gaze while her hand slowly reaches out to take mine, and the instant our palms connect, I feel *home*.

Grounded in the midst of a storm.

"I'm Annika Williams," she says, her voice wobbly, "and I have every intention of being a very high maintenance friend, because I need more than I can give right now."

"Just so happens I owe a lot more than I have any right to ask for."

"You really do."

She wheezes out a small laugh while I smile and pull her hand to my mouth, because I can't help myself.

I *want* to ask her to be more.

But I need to earn this.

And I will.

She stiffens as my lips graze her knuckles, and Sue butts his head in and *maa*s in my ear again.

"Alright, alright," I grumble to the goat while I release Annika's hand.

Letting go shouldn't be this hard.

But I've already said goodbye to her too many times.

I don't want to let her go again.

"Mama's appointment is over in twenty minutes," she says quietly. "And for the record, I'm sorry too. I should've called when I got home. Or…a few years ago."

Where would we be if she'd called a few years ago?

I ignore the question, because it doesn't matter.

"To Sarcasm we go." I put the truck back in gear and slide one more look at her. "Were you really going to bike all the way back?"

"Think I couldn't do it?"

"Think I would've liked watching."

"Not enough women in Shipwreck?" she asks lightly while she reaches back to scratch Sue's head again.

"Turns out I have very exacting standards."

I could definitely get used to the feel of that gaze studying me. In a car in the rain. At a table over the perfect fudge lava cake. In my bedroom.

One whiff of Annika Williams, and I have it bad all over again.

She's my kryptonite.

"Hope you have the determination to match," she murmurs.

It blends in with the raindrops pelting the truck roof, but I hear the challenge.

And I smile.

Because you know what?

I'm damn sure up to it.

17

Annika

By the time Grady pulls up in front of Mama's small double-wide, I can't decide if this energy crackling between us is suppressed sexual tension, or if it's the next phase in our bakery war.

Or possibly both.

"Thank you for the ride," I tell him. I'm still soaking wet. The rain is letting up, though, so I shouldn't get too much wetter on the walk into the house. I turn to the goat. "And thank you for sharing your seat."

He tries to lick my ear.

"Sue. Not on the first date." Grady pulls the goat's head away and scratches under his chin, which makes his leg shake.

Just like a dog.

These two are so weirdly but perfectly adorable.

I climb out, and Grady does too. The sun's peeking out

through the blue-gray haze covering the top of the green mountains, making the lingering raindrops glow and shine as they dive gracefully to the ground while he pulls my bike out of the bed of his truck.

"Get your phone number?" he asks me casually, like it's no big deal, but I recognize the tightening of his knuckles around the handlebars while he pretends to be testing the shocks.

He's nervous.

And it's ridiculously endearing.

"Annika?" Bailey calls from the front door. "What's *he* doing here?"

"Don't worry," I call back to her. "I didn't tell him all about the chocolate ketchup cookies we're making tomorrow."

Her face pauses mid-lip curl and her eyes light up. "*Dammit*, Annika. I *told* you not to tell anyone our secret magic ingredient."

"I also didn't tell him about the baked beans and the crumpets," I report.

"God, I missed you," Grady breathes. "And it's really fucking hot when you talk about horrible baked goods. It shouldn't be, but it is."

My whole body flushes, and I'm tempted to blurt out that horrible baked goods are still my specialty, but I don't yet trust everything about this situation.

I rattle my number under my breath to Grady, then thank him again and take my bike.

"Quit staring at my sister's ass," Bailey calls.

Not that I needed confirmation that he was watching me go.

My butt was tingling.

And not from the rain making my pants wet.

I barely resist turning to watch him watching me, and I don't take a full breath until I hear his truck door slam and the engine roll over.

Bailey trots around the side of the house to the shed with me. "What were you *doing* with him?" she hisses.

Flirting probably isn't going to win me any points with my sister.

"I got caught in the rain, and it was either take a ride or be late."

"I don't trust him."

"I know."

"He's trying to put our bakery out of business before we even get it off the ground."

Our bakery.

If it fails, I'm not just letting down Mama. I'm letting down Bailey too.

"It's not working, is it?" I say. "We can't let other people dictate our success. Only *we* can do that. And you, baby sister, are kicking ass and taking names in the baking department."

"Are you trying to distract me with flattery?"

"Is it working?"

"You're close. Call me a culinary genius ahead of my time."

"You're like the love child of Giada and Martha."

"But prettier?"

"Duh."

"I'm still pissed that you're fraternizing with the enemy."

I pull open the shed door and roll my bike in as the sun

breaks all the way through, chasing away the afternoon rain shower. "How's Mama?"

"She accidentally reprogrammed her voice assistant to answer to *Goddess of my Loins* and really needs to go blow off some steam, but she doesn't think throwing a bowling ball around in her current condition will do any good."

She follows the announcement with a good swift kick to a clump of grass, and I instinctively pull her into a hug while her breath goes ragged and her shoulders tremble.

I could tell her that Mama's tough. That she'll adapt and re-learn how to do almost everything she used to, and a few months from now, we'll never remember a time that *this* wasn't normal.

But it won't help.

It's not helping me right now either.

"It's not fair," she whispers through a hiccup.

"When life kicks you in the balls…"

"I know. I know. Too bad for life, because you have a vagina of steel. My vagina's feeling a little bit more like an overripe kiwi though."

"Please don't ever say that again."

Her watery laugh eases the sting in my own eyes, and I squeeze her tight again.

"Don't tell Mama, okay?" she whispers.

"Naturally. You want to take her bowling?"

"Annika. *We can't.*"

"Don't tell me we *can't* anything. You know she'll still kick your ass."

"But what if she doesn't?"

"She'll still have fun. And that's the important part. Adjusting and figuring out *she still can*, despite the roadblocks."

Mama's always been dauntless. There's not a single roadblock that she hasn't overcome in her life, and starting as a teen mother, she's had to overcome a lot. The idea that she'll be robbed of her bravery and her joy in her mid-forties is breaking my heart, so I have to believe she'll kick being blind in the groin and come out on top in this too.

I have to.

Her mobility specialist tells me she *will* be able to frost cookies again someday. And probably bake, all of it, start to finish. The tools are out there to help her.

The social worker is helping us get everything lined up for her to go on disability while she's being retrained.

We can get a guide dog.

She *will* be able to live a full, independent life again.

But we have to give her time to learn how.

And once she's settled again, then I can stop and figure out what the future holds for *me*.

My phone buzzes in the zipper pocket at my waistline, and my heart gives a big ol' thump that has nothing to do with Mama, and everything to do with something else.

Hope.

And I don't want to think about what I'm hoping for.

Bailey pulls back and wipes her eyes. "Can I take your bike for a spin?" she asks.

"Wear the helmet."

"Yes, Mamika."

She dutifully snaps on the helmet and pulls my bike back out, now that the rain has stopped completely, and I head for the house. Once she's out of sight, I peek at my phone and read the text message that came in.

Testing…Master Baker here, checking in on my high maintenance friend.

I smile softly.

No shortage of ego there.

But then, there never was. Not really.

For either of us.

We both knew who we were going to be.

A new message pops up while I'm still smiling over the first.

By "high maintenance," did you mean you need regular deliveries of MERs and someone to shine your combat boots, or did you mean someone to vent to, or did you mean something else that my simple male brain hasn't thought of yet?

MERs?

What is he—*oh*.

I snort-giggle to myself while I ease in the back door, typing as I go.

He means MREs.

Meals Ready to Eat.

I mean I expect you to let me vent without offering a solution. And also deliver four dozen dandelions to my front door every morning beside the Army-grade black coffee you'll have to drive up to Fort Belvoir to get.

I don't expect any of that, obviously, beyond perhaps having a sympathetic ear.

And after the coffee that Hazel over at Rise and Grind brought me this morning was *so* delicious, I don't think I could drink Army coffee sludge ever again.

Especially Army coffee sludge that would be cold after the two-plus hour drive back from northern Virginia, probably more after traffic.

But when the bubbles appear that tell me he's typing a text back, anticipation puts a lightness in my heart that I haven't felt in weeks.

"Bailey?" Mama calls.

"It's Annika," I reply, crossing through the small kitchen and into the dim living room. I turn the lights up a smidge and sit next to Mama on the ivory couch. She has a crochet needle in her hand and she's fiddling with a ball of yarn in her lap. "How was your session with the mobility specialist?"

"What color is this?" she asks.

"It's your hunter green wool," I tell her.

Her chin wobbles. "The one I was going to use for a scarf for you."

"Mama—"

She grabs the yarn and hurls it across the room, then flings the crochet hook after it. The metal hook clatters against a picture of the three of us on the wall, and the glass shatters and the whole thing tumbles to the floor.

Her head drops into her hands as if it's being pulled by the devil himself.

My chest caves in, but I don't have time to feel for *me* right now. "Mama. Let's go bowling."

"I can't *see*, Annika."

"But you can still *feel*. And I know you can still throw a ball."

"I *can't*. And now I made a mess that I can't clean up because *I can't see*."

I wrap my arms around her and squeeze tight while a sob wrenches through her, because I don't know what else to do.

I can't give her back her vision.

She doesn't want to hear that I'll clean up the mess, or that it was her favorite picture of the three of us, all of us wearing beaver teeth and bunny ears after a fun run that I talked them into doing with me when they came to visit me in Texas last spring.

She doesn't even complain about me being cold and soaking wet.

Mama not retreating into mama mode is scary.

"Where's Bailey?" she gasps between sobs.

"She's out, Mama. Getting some fresh air."

"She can't see me like this. Help me to my room. Tell her I'm napping."

I can't help her to her room until I get the glass cleaned up, because we'll both step in it, so instead, I keep hugging her. "She's biking over to a friend's house. We have time." And I need to text Bailey to tell her to stay out for a while.

"I'm sorry, Annika. I'm so sorry."

"Stop. Don't be sorry. This isn't your fault."

"It *is*. And now your life is upside down and Bailey's life is upside down and you're here trying to hold together *my* life when you should be enjoying yours."

"Mama. *Stop*. There's no place I'd rather be."

"You should sell the bakery."

"*Mama*."

"No. *No*. It's not your dream. It was mine. And now —now—"

"Now, it's all three of us, together, just like we should've been the last ten years."

She shakes me off, and I hate that I have to let her go, but the doctors and therapists have all warned me that she needs to grieve, and that I need to let her.

I can't do it for her.

But I need to do it for me too.

I need to grieve for everything. And I need to let her re-learn how to live.

18

Grady

It's a hell of a lot easier to sweet talk a pastry than it is to figure out if I'm texting Annika the right messages, especially since she's only replied once.

The smart thing to do is to take a win as a win and get my ass back to Shipwreck. I have a business that I need to get back to.

Instead, I'm sitting in my car outside Duh-Nuts, watching my phone to see if she's going to reply again to my egotistical suggestion that I make better coffee than the Army.

I don't doubt it's true, but I also don't know if she'll see it as a fun comment, or if she'll think I'm insulting the coffee she makes at Duh-Nuts.

Want to know the last time I overanalyzed my conversations with a woman?

Ten years ago.

DIRTY TALKING RIVAL

When I asked her to give me a chance and she shut me down cold.

I grew the fuck up the last ten years, yet here I am, twisted in pretzel knots over Annika.

Maybe I didn't grow up at all.

"This better not be just about you," I tell my cock, which has been asking to come out and play since the minute I realized that black spandex-clad ass tangled in the bushes belonged to the woman who's haunted my dreams for half my life.

My heart gives a jolt at the sight of her approaching the shop on her bike, but I quickly realize that's not Annika.

It's Bailey.

She has the same long dark hair and slender build, but she's thirteen, and the differences become glaringly obvious as she gets closer and her features come into sharper focus.

Specifically, the curl in her hair and the glare she's aiming at my truck.

She hops off the bike and walks it straight to the passenger window, which she raps on without hesitation. I roll down the still-wet glass and smile at her. "Hi."

"Don't *hi* me, dirty old man. What are you doing here?"

I glance at the bakery behind her.

It's cute in a run-down kind of way, the green and white striped awnings over the large glass front windows faded, just the same as the giant *Duh-Nuts* sign and its bubble letters over the door.

The windows are shiny and clean, the window boxes overflowing with small lavender flowers that probably have some kind of fancy name, and I can see the gold bells dangling on the metal handlebar inside the glass door.

The *Closed* sign is quaint and old-fashioned, complete with a clock indicating what time they'll open in the morning, but overall, it feels like it needs a fresh coat of paint and a logo redesign to really hit it out of the park.

"How's your mom?" I ask Bailey.

If what Annika and I escaped in the woods was a light summer sprinkle, there's a whole freaking sharknado-cane brewing in Bailey's face.

"That's none of your business."

Swear she adds *shithead* under her breath.

"You remember that time you tipped Annika out of a canoe out on the lake?" I ask her.

She stiffens, which tells me she probably at least hears the story often enough to know what I'm talking about, even if she doesn't remember, because she couldn't have been more than three when it happened. "I remember that time you changed all the rules on her and chased her away to the Army."

I grin. Not because it's funny—the idea that if I'd been enough, Annika wouldn't have left, has crossed my mind more than occasionally in the last decade—but because she reminds me of Tillie Jean.

"She couldn't bake back then," I say.

"Or maybe your taste buds were underdeveloped."

"You going into high school this fall?"

"Why? Trying to protect your ego by telling yourself you're losing an argument to a high-schooler instead of just some thirteen-year-old punk?"

She might not be wrong about the part where I'm losing this argument. "I was at your second birthday party.

Brought you this blow-up bouncy horse thing. Last I knew, you still slept with it."

"Oh, now you're talking about an underage girl sleeping?"

"Trying to be a friend here."

"By scoping out the competition? I might be young, but I'm not stupid. You don't want to help. You want to not get beat."

"What's going on over here?"

The plumber guy ambles up the street toward us, brows lowered dangerously.

"This Shipwreck shithead is spying on us," Bailey tells him.

"That true?" He peers into my truck too and frowns at me.

I think.

His eyes are definitely frowning.

His mouth is swallowed by the giant Scottie dog on his face.

I mean his beard.

Promise.

"Yep," I concede. "You caught me. I'm a shithead. Spying on the closed bakery. Thought maybe I'd see whatever ingredients you're using in tomorrow's bakery wars."

Dammit. I need to talk to Annika. Because I'm getting an idea that could help *both* of us, but I can't do it without her.

Not if I want her to have any shred of respect left for me, and I'm pretty sure right now, she doesn't quite have enough respect for me to fill up a balloon, let alone a life raft.

PIPPA GRANT

And while it'll definitely benefit me, I'm hoping it'll benefit her more.

"Does your mama know exactly what you're up to?" the plumber demands, hands fisting the window ledge of my truck like he could crush it, which he might actually be able to do.

He's probably fifty-five, maybe sixty, but right now, I don't want to test if his stomach is thick with the remnants of thirty years of eating cake, or if it's pure muscle.

Possibly both, I decide.

"She's trying to get me help," I assure him. "Nice chatting."

I lift a hand, glance at my phone one last time, hoping for a message from Annika, but no luck.

"Don't come back," the plumber says.

"Oh, right. The whole *this is my territory* thing," I agree solemnly. "Since you all in Sarcasm honor it so well too."

Bailey's eyes bug out, like I'm not allowed to use sarcasm while in Sarcasm. "Don't be a smart-ass."

"*Arr*," I say, like the long line of non-pirate pirates that I come from.

I wink.

She glares.

The plumber guy goes for his phone.

And I drop my truck into gear. "Okay, okay. I'm going."

"Leave my sister alone," Bailey says.

I probably should.

But I don't know who's helping her through all of this.

And if I want to be the kind of friend she deserves, then I need to fully extract my head from my ass and be the kind of friend she fucking deserves.

19

Annika

Despite a long nap this afternoon, Mama also insists on an early bedtime. I'm finally able to sit down with a chocolate chip cookie that I pilfered from Duh-Nuts this morning, catch up on our financials, and then read Grady's texts again.

Not to brag, but I make some damn fine coffee. You should try mine before deciding you actually prefer Army coffee.

That wasn't an insult to any coffee that might be produced in Sarcasm, by the way.

Annika?

I'm debating what to say—it's been *hours*, which probably means that conversation has died and now I have to start a new one—when Bailey flops into the kitchen in an oversize Half-Cocked Heroes T-shirt and dancing skeleton pajama pants.

"We forgot to do laundry," she announces, then drops

her voice. "And I got all the sugar crystals set up for the geode donuts tomorrow, but if Mama's not up to kneading the dough, we should probably only do a half-batch to save some for Thursday."

"She'll be up for kneading," I reply with far more confidence than I feel.

This is normal, the therapist replied when I texted her an SOS this afternoon. *If she wants to talk, I'm here. You and Bailey and your mama aren't alone, Annika. But good and bad days are part of the grieving process. So long as the good days outnumber the bad, she's on track.*

Nothing feels *on track*.

Except possibly that other text message thread that I closed up as soon as Bailey walked in the door.

Being friends with Grady again—even tentative friends—is the first *right* thing about being home.

"How are you feeling about the fryer?" I ask her.

"I'm ready for blow torch lessons," she replies.

"Do you want a day off? You haven't talked about hanging out with Sophie or Adriana at all lately."

"Sophie's at some lame sleepaway camp, and Adriana is mooning over Brantley Constantinos." She screws her face up with her tongue out, clearly indicating what she thinks of relationships, which is good.

She doesn't have to make the same mistakes I made and refuse to date, but she's thirteen.

There's no reason to rush this relationship stuff.

Just like going to the movies or a dance with a boy doesn't mean she has to have sex with him. Which Mama and I have both reminded her on a regular basis since the day she first asked where babies came from.

"What about a day to just go hang out at the pool?" I ask.

"Skin cancer."

"Sunscreen."

"Drowning hazard."

"Wear a snorkel."

"Metabolic insufficiency."

"*What?*"

She rises and heads for the refrigerator, perusing without taking anything out. "I don't want to go, okay?"

And it hits me.

Metabolic insufficiency.

She thinks she's fat and doesn't want to go out in a swimsuit.

"Bailey—"

"I like baking, okay? I'd rather be making food art and setting myself up for a successful future in a career I love than frolicking in water that half the town has peed in while the popular cheerleaders sit in the lifeguard chairs pretending to care about if people drown."

I am in so over my head. "If you don't like swimming, just say so. But if you don't want to go because of what someone might say—"

"I'm Maria Williams's daughter. I don't give two fucks what anyone might say." She slams the fridge door, battles a bunch of bananas on the counter until one finally loses the wrestling war she's waging with it, and then peels it from the bottom, monkey-style. "I just don't like swimming. It's *boring*. All we have is a box of water. Shipwreck has this huge awesome waterpark with a waterslide and a lazy river and one of those massive buckets over a water jungle gym. But we don't. Because we're Sarcasm. We're *better* than gimmicks."

"Oooo-kay," I say slowly. "Better than gimmicks. Got it."

"I'm getting a pimple, so I need extra sleep. Can you check on Mama before you go to bed?"

"Of course."

"And don't forget to lock the door. Someone was snooping around the bakery earlier. I don't want him thinking he can come in here either."

She gives me a meaningful glare that suggests exactly *who* was snooping at the bakery, then bends to hug me. "I'm glad you're here, even if you make me really mad sometimes."

"Same." I think I have emotional whiplash, and I'm not entirely certain what happened—probably hormones crossed with exhaustion—but I pick up the peel Bailey left on the table when she hugged me, toss it in the trash, and wait until I hear her finish in the bathroom and close her bedroom door before I slip out into the night, ignoring the big blue BEDTIME sticker on my calendar for right about now.

I love the stars here.

And the sky.

It's purple velvet dotted with glitter, and I swear, there's not another night sky in all the world like this one.

Technically, it's the same sky, but lying on my back in Mama's small patch of grass, tucked in by the mountains, with the crickets chirping and the cicadas whirring, the air turning just this side of chilly after a long hot day, the promise of dew wafting through the breeze, it's different.

It's *home*.

It's reliable when everything else is upside down.

I should go to bed too. Getting up at four AM to dash to the bakery every day before getting Mama to her appointments is taking its toll, which is saying something, considering the schedule I kept in the Army. But I don't want to go to bed.

I want—

I want a friend.

I stare at my phone way too long before I make up my mind, because Bailey would hit the roof if she knew I was considering calling the enemy.

Liliana is an option if I want to just *talk*. We've been texting back and forth since she stopped by the bakery the other day and then had girls' night.

But she's not Grady.

We don't have the same history.

She doesn't *know* me.

Not the way he used to.

My finger hits *call* before my brain or my heart or my liver—I don't know, maybe my liver needs a say?—can stop me.

When it rings three times, then four, I almost hang up. I can plead slip of the finger when I was checking text messages.

But a sleepy, startled, "Hello?" comes through on the other end, and it's like the last ten years haven't happened.

"Pass out watching the Fireballs?" I ask.

It's what he would've done in high school after a long track practice.

His chuckle is rueful and soothing and warm. "You got me. Sue! Dammit, Sue, get out of—*argh*. You're cleaning that up, you damn goat."

"Left out your dinner of Frosted Flakes?" I ask, hoping he says yes, because that's what he always told me his dream was.

Frosted Flakes for dinner after a long hard day of feeding people delicious baked goods.

"Lucky Charms. Close enough."

"Chocolate milk?"

"You calling me predictable?"

"I could go for predictable," I confess quietly while a mosquito buzzes past my ear.

"You still have your plans for tomorrow color-coded on a flow chart that's been printed and hung on the refrigerator?"

I'd call him an ass, except I do. "No, I work in black and white gradients now."

His chuckle sends a pleasant buzz arrowing between my legs. "What's tomorrow? Wednesday? Is that still blue sock day?"

"No."

"Fucking Army."

I smile up at the swath of stars sparkling above me. It's a sad smile, but it's a smile. "You know why I did that, don't you?"

"Because you were awesome?"

"It was the only thing we ever splurged on. Bought new. Socks, underwear, and good shoes. But Mama shopped the sales like it was her full-time job, so when she found these horrifically ugly socks in the clearance rack for pennies on the dollar just a few weeks before I started high school, she bought *all* of them. I think I still have a couple unopened packs buried in the bottom of my drawer in my room here. But when I told myself Thursdays were red sock day and Tuesdays were gold-and-black stripe day and Fridays were mismatch day, they were…"

"More bearable?"

He still sounds so sleepy. Like if he were next to me, he'd curl his head onto my shoulder and fling an arm around my belly, and I could sniff sleepy Grady and run my hands through his hair and just *be*.

"Yes," I whisper.

I want to just *be*. No worries. No stress. No Army. No bakery. Mine or his.

"You know you started a fashion trend."

How many times did he tease me like that in high school? And how many times did I tell myself that that's what friends did, and how many times did I ignore that little voice whispering, *he teases you because he likes you, Annika*.

Of course he liked me.

We were friends.

Best friends.

"Annika?"

"How was culinary school?" I don't want to talk about *me*.

I want to know what I missed.

"It was…hard, but fun," he says.

"And you came home and bought Crow's Nest?"

"Tell you a secret?"

"Is it actually a secret?"

"Ahh…I guess that depends on where you're from."

"Mm-hmm."

Lightning bugs dance overhead, blinking on and off, and I sigh happily while Grady's voice drifts into my ear.

"Cooper co-signed the loan," he says slowly. "It's basically half his."

"That makes sense."

I can *feel* him going tense. There are miles and practically a mountain between us, but the space doesn't matter. I *know* it bothers him that he couldn't do it all on his own.

"I'm saving up to buy him out. Slowly. So fucking slowly. Or at least get a new loan without his name on it. So if I ever fuck it up, it doesn't hurt him. It's just…taking longer than I expected."

"I co-signed on Mama's loan," I tell him. "Family helps family."

"Yeah, but…"

He drifts off, and when I hear a quick inhale, I know he's dropping it before he says something stupid like, *yeah, but my family could afford to send me to college, whereas yours could end up bankrupt with nowhere to turn if your bakery doesn't work.*

"You still like that soft serve crap?"

I bust out laughing. "You still call it *that soft serve crap*?"

"That's what it is."

"It's *delicious*."

"If I hold my nose and go get a cone, will you meet me at the ninth hole?"

My muscles tense and the grass beneath me suddenly feels like pins instead of a soft cushion. "You want me to sneak onto a golf course after dark?"

"I know the manager. It'll be fine."

"I'm not fully discharged from the Army yet, and I'm not going out with a trespassing charge on my record."

"Are you objecting to the golf course, or are you objecting to ice cream with me?"

A strangled answer slips out of my mouth, because I'd love to have ice cream with Grady. And talk. And catch up. And *talk*.

But you don't grow up knowing the world is just waiting for you to fuck up and put a toe out of line without developing a healthy respect for playing by the rules.

I knew exactly what my middle school and high school teachers were thinking every time they asked if I was Maria Williams's daughter.

Another wild Williams kid. Wonder if this one'll party out in the cornfields until she gets herself knocked up too?

It's part of why the Army was a good choice.

I knew the rules. I could follow the rules. And we were all equal when we pulled on our boots every morning.

Nobody else could point to my pants and giggle because they dropped those same pants off at Goodwill last week. Drill sergeants didn't care if you came from money or grew up in an orphanage. They didn't give me the side eye because my mama was a little wild before she got pregnant.

"How about I call the sheriff and ask special permission to sit in the clubhouse parking lot and catch up with an old friend?"

His exasperation is almost cute.

"The sheriff's from Sarcasm," I remind him. "You'd basically be asking for both of us to be led away in cuffs."

"Dammit," he mutters.

"Sarcasm Cellars," I say. "I have a connection there. You bring the soft serve. I'll be there as soon as I can sneak away."

20

GRADY

TURNING FLOUR, sugar, and butter into foodgasms takes skill, concentration, and sleep, but tonight I have none of those.

Except concentration.

I'm sitting in the bed of my truck in the far corner of the winery's parking lot, soft serve ice cream piled in a cake cone and melting in a cup next to me, my own waffle cone of mint chocolate chip that I got from Shipwreck's Sea Cow Creamery half-gone, and I'm beginning to wonder if I've been stood up when headlights cut through the darkness, blinding me and making me wince.

A minute later, Annika steps out of a Ford Focus next to my truck, and my heart leaps into a drum solo. I can only make out her outline, but I still know it's her.

She doesn't say anything while she boosts herself up onto the tailgate next to me in the dark, and I just as wordlessly hand her the goopy mess of sub-par ice cream she's always loved.

I'm a food snob who eats cereal for dinner.

And I'm okay with that.

"Oh, this is good," she moans, and I suddenly don't care an ounce what she's eating, because she's humming in the back of her throat and I'm at full mast and my cock is going for some kind of world record for speed and height.

And possibly density.

"You're so weird," I force out.

It's normal. Or what used to be normal.

She snorts into her soupy soft serve, and I watch her dark profile as she wipes her nose with her hand.

"Napkin?" I offer.

"Probably useless until I'm done. Did you bring a sink too? It's dripping down my arm."

I picture myself licking all that fake ice cream stuff from her wrist to her elbow, and I have to shift to give my hard-on more room. "Yep. Up in the cab."

She licks the side of her hand, then goes back to the ice cream, and even in the dark, when all I can make out are shadows and shades of black and gray, watching her head bob over the cone makes me break out in a sweat.

Does she know what she's doing?

Or is she as oblivious as High School Annika was?

"Need help?" I ask.

She freezes, then slowly twists her head to study me. I can pick out the outline of her lips. The angle of her delicate nose. The arch in her normally stoic brows.

Probably I should get that frog out of my throat before I talk again.

"Rocky road in a waffle cone dipped in chocolate?" She nods toward my hand.

"Mint chocolate chip."

Her smile is just as breathtaking in the dark as it is in the light. It's like my soul can feel it.

"Would've been my second guess. And what's on your menu in the morning?" she asks, and I wish I could see her face more clearly. Know if her eyes are getting calculated, or if she's just testing me.

"Banana pudding donuts. Town favorite. Sure sell-out. You?"

"Bailey wouldn't tell me, so I don't know."

"Bailey wouldn't—" I cut myself off with a bark of laughter. "Holy shit. You still can't bake."

"What? I can bake. I can bake your ass off."

"Christ, Annika. You're fucked."

"And thank you so much for helping by starting a *bakery war*."

Shit. *Shit*.

"Good for business," I venture.

"Hm."

Dammit.

She can't bake. *She can't bake*.

We're both fucked.

And it's my fault.

My ice cream is sitting in my stomach swirling itself into a lava whirlpool that's gonna leave me with indigestion for weeks.

"You have help?" My palms are sweating and I couldn't take another bite of ice cream if the fate of the world depended on me finishing this cone. My boner's still going strong, though, so maybe all's not lost.

Or maybe I shouldn't use it as a crystal ball, because it's a dick. "Other than Bailey."

"Everything's fine," she insists.

She's running a bakery with a thirteen-year-old and a woman who went unexpectedly blind.

She's *not* fine.

And I'm sitting on an email from a reporter who wants to cover the greatest bakery rivalry Virginia's ever seen.

I'd *crush* her.

Unless—

"Sales good?" I ask.

"I'd like to be friends, which means we can't talk about this."

Friends. Being *friends* can bite me.

I'm gonna be her fucking hero.

Decision made.

Several, in fact.

Right here, right now.

I don't just *bake*. I create *masterpieces*. Foodgasms. That won't change in two weeks. In six months. In ten years. I will *always* be a master baker.

Maybe I'll keep my own bakery if I can manage to keep my profits on an upward trend.

But what I do in the next thirty seconds will determine if I can ever be anything else besides a master baker.

"My sales are up since we started taunting each other," I tell her.

"How terrible for you. My mama threw a crochet hook through a picture and nailed it right through picture-me's nose."

"Huh. Makes you wonder how often she did that when she could still see what she was aiming at." Shit. It's exactly what I would've said ten years ago, and exactly *wrong*.

"I mean—" I start.

She shoves her soupy ice cream cone in my ear before I realize she's moved.

I yelp and leap off the tailgate, spinning like I can locate a shower, a laugh starting deep in my belly, because that's Annika.

My Annika.

Not taking any shit from anyone. Including me.

And if I still know her, she's about to apologize for it.

"I'm *not* sorry," she informs me as though she's reading my mind. "You asked for that."

There's cold fake ice cream dripping down my face and flooding my ear and catching in my stubble, and I'm suddenly bent double.

Cracking the hell up.

"I did," I agree on a wheeze.

"*And* you ruined my ice cream cone, because I don't want to eat your earwax."

"Here." I hold out what's left of mine while I use my shoulder to wipe my ear. "You earned it."

"I earned a whole fucking soft serve machine getting delivered to my bakery, *that's* what I earned."

My laughter dies away.

She's right.

She deserves all the credit for bubble waffles topped with soft serve coming to the Blue Ridge Mountains.

Because she did all this on her own. She rose above where she started, joined the military, went to college—yeah, the rumor mill crosses town lines, and I know she has a college degree—co-signed on a loan for her mom to have her dream, and now she's starting fresh all over again.

Without complaint.

Without a baking bone in her body.

And I'm standing here without a worry in the world beyond some hurt feelings over a ten-year-old leap that ended poorly for me, knowing that if I fuck up my own bakery, my family will bail me out.

I won't lose my house.

My family and the whole town will rally around me until the problem of Grady Rock fucking up is solved.

I'm a spoiled rotten shithead.

A spoiled rotten shithead whose sales are up because of a rivalry with my former best friend.

"I can help you," I offer.

"I didn't ask for your help. And I don't entirely trust it even if I wanted it."

"Okay."

Even with the parking lot in near darkness, I can see her suspicion blooming.

I can also see her outline as she twists and searches the truck bed, probably for napkins.

"Annika."

"Don't say my name."

I step closer, until my hands come to rest on her knees. "You know the only thing people love more than donuts and cupcakes?"

"Good revenge and eight hundred thread count sheets?"

"No, they—"

"Playing with babies and the smell of rain?"

"Also good, but—wait. You like babies?" She was

jumpy around Bailey when we were kids, and didn't like how much she cried, and also confessed once that she hated how jealous she was of all the attention Bailey got, and she knew it was irrational, and she couldn't tell her mama, but she also couldn't make herself *not* feel it.

I'd told her I felt the same about Cooper, who's only a year younger than me and hadn't been a baby in years, we both laughed, we both knew we were each completely serious, and neither one of us talked about it again.

At least, to each other.

I've never told another soul, but I don't know what she's told all the people who came in and out of her circle while she was gone.

"You said *people*," she reminds me. "I'm being general. People like babies. People also like the first sip of coffee in the morning, sleeping all through the night for the first time after a cold, and spring flowers."

"People don't love spring flowers more than cupcakes and donuts."

"Yes, they do. Not everyone lives and dies by the scent of sugar in a fryer or an oven."

I squeeze her knees, because she's trying to distract me, and I want to kiss her for it, but that clearly didn't end well for me the last time, so I need to keep myself under control.

For at least another minute.

"Gossip, Annika. People love gossip."

"People are assholes. And shitheads."

"We keep up the rumor that we're feuding, and both our bakeries will be full to bursting with people wanting to know which of us insulted the other and how we feel about me making prettier baked goods to combat those unicorn pirate cookies you put together, and about your banana pudding getting written up in the *Blue Lagoon County Gazette* and taking my sister's crown."

She smirks, and yeah, I can totally see the smirk in the darkness. "That really hurts, doesn't it?"

"If someone with taste had written the article—*ow*."

Her playful shove didn't hurt, but the motion has her leaning closer to me, and I can smell my mint chocolate chip ice cream on her, and I want to dribble it all over her skin and lick it off and *fuck*, I'm so hard my nuts hurt.

"You know why we got along so well in high school?" she says.

"Because I was fabulous and you were the only person who could see it?"

"Because your body might've been born in Shipwreck, but your soul belongs in Sarcasm. But only because there's not an Egoville around here."

"Whoa, now—"

I cut myself off when she laughs.

I missed that laugh.

I missed it all the way deep down to the pit of my soul, which hasn't been fully settled since the night I confessed to her how much I liked her.

It's not settled tonight, either, but it's swirling with two things that have been in short supply the last decade.

Intrigue and hope.

"So you propose we be secret friends who are publicly at war to keep the gossips going and make each of our bakeries thrive with people wanting to weigh in on whose muffins are best?" she asks.

I can't read her tone.

It's too flat.

Like maybe I've stepped in it all over again.

"And I can teach you how to bake so you can keep up," I offer.

"You are *such* a jerk."

"I'm a little off-center these days, but I'm serious about helping, and if you really can't bake, you need help. Take my help. Or at least promise me you have a plan better than letting your mama and sister continue to take care of all the baking."

"Why?"

"Because your bakery will fail if Bailey and your mama are your entire plan."

"No, I mean why do you care so much?"

"Because we're friends."

"Friends."

"Annika. You know you were my best friend."

"And you can be satisfied with that? With just friends?"

Not likely. "I—I missed you. And I always liked your mama and your sister, and I don't know what it's like to go suddenly blind, or to put your whole life on hold to care for someone who has. I've had this rock in the pit of my gut since I heard what happened, and baking is the only thing I know to do to fix anything. Baking is the only thing I've ever done *best*. Besides be your friend. Which I've been pretty shitty at the last week."

"That wasn't an answer."

"I liked you. In high school. A *lot*."

"I'm not that girl anymore, and you're not that boy."

"Not even close," I agree. "But this?" I squeeze her knees again. "I want to find out what *this* is. And who we are now. I'm not the same man I was two weeks ago either. Not since you came back."

"I don't have *that* to give right now, Grady. My plate's a little full."

"You're trying to keep a gallon of soup from overflowing a teacup. I know. So let me help. You don't have to do anything besides agree to let Bailey tell a reporter how terrible I am and not let it slip that we're talking behind the scenes."

"And what kind of lesson is that for Bailey?"

"I'll say terrible things about her too."

"No, you won't."

"Okay, I probably won't," I concede.

"Probably?"

"Definitely." My fingers inch up her firm thighs, and she doesn't bat me away. "You know that feeling when you realize you were a better person in high school than you are today?"

She doesn't answer, because of course she doesn't feel that too.

Nope, that's just me.

"What would your family say about you helping me?"

"Tillie Jean would probably blow a gasket. Pop would double down on his efforts to find me a girlfriend. But Ma would be thrilled."

Her thighs go tense at the word *girlfriend*.

So I still have a chance.

"Just think about it," I tell her.

"Do you know what I really need right now?"

"A double shot of tequila and a triple fudge cupcake?"

"No. *This*."

21

Annika

This is probably the worst idea I've had all day, but I can't help myself.

I need a hug.

Grady's body goes tense as I wrap my arms around his waist and drop my head to his chest, but only for a split second before he releases that tantalizing hold on my legs to step between them and hold me close.

He smells like sugar and sweat and fresh-mowed grass, and I grip him tighter and just breathe.

I don't realize how tense I've been until my shoulders start to droop. He strokes my hair, and when he reaches my neck, the ever-present tension that I don't even notice anymore bleeds away.

Just a little.

Like a pinhole leaking air out of a blimp.

But it's a start.

Right here, in this little cocoon, I don't have to hold anyone else's world together.

I can just let go.

Not for long.

But for long enough.

"Are you shoving the rest of my ice cream cone into the back of my shirt?" he asks softly while his hand trails down my back, sparking unwelcome shivers of delight beneath my tank top.

"I'm working on getting it down your pants," I reply while I angle my head, my ear over his pounding heart, drinking in the deep rumble of his chuckle, and melt deeper into him, seriously debating just dropping the rest of the cone because I don't want it.

I want *this*.

My nipples are tightening and there's a longing pull deep between my thighs, but I ignore them both.

Or try to.

Just a hug, I remind my body.

It snorts out an indelicate *yeah, right*.

"You're very tense," he murmurs.

"I've had a shitty month."

He holds me tight with one arm while he uses his other hand to gently knead my neck.

"Biscuits," he muses.

"What?"

"Biscuits. Your neck is tight as over-kneaded biscuit dough."

"Thank you?"

"I'm an expert in biscuits."

"You think you're an expert at everything."

"Shh. Let the master work. And for the record, I'm

awful at fishing and curling."

"You took up curling?"

"No. That's why I suck at it. Now be quiet so I can fix your neck."

How much experience, exactly, has he had at *fixing necks*?

How many other women has he used this line on?

My shoulders bunch, but then he presses his thumb right into a tight band in my neck, stroking up and down with firm, sure strength, and murmurs, "Patience, sweetheart. A little love is all we need here. I know you're already overworked, but I added more cream, and now I'm gonna stroke you just the way you like."

"Are you talking dirty to my neck muscles?"

"Sshh. Don't interrupt the master baker."

"But—*ooooohhh*." He hits a spot just right, putting me on that precipice between pain and pleasure, and release is *so* close.

"That's right, baby. You stay right there and let my hands make you feel good."

I whimper, because *damn*, this does feel good.

Also?

If he can work his way around my neck that well, what could he do to the rest of my body?

"Good girl," he croons. "That's right. Let the master baker take care of you. And I'll take care of *all* of you."

This should be hilarious, but there's nothing funny about the ache in my clit right now.

"Time to flip over, baby." He cradles my head and guides me to turn my neck, and a stiff pain hits me at the base of my skull as I twist into that spot that has a hitch in it.

But his other thumb finds it, and he puts just the right amount of pressure on the ball of tension to start to loosen it.

"Somebody's been a bad, bad biscuit," he whispers. "Does she need punishment?"

"I can't decide if I love you or hate you right now," I say.

I think.

It might've actually come out as a garbled plea for him to not stop.

In Klingon.

I squeeze him tighter and scoot closer, my thighs closing around his, my stomach lining up with—oh.

Oh.

Is *that* what he was packing back in high school too?

Maybe he stuck a cannoli in his pants.

A very large, magic cannoli for a world's largest cannoli competition.

Yep.

That's what I'm going to tell myself, because otherwise this hug is going to turn into something more than Grady dirty-talking the tough biscuits in my neck.

"You know what I do to bad biscuits?"

Please tell me you spank them. Please please please tell me you—no.

Bad brain.

Bad brain.

I mumble out a whimper that ends with an upward lilt.

"Sometimes I have to eat them."

My breasts are heavy and my panties are soaked and I need to leave so I can go home and have some private time with my fingers.

In the shower.

While I fantasize about Grady's cannoli.

And about him eating me.

I'm about to bolt when he hits that spot in my neck just right and the tension takes wing and floats away into the night.

"Oh my god, you're so good at this," I say.

And this time, I think I actually managed the real words.

"Better?"

"Mmm."

My scalp tingles beneath his lips, which are hovering right over my crown, my skin on fire with a desperate need for something my brain can't agree with, but I can't let go of my grip on him.

And I might be trying to subtly check out his cannoli more, because *dear god*, if I'd known about that in high school, I either would've been scarred for life or in very, very deep trouble.

Probably the latter.

Definitely the latter.

I wasn't afraid of sex, the act.

I was terrified of the consequences.

He has to feel me arching against him, but he doesn't thrust his hips or push himself into me.

But he does slide his fingers through my hair, combing them down my back, playing with the ends and tugging lightly, setting the nerve endings in my scalp back to dancing again.

"Cooper's gone a lot," he muses. "Like right now."

"Hmm?"

"He has these zero gravity massage chairs for living

room furniture at his place up on the mountain. And I have the security codes to get in."

"Are you bribing me with a massage chair?"

"Yes."

He sweeps his hand through my hair again, and I bite my lip to keep from moaning at the electric sensation of having this man and his talented hands playing me like a bowl of cookie dough.

"What do you want?"

"My friend back."

My eyes drift shut, and I squeeze him harder.

Maybe it really is a giant cannoli. Or maybe getting racked in the nuts with a softball makes a guy swell for a long time.

Or maybe he's trying to do the gentlemanly thing and take care of me first.

I don't *need* someone to take care of me.

But I'm so damn touched that he's doing it anyway.

Because *this* is the Grady I missed.

The one who didn't need every day to be even, because it all worked out in the end. He'd talk me off a ledge when I got spun up over missing writing down a homework assignment, and I'd assure him that the best people in life were often the ones overlooked in high school when Cooper would do all the things Cooper used to do.

He showed me that the world could be fun even when I was driving myself toward succeeding at adulting before I was old enough to vote.

I like to think I showed him that it's okay to come in second, so long as you're giving your best to the things that mattered.

I should take his offer of continuing our rivalry. We should play the reporter who wants to cover our bakeries.

It would set Mama and Bailey up for success.

I can't afford a full-time baker without raising sales, but I can't raise sales without a full-time baker.

"Okay," I whisper, and I don't know exactly what I'm agreeing to.

Being friends? Yes.

Letting him help me? Probably.

Kissing him until we're pawing each other's clothes off and I'm begging him to do to my clit what he just did to my neck?

I don't even stop to think, because if I do, I'll change my mind, and I don't want to change my mind.

I want to kiss Grady.

I lift my head and straighten my spine to reach for his face, and my lips are a breath from his when my phone rings, the sound splitting the night air.

We leap apart. I smear the ice cream cone across his shirt and drop it in my haste to dig my phone out of my pocket. "Oh, shit. Sorry. Sorry. I didn't mean—*Bailey*."

My sister's picture lights my screen, and I don't hear whatever Grady replies as I swipe to answer and lift the phone to my ear.

I shouldn't have left home.

Or I should've told her where I was going.

And instead, I'm taking a panicked call when she should be sleeping because she woke up and realized I was gone.

It doesn't matter how much I want to kiss Grady, because my life isn't my own.

Not right now.

22

Grady

Sue reads me the riot act when I get home. Apparently he doesn't like being home alone any more than Bailey does.

Maybe I should drop the goat off with Annika's family the next time she calls me for an ice cream run late at night.

If there's a next time.

I hope there's a next time.

I give Sue an extra bowl of goat food and head around the corner to the laundry room. Need to get the goop out of my ear and take care of this boner that won't quit.

"Is this normal?" I ask the goat, who's ignoring the goat food in favor of trying to eat my shirt, since it, too, has ice cream all over it. "Is it normal to be hung up on the same woman after not seeing her for ten years?"

"*Maaaa*," he replies sagely.

PIPPA GRANT

I wrestle him for my T-shirt and toss it straight in the washing machine in the small room off the kitchen.

He tries to go in after it, and I end up wrangling him all the way to my bedroom, where he starts going after my ass.

"Down, you damn goat."

I'm twisting around, realizing I have mint chocolate chip streaked down the back of my leg and need to toss these pants in the wash too, when my phone rings. I lunge for it and don't even look at the screen before I answer.

"Annika?"

"Whoa, dude. TJ's right. You got it bad."

"I said, *way to haka*," I improvise, because I'm not admitting to Cooper where I went.

He'd get it—back in high school, he was hung up on Ariel Bodine, and Jericka Jones, and the cafeteria lunch lady, who was a recent college grad and really fucking hot, among other women—but that doesn't mean I want to talk to him about it.

He's laughing, which isn't reassuring. "So if I called Pop and told him I just met this girl in San Diego who'd be perfect for you—"

"Quit eating my pants, you asshole," I tell the goat while I try to strip out of them.

He head-butts my boxer briefs, then licks the back of my knee.

"You need some private time with your goat?" Cooper asks.

"Nice win. Fireballs needed that. Why are you calling me so late?"

"Make sure you're doing okay."

I dodge Sue and head back to the laundry room with

my jeans, realizing this isn't going to end well for my hard-on, because the goat won't get off my tail. "Doing fine. It's almost midnight."

"Yeah, and you're awake. Got a text from Nana. She saw you leave home when you were supposed to be going to bed and wanted to make sure you weren't planning on driving over a cliff so you didn't sully the family name by getting involved with a girl from Sarcasm."

"Why didn't Nana—never mind."

"Yeah. Tuesday night, man. Business sock night."

"Tuesday's shower sex day, and Pop wore the striped ones today." I have no idea what Pop wore today, but if Cooper's going to throw *business sock night* at me, I'm going to one-up him.

"Nana told me she spent the afternoon at the spa. Coochie smoochie day."

Don't need to think about Nana having a Brazilian, and I don't know if he's blowing smoke up my ass, but it's helping the boner situation, so I'll go with it.

"Reminds me. Knock before you go into the bathroom next time you're in Crusty Nut. Although, that was an appropriate location, given how old Pop is, and how crusty his nuts must be."

"You think vaginas get loose and hang low like dicks do? *Ow*. Fuck. *Fuck*, Darren. You don't like hearing about my grandparents doing it like rabbits, go back to your own room."

"Or maybe you shouldn't talk about your elders having sex," I say.

"I'm calling to talk about *you* having sex," my little brother replies. "Specifically, with your soulmate."

"My sex life is none of your business."

"It's none of anybody's business but you and your hand lately. Which we need to change, because you can't knead dough right unless you're giving each of your hands equal whack-off time. Does that make you ambi-whacks-trous?"

"I'm hanging up."

"Some reporter lady from one of those regional magazines called my agent and wants my opinion on a bakery I co-own having a war with a bakery in Sarcasm. Just want to know what I'm supposed to tell them."

"Nothing. You're supposed to tell them *nothing*."

"I got caught in Duh-Nuts. Dude. I can't tell them *nothing*. So I want to know. Are we on team Grannika, or team Enemies Forever?"

"*Grannika?*"

"You'd rather be Annady? That has a ring to it too."

"It's a good thing you're pretty," I grunt.

"And talented. Don't forget that part. You see that home run I hit tonight? Four hundred and *twelve* feet."

"You're a baseball god. I have to go to bed or nothing's getting kneaded in the morning."

"Where'd you go?"

"To the laundry room to—*dammit*, Sue, let go of my underwear."

"How does Annika feel about your goat?"

"You know where she works. Why don't you call and ask her?" Fuck. Now I need to warn her that Cooper might be calling.

"Does that mean things aren't great in Grannika-ville, or does it mean you're trying to throw me off the scent?"

"Don't you have a curfew?"

"Gods don't need them."

"But you do."

"Oh, *snap*. Nice one. When are you seeing Annika again?"

"What difference does it make to—*Sue, get off the fucking dryer.*"

My goat snorts at me, turns, and drops goat pellets all over the top of the dryer, and they fall to the floor.

Yeah.

That kind of goat pellets.

My brother does that laugh where he sounds like a hyperventilating hyena, and I turn around, bare-ass, and walk out of my laundry room, wishing Annika was here, because she'd be laughing too, but if she laughed, I'd laugh.

Her happiness makes me happy.

She's not happy right now.

She's a flaming ball of tension over shit that isn't her fault but that she still has to clean up.

Sue *maaa*s at me indignantly, like it's my fault he's stuck on the dryer.

"You ever wonder if you and Annika will end up like Pop and Nana? Having business sock day, running the pirate festival, walking your goat through town, horrifying your grandchildren by having sex in public…"

No.

I've never wondered.

I've just *known*.

Deep down in my gut, I've always known it was her or no one. Even when I dated other women, I'd think about the future, and I'd see Annika.

She snuck into my head when I was fourteen, and I

found the woman I've been soulmates with from the dawn of time.

"Playing matchmaker for my loser brother who can't date one woman at a time to save his life..." I finish for him.

"You date. I hook up. We're equally right in our own ways, and I wish you'd accept my promiscuity the way I accept that you have a self-righteous stick up your ass."

I step into the bathroom and crank the hot water. "I'm going to bed."

"Grady. Bro. Listen. You want her, go for her. Fuck anyone who doesn't support you. Let love win, man. Let love win."

"Who are you, and what did you do with Cooper?"

"I just had a very philosophical discussion with a Louisville Slugger, and that's what the wood told me."

"Thanks for the pep talk."

"Me and my wood are always here for you. And for Annika."

"Keep your fucking wood away from Annika."

He hyena-chuckles again. "When you have babies, I want the first named after me."

"Arrogant bastard?"

"Fuck, yeah. That kid'll grow up to go places. *President Arrogant Bastard Rock*. Got a ring to it, doesn't it?"

Steam is rising in the shower, and I'm grinning as I hang up with my brother, because he might be obnoxious, but he's still my brother, and he's fucking hilarious.

So long as I don't think about owing him money if my plan doesn't work and he has to bail me out.

As soon as I step into the hot water, all that melts away though, and Annika's face pops into my head, those eyes searching mine, her nimble fingers pushing down the straps on that tank top, and in this fantasy, she's not wearing a bra.

Or panties.

I grip my cock and stroke, eyes closed while the water pounds down on me, imagining her in the shower with me, her hands roaming my skin, her mouth claiming mine, her legs wrapped around my waist while I pound into her.

But it's not enough.

I jerk harder.

I don't know what she likes. I don't know where she's most sensitive. I don't know if she's hot and hard or slow and deep.

I don't know if I'll ever get a chance to find out.

But I want to.

I want to slather her in brownie batter and lick every inch clean.

Her toes.

Those sexy as fuck calves.

Her thighs.

Her pussy.

My balls are tight, and I can feel myself getting close to release.

Is she bare? Does she wax? Or does she have a pretty triangle of curls?

What color are her nipples?

Will she scream when she comes, or is she a quiet, gasping moaner?

I hear her pleading my name, imagine her straddling me and taking me into her hot core, and I groan in relief and despair as my cock jerks and I come in the shower.

Alone.

Just me and my hand.

Cooper's right, the fucknut. I have more of a relationship with my hand than I've had with a woman in too long.

But I have to earn my way back into Annika's life.

I've been a shit.

Time to fix it. Time to be the man she needs me to be.

I'm going to earn her, and I'm going to help her bakery succeed.

No matter what it takes.

23

Annika

I hate caving, but sometimes, it's necessary.

My stomach is in knots while the morning rush dies down, and I keep looking at the cupcake clock hanging over the front door, because at exactly ten AM, I'm expecting someone.

Several someones.

And I have to talk about *everything*.

Bare my soul.

Confess my deepest fears.

And also lie my ass off and take responsibility for the delicious donuts that Bailey and Mama tweaked with a new recipe over the weekend, and that Bailey filled with cinnamon-spiced fudge pudding and topped with a salted caramel glaze.

But she didn't stop there, because Bailey is physically incapable of not going to extremes.

Which is why today's dragon donuts—as she named them—feature not simple salted caramel glaze, but a glaze that she's somehow managed to make look like dragon scales.

None of the bakers I've interviewed—all two of them who have answered my ads—can do *that*.

My phone dings, and I pull it out quickly to check the message.

Holy fuck, Annika. She'll be TEACHING culinary school before she's sixteen.

Grady's attached a screenshot of the Duh-Nuts Instagram post about our dragon donuts, and I can't help a huge smile from stretching so big my cheeks instantly hurt.

She gets a childhood first, I type back.

Not that I have to argue with *him* about her childhood.

I spend enough time arguing with *her* about it.

"Who are you texting?" she asks behind me.

"Liliana." I pocket the phone beneath my apron and turn to find her watching me from the doorway to the kitchen, a fresh tray of dragon donuts in hand, her suspicion stronger than it's been anytime in the last week since Grady and I quietly made up, and then agreed to lie to everyone about making up.

But aren't sales better? he'd said. *People love a train wreck more than they love hearing about two friends making up.*

And thus we stay a secret.

For the bakery. Bakeries.

We're both benefitting.

"Are those the last?" I ask Bailey with a nod at the donuts.

"We have one more tray. You don't normally blush when you're texting with Liliana."

"I'm nervous. I hate reporters."

"No, you don't."

I do when I'm lying to them. And I've been lying to Bailey and Mama too. In the name of Mama's dream and Bailey's future, but still lying.

Who are you texting, Annika?

My friend from the Army/first duty station/basic training/that karaoke bar I used to go to in El Paso.

That peanut butter cupcake recipe was perfect, Annika. Where did you find it again?

Pinterest.

What's that you were eating?

Not a coconut pecan chocolate cookie from a bag that I found on the back door that almost certainly came from Grady, who texted late last night after everyone else was in bed, to tell me that cookies make life better and I should go check the back porch before the local raccoons or possums did.

I hate lying.

I hate it to my core.

But if that's what it takes to keep raking in sales while I try to find a new baker who can do what Bailey does when she goes back to school in just a few weeks, then that's what I'll do.

"Today, I hate reporters," I tell Bailey. "I don't *like* fighting wars."

"You were in the Army."

"I'm basically a human resources Excel manager and paper pusher, and that was for a noble cause. This is just a petty rivalry between two towns, and none of us can actually remember why we hate the other."

"It's because Shipwreck lied about being founded by a pirate and tried to poison the founder of Sarcasm," Mama calls from her seat at the worktable, where she's shaping snickerdoodle cookie dough, which she can do by feel, though she seems to lose the cookie scoop every few cookies and has to pat around to find it again.

But this is progress.

Just like getting her out bowling Sunday night.

"That happened three hundred years ago," I call back.

"A hundred and fifty," she says. "And don't say that to the reporter. We don't need those Shipwreck shitheads thinking we've gone soft. Even if they're not actually the shitheads everyone in Sarcasm calls them. I'm just getting in the mood to tell a good story."

There's a knock at the back door. I take the tray of donuts to put them in our display case while Bailey scampers off to answer the knock.

Our supply truck came yesterday, so I'm not entirely certain who's knocking on the back door, but I hope it's not Grady.

Surely not.

He knows the reporter is coming to see me today after she leaves Shipwreck, and if we're going to keep up a pretense of being at war, he needs to not be here.

Although, Bailey is definitely still at war with him, even if I think Mama still secretly likes him.

And I have this feeling his family wouldn't take too kindly to seeing me either.

Especially Tillie Jean, and not just because someone started a Facebook page dedicated to keeping score in who's winning, and is now taunting her mercilessly about the banana pudding thing.

I shake my head, because I'm being dumb worrying about who's at the back door.

It's probably Roger. He's been stopping by and offering to visit with Mama just about every day.

"Oh em gee, are you serious?" Bailey squeals as the doorbells jingle on the front door.

My stomach drops so hard, I swear it lands on my big toe.

Not because Bailey's squealing, but because the woman walking through the front door is dressed in black slacks, a maroon blouse, and flats with a leather messenger bag tossed over her shoulder, and she smells like a reporter.

Not that I know exactly what reporters smell like, nor can I actually smell her over the scent of donuts and cupcakes permeating the walls, but she looks like she smells like a reporter.

And she has a photographer with her.

Not the same photographer as the morning of the Cooper incident, thankfully, but he's still carrying a massive camera with a lens that could probably be used to fend off a bear in an attack.

Photographers must have very strong neck muscles to be able to carry those huge cameras with the straps around the neck all day.

And I don't even want to think about the judgments they're making about our little bakery.

It's cozy, with the same ten chipped Formica tables that were here when I was a little girl, because the former owner's kids didn't want anything from inside the bakery when they finally sold it, and keeping the old tables and the glass display cases and the decorations meant there were so many fewer things for us to buy immediately.

Bailey and I repainted the dining room walls a buttery yellow between Mama's doctor appointments not long after I got back, and we washed the windows, but they need washing again. Our coffee machines are used—clean, but clearly loved—and one of the overhead lights is buzzing.

Which means the biggest thing I have going for me right now is my smile.

The Army trained me to make mediocre coffee, do paperwork, fire an M-4 rifle, and complete my physical fitness tests with time to spare.

They did *not* train me to smile to get my way.

Still, I dial it up as far as it will go. "Hi. Welcome to Duh-Nuts."

The woman glances around at our donut pictures hanging on the walls, then back to me. "Annika?"

"Yes. You must be Bridget. Nice to meet you. Coffee?"

"Oh em gee, *Annika!*" Bailey barrels out of the kitchen and smothers me in a shoulder-hug from behind. "Thank you thank you *thank you*. Tell me you have bubble waffle makers coming too, and I swear, I will love you *forever*."

"I—"

She pulls back and moves to the back counter and starts rearranging the cake plates and coffee cups. "Here," she says to someone in the doorway. "You can put it here."

A guy in blue work pants, a gray polo with a delivery company logo, and work boots joins us from the kitchen, pulling a dolly loaded with a brown box wrapped in white shipping bands. It's about the size of a dorm fridge, and I'm more than a little confused.

And possibly on my way to a panic attack, because *this is not on the schedule for today*.

In fact, it's not on my schedule for *any* day.

There's a reporter standing in my bakery.

With a photographer capturing all of this.

And I have *zero* idea what's going on.

"What—" I start.

Bailey's gaze catches mine, and the excitement making her brown eyes dance fades. "You…didn't order a soft serve machine?"

I make a noise that might be *of course I did* or it might be *what the hell are you talking about*, and it makes the delivery guy stop and squint at me. "You Annika Williams?"

"Yes."

"And this is Duh-Nuts? Like the lady in back said?"

"Yes. Yes, of course."

"Then is this young lady right about where you want your countertop ice cream maker?"

Oh.

My.

God.

No he didn't.

And by *he*, I do *not* mean the delivery guy.

"Did my mama sign for that already?" I ask quietly.

"Yes, ma'am. Right here."

I look down at the delivery invoice, and yep, there's Mama's scrawled signature crossing four lines of text near the bottom of the delivery order.

"She can't see," I babble while I scan the rest of the document.

"Yes, ma'am," he replies.

And there it is.

Grady Rock.

I'm going to kill him.

Or possibly hug him.

Or most likely do both.

I can't keep this. Not the soft serve machine, and not the shipping paperwork with Grady's name on it, because if Bailey sees it, she'll blow a stack, and we need to save the stack-blowing until *after* the reporters have left.

"Cost half as much as the machine cost to ship it back," the delivery guy muses.

As if he's been *coached* on what to say.

"*Bubble waffles!*" Bailey shrieks again.

The reporter is taking notes.

The photographer is snapping away.

And Mama slowly makes her way to the doorway too, white cane catching on the corners of the worktables and the doorway. "Bailey," I say, and I jerk my head to her.

Bailey leaps to help her "Mama! We'll do *bubble waffles!*"

"Oh, I'll bet they don't do bubble waffles in Shipwreck."

"*Squee!*" Bailey says.

Seriously.

She's so excited she *honestly* says *squee*.

"Bubble waffles?" the reporter asks.

"Bailey—" I start, because she doesn't know this is the reporter she's talking to, but she rolls right over me, leading Mama out to one of the tables as she goes.

"Oh my gosh, you've never heard of bubble waffles? Mama, step left, you don't want to run into the counter. There. Bubble waffles are like waffle cones but ten million times better. They're from Hong Kong but they're *exploding* all over the world, and we're the *very first* bakery in this area to offer them."

So maybe she *does* know this is the reporter.

"And you are?" Bridget asks.

"Bailey," I say quickly. "My baby sister. Bailey, this is Bridget, from *Virginia Blue Magazine*. And Bridget, this is my mama, Maria. She owns Duh-Nuts."

"Co-owns," Mama says, her hand outstretched and floundering like she wants to shake. Bridget quickly closes the distance between them and takes Mama's hand in hers, the photographer with the massive neck but still no name continuing to snap away. "My daughter, Annika, left the Army to come home and run the bakery with me when I went blind right before we were scheduled to open."

"Annika's making all our dreams come true," Bailey pipes up.

"You...went blind?" Bridget asks.

The delivery guy rips a knife through the shipping band, and *oh my god*, unlimited soft serve ice cream.

Delivered unplanned *in the middle of the interview.*

Is it possible to kill a man with a hug?

Because I might want to take that option so I can get both in.

Mama's telling Bridget the short version of the story—her vision started going fuzzy and getting floaters, and she thought she'd scratched her corneas, and by the time she finally asked a neighbor to take her to the hospital, a rare artery condition had rendered her completely blind in both eyes.

But I came home, much to the horror of those unforgiving people in Shipwreck who previously had the market cornered on baked goods in this county, and now we're all doing the best we can, working sunup to sundown to make a living for our little family so Bailey can one day inherit Duh-Nuts herself.

This is bad.

This is *so* bad.

Because Grady is going to look like a first-class asshole.

He's going to look like the festering, infected asshole that develops on the asshole of an asshole creature.

And I just stand there.

While a guy installs—not just delivers, but also *installs*—a soft serve ice cream machine on my counter, and my mama and sister tell the reporter all about how Grady used to be my best friend, but he's *changed*.

And now he's out for blood.

Oh, god.

Bad doesn't cover it.

This is a horror flick.

Not even the people of Shipwreck will support him after this.

"I got him though," I announce. "I racked him in the nuts in our annual softball game."

Every head in the shop swivels toward me.

The delivery guy, who's fiddling with a screwdriver behind the machine, eyes me and takes a healthy step back.

And the four locals who are all watching the reporting go down give me the thumbs-up.

"Mama and Bailey are being nice about it," I continue, the words flowing out of my mouth before my brain has a chance to jump in and do its job, "but I'm glad we're fighting with Shipwreck. Their town is so high and mighty, acting like being a pirate town in the mountains is special, when they're just jealous that they can't move on past pirates, and that ship sailed at least ten years ago on the internet. Seriously, how many pirate memes do you see nowadays? None. But when corn went out of style, we rebranded to unicorns. Unicorn pirates aren't a thing. And also, we have the better town name."

"Sarcasm *is* a really good name," Bailey says.

Mama shushes her.

"You have a unicorn festival here?" Bridget says. "Unicorns don't seem so...sarcastic."

"That's the beauty," I babble. "It's like it's so sarcastic we go all the way to rainbows and glitter. It's meta sarcasm."

I have no idea what I'm saying, and I probably need to shut up, but this is *not* going to be a two-sided story.

Because there's literally *nothing* Grady can say that will compete with *This mean man from a pirate town called a blind lady and her teenage daughter names and tried to run them out of business.*

Which means I need to be a stark raving mad bitch if this story is going to have any balance to it.

"Meta sarcasm," Bridget repeats slowly.

"I knew Grady had a huge crush on me in high school," I add. "I led him on because he was really smart in chemistry, and I knew he'd help me if he thought he had a chance, and I really needed grades high enough to get into the Army. So I could shoot things. So it's kinda fitting that we're rivals now. We always were. He just didn't know it. Mama, are you tired? You look tired."

The door opens, the chimes ring, and Roger steps in the front door.

All of us stare at him.

Except Mama, obviously.

He looks at her, then the reporter, then Bailey, who's giving me the *are you smoking burnt cookie dough?* look, and then at the delivery guy, who appears to be wishing he'd worn a cup to work this morning, and finally, Roger's gaze lands on me.

All while the photographer keeps snapping away.

"Roger! We hate Shipwreck. Don't we?" I say.

"Roger?" Mama perks up. "Roger's here?"

"Ah, hi, Maria. Shitter running okay?"

Yep.

He just said that.

In front of the reporter.

I am officially over this entire day.

24

Grady

Usually, showing off Shipwreck is one of my favorite things.

Talking about my great-to-the-nth-degree grandfather Thorny Rock who founded the town and supposedly buried all his Spanish doubloons somewhere between the gazebo in the park at one end of town and Thorny Rock Mountain just west of town proper. The pirate festival. The people who come with metal detectors and sonar equipment to try to find Thorny Rock's treasure. Growing the town and adding a water park and miniature golf and the retreat center and outdoor adventure businesses.

The destination pirate weddings.

The hiking and rafting in the mountains just up the road.

Our part-time neighbors up on the mountainside who bring their own kind of excitement.

My family's place in the history of keeping Shipwreck fun and fresh, with my aunt and uncle helping get Davy Jones's Locker running, and the Deep Blue Retreat Center built.

My bakery.

But after an early morning tour for Bridget the Reporter and her trusty sidekick, Clicky Mick, and walking that line of being honest but not quite in answer to her questions about how the rivalry between our bakeries started, I'm ready to call it quits for the day before the morning's half over.

I don't, though, because the whole damn town has shown up at Crow's Nest at one point or another today to talk about having a reporter in town to finally show the world what assholes all those people in Sarcasm are.

It's gossip central, even when people have to wait thirty minutes for us to whip up fresh cookies and cupcakes long after we've sold out of donuts, muffins, and scones.

Georgia's rocking the kitchen like a beast, the cash register is overheating, and I'm refilling coffees and getting fresh tea, agreeing whole-heartedly that there's no way anyone in Sarcasm could fry up crème brûlée macaron donuts like the beauties I served this morning.

Yeah.

Those were perfection.

And a pain in the ass, but well worth the trouble.

And nobody blinked at paying double price for them.

We're so far in the black today I just recouped all my savings from sending Annika that soft serve machine.

This rivalry is solid gold for business.

Clicky Mick spent thirty minutes shooting the macaron

donuts from every angle before they packed up and headed to Sarcasm to get Annika's side of the story.

And I'm a fucking hero today.

Here, anyway.

Pop is holding court at the corner booth with Long Beak Silver, who squawks, "*Walk the plank, asshole,*" anytime anyone says *Sarcasm*. I tell the parrot to swab the deck, and he tells me to eat shit and die.

Our relationship is solid like that.

Pop's also entertaining some women I don't recognize but who are all roughly my age and keep accidentally spilling their sweet tea or need me to talk dirty to them.

I mean explain my favorite donut fillings and cupcake flavors.

Same thing.

And I don't enjoy it.

Not like I enjoyed talking dirty to the knots in Annika's neck last week.

Talking to her on the phone at odd hours when we're both alone hasn't been the same.

I miss her.

Some of the out-of-towners in for conferences or just to get away to the mountains for the week report they've been to Sarcasm, and their bakery is just as busy. One or two whisper reverently about the dragon donuts, and I have to remind myself not to smile.

I call it a day when I've sold out of everything and Georgia declares herself over-poached just after three.

My phone's been burning a hole in my pocket, buzzing off and on all afternoon, but I haven't had two seconds free to check it.

I pull it out as I start the short walk home, but before I

can register much more than that Annika has sent me approximately four thousand messages, Tillie Jean appears at my side.

I shove my phone back in my pocket before she can glimpse the screen. "Hey, sis."

"You're a genius, you know that?"

"Some days," I agree modestly. "Like every day that ends in a Y."

She snorts and chucks me in the shoulder. She's in her standard uniform of black pants and a white blouse with *Crusty Nut* embroidered on the breast pocket, and her hair's different.

Maybe she cut it or something.

"You're hilarious. Do you think Sarcasm put on as good of a show today?"

I hope so. "Not a chance. Even if they did, it'll all get lost in translation."

"She asked me all about Annika in high school."

"Yep."

"I'm really pissed at her. And I'm pissed that I'm pissed, and then pissed that I have reason to be pissed."

"Eat a duh-nut. It helps."

She freezes.

Oh, *fuck*.

I just said that.

"Damn Sarcasm assholes are fucking with my words," I say a beat too late.

And I keep walking.

Head down.

I'm a block from home.

I just want to get home and check my messages.

Tillie Jean's shoes slap the pavement as she rushes to

catch up to me. I keep my stride loose like I didn't just tell her to have a duh-nut.

"Grady," she says in that *I'm going to kill you* tone, which shouldn't be terrifying, because she's six inches shorter than me, at least forty pounds lighter, and I know she can't kill me, except she knows I'm afraid of hamsters and that I'm ticklish on my neck and where I keep my spare house key.

Note to self: move the spare house key.

"Is there something you need to tell me?" she demands.

"I stole your signed Lawson Perry baseball bat when we were teenagers."

She gasps.

I stop. "No, wait…sorry. That was Cooper. He was balancing it on his chin while paddle boarding on the lake. Somehow it got mixed up in his gear bag. He thought he was balancing the bat with a crack in it, so it didn't matter that it fell in the lake. We lied when you asked if we knew where it was. Probably still there, if you want to go diving."

"He—stop trying to distract me. What the *hell* are you up to? Tell me you're not talking to Annika. *Tell me you're not talking to Annika.*"

I turn up my walkway and see Sue standing in the front window of my white-sided ranch, hooves on the windowsill, nose pressed to the glass.

Probably wagging his tail too.

"Aw, fuck, I forgot to let my goat out."

"*Grady.*"

"Last time I did that, he left the fridge opened all day long after he helped himself to a can of beer, and I had to replace all my food and my couch because he pissed all over it while he was sleeping off being drunk."

Tillie Jean hits that spot on my neck, and I yelp and leap away.

She's a deadly opponent in tickle wars, and I'm too old for this shit.

"Don't you have a shift to work?" I ask.

"You think anybody's going to care when I show up and tell them you've been talking to Annika Williams?"

I keep a close watch on her while I shove my key in the lock and push into my house. "Even if I was—and I'm not saying I am, I'm saying *if*—what's it to you?"

"She stole my banana pudding recipe."

"Cooper said they put almond extract in it. That's not your recipe."

Sue charges me, and after a quick pat on his head, I step aside to let him ram into Tillie Jean, who's so worked up that her nostrils are widening and I wouldn't be surprised if she shot flaming boogers at me.

And while she wrangles with the goat, who's shoving his snout into her crotch, I catch movement out of the corner of my eye.

It's a flash of color diving into the little nook off the living room that leads to my bedroom.

Huh.

And there's a red Ford parked in the alley behind my house.

At least, I assume it's a Ford. All I can see is the angle of the roof, but the angle looks like a Ford.

Interesting.

The man downstairs is already peeking his head up, because now I can smell her too.

Coconut.

Like the sunscreen she used to slather herself with when we'd go to the lake. *Just because I'm naturally bronze doesn't mean I can't get sunburned*, she'd say.

"Get *off*, you mangy goat," Tillie Jean says.

"He likes you. He wants you to take him for a walk."

"Quit distracting me. *Grady*. She broke your heart, she tried to break your testicles, and she's giving you a big middle finger wrapped in a donut. She's probably the one running that Facebook page keeping score in the bakery wars. *Move on*."

"Is that a cake donut or a yeast donut?"

"*Ugh*. I can't help you if you don't let me."

I suppress a smile. "And what's you helping me gonna look like? Me on a leash going out with Pop's mailman's cousin's sister-in-law's best friend's grandma's next-door neighbor? Because you know he's moving on to you next. I'm doing you a favor in playing the heartbroken fool. Quit nagging me, and I'll milk it for at least another two months. Maybe three. Who knows? Maybe you'll find your own true love in the process so Pop turns his talents on Cooper."

She snorts and heads to the kitchen. "I'm so mad at you right now."

"And yet you're still here."

"I need cookie dough."

"I don't have any—oh. Huh. Look at that. Right on top in the freezer."

She slams the bottom freezer drawer shut and rips into the zipper top bag of chocolate chip cookie dough balls.

"There something you need to talk about, TJ?" I ask.

"Because now I'm thinking you're acting like *you're* having troubles in love."

She snorts around a mouthful of frozen dough, and saliva dribbles down her chin.

"Tillie Jean. You keep secrets too?"

"Oo aab oat oo owa oor."

She points, and *shit*.

Yep, I've got goat poop on my kitchen floor.

Better than on the carpet in the living room.

"What's his name?" I ask.

I get the eyeball of *I'm going to shave your testicles and rub them down with Icy Hot* and then she stomps back to the front door. "I 'afta go to work."

"Hey! That's my dough," I call after her.

"You can have it back when you tell me you're not talking to Annika Williams."

"I'm not talking to Annika Williams." Right now. This exact minute. Not directly.

If she's hiding in my bedroom and listening in, that's not actually my fault.

Tillie Jean's eyes narrow.

I hold out a hand and twitch my fingers, a silent order for her to give me the bag of dough.

She rolls her eyes and marches it out the front door after distracting Sue by tossing his favorite stuffed teddy bear across the room, sending him galloping after it.

And I suppress a grin while I watch her stalk down the street back toward downtown.

She's so easy to play.

But I don't like the idea that she's having issues with a guy. I need to look into this.

I whistle softly while I lock the front door, then send Sue out back to have some outside time.

I *didn't* leave him in the house today.

Which means my damn goat helped *someone* break into my house.

With my sister and the goat taken care of, I turn the corner into my bedroom.

Empty.

Just the rumpled blue sheets on my king-size bed and the dust bunnies peeking out from under the massive oak furniture my parents insisted I take when they downsized a few years ago.

That red Ford Focus is still in the alley behind my house. Window's closed.

So I turn into the bathroom.

Seems empty too, but there it is.

Coconut.

And I don't think it's drifting in on the breeze from the open bathroom window.

I tug on the Jolly Roger shower curtain, and Annika screams and yanks on the faucet, holding out the shower head on a hose like a gun, and I take a blast of cold water straight to the face.

Instinct sends me ducking for cover. "*Aah!*"

"Oh my god!" she shrieks. The water sprays in an arc, splattering across my mirror.

I dodge the spray. "Turn it off!"

She doesn't. Oh, no. She waves that shower nozzle all over. "I thought you were Tillie Jean!"

"She left! You heard her leave!"

"You still scared me!"

"This is *my house*! And you were going to shoot *my sister*!"

"She hates me!"

"*It's my house!*"

"Your goat let me in!"

"*Turn it off!*"

She wrenches the water off and points a finger at my chest.

"*And you damn well better fucking appreciate everything I did for you today, you—you—you—ICE CREAM MACHINE SENDER.*"

Oh.

So *that's* what this is about.

I slip on the wet tile, grab the towel bar for support, and it gives an ominous creak and pops off the wall.

But even though my heart is still operating in *there's a saber-toothed tiger chasing us* mode and my brain is demanding to know how the *fuck* Sue let her in my house, I huff out a chuckle and I grin.

Oh, yeah.

She's mad.

Because I did something nice for her.

Took most of my savings, but it was worth it. Especially knowing how far ahead it'll put Duh-Nuts in our bakery war.

After how well Crow's Nest did today, I'd feel guilty if I *hadn't* sent her that ice cream maker.

Our fight is seriously solid for business.

I get my footing back and pull off my soaking wet shirt. "Huh. Got there early."

"You shouldn't have sent it at—what are you doing?

Are you—*What are you doing?* Put your shirt back on. *Put it back on!*"

"It's wet."

She fans her face, and huh.

Annika's cheeks are adorable when they flame up.

She broke into my house.

And I'm completely good with this.

I nod to her tight gray Rolling Stones shirt, which is also soaked, and therefore happily showing me the outline of a bra that can't quite contain her chilled nipples.

Lace.

That has to be lace.

And I want to know what color it is.

"Yours is wet too," I point out. "You take it off, I'll get you a dry one."

She's panting. We both are. Shower wars are no joke.

"I'm fine," she says.

Her eyes are telling a different story though.

They're wide.

Sweeping over my chest.

While she gnaws on her bottom lip and clenches her fingers tighter around the shower head and the handle.

I lean against the sink and spread my shoulders while I grip the porcelain behind me.

Let her have a good look at my bare chest. "You sure? All my T-shirts smell like me."

Her gaze snaps back to my face. "I wasn't thinking about how you smell."

The lie makes blood surge to my cock. "No?"

Her tongue darts out and makes a quick swipe over her ripe lips. "*Dammit*, Grady. You made me start lying, and now I can't stop."

"If it helps, I was wondering what color bra you're wearing."

She flicks her wrist, and I get another spray of ice-cold water in the chest.

But her eyes—those eyes are dancing.

Intrigued.

Angry.

And still drinking me in while I shove off the sink and close the small gap between us to wrench the shower head out of her hand and step into the tub with her.

Backing her against the tile wall, my chilled skin soaking up the heat radiating off her body.

"You need to stop doing that," I murmur.

Her hands skim my chest and come to rest over my thundering heart while I anchor my hands on either side of her. I haven't seen her in over a week, and that's too long.

Entirely too long.

"I'm *very* angry with you," she breathes, her focus shifting to my mouth again.

"Why?"

"You want a list?"

"Yes." The longer, the better. She won't leave while she's ticking off my sins.

Her lashes lift, and those big brown eyes study me like she knows it.

But she doesn't call me on playing games.

Not Annika.

No, she tilts her hips against my thigh and strokes her palms down my chest. "I can't afford an ice cream machine."

"You didn't buy one. Next problem."

"Grady."

"Did Bailey like it?"

"Did—*what?*"

"She's making bubble waffle plans, isn't she?"

"You hacked her Pinterest account!"

"Annika. I'm a master baker. Not a master hacker." I angle my jaw closer to her, and whisper, "Plus, she mentioned it that first day I saw you in Duh-Nuts, and her Pinterest boards are public."

"You—"

"What else?"

She doesn't push me away when my cheek brushes hers.

Her fingers dig into my skin though, and her breath goes shallow. "You made me lie to defend your honor."

"You had to *lie* to defend my honor?"

"I had to lie to make *me* look bad since *you're* the idiot who started a war with a blind woman and a teenager! I told them I led you on all through high school and made you let me copy your homework assignments so I could get into the Army. *I told them I was a stark raving mad bitch.* For you."

"Annika—"

"And *then* I came over here to chew you out for it, and your goat was all *I'm so lonely, I just need to go inside for a drink of water, look, here's the spare key, you can leave your note inside the house,* and then you *walked in the front door*, with your *sister*, and I heard her leave, but I was so mad at you that I decided no matter what, I was going to hose you down, and then *I lied about that too* because I didn't want—I couldn't—I can't—*ugh*. I am *SO PISSED at you!*"

She yanks me behind the neck and presses her lips to mine, and she's not just kissing me.

She's devouring me. Stroking my back. Wrapping a leg around my hips and grinding against my hard-on while she thrusts her tongue into my mouth and owns me.

Just *owns* me.

If this is Annika being pissed at me, then she can be pissed at me every minute for the rest of my life.

25

Annika

The words are *thank you*.

But I can't find them.

Because Grady Rock makes my brain short-circuit.

I spent four years of high school re-wiring myself over and over so I could resist his dimples and his confidence and his easy acceptance of me for who I was, not where I came from or where I wanted to go or the schedule I'd made to get me there.

But I can't do it anymore.

I can't resist him.

And I don't want to.

He's not perfect. God knows, neither am I. But when he walked into the shower and casually pulled that curtain back, like he *knew* I was here, and it was okay, and he was happy to see me, no matter what happened in the rest of the world today, I fell.

I quit trying to overanalyze, and I just *fell*, and it scared the shit out of me.

Because what if we don't work?

What if all this is just a leftover high school crush?

That bulge against my belly doesn't feel left over.

The press of his body anchoring me to the chilly tile wall doesn't feel left over.

The hot swipe of his tongue against mine doesn't feel left over either.

I can't stop touching him. The sleek angles of his back. The thick roughness of his hair. The chill of his wet skin. The hard plane of his thigh beneath my pussy.

He pulls out of the kiss with a low groan. "Can we do this without one of us being pissed?" he whispers against my lips.

"I'm not pissed," I lie.

Maybe?

Or is it the truth?

His blue-green eyes bore into me, and I let him, because maybe he can find the truth.

One dimple pops out, and I swear it makes my knees wobble.

Maybe I'm pissed. I don't know.

But I'm definitely horny.

"You're still pissed," he tells me, his lips brushing over mine while his hands stroke up from my hips to my ribs. "Tell me what to do to make you not pissed."

"More." My eyes slide closed, and I tilt my mouth to his, invite him in, and this time, there's no attacking.

Just soft, gentle caresses. His lips on mine. My lips on his.

Tasting.

Teasing.

Igniting my nerve endings and sending a desperate, aching pulse to throb between my legs while he suckles on my lower lip, his stubble a sharp contrast to the silk of his mouth.

"More," I whimper into his kiss.

He makes a low rumble of agreement while his thumbs brush my nipples, *oh yes more there*.

I arch into his hands, and he continues the slow rub around my hard tip, and I press my clit against his thigh, because I'm aching and needy and desperate *everywhere* and I don't care if our first time is in a shower or on a bed or under the stars, I just want him to touch me.

To keep kissing me.

To never let go.

His thick length is pressing into my stomach, and I want to stroke him and lick him and ride him and I want all the weirdness between us to go away and for there to be nothing left except two best friends who can't get enough of each other.

His tongue touches mine and *this* is everything I've ever wanted from Grady.

Ever.

Always.

I trail my hands through his hair, down his neck, over those solid shoulders, memorizing every inch, the texture of smooth skin over hard muscle, the flex in his biceps, the hard plane of his chest, the rough hair over his pecs.

I didn't come here to seduce him.

I came here to warn him. To tell him I didn't mean what I said to the reporter in the name of keeping our friendship a secret for the sake of our bakeries.

But I like this plan better.

Especially when he rocks his hips and lowers his hand to slip under the waist of my leggings, fingers drifting between my legs. I kiss him harder while I open wider to give him full access, and when he thumbs my clit, that simple touch is enough to send a wave of white-hot need spiraling out of control in my core, the hot pressure building me toward a man-made release that I haven't had in months.

Or longer.

He deepens the kiss and slides a finger between my folds, groaning into this kiss like he's found the buried treasure he's been searching for his whole life.

I grip him tight, one hand tangled in his thick hair, the other wrapped around his neck while the sensations swell and deepen and *oh my god*, Grady's finger pushing inside me has to be the single best sensation in the universe, but I still want more.

Closer.

I need to be *closer*.

I need him deeper.

I pump my hips into his hand, and he matches my rhythm, thumb to clit, fingers thrusting into me, and I'm close.

So close.

Almost—

"*Rawk!* Ride her like a pony! Ride her like a pony!"

I jerk back and bang my head against the shower wall. Pain erupts and my eyes water while Grady twists out of the kiss, yanks his hand out of my pants, and curses. "*Dammit*, Long Beak Silver, *go walk the fucking plank.*"

The pain at the back of my skull isn't strong enough for

me to be hallucinating, and if I were hallucinating, I wouldn't be sitting here with an ache in my lady bits demanding a grand finale to that intense music he was playing in my pussy, which means that really is a parrot on the shower curtain rod.

And is it…? It *is*.

It's walking crooked like it's drunk.

"I'll see you in hell, fuckwad!" the parrot says before it topples sideways off the curtain rod and dives at us.

I shriek and bang my head against the shower wall again as the bird rights itself with an easy spread of its wings and turns to glide right back out the open bathroom window.

"*Ohmygod*," I gasp.

"Grady? You in there, boy?" an older man calls from somewhere inside the house.

"I'm jacking off, Pop," Grady calls. "Go away."

I slap a hand over my mouth to keep from squealing. The idea of Grady masterbaking—*masturbating*—is enough to take my panties four shades wetter, which I didn't think was possible.

"To porn? Is it good porn?"

Grady squeezes his eyes shut. "Filthy, horrible porn."

"You think your grandmother would like it?"

"Fuck," he mutters, dropping his head to my shoulder while I decide if I want to laugh or cry. Or possibly follow the parrot out the window. He lifts his head and looks at the closed door, which is wobbling. "Yes, Pop. Nana would love it. There are mimes. I know mimes turn her on."

"Got that reporter lady with me," Pop Rock says.

"Maybe you shut the porn off and come show her your yearbook?"

"Oh my god," I whisper-shriek. I avoid banging my head on the wall one more time while I wriggle out of Grady's grasp. "She can't catch me here."

The door bursts open, and Sue comes barreling in.

Grady leaps out of the bathtub, slides on the wet floor, and yanks the shower curtain shut. "Stay," he hisses to me.

"I'm not jacking off," he calls while he rushes out of the bathroom, soaking wet, without a shirt.

He slams the door behind him, leaving me alone.

With the goat.

And an open window.

An open window that's not very large, because it's a *bathroom* window, but it's still a window.

I use the shower curtain to shield me from the door, just in case Pop decides to come in, and yes, he's Pop to me too, because he's Pop to *everyone*, though most people from Sarcasm call him *that Shithead Pop*.

"No, Pop, I just wanted half an hour to read a book," Grady says somewhere beyond the bathroom.

"What book?" Pop demands.

"*The Wicked Wallflower*," Grady answers.

"You read romance novels? And why are you all wet?"

Shit. That really is Bridget the reporter.

And where did Grady pull that book title out of? Does he *really* read romance novels?

I'll have to text him later and ask.

And then threaten to send Bailey over to soft serve ice cream his front yard if he lies to me.

Oh my god.

Who am I?

I don't do things like that.

And more importantly, I need to leave.

Now.

The window's big enough. I can fit.

If my heart quits pounding so hard. It's making my chest swell.

The bigger question, though, will be if I can get away.

Because the bird's sitting on my car.

Watching me.

"Intruder! Intruder! Intruder!" he squawks.

"Sue, go eat the parrot," I whisper.

Sue leaps up on the toilet seat and crows out an offended *Maaa!*

But it's enough.

The parrot takes off.

And so do I.

26

Annika

Bailey gives me the side eye when I get home two hours later.

My clothes are dry, my sorely disappointed lady bits have come to terms with their fate today and are holding out hope for a round two sometime in the not-so-distant future, and I'm carrying a box holding six bubble waffle makers that I had to go practically all the way to Copper Valley to find.

Apparently I guilt-shop.

And ever since I crawled out of Grady's bathroom window and took off out of Shipwreck, I've felt guilty.

Guilti*er*, that is.

For lying. For leaving Bailey in charge of Mama and the bakery while I went to dry-hump my former best friend. For those seven seconds when I hit the edge of Shipwreck and considered turning left on the state

DIRTY TALKING RIVAL

highway to run away and stick my head in the sand instead of turning right to come back to Sarcasm.

I *did* turn left, but I had to if I was going to find a store that sold bubble waffle makers.

And I came back.

That's the important part.

I came back.

"Do you know what tonight is?" she asks.

"Netflix binge night?"

She crosses her arms and glares.

"Bad karaoke in the living room?" I guess.

"*The softball game*, Annika. The softball game is in thirty minutes against Snyderville, and they need you to play, and Roger asked if he could take Mama. *On a date*. To the softball game. Where *Bridget* is going to be watching. And you *almost missed it*."

I'm missing something else too, because she shouldn't be so upset about a softball game.

Should she?

Wait.

"You...don't want Roger taking Mama to the softball game."

"She's in no condition to date."

"Bailey. She's blind. She's not *broken*. Wait. Where *is* she?"

"*With Roger*," she shrieks. "Annika, if she has sex with him, she'll get pregnant again, because she's forty-five, not past menopause, and she can't be blind and pregnant and raising a baby, and then you and I are going to be the old married couple who aren't married because *incest*, plus I'm *thirteen* and can't legally get married, but we'll still be that couple who put their entire lives on hold to raise *one more baby* that she could've prevented if she didn't get asked on dates by old plumbers who just want to get in her pants!"

I sincerely hope this is teenage hormones and not some insight she has to what Mama and Roger's relationship might've been before Mama lost her sight.

But in any case, I'm almost positive I know how to handle it.

"I got bubble waffle makers." I tilt the box so she can look in, but it doesn't help.

Her eyes fill with tears, and she collapses into a kitchen chair as if she's just found out her long-lost first love who went missing during a war has come back, but decided that he'd rather date Grady's goat because the goat wrote him letters.

I need more sleep.

"Bailey. Hey. It's okay." I sit down next to her and pull her into a hug, then pick out a clump of cookie dough that's stuck in her hair, and then kiss her head. "Roger won't take advantage of Mama. And Mama won't let him. And you need to take tomorrow off and sleep in and go play volleyball with some friends. I'll make some phone calls and get you into the gym at the high school, okay?"

"But you juuuuust got buuuuuubble waaaaaafle makers," she sobs. "I want to make buuuuuuuuble waaaaaaafles. And not be a sister-aunt."

"You're not going to be a sister-aunt."

"You're a sister-aunt."

"I'm going to pretend I'm not confused right now."

"You're just so *old*."

"Or offended."

"It's like we're not really sisters. You're more like my aunt."

Oh. "If I had a baby, you'd be an aunt."

"*YOU ARE NOT ALLOWED TO HAVE BABIES.*"

I rub my ear. Pretty sure hearing will come back in another day or two. "Bailey—"

"*No.* We have too much on our plates for babies. And what if the bakery fails, Annika? What if we can't do it?"

"Then I'll get a new job, and we'll be *just fine*. I do have a few skills that can earn me money."

"But—"

"Bailey. Trust me. We're going to be absolutely fine. Do you want to know how I know?"

"Because you're a know-it-all who's just projecting confidence to make me stop having a hormonal freak-out?"

"Yes."

She sputters a laugh and pokes me in the stomach. "Not funny."

"We're Williamses, Bailey. We survive. It's what we do."

"And kick ass in softball games?" she whispers.

"*Oh my god*. There's a boy on the Snyderville team, isn't there?"

"No," she replies so fast that my whiplash gets whiplash with the cherry of a lie on top.

I rise and scrub my hands over my face. "Who is he?"

She jumps up too, but instead of telling me *no one*, she bursts into tears again and runs out of the kitchen.

So.

I just fucked that up.

I am so fucking awesome.

I drop back down into the chair at the kitchen table and thunk my forehead against the scarred wood.

I almost reach for my phone, but texting Grady won't solve this.

He doesn't know anything more about teenagers than I do.

And honestly?

I don't know that I know anything more about *relationships* than Bailey does.

But there's only one way to learn.

And that's to *do*.

So I give myself thirty more seconds to just breathe, and then I call Roger to check on Mama, and then I go digging for my old softball glove.

I'm going to learn.

Starting with a softball game.

27

Grady

The bus ride to the softball fields is rowdy tonight. Everyone's talking about how Pop and Bridget found me jacking off to mime porn, and celebrating the Fireballs' win last night, and asking if I got myself a better cup this week.

Sue and I give them all shit right back, because that's what you do when you're part of a team. Shipwreck Lager is being passed around, and we're ready to win this week.

Halfway to the high school, Sloane moves down the row of seats until she's next to me and Sue. "Move over, goat," she says.

"*Maa!*" Sue replies.

"Lovely to see you too, but I need to talk to Grady, so we're gonna get comfortable, mm-kay?"

Sue snorts, licks up his own nose, and scoots over to plop his bony butt onto my lap.

"Good goat," Sloane says. She drops into the seat next to me and gives me the *spill it* look. "What's the real story with you and the Sarcasm chick?"

"We were best friends and now we hate each other's guts." And as soon as I get two minutes of peace, I'm texting her to see if she'll meet me somewhere again tonight, because that four minutes in the shower was *not* enough.

Especially when I know I didn't leave her satisfied.

Also, if I'm going to be covered in something when I'm making out with Annika, I'd prefer it was cookie dough.

I'm about done with just getting wet while she's around.

Now, if we'd been naked in the shower with the *hot* water on...

"Cut the bullshit," she says. "Your pop wouldn't be trying so hard to dig up everything he can find about my family and health history if he wasn't worried you were going to do something like fall for *the enemy* again."

She makes air quotes around "the enemy." She's not from Shipwreck originally—she came for a destination wedding as a guest a year ago and never left—so she clearly doesn't get the pride we take in our rivalry with Sarcasm.

"I think he's more worried we'll start inbreeding," I tell her. "You're fresh blood."

"Do you know what I always hated about Romeo and Juliet?"

"That it's a tragedy that gets billed as a romance, even though there's no happy ever after?"

She squints at me like she wasn't expecting that. "Well,

yes. But also that people couldn't just let love be love until it was too late."

"Are you trying to play matchmaker?"

"I didn't grow up with this kind of gossip. I'm trying to level up."

I hold out a fist. "Nice first try. Stay out of my love life."

She bumps. "Thanks. Also, if you like her, freaking ask her out. Give me some hope that *someone* in this town has the testicles to man up before it's too late."

I grin. "Ah, the newbie's crushing on someone, is she?"

"We're talking about *you*," she reminds me primly.

I glance around the bus, because now I'm curious.

Who does Sloane have her eye on in Shipwreck?

Maybe Tillie Jean knows.

We spend the rest of the short drive trying to trick each other into talking while I answer the occasional call about if I prefer the male or female mime to be dominant in my porn.

When we pull up to the fields, the game before ours is in the sixth inning.

And Annika's up to bat.

She swings so hard she spins in a circle, and even from the parking lot, I can see her muttering to herself.

Uh-oh.

"Yeah," Sloane says with a smirk beside me, "she's just the enemy. Mm-hmm. If you say so."

"How much is Pop paying you to get dirt out of me?"

She laughs and tosses her bag over her shoulder. "Not a thing. I do this for fun. Also, if you like her, quit being a dick and do something about it."

We head toward the field as Annika swings again, and this time, there's a solid *crack!* and the ball goes sailing.

"Cover Grady's nuts!" Pop hollers.

Tillie Jean leaps in front of me like she's sacrificing herself.

"She hit it down the opposite baseline," I mutter.

"It's *Annika*. She's not to be underestimated. It might've hooked at the last minute."

"And flown all the way across the outfield to rack me in the nuts again *here*."

Annika might be right.

I might have the soul of Sarcasm in my blood.

Sloane smirks.

Pop grunts.

And Long Beak Silver tells us all to go fuck ourselves.

That parrot needs some quality time in the brig.

We stretch and toss softballs off to the side while Sarcasm's GOATs kick some ass, and I subtly check out their cheering section. Maria Williams is in the bleachers with the plumber guy again. Bailey's not here—no, wait.

There she is.

By the snack bar.

Talking to a boy.

Oh, fuck, no, she's not.

"Forgot my water," I say to Tillie Jean. "You need anything from the snack bar?"

She scans the area quickly, like she's making sure there's not another bake stand set up this week before she shakes her head. "Nope. Thanks."

Sue trots next to me while we head to the little stand behind home plate.

Bailey side-eyes me as we get closer.

I pretend I don't see her.

The game's nearly over—one more out should do it—and then the Williams ladies will leave, and I'll find my game, and we'll school the Cedarton Sandbugs in the fine art of getting their asses kicked.

And then I'll text Annika and see what she's doing later.

If she wants to pick up where we left off.

"Yeah, my sister is getting the gym open so we can play volleyball at the high school tomorrow," Bailey's telling the boy.

Hereafter called *the asshole who better not lay a finger on her*.

He grunts in response.

It's a wimpy grunt. The kind coming from a kid who's discovered grunting is a thing, but hasn't finished puberty and can't really put the *unt* behind the *gr*.

I don't like him.

"I could text you when we get there?" Bailey says.

No boys. Boys cause pregnancy. I love my mama, and I wouldn't trade her for anything, but I'm not doing what she did.

It was Annika's mantra through high school, and here's Bailey, not even *in* high school yet, flirting.

With a boy.

"Two waters," I say to the woman at the snack bar, who's been staring at me for at least two minutes now.

"Can't. I gotta stay home and blow up my basketballs," the baby asshole says.

If he were talking to anyone other than Bailey, I'd be tempted to take the kid under my wing and teach him how to be interesting. And a gentleman.

But he's talking to Bailey, and my fingers are curling into a fist.

"Seven dollars," the snack bar lady says.

"Seven—*what*? Are you serious?"

"We doubled prices to support the Maria Williams Foundation for the Blind. We've fixed the railing on her house, but we still need to upgrade the bathroom with safety rails."

Shit.

Can't argue with that.

I hand over a ten and tell them to keep the change, because Annika's right—I look like an asshole for having a bakery war with a blind woman and a teenager.

Good thing the rest of Shipwreck is so charming.

But if the end result is more sales for Duh-Nuts, I'll be the biggest asshole Shipwreck has ever seen.

I mean shithead.

Yeah.

I'll be the shittiest Shipwreck shithead to walk the plank since Thorny Rock himself lied about having a buried treasure to convince the four residents of whatever Shipwreck used to be that he could be their new leader.

If that's how it happened.

Considering people have been looking for Thorny Rock's treasure for a couple centuries now, odds are good he didn't have one, or if he did, he didn't bury it here.

Or maybe I'm getting cynical in old age.

"Have you been by Duh-Nuts?" Bailey's asking the guy while I inspect my water bottles. "I work there. It's my family's bakery. You know those galaxy donuts? Those were my idea. And I have the whole day off tomorrow, so it's all sleeping in and hanging out. We can use half the gym for basketball and half for volleyball."

"Is Adriana gonna be there?" the guy asks.

Motherfucker.

I look their way.

Bailey's lips are tipped down, her chin wobbly, but she squares her shoulders and her eyes narrow when she realizes I'm watching. "Maybe," she says.

"She's really pretty."

I start to growl as a cheer goes up from the Sarcasm stands.

Game over.

"So maybe I'll see you there," Bailey finishes softly. "I—I gotta go."

I just stare at the kid.

Don't know how old he is—fourteen, fifteen maybe?—but he doesn't watch her go. He's scanning the crowd.

The Sarcasm crowd.

Like he's looking for the other girl.

My heart cracks in two. I want to hug Bailey and tell her she's not allowed to date until she's eighty-five and also, when she's eighty-five, she deserves better.

And I want to ask that kid what the *fuck* is wrong with him that he can't see what's right in front of him.

It's like being eighteen all over again.

Annika. You know I love you. Let's do this. Be with me.

Except she was right to leave, and this kid is just being a dumbass.

Annika trots off the field. Her gaze goes immediately to Bailey, who stomps off toward the parking lot.

The plumber guy is saying something to Maria.

If he's as smart as I think he is, he's telling her they'll

wait until the rest of the crowd clears out before they leave the bleachers.

Annika's gaze is darting from her mama to her sister.

And I can't just swoop in and fix everything for her.

I'm *the enemy*.

Here, at least.

But behind the scenes, I'm doing everything I can to make sure she and Duh-Nuts succeed.

No matter what.

28

Annika

Somehow, in the last two weeks, my life has turned completely inside out *again*.

Bailey's refusing to talk to any of us and has been crying in her room since we got home from the softball game, but she made me promise I'd have the high school gym open in the morning so she could play volleyball with her friends.

But not Adriana. She doesn't want to invite Adriana.

And I feel awful for missing the signs earlier that she needed a break.

Mama and Roger are sitting on the front porch, where he's describing the rising new moon to her.

And while I'm trying to rearrange my calendar for tomorrow and figure out how the *hell* I'm going to fill Bailey's shoes at the bakery, especially since my last remaining candidate for full-time baker canceled her inter-

PIPPA GRANT

view, I also need to figure out who, exactly, I need to talk to so that Bailey can play volleyball at the high school, and how she's getting there, and how Mama's getting to her eye doctor follow-up, my phone is blowing up with text messages from Grady.

Sorry about Pop and the parrot and my goat this afternoon. And also between our games. And after our games, which you don't know about, but which I need to apologize for anyway. Got a minute?

Hey, I know you're busy, but this is important.

Are you in bed?

Shit, you're in bed, aren't you? Sorry. Just wanted you to know what I overheard tonight—it's about Minnika.

The last one does it.

Minnika.

It's what he used to call Bailey. Mini-Annika.

I pop out the front door and tell Mama I forgot to make sure we have enough cupcake wraps to get us through this weekend—*more lying*, dammit—and when Roger assures me he'll help her inside if she gets tired before I'm back, I head off at a fast clip toward Duh-Nuts.

It's a five-block walk, so not far, but my stomach is in knots and my legs and arms and even my elbows are whining that bed is in the *other* direction.

As soon as I'm well out of earshot, I dial Grady.

"Hey. I didn't wake you, did I?"

That voice.

It's calming and soothing and deep and strong and reliable, and everything I need right now, even though I shouldn't let him be my world.

I have too many other worlds I'm running.

"No, I wasn't sleeping. I was—"

DIRTY TALKING RIVAL

I pause with the words *rearranging my calendar* on my lips, because that's not what I was actually doing.

"I was just trying to not completely and totally lose my shit because I'm tired and worried and overworked and everything I do is a disaster," I whisper.

"Where are you?"

"No. No, don't come. You can't. And I'm fine. I'll *be* fine. I just need—I need—a minute. I need a minute to let myself fall apart, and then I'll be fine."

"Bailey's taking tomorrow off?"

I freeze in front of the mechanic shop at the end of the bakery block. "How did you know that?"

"Overheard her talking at the game."

He's hiding something. He's using that evasive tone he used to use when he didn't want to tell me that he suddenly had a cousin's birthday party he had to go to when I'd finished putting my weekend calendar together and found three free hours between work and softball where we could head over to the preserve and go hiking.

"What?" I demand while I pick up my pace as I get closer to Duh-Nuts. "What did you hear? What's going on? What aren't you telling me?"

"Nothing. It can wait."

"Grady," I growl while I shove my key into the back door.

"She said you got the high school gym open for her to play volleyball. She was looking for friends to join her. That's it."

"Friends to—*you saw her with the boy*. Who is he? Where's he from? What's his name? Did he make a pass at her? Did he stare at her boobs? I'm gonna kill him. Except I don't have time to kill him, because there's not a single fucking spare five minutes in the next four days, and I don't know who to call at the high school to get the gym open like I promised her, and I have to miraculously pull donuts and cinnamon rolls out of my ass in the morning *and* somehow put out an ad for a baker to just materialize, but not anywhere that the reporter from *Virginia Blue Magazine* might see, because Bailey needs a day off and there's no fucking *point* to Mama going to see the eye doctor tomorrow because they'll say the same thing. *We're sorry, Ms. Williams. It's permanent. But can we poke and prod a little in the name of research?* You know what? No. *No.* They can't fucking turn my mother into a science experiment, because she has a *life* to live and just because she can't see doesn't mean she can't fucking *live* it."

"Annie Workman," he says.

"*What?*"

"Annie Workman. She's the high school volleyball coach. I'll shoot her a note. Does Bailey need a ride?"

"*You can't do me favors in public.*"

"Got a cousin on the volleyball team. I'll tell Annie it's for her, and I'll tell my cousin if she breathes a word of this to anyone, that I'll make sure she's pulled over for speeding, which will mean she doesn't get to drive anymore, because her parents are strict like that. Whoops. Sent the text. Already done. Next problem. You. You're exhausted. You need to go to sleep."

"I can't go to sleep. I have to have a montage."

He laughs, and *god*, it helps. "Annika. You can't montage your way to being a master baker overnight."

"*Do not take my dreams from me.*"

"God, I missed you," he says on a sigh, and I feel the

sentiment all the way from my heart to my lady bits to the tips of my toes.

I slide onto Mama's stool at the clean worktable and let my head drop onto the cool surface. "You remember."

"A man doesn't forget being told he can't montage his way into a woman's pants."

I laugh, because I told him that in the good days.

Before graduation.

Back when he was convinced he could have all the women in the world if he figured out a way to pump iron while he was experimenting in his dad's restaurant kitchen. *I'll lift weights while the cookies are baking, and run while the bread is rising, and by next week, I'll be so buff even the teachers will be falling all over me.*

He was so freaking adorable.

And because I'm *me*, I'd gone on a rant about movie montages giving us unrealistic expectations for how long it takes to go from hockey player to figure skater or sheltered daddy's girl to amazing sexy dancer, because we had all of four movies at home and Mama's two favorites were *Dirty Dancing* and *The Cutting Edge*.

And he'd just grinned at me and said, *Yeah? Well, watch me do it.*

Not eight days later, he'd walked into school in a muscle costume, announced he'd montaged himself into a beefcake, and the lunch ladies gave him free cookies that he pretended to like as well as he liked his own baking.

"Annika. Go to bed. Get some sleep. You can't take care of anyone if you're not taking care of *you*."

"Watch me." I stifle a yawn.

This worktable is weirdly comfortable. My face is

starting to stick to it, but I don't need that side of my face. It'll be fine.

"You could sell burnt cotton candy and the people in Sarcasm would buy it. Get sleep. Cancel your mama's appointment. Ask that plumber dude to take Bailey to the high school. And sell the fuck out of your chocolate chip cookie bricks tomorrow."

I smile as my eyes drift shut. Five minutes. Just five minutes of rest, and I'll be fine. I yawn again. "I need to order ice cream ingredients."

"Already on their way for delivery tomorrow. Where are you?"

"You can't order ingredients for me. And Bailey already teased that we're making chocolate chip cookie donuts and doing a chocolate chip cookie blowout for National Chocolate Chip Cookie Day, which I didn't even know was a thing, and the last time I tried to make chocolate chip cookies I set off four smoke alarms and my roommates had an intervention. With charts. *They had an intervention with Annika Cooking Disaster Charts.*"

"You know the reason you can't bake?"

"Because I'm a walking disaster?"

"No, it's because you're so good at everything else. This is balance."

"Couldn't I have balance where I suck at hula-hooping or juggling? I could live with that balance."

"Annika. *Go to bed.*"

"I can't hear you."

"About four years ago, Cooper got us all tickets to the Fireballs game."

"What does that have to do with anything?"

"Hush. Just listen. So, he got us tickets. Home game. Me, Ma, Dad, Pop…"

I don't understand what this story is about, but I listen while he talks about driving to Copper Valley. Finding their seats. Buying hot dogs.

Nothing happening through four innings.

And I don't really care who won.

Odds are good, it wasn't the Fireballs.

But Grady's talking.

And his voice is so nice.

Calm.

Steady.

Hypnotic.

He's putting a warm, pleasant buzz in my whole body.

And the last thing I remember is thinking that I'm drooling on the worktable, and that I really don't care.

29

Grady

I shouldn't take my own truck to Sarcasm—someone might recognize it—but I don't have time to go borrow one of Cooper's old beaters up on the mountain.

Not when I'll already have a hell of a time pulling off what I'm about to attempt to pull off.

When my headlights finally slice through the darkness in the alleyway behind Duh-Nuts, my pulse goes into hyperdrive.

The back door's open.

And the lights are on.

Some asshole is breaking into Annika's bakery.

I kill the engine two shops down and leap out, shutting my truck door as quietly as possible before tiptoeing to the back of the bakery.

If I'm caught here, I'm in trouble, but not nearly as

much trouble as whoever thinks they can break into Duh-Nuts and get away with it.

Gravel crunches under my feet, and I slow my pace to a crawl as I angle through the shadows to peer into the kitchen.

And relief makes me sag against the wall.

Annika's passed out cold at the worktable, her phone propped on the side of her face like it slid off her ear and didn't have the energy to go all the way to the table, lips parted, dark smudges under her eyes.

She was *here* when I told her that awful boring story about nothing happening in the Fireballs game.

I grin to myself while I ease the screen door open and slip into the bakery.

It worked.

I told her a bedtime story, and it worked.

Which means it's time for *me* to get to work.

Doesn't take long to find the recipes Bailey was planning to use tomorrow. I pull out butter and eggs and open the flour bin, though I have to hunt for the baking powder and salt.

Considering they're right there on a shelf over the flour bin and all, they were doing a damn good job of hiding.

The ovens are a newer model of my wall ovens, and I have a minute of oven envy while I flip them on to three-fifty and crank up the proofer.

But the measuring cups and spoons and bowls—these are recycled.

They have history.

They've been places. Seen things.

Made a lot of sweet, sweet cookie dough.

Reminds me of Nana's kitchen.

Used. Loved.

This bakery has good bones. Good heart. I can feel it.

While the butter warms to room temperature, I also flip on the fryer, double-check the donut recipe and find the donut dough in the fridge. Feels like silk, smells like cookies.

Fucking good dough.

I eyeball the recipe, then decide it's none of my business how she's making a yeast donut dough smell like a chocolate chip cookie.

This is the Duh-Nuts domain.

I'm just playing baking fairy tonight.

I roll it out and find the donut pin to cut them, then set them in the proofer to rise. They'll be a few hours older than fresh when the Duh-Nuts doors open, but they'll still be good.

"Sorry, Annika," I murmur when I can't put off starting the industrial mixer any longer.

Cookie dough's gotta get made.

"The marshmallow requisition is on the captain's desk!" she shrieks.

I turn back to her, eyebrows raised, and her glassy brown eyes slowly focus on me. "You're not the—*Grady*?"

"Go back to sleep."

She shakes her head and looks around like she's never seen this kitchen before. "Where—what—how—oh, *shit*. What time is it?"

She leaps up, the stool clatters to the ground, and her phone follows when she tries to grab it.

I flip on the mixer to get the butter and sugar creaming together and bend over to retrieve her phone. "Sit. Better yet, *go home*."

"What are you doing?"

"I'm not here. You're dreaming."

"I am not." She shoves my shoulder, and I snag her hand and help her wrap it around my waist.

"So maybe I'm dreaming," I say with a grin. "Not every day I get full access to a sexy woman's...ovens."

"You—" She pauses, thick, dark lashes fluttering while her arm tightens around me. "You're saving my ass."

"I like your ass. It's worth saving."

"You read romance novels," she blurts suddenly.

"I—yeah. Time to time. Tillie Jean has this singles club she runs, and—"

"Is that like a book club?"

"Yeah. Without the books. Most of the time. Until a new historical romance that she's been dying to read comes out."

She smiles.

I go lightheaded.

Not unusual.

"You're a big ol' softie," she whispers.

"There is *nothing* soft about me."

Her eyes crinkle when she smiles, and yep.

Lightheaded again.

She turns into me so we're toe-to-toe, thigh-to-thigh, hip-to-hip.

Right back where we were in my shower earlier.

Complete with my hard-on aching and ready, because that's all it takes.

Just one look from Annika. One touch. One whisper of her voice.

"I'm glad you're home," I tell her.

"I'm getting there." She loops her free arm around my neck. "You know I don't have time for this."

"For a visit from the master baking fairy?"

"For a relationship."

"This? This isn't a relationship. This is two old friends trying to have sex while one bakes cookies for the other."

"So it's just sex and cookies."

"And donuts." I kiss her forehead, give myself a moment to fantasize about spreading her naked on the worktable and licking her from head to toe until she's panting my name and can't remember any man except me.

She presses her breasts into my chest and tilts her pelvis against mine, and I groan.

"Cookies," I mutter.

"Cookies?"

I jerk my head at the mixer. "I'm going to tear your clothes off you and make you come so hard, the only thing you'll be able to say for a week is *Grady Rock is a sex god*, but not while I'm baking cookies."

She gapes up at me, all bags under her eyes and lips parted with lust, then she blinks and cracks up. "Cookies keep you from performing?"

"It's not *clean*." Yeah. I'm *that* wet rag in the kitchen. "And you need cookies and donuts before I can give you…well, *your* cookies."

"I can't decide if I'm pissed or amused or just plain turned on."

"I'm all three."

I let her go, because I've creamed the butter and sugar enough, and I'm not letting her sell sub-par cookies tomorrow just because I got a boner—again—and wanted to shove her up against the fridge and bang her senseless.

DIRTY TALKING RIVAL

I wash my hands—I don't fuck with hygiene when I'm baking—and I grab the eggs and start cracking them into a bowl. She sidles up beside me, her fingers trailing down my back.

"You're putting my bakery first," she murmurs, leaning her breasts into my arm, and *fucking hell*, it makes my cock leap and strain and beg for five minutes between her legs.

I can make her come in five minutes.

I know I can.

Probably two, if I whisper dirty things to her first.

I was nearly there in three just this afternoon. I know I was.

"That's right, baby," I tell the dough. "You never knew you could be this good, but you're about to get even better."

"I liked you, you know," Annika says.

I crack an egg too hard and it splatters all over the countertop.

She trails her fingers down the inside of my left forearm while I single-handedly crack the rest of the eggs into the bowl. "Does that usually happen your first time in a new…kitchen?"

"Only when I'm unexpectedly…excited."

"Wow. You must be *very* excited."

"Creamed sugar turns me on."

"You turn me on," she whispers. "I don't *want* you to. But you do."

"We're not kids, Annika. We don't have to resist this."

"But we're still not in a place to be parents."

"I'd make a damn good dad. And it's not what I want right now, but that doesn't mean I wouldn't change my whole life around and make the most of every minute."

Her fingers still.

"That's what it's about, right? Not wanting to be a single mom, like your mama was?" I drizzle vanilla into the mixer, watching the creamed sugar and butter and eggs turn into shiny satin ready for some flour, salt, and baking soda. "Or am I missing another objection that's swirling in that lightning-fast brain of yours?"

Her head tilts into my shoulder. "Why were we friends?"

Not the answer I was looking for.

But with Annika, it never was. Which is exactly why she was perfect.

"Because you're smart and I'm funny, and we're both friendly, though you're a little scary with a color-coded planner and a goal, and I sometimes forget I need to let my goat outside. We're peanut butter and chocolate."

"I'm funny too."

"Not on purpose—*oof*." I tip too much flour into the bowl when she pokes me in the gut, but I'm grinning.

Everyone else in high school thought she was stiff and bossy and driven.

But she's right.

She's funny. Smart-funny.

She made me want to be smarter.

She made me want to bake better, because her mama—her mama can *bake*.

People thought I baked because it was the one thing I was better at than Cooper and Tillie Jean, but I couldn't hold a candle to Maria Williams, and I knew it.

And Annika let me bring her baked goods every day of high school, and I swear she knew I was waiting for the day she said I made something better than her mama.

It never came.

But I have a lot more experience under my belt now.

In *everything*.

"I'm a pain in the ass," she says slowly.

"No. You're a woman with a goal. You're driven. You put your family first and you give back more than you take, because you don't want to be a drain on anyone. And you know your limits. That's not being a pain in the ass. Don't ever apologize for being a good person."

"*Oh.*"

I tap the rest of the flour into the mixer and glance at her.

She's staring into the mixing bowl like the dough's just spelled out the answer to life.

"Oh?" I ask.

"*That's* why we were friends."

"Because you put it in your planner?"

Her hand slips into mine, and she squeezes. "Because you saw me."

"At the risk of irreparable harm to my pride and ego again, I should confess that you and those eyes and that hair and that body are *impossible* to miss, and I *saw* you from day one, and I *wanted* you from day one."

"Did I see you?"

"At the risk of insulting your eyesight and taste, *duh*. Yeah. These dimples? Chick magnets. You put up a good fight, but—"

Her hand clamps over my mouth and she turns my jaw until I have to look at her.

"No one knew how talented you were," she tells me.

Heat creeps up my neck.

"Tillie Jean was the smart one *and* the artistic one.

Cooper was the athletic one. And you were *everything*, but not enough to stand out at *anything*."

"So we were friends because you like settling for second best." There's a balance to sweet and bitter, and if I don't perk up, these chocolate chip cookies are going to taste like black licorice soaked in vinegar.

"I was second string on the softball team until senior year. Didn't make top ten in our graduating class. Never promoted to junior management at the grocery store. Part of the crew instead of the cast that one time I tried out for the play. And I didn't graduate top of my class in Basic, or ever get that *number one enlisted* slot on my performance evaluations. But I wasn't *second best*, and neither were you. Because we were both playing a different game."

I kill the power on the mixer, and the background hum slows to a halt while I grab a scraper and attack the sides of the bowl. "You ever want to go back? Try it again? See what we could do differently?"

She shakes her head.

"I do."

"No, you don't."

"I would've written you all those letters I promised."

She inhales sharply.

"And I would've waited for you." Raw honesty isn't easy, but Annika won't let me in if I don't let her in.

"How long?" she whispers.

"However long it took."

Her dark eyes are studying me, and I don't have to ask if she sees me.

I *know*.

She sees me.

She always has.

"I'll still wait, Annika. As long as you want me to."

"You shouldn't put your life on hold. Mine might always be in chaos."

And that's pure Annika.

Expecting she'll just do it alone. That she's not worth the *life* that comes with another person.

Pop keeps asking when I'm going to settle down.

I didn't know it until just now, but there's a reason I haven't yet.

I've never found someone worth giving up sleep for.

Worth coming in second for.

Worth going through *life* with.

The good and the bad.

The up and the down.

The give and take.

Not like I had with Annika in high school.

"You say *chaos*," I tell her. "But the things that take us by surprise are what make life interesting."

"I like a little calm with my storm."

"It'll come." I give the dough one last ride around the mixer paddle, then unhook the bowl and grab the chocolate chips.

She watches while I give the massive batch a few strokes to mix in the chocolate, and I can't decide if she's watching my arms or the dough.

"Want a lick?" I ask.

"You know I can't resist."

Oh, I know.

I know very well.

I grab a spoon and dish out a serving of dough, then swipe it onto my finger and hold it up just out of her reach.

"This?" I ask.

"You're evil."

The longing in her voice makes my cock throb again.

"Is it my finger, or the dough that you want?"

"Both," she whispers.

Fuck.

Didn't expect that.

"Only good girls get to lick."

"That seems backwards."

"If I let you have this, you have to promise to go home and go to bed."

Her hands slide around my waist and dip to squeeze my ass. "Hard pass."

"Or you can go home without a treat first."

"This is already a treat." She squeezes again, my dick asks if we can please lose the clothes yet, and my eyes almost cross, but I know what I need to do.

I need to be the fucking good guy.

I'm not seducing Annika in the middle of her bakery when she's four days short of sleep and under more stress than the bottom layer of a ten-tier wedding cake.

"Don't your cookies need love?" She tilts her head, lids lowered, breath coming fast. "This is inspiration."

"Didn't you just tell me we can't do this?"

"That was before you threatened to deny me cookie dough and your company. And we have unfinished business."

"I'm not making out with you again tonight." Christ, *who am I?* How did that just come out of my mouth?

"But you'll let me suck on your fingers?"

"I—"

"Just one lick, Grady? Please? Let me live the dream

that I can whip up delicious cookie dough that you'd want to lick off me."

"You're playing me for dough, aren't you?"

"Is it working?" she purrs.

"Yes. No. *Fuck*. You need to go to my bed. To your bed. Alone. To sleep with me. To sleep. *Dammit*, Annika."

"You started it. You teased me with cookie dough. You've been a bad, bad boy, Grady Rock. And now you have to pay the price."

I give in with a groan, even though there's some part of me insisting I shouldn't, because if I let her lick my finger, I'm going to kiss her. If I kiss her, I'm going to have to touch her.

And if I touch her, I'm going to give her the orgasm to end all orgasms.

She won't be able to walk without thinking my name.

And I can't see where that's a bad thing.

Plus, orgasms are good for sleeping.

And she needs to sleep.

I'd be doing her a *favor*.

Her lips close around my finger and she sucks, a low moan of appreciation emanating from the back of her throat while she licks the dough off, eyes sliding shut, and I haven't come early since I was nineteen, but I'm about to blow my load right here, right now.

"Annika—"

"You are *such* a master baker," she murmurs.

The sweet hints of chocolate and vanilla and sugar linger in the air between us. Her fingers are still digging into my ass, her belly pressed against my hard-on, and I can't resist.

PIPPA GRANT

I angle my lips to hers, and she melts into me like ice over an open flame.

I was fifteen the first time I wanted to kiss her senseless.

Eighteen the first time I tried.

And I've spent over a decade with fantasies of this woman. Sometimes the fantasies are front and center, sometimes quietly lurking in the background, waiting for the right moment to catch me off guard.

But none of them come anywhere close to reality.

To the taste of cookie dough on her lips. The heat of her breath. The press of her breasts into my chest. The eagerness of her tongue.

That happy, aroused moan as I run my hands over the curve of her hips.

My shirt is suddenly jerked from behind, Annika's lips are wrenched away, and a booming voice yells, "*You!*"

"Oh my god, Roger, put him down," Annika orders.

Huh.

My feet aren't on the floor.

Also—*fuck*, my collar is straining at my neck, and that's before he gives me a shake.

"Think you can sneak in here and steal all our secrets, do you?" Roger growls. "Take advantage of our defenses being down on account of all the worry over Maria? Go back where you came from, you dingy rat."

And there's the toss.

I land on my feet and brace a hand on the worktable while Annika leaps between us. "Roger. *Stop.*"

"You deserve better than some backstabbing, two-bit *master faker* coming in here and sweet talking you out of all your mama's recipes so he can win this blasted bakery war that he never should've started in the first place."

"I can't bake!" Annika explodes. "I can't bake, and Bailey needs a week off, and Mama can knead dough and roll cookies, but she can't stand there at the fryer. It's not safe. And she can't see when cakes and cookies and muffins are done, much less frost them, because *she can't see*. So how the hell else am I supposed to keep her dream alive without help? *How?*"

"Well, whaddya think I came over here for?" he shouts back. "To do all your baking for you!"

She blinks.

I blink.

He glares, then grabs his belly and gives it a jiggle. "You think I got this gut with take-out? No, ma'am. I got this gut the old-fashioned way. I might not claim to be a *master baker*"—he tosses a sneer my way—"but I can damn sure bake some chocolate chip cookies and fry up some donuts. Don't think just because I spend my day with pipes and clogged shitters that that's all there is to a man."

Her lips part.

Mine do too, but I snap them shut, because he's right.

Tillie Jean's not just the manager at Crusty Nut. She's also a painter.

Cooper's not just a baseball player. He's been dabbling in writing a fantasy novel forever.

Pop isn't just a horny old—no, wait.

He really is just a horny old pirate.

Bad example.

But Roger the plumber—he's sweet on Maria, and his stomach does speak for itself.

He glowers. "Now. Get out. The both of you. I gotta fix

the mess this shithead made. And *you*—" He points at Annika. "Go home. Sleep. Right up until five minutes before you want to open this place. I'll have everything ready."

"I'll help," I say.

"Shut up," Annika hisses at me.

He points at me. "You. Leave first. Go. Now."

"I'm not—"

"Grady." Annika turns, and *dammit*.

I can't be one more thorn in her side. She's laying in a whole field of rosebushes right now with as much as she's dealing with.

"Thank you," she says quietly. "We've got it from here."

I don't want to leave. I want to kiss her again.

Hell, I want to take her with me.

Make her sleep for a few days.

Feed her and kiss her and touch her and eat her and plunder and pillage her between naps.

Her mouth quirks in a wry grin, and yeah, sorry, my pirate roots are showing.

Pretty sure she knows it.

"Go," she repeats.

I don't want to, but staying will only cause her more trouble.

So I have to find another way to help.

Damn good thing I have a kitchen too.

30

Annika

WHEN I GET BACK to the bakery too few hours after I left it, all the donuts are fried, glazed, and topped with miniature chocolate chips, and the last of the cookies are coming out of the oven.

"Gotta let the dough firm up in the fridge to make 'em taste best," Roger informs me.

"Thank you."

He doesn't mention Grady.

I don't offer any details.

"Made a bunch of my granny's chocolate chip muffins too. That lady could bake almost as well as your mama. How's she doin' this morning?"

"Still sleeping. Bailey too." I asked a neighbor to sit at the house in case either of them needed anything, but when I got home just after midnight, I turned off both of their alarms, because we're all running on fumes. "I can find someone else to take Bailey to—"

He cuts me off with a snort. "You stay here and sell stuff. I'll get Bailey where she needs to be. You run out of anything, you call me. I got Birch running No Shit today, and I already got three pots of coffee in me."

My eyes sting with heat. "Thank you."

"What friends are for."

Yep, that glare was full of *and that Rock boy ain't your friend*.

"I'm watching YouTube videos and Food Network," I tell him. "Maybe thirty minutes a day. But I'm teaching myself to bake. I can do it. So that we're not such a drain on everyone."

"Friends ain't ever a drain. We give and take. And your mama's always been a good friend, even if she didn't know it. Don't need to be even to be friends, but I owe her this."

I tilt my head.

I don't remember Roger much from my childhood. I knew who he was, but he doesn't stand out as someone Mama saw often.

"Used to drop off cookies at the hospital," he tells me. "When my Chrissy was—well, when she was sick. 'Bout five years ago. Always cheered me up to have someone to talk to and share a cookie with, especially after—well. I asked her to bring some to the funeral too, and she did. Brought enough to feed the whole county. Never forgot how that made me feel."

I'm not a hugger. Not really.

It's not that I don't like hugs.

It's more that I miss the cues for when they're appropriate because I spent so many years denying that I needed them.

But I can't resist hugging Roger.

He pats me on the back and tells me to sell out so his time wasn't all wasted, then promises to head over to get Bailey once he's had a shower and a shave and some real breakfast.

And Grady must have a spy somewhere, because Roger's truck has barely turned the corner before my phone dings with a text.

Master Baker lessons. You. Me. Thorny Rock Mountain. Friday night. 6 PM.

I glance at my calendar, and I realize he must've already checked it, because Friday is the only night I have nothing scheduled after four PM.

What if I don't want to learn to bake? I type back.

It takes a few minutes for his answer to come through, but when it does, it's not text.

It's a picture.

Of cookie dough on his finger.

Hello, mini-gasm.

He follows it with an address, and I send back a thumbs-up, because I don't trust myself with words right now.

I flip on the coffee and read the instruction manual for the ice cream maker before the first few customers straggle in, and I wonder if he got any sleep last night.

If his hours are anything like ours have been, he probably had to be up at three or four.

And if his day is anything like mine, he has a steady stream of regulars this morning, along with unfamiliar faces who have started to hear about the bakery war and want to see for themselves who's worth traveling from Snyderville or one of the other surrounding towns for our baked goods.

I've never felt like such a fake as I do telling everyone that *Duh, of course Duh-Nuts is the best*.

But I do it anyway.

For Mama, who called to say she was taking a morning off since Roger assured her I had everything under control, and not to worry, that he'd stay with her.

I'm tempted to text Roger a polite but firm *do not hit on my mother* note, but Mama's a grown-up.

If she wants to let him hit on her, that's her business.

Liliana pops in during the middle of the morning rush.

"How's the winery?" I ask while I put four cookies in a to-go bag for her.

"I think it's good," she tells me. "Honey's not exactly what I expected."

"Honey—the heiress?"

"Yeah. She's more down-to-earth and willing to listen and learn than I thought she'd be. And I think she reads a lot."

"Like...science books?"

She laughs. "No. Fiction. Romance novels. It's weird, but I'm starting to think she's...well, lonely."

"Are the photographers still hanging around?"

"Some, but not like they were last week. Oh, and nice game last night. I saw the highlights on Instagram. By the way, how's your mama?"

Everyone asks.

Everyone.

How's Maria?

Is your mama doing okay?

If you ladies need anything, you let me know.

My teenager could use a job washing dishes if you're ever hiring. He's cheap, and highly motivated.

Being in the Army is like being in a second family. Military life is different—people come and go, the standards are rigid, and it's often months between visits with your blood family, so having an Army family is necessary.

But I'm realizing Sarcasm is a family of its own too.

And they're very easily pulling me back in as one of their own.

Like I *fit* here.

But part of fitting here means I'm supposed to hate Shipwreck.

And I can't do it. I can't.

"Mama's good," I tell Liliana.

"I heard Grady Rock is serving *beernuts* over in Shipwreck today," one of my regulars says with a sniff. "That's so *alcoholic* of him."

"Mm. Have you heard of bubble waffles? We're adding them to the menu soon."

"I can't wait to see that article about the bakery war. Shipwreck is finally going to show themselves to be the shitheads we always knew they were."

Liliana rolls her eyes.

And I realize exactly how I'm going to sneak to Shipwreck. "Hey, do you have plans tomorrow night?" I ask Liliana.

My tone must tip her off, because she goes from *normal woman in a bakery* to *Thomasina Cruisette infiltrating a James Bond movie.*

"No," she says loudly. "Of course not."

"Great. I'll text you and maybe we can get together."

"That would be WONDERFUL."

She hands me a twenty. I get her change. And she's grinning like a woman with a secret when she announces, "GOTTA GET TO WORK NOW! SEE YOU TOMORROW!"

She turns her ankle on her heels, rights herself, assures three guys who didn't ask that she's okay, and darts out the door.

My phone dings in my front apron pocket not ten seconds later.

And as soon as I get a break in the customer line, I glance at her text asking exactly what I need coverage for, and I reply by asking her to be my fake movie night friend so I can go get baking lessons from Grady.

So that's what the kids are calling it these days, she texts back.

I swear her to secrecy, and immediately start counting down to tomorrow night.

I'm very much looking forward to seeing Grady again.

Hopefully, *finally*, without interruptions.

31

Grady

"Oh, fuck, baby, you're so damn perfect," I murmur to the raw steaks on Cooper's kitchen counter. "So juicy. I'm gonna heat you up until you beg for mercy."

Pretty sure a cow up in cow heaven just flipped me off for that, and I can't say I blame it.

I've never been able to sweet talk meat the way I can a donut. Doesn't feel right.

But I keep trying.

This better not be an omen for how tonight's going to go.

Everything should be perfect.

Cooper texted the whole family on group message to tell them he was having his house bug-bombed, and to avoid it this weekend, just like I asked him to. I told everyone in Shipwreck that I was taking Sue fishing for the weekend, and I left Georgia in charge of the bakery.

Annika reports her friend Liliana is covering for her.

Sue's grazing in the back yard behind the hot tub, and I'm almost positive that's not poison ivy he's eating.

I have all the ingredients ready for lessons on no-fail killer brownies and cake mix cookies, and I'm working hard on thinking about Nana naked every time my dick twitches in anticipation of being alone with Annika, because tonight's not about getting in her pants.

First, because she needs sleep and baking lessons more.

Second, because I can be fucking patient.

And third, because if I were planning to seduce her, I wouldn't do it in my brother's house.

Now all I need is for Annika to get here.

The grill's hot. Got corn on the cob and watermelon prepped too.

And because Annika's never late for anything, I catch the flash of the sun reflecting off a windshield through the front windows right at six o'clock.

I hit the front door and pull it open as she's climbing out of her car.

Her dark hair is tied back, and a baseball cap shields her eyes. She's in tight low-rise jeans with her phone sticking out one pocket and a tank top that keeps lifting to show a sliver of her belly over the white long-sleeve blouse she has tied at her waist.

And she's in hiking boots.

The first time I saw her, she was in boots.

They make me happy, she'd said.

Her happiness made me happy.

And now that I've finally figured out the magic of making her happy, I never want to stop.

"Get all dressed up for baking lessons?" I ask with a grin.

"If you're looking for makeup and a slinky dress, you asked the wrong girl to stick her hands in dough with you."

I clench my eyes shut and try to think of my Nana naked, but all I'm coming up with is Annika in my shower, her cheeks flushed, my fingers in her hot, tight pussy, and I shouldn't have borrowed my brother's house.

Screw the brownies.

And the steak.

"Grady?"

"Hold on."

Pop.

Yep. Think about Pop. Crusty nuts and saggy vaginas.

Okay.

This is good.

I toss a mime into the mix, and yep.

That does it.

Situation temporarily contained.

I open my eyes again, and Annika's giving me the lifted brows of *what the fuck have you been smoking?*

"Making sure I didn't forget anything before we pop the wine," I lie.

She smirks. "You were thinking about me naked."

And there goes my dick.

"Trying *not* to think about you naked," I correct. "I'm teaching you to bake. In my brother's house."

"Did you say he has massage chairs?"

She glances around the interior of the cabin mansion—yeah, *cabin mansion*. It's like a cute mountain cabin on steroids with high ceilings wired for surround sound, with those four massage chairs on the plank wood floor in the living room, the kitchen taking up the entire back corner with its rustic cabinets and gleaming granite countertops and island big enough for four chefs—or one horny master baker and his prodigy—and a loft bedroom overhead.

There are also six guest bedrooms in the basement, and a pool house with another guest room around a path out back.

I gesture to the closest chair, which looks like a designer leather torture machine with those leg slots and the arm liners and the thingies that can knead a man's neck right off if he's not careful with the remote. "Want a go while I grill some dinner?"

The other day, in my shower, she was looking at me like she wanted to jump my bones from here to the next century.

That's nothing compared to the lust in her eyes now.

Part of me wants to punch Cooper for having better toys than I do.

But I tell myself the bigger part of me wants Annika to be happy, and that what was left of my savings was better spent getting her an ice cream machine than a massage chair, so I tug her hand and guide her to the chair closest to the open kitchen.

"Just don't hit the red button," I tell her as I explain the remote. "That'll basically make you launch into space."

She settles into the chair, and I'm not three steps away before she moans in pleasure.

And hello, hard-on, we meet again.

"Are those steaks?" she asks on a blissed-out sigh.

"Top sirloin."

"So you don't have cereal *every* night for…*oh, god, that's good.*"

She whimpers and sighs and moans and I'm pretty sure my dick could best a marble rolling pin in a sword fight right now.

With the open floor plan, I have a clear view of her while I finish prepping the steaks with salt and pepper. There's a smile curving her lips, and if it were possible for a person to sink through the leather, she'd be doing it right now.

Her shoulders visibly relax, her chin droops, and by the time I've pulled the corn out of the fridge to add to the pile to take to the grill, she's passed out cold.

I wouldn't say she's snoring, but that's mostly because she'd probably hit me if I did.

But who falls asleep after seventeen seconds in a massage chair?

An exhausted, overworked, over-stressed Annika.

I toss the steaks and corn back in the fridge.

Leave the baking ingredients sitting out.

And I claim the chair next to her, lift the footrest, and flip on the TV.

She doesn't stir.

In fact, she doesn't stir for three solid hours.

By then, the Fireballs are getting their asses kicked in Milwaukee, which makes her startled exclamation of, "We forgot to put gravestones in the peanut butter bin!" a relief.

It's a good distraction from the sight of Cooper growling on the wide-screen TV. He's about to blow his stack tonight.

Can't say I blame him.

He's playing his heart out, and they just can't pull it off.

"Good nap?" I ask Annika.

Just like the other night at her bakery, she looks around wildly as though she's trying to find the bear waiting to pounce on her. Her chest lifts as she sucks in a big breath, then blinks at the dark windows over the dining room table just off the kitchen.

"What time is it?"

"Little after nine. Hungry?"

She fumbles with her pockets, and I grab her phone off the end table between us and hold it out to her. "No texts," I tell her. "No calls either. They're good."

She breathes out a long, slow breath. "Wow. Sorry. Didn't mean to fall asleep. This chair is like the sleep whisperer."

"You're tired."

"Whoa. Is that really the score?"

She points to the TV, where the Fireballs are down by twelve, and I wince. "Yeah."

"How's Cooper doing?"

I gesture around the room. This house is basically an oversize man cave, complete with a stone fireplace in one wall and a hot tub and designer fire pit out back before you get to the pool. "He's somehow managing to find a way to deal."

She rolls her eyes, a smile lighting her face. "Money can't buy happiness."

"Yeah, but at least he's close by during the season. We cheer him up. Or torment him the old-fashioned way." I drop my footrest, because she's getting dinner whether she likes it or not. "Pretty sure he has some master plans of finding a way to circumvent management to turn the team around, but so far, it's not working. Maybe next year. Don't get up. Give me twenty minutes, and we can eat."

"And then bake," she sighs.

An ugly thought strikes me. "You don't like to bake."

"Sure I do," she lies.

"Annika."

"Grady. I'm *terrible* at it. And it's not like I haven't had practice to try to get better. *I burned water*. Who burns water? But it doesn't matter. Mama needs me to bake, so I'm going to learn to bake, and this conversation didn't happen, because it's not even a conversation. It's a blip. Like four breaths. And poof! It's gone. Are we starting with cookies? Those are *my favorites* to turn into coal. I never know exactly what shape the coal will be, so it's always a fun time."

It shouldn't be a struggle to wrap my brain around the idea of someone *not* liking to bake. Being bad at it, fine. But not liking it?

Tillie Jean only likes to bake brownies. Ma doesn't bake anything. Dad prefers grilling hamburgers and frying up gold nuggets to baking the bread that Crusty Nut is relatively famous for—after the gold nuggets and banana pudding and those bacon gouda cheeseburgers, anyway—but actively *not liking* to bake is just...

It's so...

I look at the flour and cocoa and candies and butter waiting for us in the kitchen.

Then back to Annika.

"You need a baker."

"*There aren't any*. Not in this part of the mountains. I interviewed someone off the street this morning who came in and told me it'd always been her dream to work in a bakery, and I asked what she baked, and when she said her in-laws rave about her cookies, I asked what her secret ingredient was, and do you know what she told me?"

"Love?"

"*Marijuana.*"

I scoff. "Everybody knows that's better in brownies."

"*Grady.*"

"Okay. Okay. We can fix this."

"We can't. But you're going to teach me how to bake anyway, because *this can't fail.*"

My heart clenches. "What were you going to do? Whenever you got out of the Army?"

"I don't know." She rubs her eyes and sinks back into the chair, fussing with the remote. "I'd started thinking I'd stay in another ten or twenty years. Eventually retire when I had to. Guaranteed pension for life, plus the opportunity to work another job. Something administrative. Or in contracting. There's always work for contractors in the government."

"But what do you *want* to do?"

"Stop you from asking annoying questions that are irrelevant to my current life situation."

I smile, but I don't feel it. "Okay. How do you like your steak?"

"I don't know. Medium something? Whatever."

"You don't—" I cut myself off, because *of course* she doesn't know.

She grew up poor, and I know the Army doesn't pay shit for the first few years. Maybe more.

She's probably never had a truly good cut of steak.

"It was always either mooing or super tough whenever

I had it at the dining facility and on deployment they boil it first," she grumbles. "I like chicken. At least I know to expect it to be rubber."

"One Grady Rock steak special coming up. And if you hate it, there are Cocoa Krispies in the pantry."

She curls into the chair and gives me a small smile. "Sorry I'm being a butt."

"Thanks for being comfortable enough to be a butt."

I tug her hair and kiss her forehead, then head to the kitchen.

Maybe she'll like dinner.

Maybe she won't.

But she's staying.

And that's all I care about.

32

ANNIKA

My limbs are so heavy, I think someone must've put lead weights in my fingers and toes while I was sleeping. But I manage to pull myself out of the massage chair—I am *so* getting one of those if I ever win the lottery, which I won't, since I don't play, but a girl can still dream—and I make my creaky bones move to the kitchen area to dig for forks and knives and plates while Grady steps outside and fires up the gas grill.

Sue comes back inside with him, and I swear the goat is panting like a dog.

I scratch him behind his ear, and he circles the two of us until I'm somehow getting a Grady hug again.

"Why is there a box of cake mix on the counter?"

"Annika-proof cookies."

I snort.

Sue snorts.

Grady rubs my neck, and *oh*.

How long has his cannoli been back?

Inspecting the baked goods in his pants seems a much better use of a free evening than baking.

Except it's not. Because I need to be able to keep the bakery going until we can find a more permanent solution.

The bakery is the only thing Mama gets excited about.

Well, that and Roger.

"You do any of the decorating?" Grady asks.

"I tried. Bailey told me it looked like a small dog pooped on her perfect peanut butter cupcakes, and to please just stand back and look pretty and let her do the heavy lifting."

He doesn't answer, but he does trail his hand up my neck until he's teasing my roots, and this isn't how Mama told me babies were made, but he's turning my scalp on and making me want to rip all my clothes off and offer him my whole body for physical inspection.

I wonder if he feels this good when I touch him.

I assume so.

And that cannoli poking my stomach would suggest so.

But I let my hands take a little field trip to the land of Grady's rock-hard ass and give it a stroke over the denim covering his skin.

His cannoli pushes harder into my belly and his breath catches in his chest.

Pulse is definitely picking up. I can feel it under my ear.

I give his cheeks another test squeeze.

"Annika," he warns.

"You didn't invite me *just* for baking lessons," I whisper.

"You're tired and stressed and I'm not going to take advantage of that."

"But you want to?"

"*No.* I want you to be happy with everything settled, and for you to still want me to strip you naked and make love to you until the sun comes up. I don't mind being your stress relief, but I want to be *more*. I want *us* to be more."

"You're already more."

I could do without the lying part, and the sneaking out here when my family thinks I'm with Liliana part, and even the part where he wants to talk about what *my* dream career is, because I don't know.

And I don't like that I don't know.

I've been out in the world for a decade.

Shouldn't I know what I want to do with my life by now?

Not that I currently have much of an option, but if I did…what would I do?

The timer goes off on his phone, and he squeezes me tight for a second before he lets me go. "Time to flip the steaks."

I finish setting the table while Sue watches.

He's a friendly goat.

Doesn't seem prone to leaving messes inside.

I wonder if Grady trained him, or if goats are more domesticated than I thought.

Wait.

Have I ever thought about goats being domesticated?

"Annika? Can you set the oven to three-fifty?" Grady asks through the sliding screen door.

"Afraid to come in and do it yourself?"

"Yep. Also, it's step one in baking no-fail brownies."

"You realize you just cursed us by calling them no-fail brownies?"

His dimples pop out—both of them—and why didn't I let him kiss me on graduation night?

Why didn't I tell him how much I was going to miss him?

That when I was ready, he'd be the one I wanted?

That I'd be home in four years, that I'd go to college in Copper Valley, that there was no one else I'd want by my side as a partner to deal with anything horrible that ever happened?

"Annika?"

I leap toward the double wall ovens. "Three-fifty. Right."

Sue trots beside me and *maaa*s at me when I stare dumbly at the controller. "Upper or lower oven?"

"Your choice."

I don't want to pick.

If I pick wrong, I'll ruin his no-fail brownies.

If I'd let him kiss me, I wouldn't have been able to get on that bus to head off for basic training.

"I'm really mad at you for being a dick when I got home," I call to him.

"I'm mad at me too."

It's not flippant or sarcastic.

It's quiet and regretful.

"I'm mad at me for being afraid of leaping and trusting you," I add quietly.

"Leaving took more courage than staying stuck in high school. You needed to go. I needed to go. We needed each other to go."

"If I was home just to help my mama open a bakery, and she hadn't gone blind, would you still be helping me?"

He doesn't answer right away, but instead watches me through the screen door while I watch him right back.

"I missed you," he finally says, "and I'd like to think I would've pulled my head out of my ass, but I don't know. I'm glad you're here though. And I appreciate the second chance."

"I never had another best friend."

"I never wanted another best friend."

His alarm goes off again.

"Three-fifty. Just pick an oven."

I pick the top one, but I think I accidentally hit the buttons to turn on the bottom one.

That's basically how I roll in kitchens.

But Grady's going to help me.

He's not the enemy.

He's my friend. He cares. And he knows how to fix this.

He knows how to fix *me*.

"I shouldn't make relationship decisions when I'm tired and hungry and worn down," I tell Sue.

He rolls his eyes like *duh, lady, stick with the people who love you when you're at your lowest, because they won't let you down.*

"You're very wise for a goat."

He snorts and licks up his own nose again.

"And also a little gross. But I'll forgive you, because you're a goat. Like the GOAT of goats."

He tilts his head.

"That's the Greatest Of All Time of goats," I explain. "It's an acronym—and you're a goat. And probably don't care. If I don't like my steak, do you get to eat it?"

"He'd eat toilet paper and think it was foie gras," Grady tells me as he slides open the screen door and steps inside with two perfectly grilled steaks and two aluminum foil packets in the shape of corn on the cob.

My belly suddenly gives a rumble, and I realize I haven't eaten since breakfast.

That was probably a mistake.

"C'mon," Grady says with a grin. "It's time to eat."

33

Grady

While we eat, we tell each other stories about things we've done and seen the last ten years, falling back into those easy patterns of listening, teasing, and sharing, no judgment, just curiosity.

We pretend we're not playing footsie under the kitchen table, and Annika finishes every last bite of her steak, and then eats four more bites of mine before she finally leans back in her seat with a contented sigh. "Okay. I'm sold. Steak is delicious when it's cooked right, and I'm positive the only reason I've never been able to bake is because I've never had a meal that delicious to warm me up. Watch out, ovens. I'm coming for you now."

"That's the spirit."

We clean up quickly, shoulders bumping, hands touching, with Sue trying to push us into each other at every opportunity until I finally kick him out of the house.

I turn back around and find Annika at the island, staring down the flour, butter, and cake mix box. "I will own you," she growls to it.

I stifle a laugh. "I see where the first problem is. Here. Watch."

I stop behind her and press her body to the countertop, then guide one of her hands to the cake mix box, which we pet like it's a dog. Or a goat. "Repeat after me. *Hello, lover. Let's make some music.*"

"Are you talking to me or the cake mix?"

"You're not repeating. Let's try again. *I can't wait to sink my fingers into your silky depths.*"

"Okay, hot flash in the hooha, but is cake mix really silky?"

If I weren't already hard as one of her normal baked creations, that would've done it. But I ignore my needy cock and slide a finger under the box lid to pop it open, then pull out the bag inside and slice it open with a knife out of the knife block. "Here. Feel."

She twists her head to look at me.

"*Feel*," I repeat.

I dip my hand into the bag and crumble the fine powder between my fingers. After a moment of hesitation, she does the same.

"Soft," she says.

"Don't tell me. Tell the mix."

She giggles.

Home fucking run.

"You're so soft," she says shyly to the cake mix. "I kinda want to just keep fingering you."

"That's it," I murmur while my cock pulses.

"This is so wrong," she whispers.

"But it *does* feel good."

"Silky," she agrees. "And powdery. I better not get pulled over with powder all over me on the way home."

"And I'm going to stir you until you give me all the good stuff," I say to the mix.

She snort-giggles this time. "I am *not* saying that while my mama and sister are listening, so I don't know how this is going to help me bake anywhere *else*."

"It can hear your thoughts."

"It's *cake mix*."

"Annika. You're right. You have to bake. Do you want to do it the easy way, or do you want to do it the flaming brick of moon rock way?"

"Okay, okay. You're so beautiful and powdery and not at all drug-like, and I want to make you wet."

My aching cock surges against her, and she goes still.

"Did I do that?" she asks.

If I answer her, we're not getting our baking lesson done. "Pour the mix into the bowl and tell it that it's about to meet its soulmates."

"Oh, baby, you get to have a seven-some for life," she croons while she tips the bag into the Pyrex mixing bowl.

I swallow hard. "Threesome," I correct. "But it'll be good."

"Seriously? Only three?"

"Cake mix, eggs, and oil."

"What about butter?"

"You master this first, and we'll talk about what you and I can do with butter."

"I feel very turned on right now."

"Tell it to the eggs, baby. Tell it to the eggs."

I could get addicted to that giggle.

"Crack the eggs, but promise them it'll be worth the pain," I tell her.

"I can't crack eggs."

"They're *eggs*."

"But you're watching. And I saw you do that one-handed egg thing the other night and if I tried that, I'd explode egg all over the kitchen."

"Baking is a lot like sex. The messier, the better. And I'll never object if you use both hands."

"Hoo, boy, did you know nipples can have orgasms?"

Shit. My pirate mast just tried to raise another flag, and based on the way she's rubbing her ass against it, she knows exactly what she's doing. "You can't say orgasm."

"You mean when you're denying both of us *orgasms*?"

"Crack the eggs, Annika. The cake mix needs some love."

"It's not the only thing in need of some love. Is steak an aphrodisiac?"

"Eating is an aphrodisiac."

I reach around her and grab an egg, and I crack it single-handedly into the bowl.

"That's really sexy. Do it again."

"Annika—"

"The cookies will feel the love if *we* both feel the love, right? Do you work out, or are your arms this incredible because you spend all day working with your hands?"

"Both."

My voice is strangled, and having her so close isn't helping.

Nor is her mouth.

It's like someone has turned off her filter and she's

either legitimately into me, or she's trying to drive me crazy and she's going to bury me in this bakery war.

I don't care if she buries me.

Hell, I *want* her to bury me.

So long as I get to bury myself in her along the way.

Show her I can be what she deserves.

What she needs.

Finally convince her she can't live without me. Because now that she's back, I don't know if I can live without her.

I swallow hard and crack the second egg.

"I could watch you do that all day long," she whispers.

I palm her belly and pull her closer against me. "Grab the measuring cup and oil. We need a third of a cup."

"Mm, oil. So slick and lubey."

"Are you trying to torture me?" I murmur into her hair.

"Like you can talk, Mr. Food Porn. You feed me things that make my mouth happier than it's been since the dining facility fixed their soft serve machine, and then you go and put those hands that bake so well on me, and you think I can resist?"

"The oil, Annika." I'm holding on by a thread.

Do I want to boost her up on the counter and sprinkle cake mix all over her breasts and lick it off her?

Yes.

But she needs to learn to bake, and I'm trying to do the noble thing here, and it fucking sucks, but she needs this.

"Are you this bossy when you're naked?" she murmurs while she pours the oil.

Christ. "Are you talking to me or the cake mix?"

"Oh, I don't know. Maybe one of you. Maybe both of you. Is baking like getting involved in BDSM? Because I don't know much about the lifestyle, but I know I'm about to beat this cake mix until it begs for mercy."

And now I'm picturing her in assless leather chaps, bent over the island while I slap her cheeks, and that's never really done it for me before, but I'm having to concentrate damn hard on just breathing to keep from blowing my load in my pants.

"Is there a magic trick to stirring the dough?" she asks.

"Batter," I rasp out, momentarily confused, because she's short-circuiting my brain.

"Butter? You smear it with butter?"

"*Annika.*"

"I'm not a cock tease, you know," she says. "I'm just enjoying the foreplay."

"We don't have to—"

"But don't you *want* to?"

"I *want* to earn you. To deserve you. And since you've been home, I've done a piss-poor job of it."

She frowns up at me, studying me like she's looking for the *real* me, the kid who used to wait for her by her locker in the morning, or maybe the me who almost kissed her at our sophomore homecoming dance when she showed up in a second-hand dress that some of the rich girls were whispering about because it was one of their hand-me-downs, or maybe the me who used to compete with everyone for everything until the first time she tried one of my cookies, when she looked at me and said, *you need to quit trying to beat your brother in baseball and put your heart into doing what you LOVE. And by that, I mean bake, because this is almost as good as my mama's.*

Or maybe she's looking for the guy who learned his

lesson about pushing too hard, too fast, and who would wait for years so long as he knew he had a chance.

I fell.

I fell hard at fourteen.

And I never got up.

"We need to mix the dough," I tell her.

She breaks eye contact and reaches for a wooden spoon, and I cover her mixing hand with mine and guide her through the strokes.

My pulse is whipping like a KitchenAid dialed up to ten. I can't smell the cake mix, because I'm consumed with the scent of her shampoo. My hands are shaking, and my cock has never been this hard.

"Is it supposed to be this thick?" she asks, and I don't know if she's talking about the dough or my raging hard-on poking her back.

So I just say, "Yes," and we keep mixing.

While my hand drifts lower on her belly.

Her breath is coming faster too now. "Are you a two spoons guy, or a scoop guy?"

"I'm a *you* guy." I pull open the drawer to the right of us and feel blindly for the cookie scoop I saw earlier while I press my lips to the side of her neck. "But here. This'll work for the dough."

I shift to her other side and reach under us for a cookie sheet, then press my lips to the other side of her neck on the way up.

She wants foreplay.

I can do foreplay.

For days if I have to.

So long as she feels good.

"I thought this was fun when I was just torturing you, but I like this too," she whispers.

"Scoop the dough, Annika. You know how to space them?"

"I know lines."

"Do you?"

"On graphs and charts. Yes. Here?" She presses back into me again. "Here, I don't want lines."

Her hands shake while she scoops the dough into even lines of cookie balls on the pan.

Probably doesn't help that I'm stroking her neck with my fingertips.

"Okay," she finally says. "These beautiful balls of foodgasms are ready to get hot."

"That's the spirit," I murmur. "Slide them into the oven. And set a timer."

"I *do* set timers," she informs me.

"Ten minutes, then check them."

"That's not very much time."

"It's a lifetime for a cookie."

I step back so she can turn and put the cookies into the oven, and that smile dancing on her lips puts a smile in my soul.

She's so fucking gorgeous.

"You're going to love it in here," she tells the cookies. "It'll change your life."

She closes the oven, stares at the controls until I'm about to step in, and then she hits all the buttons right to set a ten-minute timer.

I pull a second cookie sheet out of the cabinet and gesture her to it.

She plants a fist on her hip and cocks it. "Are you kidding me?"

"Still more dough. Shame to waste it."

"There's ten minutes that we could make out."

Hells to the yes, my cock agrees. My hands itch to grab her. My hair asks if she'd put her fingers through it again. And my lips are aching to touch hers.

"Is this a test?" I ask.

She shakes her head and goes back to the cookie dough, flinging it onto the sheet.

"Whoa, hey." I slide behind her again and wrangle the scoop away. "Gentle. We love the cookies. Remember?"

Her lips twist in a *gotcha* smile. "Oh. Whoops. I forgot."

"Annika Williams, are you *trying* to get me to touch you again?"

"Why would I do that? I'm a strong, independent woman who doesn't ever need *me* time or to be spoiled or taken care of by another person. I can carry the weight of the world without rest. I don't need hugs or kisses or pampering. Or to have my ego soothed. Or reassurance that I'm attractive and a good friend and that you still want to get into my pants."

"Pampering?"

"Of everything there, you want to talk about *pampering*?"

"The rest of it, I can handle. I know about egos and kisses and getting in your pants. But everything I know about pampering a woman, I learned from my sister. And the internet."

"Do I want to know what the internet taught you about pampering a woman?"

"I know it involves goop. And skin. And cucumbers."

Her shoulders shake while she suppresses a laugh. "You know that wasn't a euphemism, right?"

"So women don't want my cucumber on their eyes?"

"Probably not random strange women you pass on the street, no."

"What about the goop?"

"You want to know about the goop?"

"I should be informed if I'm going to be in charge of making sure you get pampered."

"It's like—here. I'll show you."

"You have goop here?"

I catch the glint in her eyes a moment too late as she twists in my arms. "Yep. I have goop here."

I duck, but I'm too late.

She's smeared cookie dough all over my face.

"Goop!" she shrieks, eyes dancing, mouth laughing as she grabs the bowl, tucks it under her arm, and dashes around the other side of the island, feet braced, hand buried in the yellow dough while I stalk around, trying to get closer, the raw cookie heating against my skin and dripping to the floor.

I crook a finger at her while we dance around the island. *Fuck*, she's so pretty. And that smile is my life.

It is.

She's my life.

Her happiness.

Wanting to make her happy is shifting everything back into place.

"Your turn," I tell her. "You want goop on your face. I need to pamper you and give you your goop too."

"*Sshh*," she chastises, switching direction around the island when I fake to the left, then re-centering herself when she catches the ploy. "Don't call the dough names. It doesn't like it, and then you'll ruin my cookies."

"I'm gonna give you your cookies."

Her cheeks are flushing deep, her eyes crinkling at the edges, and her smile lights up the whole fucking mountain. "You have to catch me first."

I take off at a run around the island.

She shrieks and runs too, but I stop and dive over the island, sending the flour bag and salt canister and the cookie sheet with three ugly dough balls flying.

"Gotcha!" I announce as I grip her arm.

She rubs a handful of dough over my cheek and lips, and I grab my own handful to smear across her neck.

"*Ah!* You got me."

"You started it."

She's cracking up while I lie there splayed half across the island and smear dough into her hair, which is only fair, since she's rubbing it in my hair too.

I crawl the rest of the way across the island, twist, and drop to the ground, then bend and lick the sweet dough off her neck. "*Mmm*."

Her breath catches, and she licks my cheek.

"Oh," she whispers. 'That's good."

"Put the bowl down, Annika," I whisper.

"We should bake naked so I can rub this all over your chest and lick it off." Her mouth is working my cheek while she talks, and I don't answer, because I'm devouring her all the way down to her collarbones.

"Grady?" she whispers.

It's a plea and permission all in one, and I don't answer.

Instead, I pry the bowl out of her grip, and then I toss

her over my shoulder. "You know what I do to dirty girls?" I ask.

"I hope it's strip them naked and lick them clean," she replies.

Yeah.

I'm a complete and total goner for this woman.

34

Annika

I'VE POSSIBLY LOST my mind, but there's nothing that feels more *right* than helping Grady peel his shirt off in the huge master bathroom on the second floor.

"You have dough in your hair," I tell him with a giggle when he reaches for my shirt hem.

"I want to put dough in your belly button and lick it out."

My giggles die away as he pulls my shirt over my head and I wrap my arms around him and attack him with a kiss.

He tastes like cake-cookie dough and Christmas morning, and his hands are hot and big and strong against my back, pressing us together while he kisses me back like a starving man given a brownie sundae.

And that bulge in his pants is still holding strong.

Poor guy has to hurt by now.

My fingers get caught in the sticky mess in his hair, and I'm giggling and panting and aching for more all at the same time.

And suddenly my bra is gone, and I shiver in anticipation.

The happy tingles spread over my entire body when Grady palms my breasts, rubbing lazy circles around my nipples. He pulls out of the kiss with a groan. "Years, Annika. I've wanted you for *years*."

"Half my life," I confess. "Tell me you have a condom."

"Six. Back pocket."

"Optimistic much?" I ask through a giggle while I dig out a stack of foil packets from his pocket.

"Should've been a Boy Scout. Oh, missed a spot." He bends and sucks at my neck, and my breath catches at the pressure, and I suddenly need to get out of my pants.

And I need him to get out of his pants.

I make quick work of his button—yes, while gripping all six condoms, and I suddenly realize he might mean to use them all at once for sextuple protection, and then I'm giggling again, and he sucks harder on my neck, right in that sweet spot where it meets my shoulder, and then I'm freeing his cock and *lord have mercy*, he could win any cannoli contest hands-down.

I grip his silky length in one hand and stroke, and he makes a strangled noise and pushes me back until we're in the walk-in shower.

"Pants. Gone," he orders. "Two seconds. Water."

"Hot water?"

"Fuck, yes."

He takes the condoms and puts them on the soap ledge, and then he's kissing his way down between my breasts, over my belly, and lower while he tugs my leggings and panties off.

"So fucking gorgeous," he murmurs to the curls between my legs, and my breath catches as he inhales. He lifts my foot to pull off my pants, and presses another line of kisses down my inner thigh.

"*Grady*," I whisper.

"Sssh. Let a man live out a fantasy."

"You—"

I end with a strangled moan when he kisses his way back up my thigh. "You're getting your cookies tonight, Annika. No excuses."

My skin is on fire. My toes are already curling. He's touching my hips. My ass. My legs.

Kissing my other inner thigh and making my knees quiver. My clit is pulsing and heavy. My pussy is hot and ready. Cool air brushes my most sensitive parts when he lifts my other foot to tug my pants the rest of the way off, and then he pushes me against the wall, carefully parts my legs, and leans in to kiss me.

There.

I gasp at the intimate touch of his tongue against my seam, but *oh my god*, that's good.

"So good," I pant.

"You're wet," he murmurs before he licks me again.

"All—night—you—want—*Grady!*"

His tongue swirls around my clit, and I fist my fingers in his sticky hair. His stubble against my sensitive skin is electric and perfect and I buck my hips into his mouth and spread my legs wider, because *more*.

"I could fucking live here," he says, and that's the last coherent sentence I hear before he unleashes his magic tongue and devours my pussy like it's the cupcake that's been taunting him for days, and he's finally been given permission to eat.

He licks and suckles and teases, and I gasp and moan and just *feel*.

I let go.

I let *him* take care of me, with my foot hooked over his shoulder and his fingers lightly scraping my hamstrings while his mouth—*oh*, god, his mouth is playing my pussy like he was born with his face between my legs, and just when I think I'm about to come apart in a million shiny pieces of glass, he sucks my clit hard and slides two fingers deep inside me and crooks them just right, and my body goes off like a bottle rocket.

The spasms hit me so fast, so deep inside, that I don't have time to think.

Just feel.

Close my eyes.

I think I call him a sex god for all the ages, but I'm not sure, I just know that's my voice echoing off the tile walls and I'm clenching so tight around his fingers and my clit is doing backflips of joy and he's licking me clean while my body keeps riding wave after wave of ecstasy, which looks like cupcake fireworks over rainbows made of unicorn horns that shoot glitter and turn the whole world into one big, happy, shiny party of joy.

If there's a heaven, it's here.

"That's better," Grady murmurs as he pulls his fingers out of my pussy.

I whimper, because I'm suddenly empty, but when he licks my juices off his fingers, I don't care that I just came so hard my right eye can't quite focus, even though I dimly know my vision is really important for some reason.

"You are so fucking sexy," he tells me.

"I don't know how many cupcakes you practiced on," I pant, "but good job."

He grins, lids heavy, and shoves to his feet, shucking his pants as he goes. They join my pants outside the shower, and he flips on the overhead nozzle.

"You're still all dirty," he informs me, shielding me from the cool spray and licking my neck and exploring my body with his fingertips until the glass wall fogs.

I bite his shoulder and explore on my own, letting my fingers learn the curve of his arms, the hard planes of his chest, the dip of his belly button, the thick length of his cock.

"I always knew you'd be amazing," I whisper while I squeeze him.

He grunts. "Careful. Let's get you cleaned up."

"I don't want to be clean."

His lips twist in a grin that brings out his dimples, and I'm fairly certain I could live every day for the rest of my life with those blue-green eyes raking over my body like that.

"How about dough-free?" He guides me into the shower spray and combs his fingers through my sticky hair. "Clean hair, dirty girl?"

"Do I get to be dirty with you?"

"As dirty as you want."

He grabs a bottle and squeezes a dollop of shampoo into his hand, then slowly starts rubbing it into my hair, his fingers massaging my scalp, making my eyes drift closed as my fingers keep exploring his wet skin.

"We're always wet," I whisper.

"I like you wet."

"I need to wash your hair too."

"Patience, my eager apprentice."

I giggle and trail my hands down to grip his cock again. "*Apprentice*? Excuse me, mister, who do you think has more experience washing hair?"

"Fuck, Annika, I love when you touch me."

"Mm," I agree, stroking his length while his fingers tighten in my hair. Bubbles drip down my back, and as I stroke him, he tilts my head back, kissing me while hot water rains down on both of us.

"Can't—much—longer," he gasps, which is fine with me, because having him in my hands is making me want him inside me, and never in my wildest dreams did I think I'd ever let myself stand naked in the shower with Grady, his impressive hard-on straining for me while my very happy lady bits asked to please invite him in, and not for tea and crumpets.

"Does it hurt?" I ask.

"The part where I'm not inside you? Yes. Yes, it hurts."

He's trying to smile, like he's joking, but there's so much heat and need darkening his eyes that I grab one of the condoms.

"I don't like it when you hurt," I tell him.

"I don't want to hurt *you*."

"Best friends?" I whisper.

"Annika. *Everything*. You're *everything*."

I roll the condom down his hard length and press up on my toes to kiss him again, because now that I've kissed him, I can't stop.

I don't want to *ever* stop.

I don't want to fight a bakery war. I don't want to go home to Sarcasm tonight. I don't want to lie and hide.

I just want *Grady*.

He lifts me so I can wrap my legs around him, and once again, my back hits the cool, slick tile, but this time, there's nothing between us.

No clothes.

No hesitations.

No secrets.

Not between *us*, anyway.

This is just me and my best friend. The man who's known me for longer than anyone outside my family.

Who shows up at midnight to bake cookies for me.

Who listens when I need to vent my frustrations and worries.

Who I've been in love with forever, no matter how hard I've tried to deny it.

The head of his cock nestles between my thighs, nudging me apart as he slides in slowly, not just filling my body, but adding the final piece to my soul.

"Annika," he gasps, his head dropped to my shoulder.

"Deeper," I urge, tilting my hips into him. "I want all of you. I *need* all of you."

He pulls back, then thrusts all the way in, slowly, carefully, so I can feel every inch of him against every inch of me, and *oh my stars*, I need him.

His body. His heart. His friendship.

His love.

Love isn't a secret, doubt whispers to me.

I squeeze my eyes shut and roll my hips into his as he strokes inside me again, faster and faster, whispering all the confessions I've wanted to say to him too these past ten years.

I missed you.
I needed you.
I want you.
You're beautiful.
So perfect.
My match.
My only.

I'm gripping his face, kissing his chin, his nose, his dimples, all the dough in his hair melting into streams of sweetness down his body while he thrusts harder, every press of his hips into mine spiraling me higher like a wind-up toy until he lifts his head, that hooded blue-green gaze boring into me, saying everything neither of us will put into words.

I love you.

My release springs free from the deepest part of my soul, my pussy tightening around his thick length until I'm certain he's left an imprint.

"Annika," he cries, and I feel him pulse inside me with his own release, the thickening against my already swollen walls sending corkscrews of pleasure shooting through my hips and belly as I spasm around him, letting go of every ounce of hurt, of pain, of regret, all of it washing down the shower drain while Grady loves me.

His hands gripping me tight.

His body pressed deep inside me.

His forehead drops to mine, dark lashes lowered while he catches his breath.

"Once could never be enough," he murmurs.

I bury my face in his neck and hold on, because he's right.

Once isn't enough.

And—"*Ohmygod*, the cookies!"

His gaze connects with mine, and we both start laughing, which makes him wince, because he's still buried inside me, and apparently feeling sensitive.

"Tell me you ruin cookies all the time," I say.

He wiggles his brows. "Did I ruin *these* cookies?" he asks with a playful thrust of his hips before he pulls out of me.

I kiss him hard once more, then push him under the shower spray. "Wash up, Master Baker. We're gonna need a round two."

35

GRADY

I CAN'T REMEMBER the last time I couldn't wipe a goofy smile off my face, but as I dump the burnt cookies and clean up the kitchen while Annika's digging through some women's clothing I found in one of the spare bedrooms downstairs, I realize I'm also whistling.

She stayed.

She seduced *me*.

I have my best friend back. We're good. We're better than good. And I'm just getting warmed up with being everything she needs me to be.

She steps out of the basement stairwell across the room with a wrinkle-nosed smile, and I bark out a laugh when I take in her socks, which go all the way up to her knees over purple leggings.

"Rainbow stripes? Not so sure those go with your boots."

"Don't judge, Mr. Leopard Print Robe."

"I put that back in the closet."

"But you still put it on first." She's in a Thrusters T-shirt—the pro hockey team in Copper Valley—and her damp hair is dangling over her shoulders, leaving small wet spots on the gray cotton where it touches.

She tugs at the back of the leggings like they're a size too small. "Best I could find. Thank you. For starting the laundry. I could've gotten that."

"Annika."

"I said *thank you*. You can't expect me to not add that I could've done it myself. So say *you're welcome* and let's move on to seeing if I can burn these no-fail brownies you swear are Annika-proof like those cookies. Which smell awful, by the way."

Yep.

She's hilarious, and she doesn't even know it.

"My fault on the cookies. If you'd been alone, you would've heard the buzzer."

"If I'd been alone, I probably would've been lost in a podcast about DNA testing and the scandal and drama that goes with it."

"Really?"

It's not often she goes ruddy in the cheeks, but there it is. "Guilty pleasure."

"Why guilty?"

She joins me by the sink and takes the cookie sheet to dry it. "It's all these people who think they're someone, and then they find out they're someone else, and it's... well, it's hardcore *who did your mom really sleep with* gossip on top of *how many siblings do I have* and *was anyone ever going to tell me*? And all these other people having their lives turned upside down when they find out their dads slept around and they have seven siblings or some rare genetic disorder in the family that doctors would've missed without the missing family link…"

She ducks and turns to put the clean cookie sheet away in the island cabinet.

"You ever do it?" I ask.

I know the answer. She told me she refused to spend $30 on a pedicure when she got back from a deployment, because she could scrub the dead skin off her own feet for the cost of a pumice stone.

No way she's dropping a hundred bucks just to find out her mama's her mama.

"Yeah," she says quietly.

I'm not fast enough to stop my brows from meeting my hairline, and she gives a self-conscious laugh as she straightens. "I knew my grandma ran away from home in New York when she was seventeen because her dad was an abusive asshole, and she married an abusive asshole of her own who mysteriously disappeared when my mama was four, but I didn't know…"

She trails off, and it's not hard to jump to where she's going. She didn't talk about it much in high school, but I was with her once when she saw him. "You wanted to confirm who your father was."

"No. Mama wouldn't have lied." She shakes her head. "That was never the question. I just…if any of *them* ever take it, I want…I want them to know. I want *my* record to be there too."

Them.

She has siblings.

Not just Bailey.

"He's...?"

"Married. Three kids. Happy family in Copper Valley. Soccer teams and honor roll and new gaming systems for Christmas, last I heard. Why's the oven still on? We're not seriously making brownies tonight, are we?"

"You want them to know he didn't help you."

"Mama," she corrects. "He didn't help *Mama*. She didn't get pregnant by herself, but raised me by herself while he denied even knowing her. That's not okay. It's *never* okay. I know he was a teenager, but you know what? So was she. And she did what she needed to do. Alone. Maybe I'm being petty in hoping they find out, but I do. Are we making brownies or not?"

"You're fucking amazing, do you know that?"

"Queen of the tooth-cracking brownies and flaming granite cookies with a side of a thirst for vengeance buried deep. I know."

I hook an arm around her neck, kiss her hair, and tug her to the island. "C'mon. Brownies. You can do this, and they'll be ready before your clothes are done. Remember the first lesson?"

"Yes. Talk so dirty to the dough—"

"Batter, for real, this time."

"—to the *batter* that I get arrested for exposing a thirteen-year-old to sexual harassment in the workplace."

"That's the spirit."

"Oh my god, Grady."

I grin. "All you have to do is *feel* the love. You don't have to say it out loud. But I highly encourage it while you're here. Here. My favorite recipe from school. I tweaked it, but people would know something was up if you had brownies identical to mine."

"You know what would be awesome? If we didn't have to pretend to be enemies in public and sneak around to see each other. *That* would *rock*."

"It would, but Annika, look at how many customers our war is bringing in. We'll come out one day. But right now—get Duh-Nuts on solid footing. Save up for the lean times."

She sighs. "I know. I just—it would rock. That's all I'm saying."

"I rock."

"You are a Rock."

"In so many ways."

I grin.

She laughs.

And we manage to get a pan of brownies in the oven before we fall back into making out in one of the massage chairs in the living room.

I don't want to let her go, but eventually her clothes are clean again, and she's walking herself to the door whether I like it or not, so I trail along, not wanting to let go.

Not when I've waited this long for *us*. "Come camping with me tomorrow night. When you're done with…what's on your calendar tomorrow?"

"Roller skating."

"Whoa. Your mom's up for that?"

"No, it's—Bailey set me up on a date with Roger's son."

I see red. And green. I growl and tighten my grip on her hand.

"We're not dating, remember?" she says. "We're *keeping up pretenses*."

"You—he—fuck that."

Her laughter breaks through the Incredible Hulk act I'm pulling. "Grady. Hi. I'm Annika Williams, and *of fucking course I'm not going*. But thank you. I like this possessive growly thing you have going on. It's oddly erotic."

She pushes up on her toes to brush a kiss to my cheek. "Let's see if I'm still standing tomorrow night before I promise anything, okay?"

"I can pick you up."

"What would I tell Mama and Bailey?"

My heart's still thundering out a howl at the idea of her going on a date with anybody, but I'm slowly getting it back under control. "Who's your friend? Liliana, right? Wait. The same Liliana who told everyone I had lice freshman year?"

She tilts her head. "I don't—oh. Yes. That Liliana. She grew up."

"She—" I stop, because reminiscing about someone who also replaced the C with an extra P when the cheering squad had a Cooper Rock day with letter flash cards—thus making it a *Pooper Rock* day—isn't going to move us forward here. "Have her tell your mama there's an overnight at the winery or something."

"I'll see what I can do," she says, but her brows furrow. "Thank you for tonight. I—*we* needed this."

I grab her in a tight hug. "You could stay tonight too."

"I can't, Grady."

Three words, seven million meanings, and most probably things that are racing through her head. *I have responsibilities. Bailey will worry. Mama will worry. I don't have a good excuse. I'm terrified of how quickly I'm falling in love with you.*

Okay, that last one's all me.
And I'm not terrified.
Not of falling in love with Annika.
Not when she's finally letting me in.
But I do steal another kiss before I let her go.
I don't know when I'll get another.
But I know one thing.
It won't be soon enough.

36

Annika

My body is both bone-tired and also more relaxed than I've been in months when I finally park my car in front of Mama's little house.

The new wood on the railings that Roger and the neighbors installed stands out in the dark, and I sigh softly to myself, because it's stupid that Shipwreck and Sarcasm fight when they both have residents who care so damn much.

Why can't they care about *each other* like that?

And why can't they support two bakeries without them having to be at war first?

I let myself into the house and close the door softly behind me, then yelp at the figure on the couch.

"You're *late*," Bailey says.

She switches on the lamp and crosses her arms. Her

foot hangs loose over her knee, tapping out an expectant beat.

"Fell asleep during the movie," I lie.

Her nose quivers, and *oh, shit*.

Can she smell the fabric softener? It's different from the no-perfume stuff we use here.

"Is that brownies?" she asks.

I almost sag with relief. "Liliana tried to teach me a few tricks. How's Mama?"

"We had a dance party with Roger and Birch. She can still shake it. You should've texted that you were going to be so late."

"Sorry. I thought you'd be in bed." I sit next to her, and she curls into me, leaning her head on my shoulder and wrapping her arm around my stomach. "Why *aren't* you in bed?"

"Boys are stupid."

"I know, but you can't change it, so you shouldn't lose sleep over it either."

"And hormones are stupid."

"Hashtag truth."

"Annika. We've talked about you saying *hashtag*. Don't do it."

I stroke her hair and smile. "Sorry. Tell me about your hormones. You want some brownies? Liliana sent me home with a few." *God*, I hate lying, but Bailey would bolt if she knew I was with Grady all night—plus Grady and I agreed on the whole *we need to be a secret for the benefit of our bakeries* thing—and right now, she clearly needs someone to talk to.

I'd rather it's me than one of her friends, who are all nice enough, but also in the throes of puberty.

"We should make brownies at Duh-Nuts. *Oh my god.* Annika. We should make *brownie donuts.* No. *Caramel brownie donuts.*"

"Or peanut butter brownie donuts."

"Who are you, and where did you gain this amazing baking inspiration?"

Huh.

Maybe sex with Grady is good for my culinary creativity.

Actually, no.

I'll keep the sex part but leave the culinary part to him.

I'm really not built to be a baker.

"You must be rubbing off on me," I tell her. "So. Tell me about the boy."

"I like talking about brownie donuts better."

"You like him and you wish you didn't?" I press quietly.

It's a relatable emotion, though I'm finally in a place where I *don't* wish I didn't like Grady.

I like liking Grady.

I like kissing Grady.

I just don't like keeping Grady a secret, even if I can see his reasoning.

Bailey sighs and sags deeper against me. "My logical brain says it's stupid to like boys. Boys haven't been good to our family. But every time I'm around him my heart starts beating like I sampled too many chocolate-covered coffee beans and my belly gets all fluttery and I get so tongue-tied that I feel like I'm talking out of my elbow."

"That sounds like a crush."

"I don't *want* to have a crush. Crushes can destroy your whole entire future. Look what they did to Mama."

My hand stills in her hair. "I don't think Mama would say she feels robbed of the life she was supposed to have," I say quietly, the revelation rocking me deep in the pit of my stomach as the simple truth of it finally penetrates past my *logical* brain and into my *feels*.

"She spent her whole life raising you, and then me, and now she's fucking *blind*," Bailey whispers. "She *was* robbed."

"Do you remember when you two came to visit me in Texas three summers ago? When it was so hot, and we went to that giant water park?"

"That was so fun. I hate Shipwreck. They have a water park like that."

I stifle an eye roll. "You were going down the waterslide over and over and over while Mama and I did the lazy river. And she was asking about my job and my life and I was catching up on how you suddenly decided soccer sucked but volleyball was life, and that you had three new friends who would come over and have dance marathons with that old Wii that Mama picked up refurbished on sale after Christmas—"

"Oh em gee, when we all dressed up in boas and pretended to be llamas invading a unicorn dance-off?"

"*Yes*. And she was laughing so hard she fell out of her tube on the lazy river."

"Well, yeah. Adriana's llama impersonation isn't something you can forget," she says with a giggle.

"Mama loves being our mama. She's so proud of you. And so proud of me. She didn't plan on being a single mom so early in life, but she fucking *rocked* it. And she probably hasn't loved every minute, but we *are* her world. And we're pretty awesome. Because of her. I don't think

Mama regrets the life she didn't have. She's too busy enjoying the life she *does* have."

"I'm too young for philosophy," she says quietly.

"No, you're not. But listen—it's okay to have a crush on a boy. It's okay to go on dates. It's okay to kiss a boy once you're twenty-four."

She giggles and pokes me in the ribs, and I squeeze her tighter in a big hug.

"You know where babies come from. When you're thirty-seven and ready, you know how to be safe and protected."

"Now you're being ridiculous."

"Hush. I'm coping with the fact that I need to take you bra shopping this weekend."

She sighs. "It's all the baked goods. It makes them grow."

"It's the hormones and genetics."

"They suck."

"They really do. They make us like boys who don't like us back, and they make us cranky for no reason, but they also inspire us to binge-watch *Gilmore Girls* while eating chocolate ice cream, so they're not *all* bad, right?"

"Are there boys you've liked who didn't like you back?"

"I'm about the worst role model for healthy relationships with boys. I denied any feelings for anybody until it was too late and I lost them."

"That Rock boy," she whispers.

It's my opening.

I should tell her.

I *need* to tell her if he's going to be in my life. In her life. In *our* lives.

"You're better off without him," she announces quickly. "Mama says he would've married you, but then he probably would've divorced you and left you with three babies to feed."

It's a sock to the gut. "Mama did *not* say that."

"No, but she should. Annika. He's a Shipwreck shithead. People from Shipwreck don't marry people from Sarcasm and have happy ever afters. It's a rule. *Especially* when those shitheads are trying to ruin our bakery." She pushes up and frowns at me. "We really need to find a full-time baker. Because if he ever actually ups his decorating game, we're toast. Adriana snuck me one of the shithead's banana pudding donuts the other day, and Annika, it's bad. I mean, the donut was good. The donut was orgasmic."

"How do you—never mind. Don't want to know."

"He can outbake us," she whispers.

"He's had half a lifetime more experience than you have," I whisper back. "This will all be okay. I promise. Trust me?"

"No. Because so far in my life, you've never let me down, which means it's inevitable that you will someday, because you're human, which you can't help no matter how hard you try, and I think I might die if this is the thing that you finally let me down with. So I'm just going to not ask you to take it on anymore."

"That...didn't make any sense."

"We need a better baker, Annika. Roger can only help for so long, and since you won't homeschool me..."

"Bailey?"

"What?"

"Go to bed and worry about boys. I'll take care of the bakery. Even *I* can't screw up bubble waffles, right?"

She opens her mouth, then closes it.

And then she leans over to hug me. "I love you anyway," she says.

She turns the light out on me and heads to her small bedroom, and I pull my phone out.

Parenting sucks, I text to Grady.

I don't give him a chance to reply before I add, *And if you know anyone who can bake better than you can, I need to hire that person STAT.*

He doesn't answer.

Probably sleeping, or heading out with Sue to whatever campground he's supposed to be at.

But he'll get my message eventually.

Probably.

Hopefully.

And then he'll help me fix this.

I could fix it by myself. I really could.

But I don't want to anymore.

37

GRADY

Sue and I are playing fetch at the edge of the lake while the sun sets on our little campsite, and I keep checking my phone.

The last text I got from her was a picture with the caption *SOS*.

She managed to blow up a bubble waffle maker, and I don't know what she used as batter, but it might've been liquid fire.

The Duh-Nuts Instagram account has a picture of a gorgeous bubble waffle cone filled with pink soft serve, so I can only assume Bailey took over from there.

My entire family—from Cooper to Pop to Georgia, who counts as family because of how long she's worked for me—all texted individually today to assure me that Crow's Nest was running a healthy business and we should consider adding a tea service once a week to up our game.

All of them.

Same message.

Even from Cooper, who's still on the road.

"Duh-Nuts is doing good," I tell Sue.

He rolls his eyes, like *Duh, Grady. All that free publicity plus BUBBLE WAFFLES AND ARTISAN SOFT SERVE.*

Or he might have a booger in his eye. He's gotten to where he can almost lick his eyeball like he can lick in his own nose, so who knows?

Either way, *artisan soft serve* is just wrong.

He suddenly lets out an excited *Maa!* and takes off for the path that leads to my little campsite, and a minute later, he's herding Annika into the clearing.

My whole body lights up like a neon sign. "You made it."

"I'm a disaster."

She slumps into my waiting arms, and Sue circles us, *maa*ing like he's trying to tell Annika every last one of my sins and a few of my redeeming qualities.

"You smell like heaven."

"I showered four times to get the smell of smoke out of my hair. The fire alarms went off and all the shops on either side of us had to evacuate too. The entire Volun-told Fire Department showed up, and then the mayor, and then *Honey freaking Wellington* and all of the paparazzi. Mama almost tripped trying to get out. And then, when we got the all-clear, the whole damn town showed up and our old gym teacher helped Bailey make everyone bubble waffles and we ran out of soft serve and now we have fifteen —*fifteen*—orders for specialty cakes *the weekend after school starts* and three have to be perfect, but the other twelve literally told me that they'd never know the difference if I bought a dozen cakes from Walmart over in Snyderville and jacked the price up and sold them as my own and *who does that*?"

"*Maaaa!*" Sue says indignantly on her behalf.

It's so fucking good to have her back where she belongs. "Want me to make it all better?"

"Yes."

"Hungry?"

She tilts her hips into me. "Yes."

"Me too."

I toss her over my shoulder, and she laughs—or maybe sob-laughs, but she also slips her hands down my pants and scrapes her nails over my ass, so I duck and carry her into my tent and toss her on the air mattress.

She bounces and laughs and quickly wipes her eyes.

"Whoa, what's this?" I settle next to her and touch my thumb under her lashes, where there's still moisture from her tears. "Aw, Annika."

"Shut up and make it better," she whispers.

She grabs me by the ears and pulls my face down until our lips brush, and fire erupts in my veins.

"I love kissing you," I murmur against her mouth.

"We waited too long," she whispers, still softly rubbing those silky pillows against the rough stubble around my mouth. "*I* waited too long."

I should've shaved. "You're worth it."

"We should have memories, Grady. We should have memories of making out in a canoe on the lake and almost getting caught under the stands at the stadium and coming in last in the voting for prom king and queen because we're *so* not prom king and queen material, except *someone* would've nominated us just to watch us lose."

"We have memories." I brush my lips over her cheek and along her jawline. "We have my favorite memories. You were my whole high school experience, and I wouldn't trade it for anything."

"But we could've been *more*. I was just too afraid."

"Are you afraid now?"

"No." She sucks my lip into her mouth, and my eyes drift shut while I lose myself in her.

Her skin.

Her eager mouth.

Her lean, strong legs.

She tugs at my shirt until she's sliding her nimble fingers over my chest and around to scrape down my back.

I shift to reach between us, and the mattress bounces her up, and our noses bonk.

"Oh, shit," I grunt. "You okay?"

She tips her head back and laughs while she rubs her nose. "Yes. You?"

"Didn't feel a thing," I lie, mostly because I'm more interested in getting back to kissing her.

She twists to her side and puts her elbow into the mattress, and the mattress flips me up.

"Crap," she mutters.

But she's smiling, and her smile makes me smile.

"Race you naked," I say.

I push to sit, and Annika topples into me. "*Aaah!*"

"*Maa!*" Sue agrees as he charges into the tent.

"Sue! Out!"

"*Maa!*"

I reach for him, but he dodges me and leaps onto the

air mattress too, and I slide right off the damn thing while Annika shrieks and dodges the goat's hooves.

I leap up as something flaps at my ear.

"Bird!" Annika yells.

Sue leaps for it. "*Maa!*"

I duck away from the bird and reach for Sue again as a loud *pop!* erupts at the head of the mattress.

"Shit," I mutter again.

Annika's curled into herself laughing so hard she's crying, hovering in a corner of the tent away from the bird and behind my goat, and this is *not* what I had in mind.

And that was my good air mattress.

I finally manage to wrangle Sue out, and the bird follows, aiming an indignant chirp at all of us while it takes to the dusky skies.

I lean over and peek in the tent.

Annika's clutching my pillow to her chest and still giggling.

"I gotta tie up my goat. Strip, and I'll be there in two minutes."

She tilts her head to smile at me, and I grab my backpack to dig out Sue's leash.

Except it's not in my backpack.

Dammit.

"Gotta dash up to my truck," I call to Annika.

"Mm-kay," she replies.

"Feel free to be naked when I get back."

I dash up the path, Sue on my heels, and ten minutes later, I'm back, panting. Dusk is falling heavily now, with the trees becoming dark shadows and the leaves overhead rustling in the late evening breeze. I fire up my phone's flashlight and use it to tie Sue to the nearest tree, then crunch over the leaves to the tent.

"Hey, beauti—oh."

Annika's still curled around my pillow.

She clearly moved at some point, because she's in nothing but a lace bra and matching panties, but she's also passed out cold.

She's sleeping so hard she's snoring.

Not half-hearted snores like last night either.

She's a gone full lumberjack.

It's fucking adorable.

And worrisome.

She went from rolling with laughter to passed out cold in under ten minutes.

She needs help.

Not the *teach her to bake* kind of help either.

She needs hostile kitchen takeover help.

I was thinking I'd just spend the next few weeks baking double and delivering her everything she needed, but that won't work.

I can't run her bakery and mine at the same time. Not while we're supposed to be in the middle of the rivalry of the century.

But I know people.

I know lots of people.

People who can help.

"You sleep," I whisper while I pull my sleeping bag over her. "Sorry I didn't think of this sooner, but I've got your back, Annika. Just hang in there."

Her life's going to get easier very, very soon.

I'll make sure of it.

38

Annika

I SET fire to the cupcakes again.

I set fire to them, and they're exploding like lava out of a volcano, spewing glitter and candy eyeballs across the kitchen, which is currently in the inside of a palace with walls made of licorice, and the Queen of England is laughing in the corner with Mama's imaginary python while—

"*Stop*," I gasp, sitting straight up.

My skin is sticky, my bedroom walls are nylon, and—

"Camping," I mutter to myself.

I'm camping.

With Grady.

Except he's not in the tent—though his shirt is on the ground next to me—and I smell wood smoke.

Not flaming cupcakes.

"Annika?" He peers into the tent, Sue right behind him. "You okay?"

I brush my hair out of my face and realize I'm nearly naked. "What time is it?"

"Five-thirty. You want banana boats for breakfast? Or eggs? I can whip up some eggs."

I blink slowly at him. "Did we have sex last night?"

He grins, and *gah*, those dimples are killer first thing in the morning. "No."

"Is today Sunday?"

His grin gets bigger, his dimples deeper. "Yes."

"Did we cuddle?"

"You threw me over for Sue."

I know he's teasing, but I really want to know.

"See that pillow?" he asks, pointing across the tent.

I squint. I know that pillow.

"You were sleeping *there* when I crawled in here last night."

And I ended up here.

Which shouldn't be surprising, since I can wreak havoc on a king-size bed all by myself. "I'm…a loud sleeper."

His brows furrow for a minute, then his grin comes back. "Not as much as you might think," he tells me. "And you're going to dash out of here in three seconds, aren't you?"

"Ohmygod! Yes."

Five-thirty.

He said it's *five-thirty*. Bailey and Mama will be at the bakery, and we have *got* to schedule a down day once a week, because none of us can keep working these hours.

I throw back the sleeping bag, realize I'm in just my bra and panties, and then shriek and cover myself again.

Sue bleats at me. Grady ducks his head and grins, then scoots out the tent door. "One banana boat to go, coming right up," he tells me. "Where'd you tell Bailey you were going?"

"To get in touch with my Army roots eating tree bark and pissing in the bushes. Her friend Adriana's mom stayed over in my room last night."

I yank on my shirt, realize it's not my shirt, but Grady's Crow's Nest T-shirt, and I grunt to myself while I rip it back off, sniff it, sniff it again, and then debate stealing it, because it smells like cupcakes and campfire and Grady.

He wouldn't notice if I shoved it down my pants for the walk back up to my car, would he?

And if he did notice, would he care?

I shimmy into my shorts and decide that Bailey would care when she found it stuffed in my pillowcase, and so I give up my dreams of sleeping with Grady's scent and yank on my own old Army T-shirt.

I pull on my hiking boots and slide out of the tent as he pulls a skillet of scrambled eggs off the fire.

"Those aren't banana boats."

"Or cereal," he agrees. "You must be special to get the egg treatment. Coffee?"

I can't say yes. I have to go.

But coffee.

With Grady.

Over eggs.

Before banana boats.

I pull out my phone and text Bailey. *Overslept. How's the bakery?*

I get a text message back in four seconds.

It's a picture of the kitchen, with Roger running the

fryer, Mama rolling cookie dough, and Adriana and her mom frosting cupcakes.

Guilt eats the rest of the lining of my stomach.

Go eat more tree bark. We've got this. And you better not have actually snuck out to sleep with that Rock shithead, Bailey adds.

I wince, then turn around and snap a selfie of myself with the lake in the background, hair a mess, with no goats, Grady, or camping gear to be seen.

Just me and the bugs and the fish, I type.

I erase it and re-type it seven times before I finally hit send.

"I hate lying," I tell Grady as I settle on a log next to the campfire.

"Because you're a good person."

"Your line is *it's not for much longer, Annika, and then I'll charm your family and you'll charm mine and this stupid war between Shipwreck and Sarcasm will melt into nothingness and we'll all laugh and eat ice cream while both of our bakeries thrive because they're built with love*."

He grins over his eggs. "That's a beautiful sentiment."

Which isn't a *yes, Annika, of course that's what we'll do*.

Of course it's not.

As far as he's concerned, this is just reunited friends with benefits.

He'd have to be insane to want more with me right now.

Plus, it's all that I've told him I want. *I'm high maintenance. I don't have time for a relationship. I can't even stay awake for ten minutes to have sex with you in a tent*.

I'm a disaster.

So maybe I need to quit riding the crazy train while I'm

around him, and then I'll get to keep having the occasional sleepover that ends with these eggs.

"Hey. We'll get there. Eventually. Okay?"

"What did you put in these? Crack and cheese?"

"Butter. Lots and lots of butter. And my secret spice mix."

"Tell me it's not marijuana."

He chokes on his eggs and keeps laughing through a coughing fit.

"That's not a *no*," I point out.

Sue plops on his haunches next to me and lays a head on my shoulder, staring forlornly at my breakfast plate.

"Don't look at me, buddy. When I fry eggs, they come out of the pan tasting like raw tuna."

"You," Grady rasps out, pointing at me with one hand while he pounds his other fist into his breastbone. "Stop talking."

"He has an overdeveloped sense of humor," I murmur to Sue. "Because I'm clearly not that funny."

He doesn't need the Heimlich, so there's not much I can do beyond keeping an eye on him and continuing to eat his orgasmic eggs.

Is there any food he can't turn to magic?

I sip the coffee, and yep.

Also orgasmic.

"Forget the bakery," I tell him. "I'm moving to this tent, and you can just make me eggs and banana boats and coffee every day for the rest of my life."

I blink, then blink again as my eyes get hot, because I'm realizing I don't want to go to the bakery today.

And that makes me feel so horribly guilty, because Bailey and Mama need me.

There'll be plenty of time for what I *want* after what they *need*.

Mama didn't ask to go blind. I can't do this. I can't put my little whines ahead of hers just because it's been a few days since I've had a break.

And I had a break. I had a break just last night. And the night before.

A really *good* break.

Sue licks my ear.

Grady slips to my side on the log and pulls me close. "Running too hard," he says into my hair.

"I can sleep when I'm dead."

He snorts. "The Army was *not* good for you."

"My hardship discharge paperwork came through."

"On a Sunday morning?"

"No. Thursday. I've—I've been in denial. Because I don't know if I can run a bakery for the rest of my life, and now I don't have the one other thing I was *good* at. God, I sound like such a selfish cow."

"You are *not* a selfish cow. For one, you walked away from your own life to take care of your family. And for two, your moo is terrible."

"*What?*"

"Remember that year we went to the state fair and every time you saw a cow, you were like, *pppp-prrrrreeewwww*?"

He trumpets like an elephant, and I snort-laugh through my tears. "What are you talking about?"

"Oh, no. Don't play the *I don't remember* card. It was after freshman year, and those kids from Snyderville were all *my goat is better than your chicken* and you turned around and told them all that our elephant would kick their goat-riding chickens into the next county?"

Oh, shit.

I *did* do that.

That was a fun day. Cotton candy. Fair rides. Pretending the animals could talk to each other and making up conversations in the barn.

Cooper telling everyone who would listen that he was a cherry pie master and they needed to go to the food tent, even though it was Grady's cherry pie that won a blue ribbon.

God, I missed their whole family.

And now they hate me.

"I must've had one too many Red Bulls that day," I tell him.

"Or you're just fun to be around, and we have all kinds of good memories from high school."

"I don't want to go back to the bakery today," I whisper.

"So stay. Sue and I are just hanging out for a few more hours. Fishing. Swimming. Fantasizing about your breasts. You're welcome to join us."

"I don't think I'll be fantasizing about my own breasts."

"You should. They're spectacular."

Twigs crack behind us, and his head whips around. "Oh, shit. I think that's my mom," he whispers.

I don't think.

I just dive for the tent.

Sue *maas* indignantly.

And I have a split second of thinking *what the FUCK am I doing hiding from Grady's mom?* when I hear her voice.

"Grady? Hey, honey. I wasn't sure I'd find you here."

"You're up early."

His shadow moves to give her a hug, and I smile.

He still loves his mom.

That's so sweet.

But I'm the enemy.

That's not so sweet.

Sue paws at the tent.

Grady grabs his collar and drags him away. "You want some eggs?" he asks.

Mrs. Rock stops. "Is that—why do you have two plates?"

Haha, Ma, funny story—I'm madly in love with Annika, I always have been, and I'm moving to Sarcasm to help her until her mama's adjusted like the specialists all say she will.

I grab the pillow and stifle my sigh in it while he replies, "One for Sue."

"You spoil that goat so much." I can hear her smile, and it makes me want to smile too.

And then I want to sob, because she used to like me.

Before I tried to steal the banana pudding crown.

"What's up?" Grady asks his mom.

"Your grandfather got a call from that reporter in Copper Valley—the one you had a crush on when you were a teenager?"

"Thanks, Ma. Needed that memory this morning."

"She got wind of your bakery war with the Williamses and wants to cover it. Pop suggested a bake-off with celebrity judges over at the retreat center. A live competition. Star Knightly loved the idea, but she wants a neutral location."

"Ah, that's...great," Grady says.

DIRTY TALKING RIVAL

"I don't know if that Duh-Nuts crew has agreed to it yet, but they'd be silly not to. Think of the publicity."

"Yeah," he says slowly.

And I wait.

I wait for him to call it off. While I cower and hide from his mom in a tent not seven feet away.

We're both hot messes, aren't we?

"*Maaaa!*" Sue yells.

"Mind your manners, young man," Mrs. Rock says.

Sue snorts.

Pretty sure the goat's telling us all we're being idiots.

He's not wrong.

"Star at the news station needs an answer by noon, and you weren't answering your phone."

"I—we'll pack up and think about it," Grady tells her.

"Don't think too long. Your sister's internet shopping for a new dress, and Georgia's plotting an improvement to your banana pudding donuts."

"*What*? Those are fu—freaking perfect just as they are."

"They could be prettier. Those Duh-Nuts girls know how to make a pretty pastry. You don't want to fall behind."

"Ma—"

"I always liked Annika, but she's still a Sarcasm asshole. Can't change where you come from. And she stole your sister's banana pudding recipe."

I stifle a groan.

"I'm going to go walk around the lake. Such a lovely morning for it. Who's a good goat? Who's a good goat who wants to go on a walk with Grandma?"

"Ma," Grady sighs.

"What? You're not giving me *real* grandchildren, and I can't walk your sister's fish."

"You could put it in a wagon. Bowl and all."

"And your grandfather's parrot would decide to be pescatarian for the day. Foul-mouthed bird. Hmm. We'll have to keep it away from the reporters. Bye, honey. I'll bring my grand-goat back in a bit."

I stay in the tent with the pillow over my face until I hear the door zipper a minute later.

"Sorry," Grady says, offering me a hand to help me out of the tent. "She needs a new hobby."

"What are we doing?" I ask him.

"Camping."

"Grady."

He swipes a hand over his face. "We're using our rivalry to make your bakery more profitable while getting to know each other again without any pressure."

"That wasn't pressure?"

"Without open hostility," he corrects. "The Shipwreck-Sarcasm thing…they'll get over it. Eventually. It's just been like this for so long—"

"Yeah. I get it." I shake my hand loose. "Thanks for breakfast. I need to get back to Bailey and Mama. *Especially* if news crews are calling."

"Annika. We don't have to say yes."

"Yes, we do. We're at war, aren't we?"

He winces.

But he doesn't call off *the war*.

He might as well be doubling down.

"I have a plan," he tells me.

"I don't want a *plan*, Grady. I want a *life*." I sigh and squeeze my eyes shut, then push up on my tiptoes to kiss his cheek. "I'll talk to you later. Gotta go. Before your mother sees me."

Once more, he doesn't say *screw my family, you're important too*.

Nope.

So I head up to my car.

And drive back to Sarcasm.

Where I do the exact same thing I'm pissed at him about.

I pretend he's the enemy.

We are such a hot mess.

39

Grady

Monday morning dawns cloudy and rainy and ugly, but I'm still smiling while I sweet talk the lemon tarts that I'm decorating with fresh meringue and candied mint leaves.

"So creamy and silky and perfect. You know you're the queen. The goddess. The foodgasm to end all foodgasms with that perfect mix of tangy and sweet and—"

"If you don't stop talking to those tarts, I'mma have to quit," Georgia informs me. "Your smile says you got laid, but your mouth says she was really damn easy, because does that actually work for you?"

So phone sex late last night wasn't the same as the mind-blowing experience of having Annika firsthand Friday night, but it was still damn good.

"Nope," I say to Georgia. "The women hate it. So last night, I resorted to meerkat por—never mind. Workplace. You want to snap a picture of these beauties, or should I?"

She's been handling the morning rush while I finish the tarts and the goat puffs.

Yeah.

Goat puffs.

I made cream puffs with goat faces so I can up my Instagram game this morning.

Or possibly lower it by seventy million points.

They're ugly-ass goats.

Bailey's pie cupcakes next to the killer brownies that I'm telling myself are inspired by Annika's Friday evening trip up to Thorny Rock Mountain make my goats look like something a kindergartener did.

Georgia huffs. "You are *not* taking pictures of those for Instagram. Are you *trying* to lose this bakery war?"

"They looked better in my head."

"You are so off your game."

"Don't knock the goat puffs until you try them. Next. Level. Eat one and tell me they suck. Go on."

She eyeballs the full tray of double cream puffs with white chocolate piping for horns and dark chocolate for eyes and nose, then takes one and bites into it.

"Ohmygah," she moans.

"See?"

"Wha di ya puh inee?"

"What did I put in these? Secret ingredient. Creamy, right?"

"Perfection," she says before shoving the rest of it in her mouth, then dropping one in her apron pocket.

For later, I presume.

"Fine. We can sell these. But we're going to have to give out samples, because nobody's buying these on looks alone."

"They would've a month ago."

"A month ago you wouldn't have painted psycho ram faces on them."

"Rams? They're goats."

"Dude. Stick with the taste. Your decorating game is shit."

I can decorate a wedding cake that would make my mother weep. My decorating game is *fine*.

I also know how to fuck it up really well when I want to.

"Okay. Not pissed at you anymore for ugly pastries. By the way, the reporter from Copper Valley is here and wants to talk pre-game."

"*Fuck*. Dammit, Georgia. Now?"

She grins. "Five minutes ago, actually. That's what you get for trying to decorate booby cream puffs like goats."

I glance at the cream puffs again, and—huh.

Yeah, maybe I did have boobs on the brain.

I finish up the lemon tarts and wash my hands fast before heading out to the dining room, where Star Knightly, the special reports news anchor for Copper Valley's News Team Twenty-Five, is interviewing my customers about who they think will win in the bakery contest that we're still negotiating.

I don't want to talk to a reporter this morning.

Not about my rivalry with Annika's family.

"Ah, there he is. Grady Rock." Star turns a practiced smile on me, and my gut goes tight like I got into a batch of whipped cream that turned. "The man of the hour. Your fans here tell me you're going to crush the competition the way your brother crushes baseballs."

"We'll all be winners when we're eating cookies and donuts," I tell her.

Like I'm suddenly the motivational speaker of bakers.

Hard to remember to be an asshole when I'm still riding the high of having Annika toss and turn her way across the tent Saturday night until she finally settled in as my little spoon and stayed there, peacefully, the rest of the night.

I want to take care of her.

Not tear her down.

Star studies me, still smiling, but I don't entirely trust her.

"So the people who love to eat are the real winners?"

"Aren't they always? I mean, when the food tastes good."

"You don't think your competitor bakes good food?"

"Mine's better. Of course." I need to shut up.

Or one of my ovens needs to erupt in flames, or one of my customers needs to choke so I can leap in and save him and get rid of this gnawing, ugly guilt that's probably curdling the cream in my goat puffs right now.

Food senses things.

Star is still smiling at me. "Tell me about your specialty."

"His banana pudding donuts," Pop interjects for me.

For once, Long Beak Silver isn't with him.

Good.

Bailey would probably call the health department and roll that video for them if he was.

"These goat puffs are going to give them a run for their money though," Georgia says behind me.

"I like his long johns," Sloane calls from one of the

tables, where she's having pastries with Georgia's grandpa, who's been the local doc in Shipwreck since before I was born. She adds a wink, and Star's brows lift almost imperceptibly.

She's not the only one who notices.

The general murmur around the dining room from all the regulars tells me exactly what's about to get texted six ways to Sunday all across town today.

Sloane has a thing for Grady! Let's see if he's smart enough to do something about it!

"If you like his long johns, you should try his fritters," Georgia tells her.

"Ah, young love," Star says, and I don't know if she's talking about me and Sloane or me and Georgia, but either way, she's wrong. "You'll be cheering on Crow's Nest in the baking contest?"

"As if I could ever cheer against Grady," Sloane replies.

Pop beams.

Cooper walks in the door.

And pandemonium breaks loose.

"Whoa. What's with reporters in all the bakeries? And where's my banana pudding donut? A slugger's gotta eat. Dude. You made boob puffs. Awesome. But I've never seen nipples like that. Are they alien boobs?"

Georgia slides the tray of goat puffs into the display case, then holds out a double cream puff to him. "Try it."

My brother swallows it whole, but his brows shoot up and he moans in appreciation. "Holy fudgenuggets."

"Good?" I ask him.

He reaches across the display case to fist-bump me. "Like heaven in my mouth. You're going places, bro. You're going places."

Star's camerawoman gets the whole thing.

"Boob puffs?" Star asks.

"I, ah, was trying to up my Instagram game. They're goats."

"Oh, like Sarcasm's softball team is called the GOATs?"

"No, because I have a pet goat. He's a rescue. Name's Sue."

"Sue's the best goat in the whole world," Cooper says solemnly. "Gives good advice for hitting baseballs."

Star melts into a puddle of Cooper worship at his feet.

He winks at me.

It's a *you're such a dumbass* wink with a shade of *got your back so you can go text your real lady, dude*.

Yeah.

My *real* lady.

Who wasn't too thrilled that Bailey and Maria said yes to the cooking contest before she got home from camping with me yesterday morning.

I slip into the kitchen while Georgia's distracted with selling cream puffs, and I pull out my phone.

There's already a text waiting from Annika.

No words.

Just a GIF.

Of that dude from that cartoon movie who can blow his top off with flames shooting out of his brain.

I text her back a picture of Sue picking his nose with his tongue.

She doesn't reply.

And I hope I haven't just fucked up the best thing I've ever had in my life.

Again.

40

Annika

Duh-Nuts is a complete and total zoo.

There were so many requests for more bubble waffles over the weekend that we made a bubble waffle breakfast bowl this morning.

Correction:

Bailey made a bubble waffle breakfast bowl, with some kind of fancy cheese in the bubble waffle mix and then filled the cones with scrambled eggs, sausage, chives, and more cheese.

I've made so many new pots of coffee, I've lost track.

Our unicorn long johns are almost gone.

The cookie bars that were supposed to last past the lunch crowd have disappeared.

Mama's sitting at one of the tables chatting with anyone who stops by to say hi. She's attempting to crochet again today, and she's making solid progress on a potholder while she chats with an Asian woman I don't recognize and her son.

Tomorrow, Mama wants to go bowling.

And Roger insists he won't let her back out of it for anything less than nuclear disaster or one of those stomach viruses that requires her to be within seven feet of a toilet at all times.

This is good.

Good good.

Except Bailey starts school in ten days.

Ten.

Days.

I have no idea what I'm going to do without her, and I still don't have a lead on a baker.

She even told me I screwed up our weekly supply order this morning.

And she was right.

If she hadn't looked over my shoulder, we would've had ten times the butter we needed and a fifth of the flour.

And in three hours, we're playing host to *another* reporter wanting to talk about how much we hate Shipwreck and how we're going to bury them in a baking contest that will be taped live in a television studio so Bailey can't actually do the baking for me.

I'm going to have to memorize a script and then "accidentally" set fire to my fallen crème brûlée cupcakes, because disasters sell cooking shows.

Bailey told me so.

Except Bailey's going back to school the day after taping.

I'm not going to hyperventilate.

And if I say it enough to myself, maybe it'll be true.

The front door swings open, the bells jingle, and three more people I've never seen in my life stroll into Duh-Nuts.

We've had so many people coming over from Snyderville and Cedarton and even up from Copper Valley, just to check out the bakery after the *Virginia Blue* story went live on their website over the weekend, that the dining room is mostly full of strangers.

Bailey and I serve up more coffee and bubble waffles with eggs, and thank the bakery gods, I can scramble eggs without fucking it up this morning, so we're managing to hold on and get everyone's orders without too much delay.

The thing about customers is, I can't pre-schedule them on my calendar, and I can't predict when someone's going to walk in the door with an order for a dozen cupcakes or a seven-tiered wedding cake, or if they just want to ask if we use organic ingredients in our soft serve.

I'm really not built for this. I like to know what my day will bring. I like schedules and calendars and numbers.

But I can do this for a few more months.

I can.

I have to.

"Annika," Mama calls. "Annika, come here."

Bailey shoos me away from the counter, and I join Mama at the table with the lady and her son.

"Coffee?" I ask them.

"Annika, this is Amy Tanaka. She's here to interview for the baker position."

Amy smiles at me with warm brown eyes. She's petite, holding one of the white ceramic coffee mugs that now has a lipstick stain on it, and I swear she's trying to tell me something meaningful before she ever opens her mouth.

"I saw your ad in the *Grandview Rockwell Times*," she says.

I stare at her.

"The *Grandview. Rockwell. Times*," she repeats slowly.

I have no idea what she's talking about, which means, yet again, someone on drugs is trying to apply for a position in my bakery.

And this time, she got to Mama first.

Great.

"Bubble waffle?" I ask.

She laughs and shakes her head. "I graduated second in my culinary arts management program at the Art Institute of Virginia six years ago. The *shithead* who stole my first place slot needs to go down. You're at war with him. I want in."

She glances at Mama, in her dark sunglasses, her face pointed roughly toward the kitchen door, where Roger is working on a leak we have under the sink.

And then Amy winks at me.

To quote Bailey, Oh em gee.

"The...*Grandview Rockwell Times*...sent you?" I repeat.

"Sure. Let's go with that." Her glance briefly travels to her son, who doesn't look much older than seven, but whose nose is buried in the thickest Harry Potter book. "I'm in the middle of a D-I-V-O-R-C-E that is U-G-L-Y and I need a new job outside the city. I want four weeks of paid vacation, I'll work weekends when I don't have my son, but not weekends when I do. I can start tomorrow if you can find me a babysitter."

While I continue to gape, my mind whirling, because

did Grady really just send me a baker?, she pulls out her phone.

"My resume," she adds dryly.

There she is.

Amy Tanaka. Arms crossed in a white chef jacket in front of a massive wedding cake at the Madison Towers Hotel in downtown Copper Valley.

"You're…a pastry chef?"

"I'm a goddess."

"She likes baking cookies best," Mama tells me. "Sugar cookies. The joy is in the decorating."

Amy nods to the kitchen. "If you'll let me, I'll prove it."

"Um…I need to check your references quick."

She hides another smile behind her coffee mug. "By all means."

I duck into the kitchen and text Grady. *Amy Tanaka?*

His response is almost immediate. *I hate her. Mostly because I spent four years wanting to BE her. She's the only person in the world who can out-bake me.*

Such ego. Only *one* person in the world who can out-bake him.

My phone buzzes again with a new message.

It's not egotistical if it's true.

It won't be true for long.

Not if Bailey keeps up her pace.

But we have a few years before Bailey's ready to fully take over. So I lean out of the kitchen and gesture Amy back.

Her son stays with Mama while Bailey shoots me a *what the hell is this?* look.

Amy stops in the kitchen doorway, her gaze sweeping over the complete and utter disaster of dirty dishes, spilled flour, splashed grease, oven door half-open, Roger grunting under the leaky sink, and she smiles. "This kitchen is loved."

"Not necessarily by me," I mutter.

She laughs. "So that's the story. Show me to your vanilla, and I'll prep you some scones that'll change your world."

Bailey darts into the kitchen. "What are you doing?" she asks me.

"Interview."

Bailey looks Amy up and down.

Amy does the same to Bailey.

"Where are you from?" Bailey asks.

"*Bailey*," I hiss.

"Virginia Beach. My *grandparents* are from Japan. Where are you from?"

"I'm from Sarcasm and my family tree is full of branches from all over the world that fell off, and good riddance. I don't care where your grandparents are from. I just wanted to make sure you weren't from Shipwreck. Is that your kid sitting with my mama?"

"She's going back to school next week," I tell Amy quickly.

I need a baker.

I need a baker who gets along with Bailey, but first, I need a baker.

"That's my son," Amy tells her. "Baxter."

"Does he bake?"

"Not yet. Do you?"

Bailey looks at me. "I don't know. Do I bake, Annika?"

"She's the queen baker around here," I tell Amy. "And way more agreeable than she comes off at first."

"Food Network?" Amy asks, ignoring me.

"YouTube and Pinterest first," Bailey replies.

"Internet generation." She rolls her eyes.

"This is *our* bakery," Bailey says.

"I can teach you how to make chocolate croissants that will make your enemies weep, and if I wanted to actually have the trouble of owning my own bakery, I'd be taking over the Madison Towers Hotel in Copper Valley right now. Marry the first time for money. Divorce settlements are way better so you can enjoy the hell out of it when you finally find love. Or so I assume. I don't have actual proof that real love exists."

Bailey's lips part, and she shoots me another look.

This one clearly says she can't decide if she's impressed, intimidated, or scared.

"Also, I'm sorry you can't do this with your mom," Amy adds quietly. "I know that sucks."

Bailey blinks. Her eyes go shiny, she blinks again, and she turns and leaves the kitchen.

"I lost my mom to a car accident three weeks before graduation." Amy's voice is even softer now. "Failed my final exams. Instructors said a good baker could work through pain. Would've failed my practicum, except Grady bailed my ass out. He deserved that number one spot. And here he is, bailing me out again when my life turns to shit."

I'm still not usually a hugger.

But I wrap my arms around her anyway.

I don't need the scones to know.

We just got ourselves a baker.

41

GRADY

I'M ON MY COUCH, Sue passed out with his snout in my lap, watching the Fireballs play their first home game in a week and a half and nodding off over an empty bowl of Lucky Charms topped with chocolate milk when I hear the sound of tires crunching over the gravel behind my house.

I don't think anything of it, because the athlete's foot spray commercial between innings is blending into the dream I'm drifting into about Sue trying out to be the new Fireballs mascot, which entails him shooting flaming boogers out his nose.

I snort-laugh in my sleep and wake myself, but something's not right.

There's a weird tapping coming from the back door.

Sue grunts.

I figure it's just the flowers, realize they don't actually have fingers and mouths, and can't tap dance across the sidewalk, much less tap on the back door, and I bolt upright just as the back door clicks open.

"'Lo?" I call.

"You found me a baker," Annika whispers behind me, and I'm suddenly fully awake.

I leap up.

Sue falls off the couch and gives us both an earful until he sees Annika slipping in from the kitchen, and then he charges.

She laughs and scratches him all over the head while he tries to leap on her. "Aww, who's a good boy? You're a good boy, aren't you?"

"You're here," I say, stating the obvious like a dumbass.

"*You sent me a baker,*" she repeats.

"I know one or two. Sometimes they're looking for changes."

The bags are heavy under her eyes, but everything else about her is sparkling. She straightens, and her loose hair falls to land at nipple level. Her shoulders are relaxed, her spine straight, her joy shining.

Instead of her normal leggings, she's in short jean shorts topped with a peach tank top that hugs her breasts and shows off her slender but strong arms.

And she's in sandals.

With pink-tipped toes.

Pink.

Annika.

But it's the giant smile curving her lush lips that sends me over the edge.

I did that.

I made her happy.

She gives Sue a final pat before closing the distance

between us to wrap her arms around my neck. Our bodies line up, thigh to thigh, my suddenly aching cock against her soft belly, her round breasts pressed to my ribs.

"Hi," she whispers while Sue prances around us.

"You're so fucking gorgeous."

"You are deliciously sexy when you're tired."

"I'm not tired."

"Thank you for saving my bacon."

I slide my hands around her waist to sink my fingers into her ass. "I like your bacon."

Sue bleats in glee and prances in a circle around the living room.

Annika's lips cover mine, and I just keep falling.

She snuck into enemy territory to come kiss me. To share her happiness.

To bury her fingers in my hair and stroke her tongue into my mouth and press her pelvis into my pirate mast.

I'm gonna marry this woman.

Swear I am.

And that's before she pulls out of the kiss to lick her way down my jaw, her fingers trailing down my body to push my shorts down over my hips, freeing my erection.

"Annika—"

"Sshh."

She drops to her knees, licks me from balls to tip, and my eyes cross.

"*Maaa!*" Sue cries.

"Bedroom," Annika orders, and fuck me.

The goat dashes around the corner like he doesn't want to watch.

"You—" I start, but she licks me again, and I forget how to use words.

"Somebody's been a very good boy," she whispers just before taking me into her mouth.

It's bliss.

It's bliss frosted on a cupcake of euphoria. A strangled moan catches in my throat. She hums on my cock, the vibrations making my hips jerk, and goosebumps break out over my entire body.

Her mouth is hot and wet, and she's sucking me deeper, until I hit the back of her throat, and *fuck*, it's heaven.

No barriers.

Her tongue rubs the underside of my dick. I fist my hands in her thick hair while she works me over, bobbing up and down, and it takes every ounce of control to not pump into her mouth.

My balls are tight. My cock is hard as steel.

Her fingers skim my ass and trail down my hamstrings, she hums again, and I grip her hair tighter in warning. "Annika—I'm gonna—"

Instead of letting me go, she sucks harder, and white-hot lightning streaks through me as I come down her throat.

She licks and sucks until I've spent everything I have in me, and doesn't let go until my legs are wobbling. Her smile and sparkling eyes as she carefully tucks me back into my shorts are everything.

Everything.

"Sit," she whispers.

My knees give out, and I tumble back onto the couch.

"*Maaa?*" Sue asks from the bedroom.

Annika swings a leg over my lap and settles on me,

peppering soft kisses on my jaw while my tongue tries to remember how to form words.

My arms though—they're doing good with remembering how to hold her.

"Thank you," she whispers again.

"Thank *you*," I manage.

"I can't stay long. Bailey's at volleyball try-outs and I have to pick her up in thirty minutes. But I wanted to see you."

Her pussy is pressing into my crotch, and I'm getting hard again. "You're welcome anytime."

"I miss you."

My grip around her tightens. "Right here, Annika."

She doesn't answer.

She doesn't have to.

I know what she means.

She has to leave. I have to stay. And neither of us know when she'll get her next break so we can sneak off together.

"*Maaa?*" Sue asks.

Annika laughs into my neck as the goat hops up onto the couch and tries to squeeze between us.

"Back, you crazy animal," I tell him.

He licks my ear and sticks a hoof way too close to the goods.

"Sit," Annika orders.

And the fucking goat sits.

"Are you kidding me?" I ask him.

He licks his nose, then snorts on me.

Annika laughs, right there in my arms, and yeah, I'd let my goat snort on me every day if that's what it took to hear that music.

I'd find her a new baker every day too.

Anything to make her happy.

Anything.

She's everything that's been missing from my life the last ten years.

All of her. Her drive. Her dedication.

Her family.

Her chaos.

She's my happiness.

And I'm going to do my damnedest to be her happiness too.

42

Annika

I've never been at a television studio before, and after today, I don't know that I'll ever want to be in one again.

They have a kitchen set up with two work stations, so Grady and I are physically separated on the set.

And then there are the three bajillion cameras aimed at us from all angles, the makeup they insisted on slathering on our faces—Mama's too—and the small obligatory crowd sitting in like we're on a talk show, but not a big one.

I'm sweating harder than I did during basic training ten years ago, and I haven't even screwed anything up yet.

"How are you feeling about your chances of beating the Crow's Nest team today?" Star Knightly asks me while Amy and Bailey fly around our workstation prepping me for making killer brownie donuts.

"*Chance* isn't something I dabbled with in the Army," I

tell Star. "Preparation and war planning, though..." I shrug, even though I feel like a total ass saying exactly what Grady and I talked about saying when discussing all the smack-talk. "Let's just say we've got this."

She smiles.

I'm pretty sure she eats conflict for breakfast.

But I might not be blowing smoke about having this contest in the bag. Or at least I won't embarrass myself. We've done seven dry runs, and I've actually turned out three batches of edible baked goods now.

I can make killer brownie donuts that we'll decorate with unicorn horns and the special white chocolate Duh-Nuts logo that we made with a mold Amy talked us into last week.

She's an angel.

An angel who can cook and who's taken so much pressure off of Bailey—and me—and who's getting along fabulously with Mama, who's starting to experiment with some new measuring tools that her mobility specialist found for her so she can do more than knead dough and roll cookie balls.

She's seated at the end of the counter where I'll be working, eyes shielded from the bright lights by her special sunglasses, proudly wearing a Duh-Nuts T-shirt in lavender, her face turning this way and that, and I imagine she's trying to catch snippets of conversations and sniff the brownie donut ingredients.

Roger, Liliana, and Birch are in our section of the stands to cheer us on.

Grady and Georgia are prepping their own station across the kitchen while his family lurks nearby.

Grady's grandparents, in full pirate regalia. His parents. Tillie Jean. Cooper.

Sue.

He brought Sue.

I give myself a minute to imagine that halfway through the contest, Grady drops his bowls and spoons and rolling pin and announces to the world that he's bowing out, not because he can't win, but because he loves me and that's worth more than any bakery.

And I'd drop my killer brownie donuts and rush past the judges' tables—where there are some *seriously* intimidating judges—to throw myself at him, kiss him passionately, and tell him that I quit the contest too, because he's worth more than chocolate.

I don't know where we'd live, because Mama can't live by herself, and Bailey still thinks Grady is the devil, and he's probably right that everyone would lose interest in coming into our bakeries for gossip because *he made me cheesecake* isn't nearly as juicy as *he stole our galaxy donuts and made them rainbow donuts*.

But I wouldn't have to sneak over to his house under cover of night like I have every night for the last week.

We could go on dates.

Take Mama to Cannon Bowl in Shipwreck, because their bumpers are new and she had so much fun bowling last weekend at the game center just outside Snyderville, except for the part where the bumpers broke and she got too many gutter balls.

Grady could come over and cook us dinner while Bailey plays fetch with Sue.

I could bake cookie bricks and offer to feed them to

Pop's parrot if he doesn't clean up his language, though I suspect Sue would actually enjoy them.

The softball rivalry next summer could be *fun* instead of *mean*.

We could unite the two towns.

We could be *not a fucking secret*.

Bakeries be damned.

"Annika?"

I blink at Star.

She just asked me a question. I think.

Shit.

"Yes?"

She looks over at Grady's crew, then back at me. "You two were best friends," she says.

I'm supposed to say *Yeah, we WERE*, but I don't want to talk smack about Grady.

I want to tell her that he gives the best neck rubs in Virginia.

That he insists on 2% chocolate milk instead of whole, because he has to run two fewer miles a week to keep in shape if he cuts out the whole milk.

That sometimes he falls asleep with his goat on his couch, and if I could put that picture I snapped of them three nights ago as the background on my phone, I'd basically have a permanent smile on my face.

But instead, I say something Amy has coached me on. "Yes, we're making killer brownie donuts. It's an original Duh-Nuts recipe, served with fresh whipped cream and a salted caramel truffle, because there's no such thing as too much of a good thing. You really went all-out with the judges, and I'm having a complete brain fart about who they all are, because cameras make me nervous."

Dammit.

That'll undoubtedly make the cut for the show news, but it's better than me calling Grady names.

I don't want to call him names.

He's talked me off six ledges this past week, and given me three times that many orgasms.

At least.

Star and I both look at the judges' table, where there are two men roughly the size of mountains poking at each other over the head of a third man who would be impressively sized if he weren't between the twins.

Although the middle guy's chin cleft keeps sparkling when the light hits him right, which is weird.

And the twins are weirdly familiar. I think I've seen them on commercials for deodorant or jock itch cream or Sharpies.

Sharpies?

Why am I thinking of Sharpies?

Anyway.

At the other table, there are two women—I think one's a billionaire, but not Honey Wellington, who was disqualified from judging since she moved to Sarcasm, which is taking sides, obviously, just like Cooper judging would've been—and there's another guy who's also familiar, but I can't place why.

"You don't recognize the Berger twins?" Star asks me.

I look back at the two identical mountains and shake my head.

"Professional hockey players," she tells me. "They're doing a charity golf fundraiser here in Copper Valley tomorrow, so we talked them into stopping here this morning before the festivities kick off. Zeus and Ares, with

Chase Jett between them. He owns an organic grocery store chain. No pressure or anything, of course."

I croak out an answer, because impressing a billionaire *grocery store owner* could mean capital investment for expanding operations and setting Bailey up to run a Duh-Nuts empire with her creations mass-produced and distributed around the nation, and oh my god, I need a paper bag.

Star points to the other table. "Then we have Daisy Carter-Kincaid. You've *surely* heard of her."

Only because Liliana squealed my ear off in Duh-Nuts yesterday. *Daisy Carter-Kincaid!! She's one of Honey's sort-of friends. She's so fucking awesome. Wouldn't YOU love to have a private jet that takes you to Europe for flings with Frenchmen and Spaniards all the time? I swear, I want to be her when I grow up. Plus—oh my god, her fashion sense. It's so DAISY. And she gives negative fucks. That's better than no fucks, you know?*

I nod to Star, and she continues down the line. "Then we have Fatima Fayad, owner of Kefta, Copper Valley's hottest Moroccan restaurant at the moment, and then Edison Rogers. He's the bassist for Half-Cocked Heroes and also happened to be in town this week."

Holy *shit*.

"That's quite the line-up of judges for a small-town bakery war," I say.

"The stars lined up." She smiles brighter. "Quite literally. Are you ready?"

Bailey and Amy both nod at me.

My stomach twists itself in knots, but I nod too.

If I fuck it all up, it's good for ratings, and Amy prepped a back-up tray of both killer brownie donuts and unicorn cookies—and they're adorable, decorated like hipster unicorns in big glasses and beanies and beards—and Bailey has an emergency batch of her banana pudding chilling in the industrial fridge.

So we'll still have actual food for judging, if we need it.

Or if we need to bribe anyone at the studio.

"Any last words for Grady Rock?" Amy asks me.

Eighteen cameras and every person, bug, ghost, and goat in the studio turn to stare at me.

"May the best baker win," I tell them all.

Star grins like I've just fed her conflict meter.

Grady fake-growls at me and mouths *you're going down*.

And even though I rolled out of his bed with jelly legs and whisker burn and an extremely satisfied vagina not six hours ago, I want to throw a fifty-pound bag of flour at his head.

Claim me.

Claim me and love me.

How much longer do I have to be a secret?

Considering he murmured, *I love having you to myself* as I was climbing out of his bed this morning and texted to ask if the bubble waffles were helping our profits enough, probably a long time.

"Judges, ready?" Amy asks the panel.

"I'm always ready," one of the hockey twins says loudly. "Bring on the food."

"Can't argue with that," Chase Jett says.

The other twin grunts and nods.

Daisy Carter-Kincaid, whose short, curly platinum hair was purple in the pictures Liliana showed me yesterday, props her Manolos up on the table, making her short skirt rise almost indecently high, and a smile that's equal parts *I own the world* and *I fucking love the world* lights her face. "Impress me, peasants. Give me a reason to get another good workout in before I fly back to Miami."

She winks at the twins like they're the workout she wants, and I swear, I get a little wet in the panties.

I want half her confidence when I grow up. And I wouldn't mind half her ability to give zero fucks.

Edison Rogers snaps his dirty blond head away from her cleavage and nods to Star when he realizes she's looking at him.

"I was born ready for this," he says in a soft Texas drawl.

Bailey squeaks behind me. "Annika! That's *Edison Rogers*! How did I not see *Edison Rogers*?"

He turns a smile and a relatively innocent wink her way, and I decide I don't have to kill him so long as the only thing he offers her is an autograph. He has to be twice her age, at least.

"Fatima?" Star says.

"I am ready," she replies with a nod.

"Thirty minutes on the clock," Star says, "and…Go!"

Controlled chaos erupts at our workstation. Bailey shoves oil at me. Amy hands me a bowl full of eggs. Mama asks if I have the special vanilla.

My hands are shaky and sweating and I almost accidentally double the oil, but Amy catches me in time. If anyone's noticed she's the same Amy Tanaka who was second in command at the Madison Towers Hotel's kitchens not two weeks ago, they don't mention it.

Grady and Georgia are joking and moving together seamlessly.

Like a team.

Like *she's* the one he should be sleeping with.

I splatter an egg all over the counter and stifle a good *fuck*, because there are cameras all over the place, and I don't need the whole world thinking I'm teaching my thirteen-year-old sister to curse like a soldier.

Or like a pirate.

I like pirates.

I've watched *Pirates of the Caribbean* seventeen times. I went to a pirate festival on the Texas coast last fall and didn't tell Bailey and Mama, and only partly because the nostalgia hit me too hard.

I'm not saying I broke up with my last boyfriend after that, but I'm not saying I didn't either.

"Annika! Too much sugar," Bailey hisses.

I jump, making me add *even more* sugar to the mix.

"It's okay," Amy murmurs. She directs me through increasing the whole recipe by half on the fly while Grady and Georgia are already moving on to—wait.

He said they were making banana pudding donuts.

But those aren't banana pudding donuts.

Those are muffins.

"Yo, Rogers," one of the hockey twins yells to his fellow judge. "You got any sisters?"

"Oh em gee, Edison Rogers is watching us," Bailey whispers.

"Are those hockey boys as tall as they look on TV?" Mama asks.

"You watch hockey?" I ask her.

"Annika, more whipping," Amy instructs while she plops a bag of flour up on the counter.

I go back to whisking the eggs and oil and sugar together. "Mama. Since when do you like hockey?"

"Since that goalie came home to the Thrusters. The one from Copper Valley. What's his name?"

"The one who wrote that really awful book that you can download on Amazon?" Bailey says.

"You people seriously can't concentrate at all, can you?" Amy mutters.

"It's the cameras. It makes us nerv—"

I cut myself off with a squeak, because I didn't look closely at the cameras.

But now I am.

Specifically, *behind* the cameras.

My blood turns into dry ice, quietly steam-freezing my bones and muscles.

My father is running one of the cameras.

His camera is trained on Grady, but he keeps shooting a look at Mama out of the corner of his eye.

"Annika?" someone says near me.

"Oh em gee, *too much cocoa!*" someone else says.

His gaze darts from Mama to me, catching me watching him. He goes ruddy in the cheeks and I realize I have his eyes.

Me.

His dirty little secret.

I have his eyes.

I don't *want* his eyes.

He quickly looks away, but I know he knows.

I know he knows that I know *exactly* who he is.

Bailey doesn't know him.

Of course Amy doesn't.

Mama would, but she can't see him, and for once, I'm glad.

I'm *so* glad she can't see.

Star Knightly is back. My body is flushing with heat and freezing up and I have to *bake donuts*, and here's put-together Star Knightly, arriving just in time to see me completely fucking up this recipe because now there are *two* men in this room who are keeping me a secret.

"How's it going, Team Duh-Nuts?"

"It's going *Duh*," Bailey says brightly. "As in *duh*, fantastic."

I start stirring the flour and cocoa into the wet stuff, like we practiced.

It feels off.

Like I have too much baggage in the dough.

I bend over the big bowls and whisper a quick, "*I love you, you're beautiful, and you're going to love your new curves*," but it doesn't help.

Georgia cracks up at the next station.

Grady's grinning like it's something he said.

Of course it is.

He probably told his muffins he can't wait to caress their beautiful mounds.

"You don't like to talk about the time you were friends with Grady Rock," Star says to me.

"Ancient history."

"Plus," Bailey interjects with a sweet smile, "who wants to be friends with someone who picks a fight with a blind lady?"

"Grady's brother told me he had a huge crush on you in high school," Star presses.

"Because Annika's fabulous," Bailey says before I can open my mouth again. I keep stirring. "He probably still has a crush on her but can't handle that he can't have her. That's how guys operate. Like cavemen."

"Bailey," Mama chides.

Amy's smirking as she drops the cake donut pan onto the countertop next to me and pulls out the bowl of chocolate chips, peanut butter chips, and caramel bits that'll go into the donuts.

"Grady Rock was a very nice boy in high school," Mama tells Star. "So polite. Much less cocky than his brother."

"Cooper earned that swagger," his nana calls from the Shipwreck side of the stage.

Cooper winks and keeps a firm grip on Sue's leash. The goat's trying to get to our side of the studio.

My sperm donor studiously ignores us.

So does Grady.

And I suddenly see my future.

Me, unexpectedly pregnant with Grady's child.

Him, moving on to someone his parents approve of.

And all that dry ice in my veins suddenly explodes when hot lava crashes over it.

I start flinging brownie batter into a piping bag while Mama extolls Grady's virtues from *before* when he turned into a Shipwreck shithead and Grady ignores us and the louder of the two massive hockey twins checks me out and Amy very quietly asks me if I'm okay.

I'm not okay.

I want to cry.

And I want to go shoot something.

I had to stay current on firearms training in the Army, though I was a paper pusher and not in the infantry, and I haven't wanted to shoot something since I can't remember when.

But I do.

I want to go run ten miles and do seven thousand sit-ups and then shoot something until my arm's about to fall off.

Because if my body hurts and my ears are ringing and I'm back in badass Army chick mode, then maybe my heart won't hurt.

Maybe I won't *care* that Grady won't publicly admit he has feelings for me.

That we've been seeing each other.

That it's like the last ten years didn't happen, and we're just as tight as we were in high school.

Except we're not.

I'm his dirty little secret.

I keep telling myself that it's because he wants my bakery to do well, but his damn sure isn't hurting for mine doing well.

And you know what?

I fucking deserve better.

43

Grady

I can't decide if Annika's game face is next level or if she had a rough morning, but her donuts smell like heaven, and I couldn't be more fucking proud.

She's in that ruffled Duh-Nuts apron, standing by her donuts while the judges sample both of our creations.

Hers are prettier with their unicorn faces piped on and that awesome Duh-Nuts logo on the bottom.

Mine probably taste better.

"Dude. Dude, try this shit." Zeus Berger shoves the plate with Annika's donuts to the guy sitting between him and his twin. "It's like having a climax in my mouth."

"Berger, you know I love you, but you can keep that to yourself," Chase Jett replies.

"Eat that donut—oh, 'scuse me, ma'am—I mean this *duh-nut* and tell me you wouldn't take this thing for a ride in the Bratwurst Wagon."

"You mean on?" Daisy Carter-Kincaid asks.

Zeus wiggles his brows at her. "You. Me. Parking lot. Bratwurst Wagon. Ten minutes. I'll show you *in*."

"We're going to have to cut this," Star says to the producer.

"You invited us, baby. You invited us," Zeus replies.

"Food," Ares grunts.

"That's right, dude. Eat the food. One finger for the donuts, two for the muffins, right, big guy?" Zeus says.

Ares shoves the donut and the muffin in his mouth together and holds up ten fingers and one foot.

Zeus snaps his fingers at Annika. "Hey, Duh-Nut lady? My brother wants twelve dozen of these nutgasms."

"Muffins are good," Chase Jett says. "Good pudding."

"Say that to my sister, and we'll end you," Zeus says.

All three men crack up.

"He's right," Georgia murmurs to me while the judging goes off the rails and Star stands there seeming at a loss. "She invited them. And they have awful taste. Is this contest rigged?"

I cut a glance at Annika.

She's not smiling.

Her mama's cracking up. Bailey's giggling. Amy's clearly holding it in.

But Annika looks like she hasn't heard a word.

Something's up.

Something bad.

"Daisy, Fatima, Edison? Any opinions."

"This banana pudding muffin is better than anything I ever had in Texas," Edison says.

He's rubbing his finger over the plate to get the last of the pudding, and licking it off.

"Bananas are too obvious." Daisy's sniffing the donut. "Give a girl chocolate, you give her life. Then your banana doesn't have to do all the work."

"Fatima?" Star asks.

"I'm fond of both," Fatima says. She's soft-spoken, but also the only one of the judges who regularly works with food in a professional capacity. "The pudding is creamy and perfectly flavored, the muffin moist, and the whipped topping complements it all very well. But the donut—the donut is simply decadent."

"You. Cooper's brother." Zeus Berger points at me with the extra donut one of the producers just gave him. He takes a huge bite. "Bro, you find a woman who can bake duh-nuts like this, you don't fight with her. You marry her."

Marry her.

My head snaps to look at Annika.

Her wide eyes meet mine for the first time all morning, and *yeah*.

Yeah.

I'm gonna marry her.

I'm gonna marry her. Take her on a honeymoon. Bring her home.

Do her baking for her.

Keep her bed warm at night.

Her yard too.

The lake.

Our tent.

We'll get six more goats and I'll help her figure out what she wants to be now that she doesn't have to be a baker anymore.

"He doesn't need to marry a woman who can bake,

you scabby sea bass," Pop barks. "He can bake everything he needs himself."

Cooper leaps between Pop and the giant hockey player, who's rising to his feet. "He's ninety-five," Cooper says to Zeus. "Going senile."

"Ain't what your grandma said about me this morning," Pop replies.

Annika's still staring at me.

"Final votes, judges?" Star says quickly.

Bailey steps between me and Annika, blocking my view of her, and says something I can't hear.

"What the hell's going on?" Georgia mutters beside me. "You don't still like her, do you?"

"*Maaaa!*" Sue hollers, and while Pops and Cooper are distracted, my goat takes off like a shot past my kitchen station to leap up and snag as many donuts as he can get in his mouth.

"Sue! Get down," Annika hisses.

Loudly.

For the whole studio to hear.

Bailey misses the fact that Annika knows my goat's name, because she's leaping to Maria's side, playing protector in case Sue goes rabid and attacks the blind lady. Annika's tugging on Sue's collar.

"Sue! Bad goat." I reach them and grab for his collar too. My hand connects with Annika's, and she snatches hers back like I've burned her.

I jerk my head up.

Oh, fuck.

Shiny eyes. Wobbly chin. Death glare that says she's pissed she's about to cry and pissed that it's my fault.

I open my mouth to tell her I'm sorry Sue ate her donuts when I'm suddenly lifted two feet in the air.

Again.

Except this time, the voice in my ear isn't Roger's.

Nope.

It's distinctly chocolate-scented and full of angry hockey grunt.

"Stay on your own side," Ares Berger says. "Goat says chocolate donuts win. Be nice to all girls."

"I was trying to get my goat," I tell him.

He grunts a displeased sound and deposits me back at my own station, then stands there blocking me from getting to Annika, arms crossed, deep blue eyes threatening to impale me with my KitchenAid mixer.

Possibly through my head.

"I'm nice to girls," I tell him.

"He is," Georgia squeaks in agreement behind me while Ma wrestles Sue back to our side of the studio. "But if you're going to kill him, could you make him sign his bakery over to me first?"

"Thanks," I mutter to her.

"All's fair in baking and war."

"Judges?" Star says again.

"Chocolate donuts all the way," Zeus Berger says.

"Banana—" Chase Jett starts.

Ares growls at him.

He snickers. "Ah, what the hell. Chocolate donuts."

"The donuts get my vote," Daisy announces.

I try to peer around Ares, but he puffs his chest wider, and there's no seeing around—huh.

You'd think a guy wearing a T-shirt featuring a cartoon

platypus saying *Eat My Bananna*—yep, spelled with three n's total—would've voted for my muffins.

But that's not the point.

And I can't see Annika as the rest of the judges—even Edison Rogers, who's clearly doing so under protest—vote for her donuts.

Georgia wants to call this whole thing rigged. I can *feel* her physically restraining herself, but the fear of Ares Berger is real.

"Congratulations to Duh-Nuts Bakery," Star says. "Annika, how does it feel to know your donuts impressed the judges so much?"

"Victory's only sweet when it's a well-fought fight." She's upset. I can hear it. She doesn't want to be here. She won, but her voice says she lost, and I don't know why, and I can't get past Ares Berger to get to her. "But I'm happy to have Mama's bakery making such a good name for itself. This one's for her."

"Aw, that's as sweet as your donuts. Maria, how do you feel?"

"So proud of my girls. So, *so* proud of my girls."

"What did you think of the donuts?"

"They're delicious, of course. Everything my girls touch turns to magic. They're the best thing I've ever done with my life."

"Wow, that is one eager goat," Star says, nodding to Sue, who's now being restrained by both my mom and brother. "How's it feel to know the decision was unanimous with your competitor's pet voting for your donuts too?"

"Sue would eat a garden hose," Tillie Jean says.

Cooper hushes her, but Pop chortles. "Likes to eat dirt too."

"Knock it off," I tell them all.

Ma gives me a funny look, but the rest of them resort to whispering whatever insults they want to fling Annika's way.

And I'm getting pissed.

Because what did she really do?

What did she *ever* do that was unforgivable?

Hell, what did *anyone* in Sarcasm do that was so bad?

Turn a bunch of goats loose during a wedding?

We don't even have proof it was them.

And it got me Sue, didn't it? He's not the brightest goat, but he's loyal, and I swear he's been on Team Annika since the minute she set foot back in Virginia, and that counts for more than him being trainable as a circus act.

"We'll get 'em next time," Georgia says to me. "When the judges aren't terrifying people who seem to have a soft spot for the other team."

Ares growls.

She jumps.

Sue *maaaa*s.

And Star calls it a wrap.

She also slips me her phone number on her way out the door, which my entire family sees.

Only Cooper hangs back and gives me the *you're so dead* look. Everyone else converges around us to help pack boxes.

Ares stands watch the whole time we're picking up.

"Dude. We gotta get to—you know," Zeus says to him. He grins broadly. "That thing. For the bet."

But he still doesn't leave.

Pop has Sue back on a leash, but Annika's gone.

You fucked up, Amy mouths to me.

Pretty sure she's not gloating.

I don't give a damn that I lost.

I give half a damn that a nearly seven-foot-tall hockey player who's as wide as he is tall is still glaring at me, because I still have some self-preservation instincts left, but I need to talk to Annika.

Apologize for my family.

Congratulate her.

"I swore she didn't look like she knew what she was doing," one of the producers is muttering to one of the cameramen, "but those donuts were amazing."

"Hey, Ares, dude. I got this. You go on and check out the rest of the city. Lots to see and do here, man." Cooper steps between us, and while Ares Berger could also snap him like a twig, the giant hockey player finally uncrosses his tree trunk arms and steps back.

He glares at me one last time, before leaving with Zeus and Chase Jett.

Most of the other judges are gone, but after most of my family departs with boxes to take to my truck, Daisy Carter-Kincaid swings her hips right up to my station, leans forward to show off her cleavage in the tight red mini dress she's wearing, and crooks a finger at me.

I keep a healthy distance. "Yes, ma'am?"

She slides a look at Georgia. "Go steal me five of those unicorn cookies the other team is hiding in their bins."

Cooper grabs Georgia's arm before she can tell off the billionaire heiress. "I'll go too."

"Yes, ma'am?" I repeat when we're alone.

"Call me ma'am again, and you'll wake up tomorrow

with your ears where your balls go. Also, next time you're secretly sleeping with the competition, own it on camera. Love makes a better story than hate every time."

She turns on her stilettos and swings her hips while she walks away before I can utter a word. When Cooper and Georgia hold out the unicorn cookies, she stuffs them into her cleavage and keeps walking, signaling her bodyguard on the way.

Not all that different from Zeus Berger shoving cookies down his pants, which he's doing right now too.

One of the crew says something to him, and he whips out a Sharpie and signs the dude's forehead.

"Got it all?" Georgia says to me.

Countertops are empty except for the tray of banana pudding muffins that are dwindling as crew move past, rearranging the set for whatever segment they're taping next and snagging snacks for later.

Maria, Bailey, and Amy are done clearing their stuff, with a few Sarcasm locals helping them like my family's helping me. Bailey's left a tray full of individual servings of banana pudding on the counter, and those are going faster than my muffins.

"Have to wonder what they told the crew with how popular they are," Georgia mutters.

"Cheaters," Tillie Jean adds.

She's back, but Annika isn't.

I don't see Annika again at all before we're shown out of the studio.

I text her as soon as Sue and I are alone in my truck.

Hey. You okay?

She doesn't reply right away, and the message doesn't even show as read.

I wait a few minutes, then text her again.

Driving back to Shipwreck. Call me if you need me.

She doesn't call.

Not before I leave Copper Valley. Not while I'm on the highway. Not once I'm back home.

Not while I open the bakery for the lunch crowd, who all want to know how the contest went.

She doesn't call at all.

She doesn't answer my calls either.

So as soon as I can, I turn the bakery over to Georgia, and I head home to check on Sue.

Then I hop back in my truck.

I don't care if somebody in Sarcasm sees me.

I need to know what's wrong.

I lost her once.

I'm not going to lose her again.

No matter what it takes.

44

Annika

It doesn't matter that Mama's gone blind, she still knows something's wrong.

As soon as we're all back at Duh-Nuts, she asks if I'll take her home. She walks herself into the house with just her white cane and the railings for guides, and she easily maneuvers through the kitchen to the living room, where she calls for me to join her.

"Mama, I should get back to—"

"Grady," she finishes for me.

The lump I've been holding back threatens to choke me and my eyeballs sting like my tears are made of battery acid. "I'm sure he's fine," I choke out.

"But you're not fine."

"I will be."

I know that frown.

It's the *don't lie to your mother* frown. I've seen it before. I'll see it again.

"I—need an afternoon off," I manage to choke out.

"Go. I'm fine. And the goddess of my loins will protect me from the cougar in the corner."

"*Mama.*"

"Yes, Maria, how may I help you?" her phone assistant says.

"Tell my daughter to take the afternoon off," Mama instructs, showing off more of her newfound technological skills with her phone, which unfortunately still only answers to *Goddess of my Loins*.

"I'm sorry, Maria, my programming does not allow me to issue orders to humans. I must wait until the coming of the computer overlord to follow this direction. Would you like me to google *tell my daughter to take the afternoon off*?"

"Goddess of my Loins, call Bailey," Mama says.

"Dialing Bailey Williams," Mama's voice assistant says.

"Mama—"

She lifts a finger and puts her phone to her ear. "Hi, Bailey. Annika's taking the rest of the day off. Do you need me to come back? No? You're sure? And Amy can handle the donut dough for tomorrow? Ah, good. Thank you. Yes, I'll ask Roger to get you to volleyball practice. Bye, sweetheart. Love you."

She hangs up and turns a smile on me. "There. Now you can't go to work."

I should be grateful.

But I have questions. And I'm tired. And I don't want to go anywhere, but I also don't want to stay here. "Do you ever think about my father?"

"Beyond being grateful that he gave me you? No, generally not. He's not worth it."

"Because he abandoned us?" I whisper.

"Because I have very poor judgment in the men I've chosen in the past, and we're better off without their influence and their baggage in our lives. I was better without him. *You* were better without him. He wasn't father material. Not that I was mother material, but I didn't have much choice, and I had your grandmother's support those first few years."

I press my palms into my eyes to try to keep the tears from slipping out. "He pretended like we didn't exist."

"All the more reason we were better off without him. Annika. What's this about?"

"Nothing." I can't tell her I saw him. There's no point. "Nothing," I repeat, stronger. "I just—are you sure you're okay? I need some fresh air. Those lights—the cameras—the interview and the pressure—"

"*Go*. I know my way around the house. I can work the microwave since you added those pads where the numbers and the start button are. And Roger will probably stop by and check on me."

"He's been a good friend," I say slowly, watching as Mama clears her throat and touches the collar on her Duh-Nuts T-shirt. "Or is he more?"

She takes a minute to answer. "It's possible that now that I can't see, I can...*see* him," she finally says.

"He's a very nice man."

"The world always manages to provide balance."

My eyes sting again, because I don't know where my balance is. "I'm going for a bike ride," I tell Mama.

"Take your time. I'm *fine* here."

I kiss her head. "Love you, Mama."

She fumbles a minute before she finds my arm and squeezes it. "You'll find your way, baby girl. Have faith."

I don't know if I will, but I know that I don't care that we won some stupid baking contest this morning. I don't care that Sue ate all the donuts I tried to ruin on TV. I don't even care that I'm almost positive someone paid off all the judges and crew because I'm fairly certain my donuts were awful, especially next to Grady's masterpieces.

I care that I've never felt more alone, and it's all my own stupid fault because I didn't tell anyone about us either.

Why am I keeping him a secret?

Because it's good for business?

Or because it'll hurt less whenever he realizes I'm not the same Annika I was?

That I don't know what I want to be when I grow up.

That I have no direction.

That my entire existence is being Mama's daughter and Bailey's sister, and beyond that, I'm just...lost.

So it's easier to be mad at him for keeping me a secret than it is to confess that I'm not really cut out for relationships after all.

Once again, I take my bike and head out of town. Out to the preserve, down the trail to the lake.

And once I get there, I toss my helmet, strip out of most of my clothes, and I dive into the lake.

It's cool. And some old fart will probably have a heart attack at me out here in just my bra and panties, but what's the difference between that and a bikini?

He can bite me.

And Grady Rock can bite me too.

He didn't keep me a secret in high school.

Being a secret means one thing.

He doesn't want to keep me.

Not forever.

And I probably don't deserve him, because did I fight for him?

No.

I didn't.

I cry enough tears to turn the lake into saltwater, but I keep swimming. Keep pushing myself until my lungs are heaving and my arms and legs feel like lead.

I'll probably have to call Liliana for a ride home, but not yet.

Because right now, I want to sit on the bank and ignore the storm clouds gathering overhead, and ignore the fact that Bailey starts school soon, and ignore the fact that Grady's whole family hates me and Bailey hates him and Mama probably knows I've been sneaking out to see him, but she lets me make my own mistakes.

Like falling for Grady again.

When I know we don't have a future.

Again.

I bury my head in my knees while I catch my breath, and I'm so focused on getting control of myself that I don't realize I'm not alone until too late.

"Go away," I force out.

Grady doesn't move. "Had a hunch I might find you here."

"Go. Away."

"Did...did I do something?"

God, I feel like such a brat.

Such a brat, and yet so *hurt* at the same time.

"No," I tell him honestly. "You didn't do *anything*. And that's exactly the problem."

"Ooo-kay."

"I'm not a dirty secret, Grady."

"Whoa, hold up—"

"I know. *I know*, okay? I could've just as easily stood there in front of all those cameras and told the whole world I love you just as much as I kept hoping you'd finally claim me in front of your family, but I didn't. And you didn't either. How much longer does this go on? How much longer do we sneak around and pretend we hate each other in the name of making freaking *money* when I don't hate you at all until I think about how much I hate that *we're fucking sneaking around*?"

"Annika—"

"*No*. Your whole *family* was there. All of them. All of them buying into the story that I'm a horrible person because I'm a Sarcasm asshole who came home to steal your sister's banana pudding trophies and your baking trophies and that I'm hiding behind my mama going blind to justify being an asshole. All while *my fucking father* stood there behind a camera like I was *no one*. I'm. Not. No. One. Just because I don't know who I am right now doesn't mean I'm no one. It means I'm someone who's a little lost. And if I'm not someone to you, if I'm not someone worth pissing off your family for, then get the hell out of my life. I don't need this."

He's blinking at me like I'm slapping him with a wet fish when it would be so much easier to just grab a dead branch to do the job, and I can't handle that bewildered, injured look in his eyes.

Not when that's exactly how I feel about our whole relationship.

Bewildered.

Injured.

A dirty secret.

To the best of my knowledge, my sperm donor's parents never even knew I existed.

They thought Mama was sleeping around with too many boys to know who my father was.

And here I am, sleeping with a man who doesn't want his family to know about me either.

And doing the same to him.

Best friends?

No.

We're not best friends.

We're each other's dirty little secrets.

"Annika—"

I shove to my feet and yank my clothes back on. "Would you tell them?" I ask.

He hesitates, his eyes dropping to the ground.

"That's what I thought," I whisper.

"I'll tell them. I will. I just need to—"

He breaks off, and I pause.

"I need to warm them up," he finishes.

"If you need to *warm them up* to the idea that you've found someone who makes you happy, then maybe they're not the amazing, wonderful, awesome people you think they are."

"There's a line," he says, and the caution's gone from his voice.

His caution in saying something to upset me, that is.

That tone's full of all kinds of warnings for me to watch whatever I'm about to say next.

But I'm past caring.

Because if my choices are Grady or my own self-respect, I know which one I need to choose.

It's not the one I *want*, but it's the one I *need*.

"Don't worry," I tell him. "I won't cross your line. In fact, I'm walking away from it. *Right now*."

Walking.

Biking.

Uphill. Five miles.

It's all the same.

"Annika," he says again, this time pulling out his *you're blowing this out of proportion* tone.

"And if you need to warm them up," I say, not turning around, "then maybe we're not actually good for each other, and we're just delaying the inevitable of having them point it out to us."

Maybe I *am* blowing this out of proportion.

I don't tend to do anything halfway.

And that apparently includes imploding relationships.

45

Grady

I don't know what the hell just happened, but I'm equal parts convinced I fucked it up, and so did she.

I follow her up the trail. She's huffing and puffing on her bike but not backing down.

She's Annika fucking Williams. Of course she's not backing down.

She doesn't give up on anything.

Except me.

I'm so pissed by the time the trailhead opens up to the parking lot that I'm not sweating from the hike, because it's evaporating right off me in waves of fury.

Everything I've done, I've done to help her.

To make sure she's settled. Solid. Not worried about her bakery failing like I've been worrying about mine.

"Want a ride?" I call.

She flips me off.

I'd do the same if I were her, because it wasn't a nice offer.

I stomp to my truck and fling myself in. Sue's not with me, which is good, because I'm pretty sure my goat would rather Annika take him home anyway.

He's practically humped her every night she's been over the last week.

But if she doesn't want me, she doesn't get him either.

"*Fuck*," I yell to myself.

Doesn't help.

I curl my hands around the steering wheel and wait, wanting to not have to watch her pedaling uphill the whole way out of the preserve.

Her legs are sexy as fuck.

And I need to not think about them.

Wrapped around me.

Tangled in my sheets.

Naked in my shower.

Dammit.

"Thanks for blindsiding me," I mutter. "Appreciate the heads-up that you woke up this morning and made a decision you couldn't fucking *tell me about*."

My truck doesn't answer.

My heart howls, so I crank the engine to drown it out.

"I'm not a fucking mind reader. And even if I was, I'm not just tossing her into the middle of my family while they think she's the devil."

And why do they think she's the devil?

Because I suggested we let them.

So that she could make a few extra bucks.

So *I* could make a few extra bucks.

Crow's Nest is doing fucking awesome since we started our feud.

It's everything I've ever wanted.

This is the best fucking month of my life.

"*Fuck*," I groan again.

I bang my head against the steering wheel a few times, and then I do the only thing I can do, since she's too fucking stubborn to take a ride.

A ride I don't want to give her, for the record, but I would.

Silently.

The ache spreading through my chest is making me short of breath, and I'm pretty damn sure my whole life just broke.

Again.

Exactly like it did ten years ago when she took off in that field and didn't call again.

Ever.

Christ, this fucking sucks.

And I don't know how to fix it.

I pull my phone out and I'm dialing before I can talk myself out of it.

"Talk to me, babycakes," Cooper says when he answers. He sounds out of breath, and he better fucking be working out, because if he's screwing a woman and answering the phone, I'm gonna beat his ass six ways to Sunday.

"Annika dumped me."

"Well, yeah. You should've told Pop and all them to go take a flying leap for being rude this morning."

"He was just being Pop."

"Yeah, and you're being a baby. Call me when you're

DIRTY TALKING RIVAL

ready to admit you fucked up."

"I might not be perfect, but she—"

The phone beeps three times in my ear, letting me know the call dropped.

"Motherfucker," I snarl, and I hit redial.

"You've reached Cooper's cell phone," Cooper says, still out of breath. "Please say the password to continue this phone call."

I grit my teeth. "I fucked up."

"Good job." He's so fucking cheerful, even with the panting, that I want to punch him in the cup. "Next step. Convince me you deserve her."

He's not helping. "Where's the *she doesn't deserve you* bit that you're supposed to say?"

"She served her country for a decade and came home to take care of her suddenly blind mother and minor sister. You adopted a goat. Which counts for a lot, don't get me wrong, but—"

This time, I hang up on him.

I can't breathe.

My heart's pounding so hard it's bruising my lungs. My windows are fogging up. My knuckles hurt from gripping *everything* too tight.

And my dick's playing itself a country song, because if I'm not sleeping with Annika, I'm never sleeping with anyone again.

Ever.

In my whole entire life.

"*Dammit*," I shout, and I dial Cooper again.

"Wow, that's some bad connection we have today," he says by way of greeting.

"Maybe if playing baseball doesn't work out, you can

be a fucking cheerleader."

He sputters a laugh. "Dude, I *do* cheerleaders. I don't *be* cheerleaders."

"Or you could be literate," I mutter. "Or an adult."

"So, you want Annika back," he prompts.

"We might not even be broken up."

"What did she say?"

My heart crumbles into biscuit dough beyond help. "A whole bunch of personal shit that's none of your fucking business."

"Ah. Wants you to get a dick extension. Yeah. That's a tough one."

"I fucking hate you."

"You've loved Annika half your life. You had a fight. She doesn't want you to get a dick extension, which—dude, bad idea. Worst idea. So if she doesn't want the worst from you, then you can fix this. Bake her a cookie or something. Or maybe grow some balls. Your choice. That's all the wisdom I have in me this morning. Haven't talked to my wood yet."

It's stupid that his wisdom is helping, but it is.

He's right.

I can fix this.

If I want to.

But how long will it last if I fix it *this* time?

She warned me.

She warned me she doesn't have time for me.

That she's high maintenance.

So I have to decide.

Is she worth it?

Is she worth possibly losing my family, my home, and my bakery? Because if I'm in, I'm *all* in.

Being all in means turning my back on my entire town if they can't deal.

Losing my bakery if they *can* deal, but suddenly don't get all the best gossip at Crow's Nest anymore.

And she *still* might not want me.

That's the one thing I've never been able to do—I've never been able to make her love me the way I love her.

And I don't know if I ever will.

46

Annika

THE SUN IS TOO BRIGHT, but it would take energy to get up out of bed and close the blinds, so I don't.

It would take too much energy to tell my phone to text Bailey to come do it for me too.

Every inch of my body aches.

My calves. My thighs. My abs. My shoulders. My arms. My teeth.

My fingernails.

My nose hairs.

I need six hours in one of Cooper's massage chairs, except I'm never seeing Cooper again, because I'm never seeing Grady again, and I don't get one without the other.

Not that I've ever in my life wanted Cooper.

And now my eyeballs are burning and I suddenly understand why my nose hairs hurt.

It's the roots.

They're in tender, swollen nasal skin.

"Oh my god, Bailey's late for school!"

I bolt straight up in bed, all of my muscles scream in agony, and I gasp at the overwhelming pain ripping through my ass.

My *ass*.

It's like I did an Ironman yesterday or something.

"Annika?" Mama says softly outside the door of my small bedroom. "Bailey caught the bus on time. Are you awake, sweetheart?"

She's tiptoeing.

She knows something's wrong, and she's tiptoeing, and will I ever stop crying?

"Yeah," I manage.

I flop back on the twin bed and stare at the glow-in-the-dark stars plastered to the cracking ceiling.

They don't glow anymore.

They haven't in years, but they're still on the ceiling.

Exactly where I put them just before I started high school, when Mama moved us into *the bigger house* so we'd have room when Bailey joined us.

The dark wood door creaks open, and Mama shuffles in with my metal water bottle in hand.

My eyelids are sneaking shut again. "I slept through my alarm."

"You needed to catch up on your sleep."

"Duh-Nuts?"

"Amy has everything covered, and Roger made our bank run for us this morning."

"Thank you," I whisper when I want to say *I'm sorry*. "I'll be fine tomorrow."

"Bailey said you looked like you wrestled a bear when you got home yesterday."

Yesterday.

God.

Yesterday.

It feels like seven million years ago and two seconds ago all at once.

I could tell Mama I overdid it on my bike. Or that I swam too long. Or that I did, in fact, wrestle a bear.

Emotionally, I might as well have.

"I've been seeing Grady," I whisper.

"I know."

"*What?*"

"Well, I *assumed* it was Grady. Your clothes smell off, but I don't know whose laundry soap smells like that, and you only smelled different after you snuck out at night and came back home."

"Oh my god," I whisper.

"You're plenty old enough to decide for yourself to have a relationship. I assumed you'd tell me when you were ready."

"I broke up with him."

I haven't checked my phone, but I don't need to.

He won't call.

He won't text.

He deserves better than my breakdowns, and I deserve better than to be his secret.

Mama pats the edge of my bed, and I move my legs —*ouch*—and nod. "Right there. That's the end. Come closer to my voice."

She takes two steps toward the head of the bed, gets a

better grip on the mattress and its orientation, and then sits.

"Why?" she asks quietly.

"I just don't have time for a relationship right now. And that's okay—it really is, Mama. Don't make that face. This isn't about you. I mean, yes, we're all adjusting, but—"

"Annika. Stop."

I stop talking.

But I can't stop the hollow ache in my chest.

"Bailey will cope, you know," she tells me. "If Grady's biggest sin is where he was born, we can overcome that."

"It's not—well, it's not *just* that."

"I always liked him."

"Not helping."

"And he loved you all through high school."

"Again with the *not helping*."

"But if you two can't find a balance with whatever happened, then maybe you're not actually meant to work out, but to learn something from each other."

"Marginally helping," I whisper, even though that's probably the least helpful thing she's said.

She's my mama.

She's supposed to tell me everything will be okay.

That we're meant to be and our problems will dissipate like the morning dew when the summer sun hits them.

But that would be a lie, and the one thing Mama has never done is lie to me.

Or pretend that life gets easier.

"You rest." She squeezes my leg. "You can't solve big problems when you haven't had enough sleep."

I don't want to rest.

I want to stretch my aching muscles and then go for a ten-mile run, because if I can just be permanently worn and exhausted, then maybe I won't have to deal with the emotions that are clogging my chest and making the rest of my life look like a bleak, dark cloud of loneliness and misery.

"Just another thirty minutes," I tell Mama.

She smiles knowingly and squeezes my leg again. "You'll get through this, baby girl. You always do."

Maybe Old Annika did.

But Current Annika?

She's still a hot mess.

47

Grady

My kitchen is a fucking disaster.

My donut dough isn't rising, probably because I forgot to put the yeast in when I mixed it.

All of my cupcakes have caved in.

The blueberry muffins I made to salvage the breakfast rush are bitter, and I told the maple bacon scones to go fuck themselves.

The sink's overflowing.

Not with dishes.

But with water, because I wasn't paying attention when I was filling it and now it's spilling all over the floor.

"Whoa, boss, you got some trouble back here," Georgia says when she bustles in a few minutes before six. She has to shout to be heard over my music, which she silences as fast as she can leap across the kitchen.

"Off day," I grunt.

"Did you sleep last night? You look like shit. Hey. Back away from the cookie dough. Sugar needs love, not a beating, remember? You want me to get rid of the TV that we set up last night to watch the morning show? I can accidentally throw a can of whipped cream at it so we don't have to watch that rigged bullshit go down."

"*Don't fucking call it rigged*," I snarl.

She grins. "Feel better?"

"No."

"Not even a little?"

I glower at her, throw my apron off, and head for the back door.

Tillie Jean bursts in. "Hey! You're not leaving, are you? I brought megaphones so we can all boo as one."

I glare at her.

She grins.

I glare harder and add a growl.

She grins bigger.

It's like they know.

They *know* Annika dumped me, and they're all so fucking happy about it.

Fuck.

That.

Fuck them all.

I turn on my heel and march to the front of my bakery.

My bakery.

I *hate* this bakery.

It's in a town full of people who hate the one woman in this world that I've loved for half my life.

The woman I measure every other woman against.

The woman whose only sin was being born ten miles down the road instead of here.

Fuck that too.

I've just hit the lights when I dimly register that those grunts I was hearing weren't coming from my baked goods that are all moaning at being mistreated.

"*Aaaah!* POPS! PUT YOUR FUCKING PANTS BACK ON! NANA! AAAAAAH!"

The two of them leap apart, stuffing their saggy bits back into their clothes, and shit damn fuck hell, now I have to sanitize every table in here.

Along with my eyes.

"Rawk! Mind your own fucking business! Rawk!"

Long Beak Silver swoops from his perch over the door and dive-bombs me, like *I'm* the one in the wrong for walking in on my grandparents doing the horizontal mamba.

Someone knocks on the glass door in the dim morning light. "Is it time?" he calls. "I want to watch the morning show."

"What are you doing here?" I demand while I shield my eyes.

"We didn't want to miss the show," Pop says.

"We're here for you, honey," Nana adds. "Since you lost and all."

Someone else knocks on the door. "Are you open yet? Turn on the TV! We don't want to miss it."

Georgia breezes past me to fling open the door. "Oven malfunction," she announces. "All we have is coffee."

It doesn't matter.

They all file in, because that's what you do.

You get up at the butt crack of dawn to file into a bakery to support your neighbors.

"Grady!"

"It's the man of the hour!"

"I can't wait to watch him spank that Sarcasm bakery back to where they came from."

All of them.

All of them.

Invading my bakery.

Flipping on the fucking television.

Cheering.

Because they think they're supporting me.

Ma and Dad file in, both of them smiling broadly at me like they know Annika dumped me, and they, too, are happy about it.

Cooper saunters in too. He showed up at my house after the game with a six-pack of Shipwreck Lager, and the two of us toasted all of our fuck-ups.

Me with Annika.

Him being only halfway through a long-term contract with a team he loved until he played for them, and a team he can't turn around single-handedly.

"I hope she sets her ovens on fire," someone says.

"Enough!" I roar.

Everyone turns to stare at me as Annika's face fills the television screen.

She was nervous as hell. Tugging at her earlobe, and she probably didn't even realize she was doing it.

I did that to her.

I made her get in front of those cameras and pretend she could bake.

I leap up onto the nearest table and I point to the screen. "I love that woman, and any of you who can't handle it can get the fuck out of my bakery."

There's a moment of total silence.

Broken, naturally, by Cooper.

"Dude. Zeus Berger is hot, but he's not a woman, and I didn't think he was your type."

I blink at the screen, where Zeus Berger is having an arm wrestling match with his billionaire buddy while the cooking is going on.

I flip my brother off. "You know I meant Annika."

"Just sayin', watch where you're pointing."

"Out. *Get out*. Crow's Nest is closed."

"Are you serious?" Tillie Jean asks.

"As a fucking heart attack. I'm done standing here listening to anyone talk shit about Annika and her family. *I'm* the reason we're having a bakery war. She didn't do a damn thing wrong, and neither did her mama. Say one more bad thing about her. Go on. Do it."

Cooper grins and flashes me a thumbs-up.

Pop frowns and pulls his matchmaker notebook out of his back pocket.

Ma wipes a tear from her eye.

Sloane pokes her head around Georgia's grandpa, Doc Adamson. "Can we get her on our softball team?"

"*Out.*"

Yesterday's contest in Copper Valley is playing out on the TV set up on the side table. It's ugly.

I'm laughing and smiling with Georgia. Looks like I don't have a care in the world.

But every single minute, I was painfully aware of how stressed Annika was.

I kept telling myself it was for the good of both our bakeries.

But at what cost to her?

"Go on," Georgia says. "You heard the bossman.

Health department violations to have people in the building with our ovens in the shape they're in. Cooper's got space up at his place for all of you. We'll be open tomorrow."

"It'll be over by the time we get there," someone groans.

"We'll turn it on over at The Muted Parrot," Ma offers.

"Wait, does this mean those Sarcasm assholes *won*?"

"Free coffee!" Ma cries.

"I'll bring gold nuggets!" Dad adds.

Tillie Jean's lip curls. "For breakfast? *Ew*. Ignore him, folks. I'm grabbing a tray of banana pudding."

My family ushers everyone out the door, all of them sending me knowing looks. Finally, it's just me and Georgia again.

Me, Georgia, Long Beak Silver, and Cooper, that is.

"What?" I snarl at Cooper.

"Just making sure I don't have to fight any domestic enemies," he replies.

"Rawk! Eat that pussy! Rawk!"

"Someone please shoot that bird," I mutter.

He swoops through the dining room and poops on my head.

"Grady, you've got it bad," Georgia says.

I start to glower at her, but she holds both hands up. "Slow down, master baker. I don't give two pirate coins who you love. I care that she's good enough for you and she loves you back. Is she worth this?"

She gestures to me in all my snarly, heartbroken glory, and I sink into the nearest chair and rub my neck.

"She's worth it," I tell the floor.

"Then get up off your ass and do something about it."

I lift my head and study her.

She rolls her eyes and puts a fist on her hip. "Can't fight love. And if you can find it with someone from a town your family has vilified for years, then maybe there's hope for the rest of us. Even if I still think they cheated yesterday."

I growl.

She grins. "You really do have it bad. Also, can you please tell Cooper not to mop the floor with me for saying they cheated? I was joking."

She wasn't joking, but I glance at my brother.

He grins too. "I can't wait to watch Pop burn that notebook. Thousand bucks says he cries."

"Who says she wants me back? He might still need it."

"Are you kidding? There's not a woman in the world who could resist your charm."

"But he'll need it for you."

"Never. I'm irresistible too. Watch this. Hey, Georgia baby, what'cha doin' tonight? Besides me?" He waggles his brows at Georgia.

She visibly throws up in her mouth. "I need a shower. And brain bleach. And a day off."

"You don't want to stay and cuddle and work up a plan for Grady with me?"

I push back to my feet and shove Cooper toward the door. "Quit harassing my assistant manager and go away."

"I'm just making sure the bird doesn't talk smack about your bae."

"Don't even say *bae* again. And take the bird with you."

"Rawk! Death first! Rawk!"

"Got a juicy steak with your name on it, bird," Cooper says while he chases Long Beak Silver around the dining room.

"You can't feed a bird steak."

"Okay, fine. The steak's for me. But I can't eat with someone who likes bugs for a snack. That's disgusting."

"You wear the same socks all season, and a bird eating a bug is disgusting?"

"We're talking about you, bro. Go get the girl. I'll get the bird out of your bakery."

Go get the girl.

Great sentiment.

"She wants you back, Grady," Cooper says. "This isn't like last time. She's not leaving. And if she does, you can fucking go with her. But it's your choice. If you don't think you can man up—"

I don't stay to listen to the rest of his motivational speech.

Because if I'm going to fight for the only woman I've ever truly wanted, I need to do it *my* way.

48

Grady

Ten miles is a long time to weigh all your faults.

By the time I reach Sarcasm town limits, I'm pretty fucking convinced I'm fighting an uphill battle with a seven-million-pound boulder.

She was right. We shouldn't have kept our relationship a secret.

I have every excuse in the book.

She had enough stress without all the gossips being gossips.

Her life's upside down right now.

It was good for business.

I won't apologize for that last one. Not when the Duh-Nuts parking lot is packed.

Running a profitable business has to be taking one more worry off her plate.

But the biggest excuse I have for keeping us a secret is one that I didn't want to face.

That fear that she'd break me all over again.

If we stayed a secret, then it would hurt less when we were through, because fewer people would know.

That's the line I fed myself.

And it was bullshit.

The only thing keeping me from hurting right now is sheer determination to prove to her that she's worth fighting for, and that I'll never stop fighting so long as I have a sliver of hope that she still wants me back.

I know Annika.

Once she's put her mind to something, she's all in.

She's decided she's done with me.

It's my job to change that, and I swear to fuck, I won't stop until I'm convinced she's not doing this out of the same fear I have.

That I'll leave.

I park around the corner in front of the Sunny Day Funeral Home—nicely played, Sarcasm—because it's the first place I can find a parking spot. The sidewalks are empty since everyone's already at Duh-Nuts.

Celebrating their victory on the morning show.

The bells jingle when I pull the door open, and realization that the enemy is in their midst gradually filters through the dining room, which is packed past capacity with people drinking coffee and eating breakfast egg waffles and chocolate-glazed donuts.

Amy looks up from the cash register and grins.

Then frowns.

Then grins again.

"What are *you* doing here?" one of the guys I recognize

from the Sarcasm softball team asks me.

"He came to rub in that he won," someone else says. "Oh, no, wait...*Ha!* Loser."

"Annika?" I ask Amy.

She shakes her head. "Not in today."

That's not good. "Bailey?"

"School, dude. That time of year."

"Maria?"

She jerks her head toward the kitchen.

"You're not going back there," someone informs me.

"Roger's with her," Amy calls. "She'll be fine. Let the man pass."

I get patted down for weapons—hello, overkill—and everyone growls at me or mocks me while I weave through the crowd to the kitchen door.

Roger the plumber spots me from his spot at the stove, where he's scrambling more eggs. "What do *you* want?" he growls.

"Who's there?" Maria's at the workbench, rolling out sugar cookie dough, which is pretty fucking amazing.

"Grady Rock, ma'am."

She feels for a spot to put the rolling pin and sits back on the stool. "Are you here to fight or make up?"

"Ultimately? Make up. But I'll fight for it if I have to."

Roger skewers me with a glare that could melt steel.

"You sound quite determined."

"I love her."

She smiles softly. "You always did."

I nod, then remember she can't see. "Yes."

"She's very reluctant to love. That's my fault."

"The hell it is," Roger mutters.

"She had other priorities," I offer. "Still does."

"And that's also my fault."

"Know what else is your fault?"

Roger spins so fast, egg bits fly off his spatula and splatter over the cookie dough.

"Oh, please tell me," Maria says wryly.

"It's your fault she's strong and smart and capable. And it's your fault she has a huge heart hiding behind her walls. And it's your fault she knows the value of real family."

"I certainly have a long list of faults." A smile teases the corners of her lips. "Maybe we should talk about some of yours."

"I can name a few," Roger says.

"I've known this boy for fourteen years. I can name more than a few. But if he's here, I hope that means he's working on fixing one or two of them. Does your family know you're here?"

"They probably have a clue."

"And what do they think of you coming into enemy territory?"

"If they're not willing to support us, then I don't give a damn."

I don't.

I don't care if everyone decides to stop coming to Crow's Nest for baked goods if I'm openly dating a woman from Sarcasm. I don't care if Tillie Jean wants to hold a grudge forever because Annika's sister can make kick-ass banana pudding.

I don't care if I find out I'm just not that interesting and *that's* why my bakery dies.

"I'd rather we put the whole damn feud behind us," I tell Maria.

"Unless it's good for business."

She's cheeky today.

"I don't care about the business. Take my business. You can have it. I just want Annika back."

"She's not here."

My heart stops.

Full-on stops.

"She—she went back to the Army?"

Not a problem. I can find her. I can go to her. I'll sell my house. I'll sell Crow's Nest. I'd sell my truck, but it would be a long walk to Texas.

Maria laughs. "No, no. She's home. Taking the day off. Roger, where are my keys?"

"You're letting him in your house?" the plumber asks.

"You're only young once, and these two have wasted enough time pretending they can live without each other. Yes, I'm letting him in my house. Besides, Annika has ten years of Army training. She'll take care of him if she needs to."

My eyes get hot when Roger hands me the key to Maria's house.

He looks like he'd rather disembowel me, but that's how some relationships go.

And I'm glad Annika has a guy like this in her corner.

I'm glad her whole family does.

And if they'll let me, I'll be the second.

49

Annika

Mama's making chocolate chip cookies. She's in the kitchen, which is in a tent on a boat, which is a little weird, but she's cooked on alligator backs before too, so this isn't outside the range of normal.

I just hope the milk doesn't spill into the snapping turtles.

Into?

Onto.

Spill *onto* the turtles.

I suck in a deep breath of cookie goodness again, and that's when reality comes crashing down around me.

Mama can't see.

She shouldn't be using the oven. Not alone, anyway.

My eyes fly open, the blank stars on my ceiling sit there and stare back at me, and I leap out of bed.

Then I remember my entire body is one huge overworked muscle of pain, and I squeak and go down.

My ass lands on the thin carpet with a jolt, and I swear on mama's cinnamon rolls, I am *never* dating again, because then I'll never be motivated to do something as stupid as making up my own triathlon of death again.

"Annika? You okay?"

Grady leans in my doorway and looks down at me, concern etched in his blue-green eyes, which are definitely more green today, and I must still be dreaming, because Grady Rock is in Mama's house.

Except this *is* Mama's house.

My old twin bed with the saggy mattress.

The stars on the ceiling.

The now-faded *Harry Potter* movie poster hiding the hole in the wall where I accidentally put a softball through it when Bailey was a baby, right next to my posters of Paris and Disney World and Australia.

This isn't a dream.

Grady's in Mama's house, looking at me like I didn't tell him to take a flying leap and get out of my life yesterday.

My heart launches into space and takes my brain with it.

"Mama?" I croak, because that's all my voice can muster.

"She's at Duh-Nuts. Are you okay?"

"What are you doing here?"

"I don't give up on the people I love. You want a cookie? Just came out of the oven. And they go equally well with milk or Jack. Your choice."

I blink at him.

Then blink again.

My vision blurs, but he's still standing there.

"Why?" I whisper.

"You always liked my cookies."

"No, why—why are you here?"

He crosses the room in three steps and squats to the floor in front of me. "I. Love. You."

I'm supposed to say something, but panic is flooding my veins while my heart tries to bat it all away with a broom like it's a mouse.

Grady loves me.

He loves me.

"And I'm not letting you go this time without a fight," he adds, that beautiful blue-green gaze daring me to tell him he'll have to fight for me.

Telling me he'll enjoy the hell out of fighting for me.

Telling me I'm worth fighting for.

Oh.

He's here.

He came back.

He loves me.

"I can't fight," I rasp out, because once I say *I love you too*, it's out, and I can't take it back, and I do. I love him. I love him and I was such an asshole yesterday and I don't deserve him being back.

"You can't?" he murmurs.

"I can't even lift my pinky finger," I confess.

He ducks his head, but I know he's grinning. "Overdid it yesterday?"

"Shut up."

"Aw, Annika." He moves to sit next to me, wraps an arm around me, and reaches across with his other hand to stroke my aching bicep like it's not a big deal that I'm sitting here about to have a mental breakdown because I told him to take a flying leap and he came back.

He came back to fight for me.

In Mama's house.

Which means she probably knows he's here.

"Hurt here?" he asks.

"A little," I lie. And then I realize what I'm doing. I snap straight and pull away, even though it makes my stomach muscles groan and puts a cramp in my back that radiates pain down my leg. *"Stop making me lie."*

"You know that selfie we took last week with Sue? When the Fireballs were losing by eight in the second inning? I shared that on the bakery wars scorekeeping page this morning."

Dammit. Now he's making my eyes water too. "You did?"

"I was never ashamed of you, Annika. You're not a dirty secret. You're my kryptonite."

"I'm a glowing piece of alien rock?" Distraction. Yes.

Definitely distraction so I can find my courage to love him back.

He strokes my back, and all my sore muscles give a shudder of relief under his careful touch.

"You're the only person in the world who can break me." His eyes are steady, but he can't fully hide the vulnerability at the confession.

And I can't leave him hanging there alone.

If he's going out on a shaky tree limb, I need to be there with him.

"I can relate," I whisper.

"It's fucking terrifying."

"Beyond terrifying."

"So much easier to pretend this isn't real so it hurts less when it's over, than it is to let myself hope we could have forever."

"I hate being afraid."

"Fuck being afraid. I love you. I've always loved you. I will always love you. Through time and space and distance, and burnt cookies and family crises and horny goats. All of it. We'll argue and fight sometimes. But I will *always* come back. Loving you is the one thing I do better than anything else, and I fucking love loving you. Even when it's hard. So yeah. I'm here. And I'm gonna shout to the world every day for the rest of my life how much I love you. Because I do. I love you."

I should be fresh out of tears, but here they come again. "I'm sorry," I choke out.

"If the next words out of your mouth are *I can't do this*, rest assured you can, and we both know you can, and I'll keep coming back."

I shake my head, and my neck muscles groan in protest and send a fiery ball of pain down my spine. "I'm sorry I yelled at you yesterday."

"I have this crazy feeling it won't be the last time."

"I don't *want* to yell at you."

"We could make up."

I grimace, because while my vagina would enjoy that, she's feeling beat up by proximity to the rest of my body.

"You can't move at all, can you?"

"I'm fine. *Fucking dammit*, Grady, I *hate* lying."

He chuckles and scoots closer to use both hands on my aching back. "That's not a lie. That's bravado. How about I feed you warm chocolate chip cookies while you soak in a hot bath, and when you're feeling human again in another week or three, you can show me around this little town you call home."

I whimper.

"Is there anywhere that doesn't hurt?"

Is there?

I take stock of my body, and yes.

There's one place that definitely does *not* hurt.

"My heart," I tell him. "My heart doesn't hurt at all."

He smiles at me, all dimpled and warm-eyed and full of love, and I realize I haven't said it back.

"You're worth waiting for," he says softly, like he knows what I'm thinking, and I thought I'd fallen for Grady Rock before, first in high school, then when he brought me ice cream, again when he figured out my secret and saved all our asses at Duh-Nuts, but I was wrong.

I hadn't fallen.

Not like this.

"I love you so much," I choke out, and it's hard, but so very, very worth it.

Because my heart takes wings and Grady pulls me into his arms, his breath going ragged while he blinks hard, and I finally understand what it means to be someone's everything.

It's a huge responsibility.

And it's one I will happily bear for the rest of my life.

50

Grady

My love doesn't half-ass anything.

Including beating herself up.

Guess it's good for both of us that I've finally found my own stubborn streak.

I run her a hot bath, help strip her out of her clothes, which I'd enjoy way more if she wasn't wincing in pain with every movement, and then I rescue the cookies from the oven before they burn to a crisp.

The bathroom is small—everything in the house is small—but I prop myself next to the tub and feed her cookies and painkillers and openly admire her naked body in the water.

"Did you put magic healing ingredients in these cookies?" she asks. "Because I'm starting to feel much better."

"They're part of the whole *get Annika better fast* package."

"Who's running Crow's Nest today?"

"We're shut down for the day."

"*Grady*. You can't shut down. Not today. Not when the—"

I put a finger on her lips, then a thought strikes me. "Does it hurt here?" I ask, tracing the delicate, plump skin.

Her eyes go three shades darker. She shakes her head and grimaces, which is both adorable and fucking hard to watch.

"No," she says. "My lips don't hurt."

"Huh. Guess that's a good thing."

Those beautiful lips spread in a smile. "Grady?"

"Hm?"

"Kiss me. Please."

"Am I going to have to do all the work?"

She laughs, then winces again. "Ow. Yes."

"You have a lot of booboos," I say as I lean over the tub. "Do they all need kisses?"

"Yes. But Mama could be home any minute, and Bailey's supposed to get off the bus at—*oh*."

I cut her off by sealing my lips over hers, and her happy, contented, chocolate chip-flavored sigh makes me smile.

So does the way she sucks my lower lip into her mouth.

The way her nipple pebbles when I skim my hand over her breast.

"Does that hurt?" I murmur against her mouth.

"Touch me more."

Her breath catches while my hand trails lower, and she lifts her fingers to my cheeks and kisses me slowly, carefully, leisurely.

I want all the kisses with Annika.

Hard and deep.

Soft and sweet.

The quick peck on the way out of the door in the morning.

The full-body, leap into my arms welcome-home kiss at night.

Stolen in the middle of the day when she swings by Crow's Nest. Or wherever the hell I'm working.

In the backyard, watching Fourth of July fireworks.

While we're both covered in face paint for matching Halloween costumes.

Over a turkey in Ma's kitchen.

Everywhere.

Every day.

I slide my hand lower over her wet body, and I start chuckling into our kiss.

"What?" she asks.

"Always wet."

She giggles, and she's gazing in my eyes when I reach between her legs and stroke.

Her eyes cross, and her lids go heavy. "Oh my god, Grady."

"Too much?"

"More."

She's slick and hot and when I push two fingers inside her, she's tight and swollen and so fucking perfect.

"I don't deserve you," she whispers.

"I'm a pain in the ass. It'll even out in the end."

She laughs, then gasps as I graze her tight clit with my thumb.

"Besides," I add, "having a naked Annika completely

at my mercy in a bathtub? Do you have any idea how many times I've fantasized about this? You are so fucking sexy."

"Look who's talking. You and your—*ohmygod,* more."

I slide my fingers in and out of her pussy while her breath goes ragged.

"That's it, baby." I add another finger, and she slips lower in the tub, her hips matching my rhythm. "You're so tight, but I know you can take more. I'm gonna fill you so good, you won't remember a time when I wasn't inside you."

"Are you—master baking—me?" she pants.

"I'm loving you."

She cries out and her walls clench around my fingers, squeezing so tight she's probably cutting off circulation, but I don't care.

I can get new fingers.

No, that's not right.

Blood flow will come back.

But making Annika happy?

That's priceless.

"I love you," I murmur as I lean in to capture her lips again while her whole body sags deeper into the hot water.

"I love you more," she replies.

We're both laughing through kisses, and that smile—that laugh—all of her.

Every bit of her.

She was worth the wait.

51

Grady

It takes a week for our schedules to line up—and for Annika to quit walking around with a constant grimace on her face—but finally, she takes me on a late afternoon tour of Sarcasm, and then we hop in my truck for an early evening tour of Shipwreck.

Bailey still hates my guts, but Annika assures me it's merely an act, especially since I *accidentally* showed her the secret to my Mississippi mud pie, and that if I keep dropping hints about what we're making next at Crow's Nest when I join them for dinner, she'll eventually openly like me instead of just confessing when she's tired that I might not be so bad.

Maria's already a second mom.

Roger and I had a chat over a beer, and so long as I'm always willing to defer to Annika being right first, then Maria, then Bailey, then we're cool.

I told him I'd agree on the condition he asks Annika for her mom's hand in marriage if their relationship ever goes that far, and he blushed so hard I could've baked a cookie on his face.

And now Annika's sitting next to me, with Sue behind us, since he wanted a tour of Sarcasm too, and we're cruising the mountain roads like we used to.

Right down to Annika's planner in her lap, though it's an actual planner instead of a converted spiral notebook with colored sticky notes. "We sell s'mores donuts best on Fridays. Is that weird?" she asks.

"I've never paid attention to what day which donuts sell best."

"You should. Your profit margins should be higher, given how much traffic you get."

"I love it when you talk dirty."

"That wasn't dirty."

"I know. But that was a hint."

Sue snorts on my shoulder, and Annika laughs at both of us.

I reach over and squeeze her hand. "They all love you."

She gets spun up in over-planning when she's nervous.

Like today.

When we're pulling into Shipwreck.

"Look at that. We're on Blackbeard Avenue," I tell her. "Home to many prominent and respected businesses all run by my immediate family, or aunts, uncles, and cousins."

"I *have* been here a time or two," she tells me.

"But have you ever played at Davey Jones's Locker? Or bowled at Cannon Bowl? Or caught a movie at The

Twisted Reel?" I point to the various locations down the street.

"Not yet."

Someone's hung a giant banner advertising our Labor Day Pirate Color Run over the street halfway down, and when we pass Scuttle Putt, a bird swoops in front of my truck and drops a load on the windshield.

Pop waves and grins.

"Swear he taught the damn parrot to do that," I mutter.

"So, he wasn't smiling because he was happy to see me?" Annika asks.

"He was thrilled to see you."

"Who's lying now?"

"He can go walk the plank."

"*Grady*."

I smile at her, because it's impossible not to. "It's a short plank. Not very far off the ground."

I circle the block and head to my house so we can drop Sue off, and also so I can get her naked before dinner with my family at Crusty Nut, except as soon as we push into the kitchen and I reach for her, my mother breezes in from the living room.

"There you are! I wondered when you would get here. I brought a dirt cake."

"Ma. We don't need a dirt cake."

"*Grady*," Annika hisses.

"Dirt cakes are for *bad* news," I hiss back.

"Wait. Does that mean I'm bad news?"

I glare at my mother.

She smiles sweetly.

"Hey, there, son." Dad strolls into the kitchen too.

"How's my favorite goat today?" He bends and rub's Sue behind the ears.

"Sue, my parents are being mean to Annika," I tell my goat.

"*Grady*," Annika hisses again.

Sue looks up at my parents, one at a time, and then lifts his leg and pees on Dad's shoe.

"*Sue*," Annika gasps while Dad leaps out of the way and Ma gapes.

I'm gonna have to clean that up. He got it on the carpet.

"Good goat." I look at my parents. "*Now* what do you have to say for yourselves?"

"We missed you, dear," Ma says to Annika.

"Glad to have you back," Dad agrees, bouncing on one leg while he tries to pull off his goat pee shoe. "And staying. Grady was nearly unbearable the first time you left."

"This is the weirdest welcome I've ever gotten in my entire life," she murmurs to me as she slips her hand in mine again.

Sue grins up at her.

She laughs.

I smile.

And my parents share a look.

A *thank god this one's settled and happy* look.

Fuck.

They're *testing* us.

My front door bangs open. "Did I miss it?" Tillie Jean calls. "Am I too late to help—oh. Um. Help cook dinner? Whoa. Dad. What'd you step in?"

Annika's dark eyes dart among all of us, and I pull her

in for a hug. "They're giving us shit," I murmur to her. "Welcome to the family. Feel free to give it back."

Her gaze meets mine, and the question in her eyes fades to pure mischief.

That's something I haven't seen on her face since we were kids, and it puts a buoyancy in my heart.

"Oh, Libby, you brought dirt cake?" she says to my mom. "I *told* Grady to tell you all I'd bring banana pudding."

Tillie Jean's eyes go wide.

Dad's head whips up, which throws him off-balance, and he topples over onto my couch.

But Ma claps her hands. "Oh, good. You're still funny enough to keep up around here. We were worried, what with all the stress you've been under. How's your mama? And your sister?"

"They're adjusting," she replies slowly, like she has whiplash from the sudden change in conversation.

"Grady, we put hamburgers in the fridge. Go fire up the grill so this poor thing can eat."

Annika's eyes go shiny. "You...like me now?"

"We always liked you." Ma smothers her in a hug. "We were just afraid to get too close, in case Grady fucked it up."

"Thanks, Ma."

"Legit worry," Tillie Jean says as she joins the Annika hug pile. "Although I'm still just mildly miffed about the banana pudding. But I'm letting it go because unlike *some* people, I don't feel the need to fight with a teenager. Oh, you still use that coconut shampoo! I love that stuff. Can you stay long enough to cheer on the Fireballs with us, or do you need to get back to your family?"

"I can stay."

"You good if I go fire up my grill?" I ask Annika.

She smiles at me from the middle of being squished by my family, and yeah.

Everything's good.

Everything.

Maybe everyone in Shipwreck and Sarcasm can let the old feud go, but if not—the people who matter most already have.

And even if they didn't, I'd still have my Annika.

At last.

EPILOGUE

Grady

Hard to believe it's been a year since Annika burst back into my life, but here we are.

Back at the softball fields.

She might live in Shipwreck now, but she's still a Sarcasm native who drives home to see her mama and sister at least five times every week—sometimes with me, sometimes without me—and she's once again playing for the GOATs.

The Greatest Of All Times.

She's my greatest of all time.

And here I am, staring her down as I wind up to toss her the first pitch.

"Don't you dare go easy on me," she calls as she steps up to the plate at the top of the third inning. We're tied, zero to zero, naturally. "I will *end* you if I think you're just being nice."

I grin, because she's all talk.

"That's not what you said last night."

"Shut up and pitch the ball, Rock," Georgia calls.

Tillie Jean audibly gags behind me.

I toss the pitch, and Annika lets it go right by.

It's rare she swings on the first pitch.

Only time she did, she racked me in the nuts, so I'm good with her letting a strike go by, even if she could've knocked it halfway to Copper Valley.

"C'mon, Grady. Give me a tough one," she calls.

I'm physically incapable of tossing her a tough pitch. Not when she smiles at me like that. The whole diamond is lit up with her glow.

Her mama and sister are cheering in the stands. Roger's there too, a permanent staple in their lives who's turned his plumbing business over to Birch, his son, so he can help Maria more in the bakery. Liliana from the winery and Hazel from Rise and Grind in Sarcasm are both in the dug-out, cheering, along with Birch.

I toss another pitch at Annika, and she swings and misses.

On purpose, I'm positive.

Two strikes.

That's not gonna do.

"Don't even think about it," she calls to me.

"Says the woman who whiffed on purpose."

"Like I'd do that."

"Oh, you absolutely would."

There's no heat in our banter this year.

Other than the *I want to take you home and get you naked* heat.

"Substitute pitcher!" my dad yells.

"I have two strikes on her," I yell back.

"But you're about to throw her three balls."

"Rawk! Three balls is one too many! Rawk!"

Annika grins.

And fuck it.

I'm not going to strike her out, and Dad knows it.

I pull my glove off and toss it in the dirt.

She frowns and steps back from the plate.

"He's right," I tell her. "I'm just gonna toss you a few balls to make myself feel better."

"Rawk! Grow some balls! Rawk!"

"He's right too," I say with a nod to the parrot.

She laughs and shakes her head. "Your balls are fine. I promise."

"No, no, they've been letting me down lately."

"Over-personal much?" Georgia calls.

"Did *not* need to know that," Tillie Jean agrees behind me.

Like they don't know what I'm talking about.

I stroll off the pitcher's mound and head for home plate.

"It's true," I tell Annika. "Time to man up."

Her brows furrow like she honestly has no idea what I'm up to.

Or what's wrong with my balls.

"Are you okay?" she asks when I'm halfway to home plate. She glances back at the umpire, like she's afraid he's going to call me off-sides, though that's not actually a thing in softball.

"I need to tell you something."

"Can it wait?"

Her teammates are starting to spill out of the dugout like they're expecting a brawl.

Georgia pulls her mask off and tries unsuccessfully to stifle a huge grin, and I know several of my teammates are pulling in closer to watch.

When I hatched this plan, I thought I'd be sweating.

But the only thing giving me any pause at all is the sudden worry clouding Annika's eyes.

"Nope. Can't wait. Not one more minute."

"Grady—"

I don't let her finish, and instead take her hand, while she's still gripping the bat in the other, and I drop to one knee.

"I love you—" I start, and that's as far as I get before realization dawns and she drops her bat and tackles me to the ground, kissing me and shouting, "*Yes!*" before I can even ask.

"Will—you—" I try again.

She grabs my cheeks and presses her lips to mine. "*Yes*," she says again.

She's laughing and straddling me and kissing me, not letting me get a word out.

I can't even get to my pocket for her ring.

"You—you—you perfect man," she gasps as she finally lets me go. "You scared me half to death. I thought you had a problem with your—with your—with your balls. And that would've been awful. I still would've loved you, but I would've been very sad for both of us."

I cradle her neck and pull her close. "Can I please ask you to marry me now."

"Can I say yes?"

"Again? Are you sure?"

She laughs and hugs me tighter. "I love you so much."

"I love you more."

"You better. Because I'm going to score a home run on you. Right now."

And because she's Annika...that's exactly what she does.

On the field. In the softball game.

But she scores a home run later too.

When we're alone.

And I promise her we'll never stop scoring home runs for as long as we both live.

PIPPA GRANT BOOK LIST

The Girl Band Series
Mister McHottie
Stud in the Stacks
Rockaway Bride
The Hero and the Hacktivist

The Thrusters Hockey Series
The Pilot and the Puck-Up
Royally Pucked
Beauty and the Beefcake
Charming as Puck
I Pucking Love You

The Bro Code Series
Flirting with the Frenemy
America's Geekheart
Liar, Liar, Hearts on Fire
The Hot Mess and the Heartthrob

Copper Valley Fireballs Series
Jock Blocked
Real Fake Love
The Grumpy Player Next Door
Irresistible Trouble

The Tickled Pink Series

The One Who Loves You

Rich In Your Love

Standalones

The Worst Wedding Date

The Last Eligible Billionaire

Dirty Talking Rival *(Bro Code Spin-Off)*

Hot Heir *(Royally Pucked Spin-Off)*

Exes and Ho Ho Hos

The Bluewater Billionaires Series

The Price of Scandal by Lucy Score

The Mogul and the Muscle by Claire Kingsley

Wild Open Hearts by Kathryn Nolan

Crazy for Loving You by Pippa Grant

Co-Written with Lili Valente

Hosed

Hammered

Hitched

Humbugged

Pippa Grant writing as Jamie Farrell:

The Misfit Brides Series

Blissed

Matched

Smittened

Sugared

Merried

Spiced

Unhitched

The Officers' Ex-Wives Club Series

Her Rebel Heart

Southern Fried Blues

ABOUT THE AUTHOR

Pippa Grant wanted to write books, so she did.

Before she became a USA Today and #1 Amazon best-selling romantic comedy author, she was a young military spouse who got into writing as self-therapy. That happened around the time she discovered reading romance novels, and the two eventually merged into a career. Today, she has more than 30 knee-slapping Pippa Grant titles and nine published under the name Jamie Farrell.

When she's not writing romantic comedies, she's fumbling through being a mom, wife, and mountain woman, and sometimes tries to find hobbies. Her crowning achievement? Having impeccable timing for telling stories that will make people snort beverages out of their noses. Consider yourself warned.

Find Pippa at…
www.pippagrant.com
pippa@pippagrant.com